P9-AGK-071

Praise for Brandon Sanderson and
The Way of Kings

"I *loved* this book. What else is there to say?"
—Patrick Rothfuss,
New York Times bestselling author of
The Name of the Wind and *The Wise Man's Fear*

"Sanderson, the author of *Elantris* and the Mistborn trilogy, once again creates an interesting world with a novel system of magic, but the best part of this series launch is the compelling, complex story of Dalinar, Kaladin, and Shallan as they struggle through emotional, physical, and moral challenges. Verdict: Sanderson is a master of hooking the reader in the first few pages, and once again he doesn't disappoint. Fans and lovers of epic fantasy will find the ending satisfying, yet will eagerly await the next volume."
—*Library Journal*

"It's rare for a fiction writer to have much understanding of how leadership works and how love really takes root in the human heart. Sanderson is astonishingly wise."
—Orson Scott Card

"Sanderson's skill and pure narrative power did not lose me at all over the course of time it took me to read the book or [over] the great page count he took to tell the story. Though it is a long novel . . . I can't say that it felt like a long tale. It felt epic and powerful, a story and world I was pleased to be immersed in during the entire reading experience of the novel.

"Sanderson has proved with his past novels he is a voice to be heard and recognized in the fantasy genre. With *The Way of Kings*, he stakes his claim as one of the preeminent purveyors of the fantasy genre—he will be spoken in the same breath as Tolkien, Leiber, Moorcock, Jordan (on his own merits and not just because he is completing The Wheel of Time), and George R. R. Martin. I have extremely high anticipation for future volumes in this series, and despite this being the first of a multivolume series, it ends with closure.

"I give this book my highest recommendation and think *The Way of Kings* will be one of those landmark novels of epic fantasy against which future novels will always be measured."   —Rob H. Bedford, *SFFworld.com*

THE
WAY OF
KINGS

Book One of
THE STORMLIGHT ARCHIVE

BRANDON
SANDERSON

TOR®
fantasy

A TOM DOHERTY ASSOCIATES BOOK • NEW YORK

This is a work of fiction. All of the characters, organizations, and events
portrayed in this novel are either products of the author's imagination or
are used fictitiously.

THE WAY OF KINGS

Copyright © 2010 by Dragonsteel Entertainment, LLC

Edited by Moshe Feder

Interior illustrations by Isaac Stewart and Ben McSweeney

All rights reserved.

A Tor Book
Published by Tom Doherty Associates, LLC
175 Fifth Avenue
New York, NY 10010

www.tor-forge.com

Tor® is a registered trademark of Tom Doherty Associates, LLC.

Printed in the United States of America

For Emily,
Who is too patient
Too kindly
And too wonderful
For words.
But I try anyway.

ROSHAR

ENDLESS OCEAN

Rall Elorim

RESH

Kasitor

IRI

RIRA

Kurth

Eila

Resh

BABATHARNAM

Panatham

DARABET

Shinovar

DESH

The Pureland

UDLAY

AIMIA

Aimian Sea

ALM

UEZIER

AZIR

Azimir

STEEN

LIAFOR

TASHIKK

EMUL

The V

CRE

Sesemalex Dar

Leewater

TUKAR

MARA

N

LEEWARD

STORMWARD

S

SOUTHERN DEPTHS

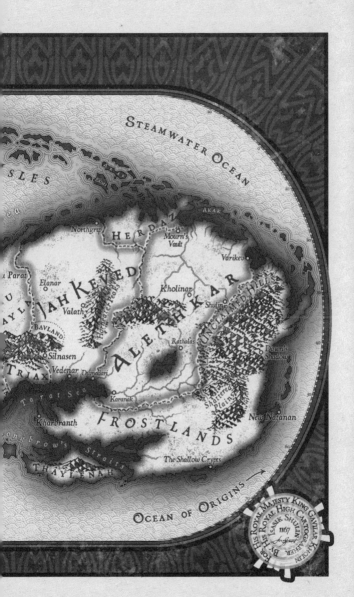

STEAMWATER OCEAN

...SLES

...Sea

...Parat

Elanar

JAH KEVED

Valath

Horneater Peaks

BAVLAND

Silnasen

Vedenar Dumadari

...TRIAX

AKAK

Northgrip HERDAZ

Mourn's
Vault

Varikev

Kholinar

Shulin

ALETHKAR

UNCLAIMED HILLS

Rathalas

Dawn's
Shadow

Tarat Sea

Karanak

Kharbranth

FROSTLANDS

Shattered
Plains

New Natanan

...ongbrow's Straits

THAYLENAH

The Shallow Crypts

OCEAN OF ORIGINS →

By His Royal Majesty King Gavilar
Kholin
By His Royal High Cartographer
Isasik Shulin
1167

THE
WAY OF
KINGS

THE STORMLIGHT ARCHIVE

Kalak rounded a rocky stone ridge and stumbled to a stop before the body of a dying thunderclast. The enormous stone beast lay on its side, riblike protrusions from its chest broken and cracked. The monstrosity was vaguely skeletal in shape, with unnaturally long limbs that sprouted from granite shoulders. The eyes were deep red spots on the arrowhead face, as if created by a fire burning deep within the stone. They faded.

Even after all these centuries, seeing a thunderclast up close made Kalak shiver. The beast's hand was as long as a man was tall. He'd been killed by hands like those before, and it hadn't been pleasant.

Of course, dying rarely was.

He rounded the creature, picking his way more carefully across the battlefield. The plain was a place of misshapen rock and stone, natural pillars rising around him, bodies littering the ground. Few plants lived here.

The stone ridges and mounds bore numerous scars. Some were shattered, blasted-out sections where Surgebinders had fought. Less frequently, he passed cracked, oddly shaped hollows where thunderclasts had ripped themselves free of the stone to join the fray.

Many of the bodies around him were human; many were not. Blood mixed. Red. Orange. Violet. Though none of the bodies around him stirred, an indistinct haze of sounds hung in the air. Moans of pain, cries of grief. They did not seem like the sounds of victory. Smoke curled from the occasional patches of growth or heaps of burning corpses. Even some sections of rock smoldered. The Dustbringers had done their work well.

But I survived, Kalak thought, hand to breast as he hastened to the meeting place. *I actually survived this time.*

That was dangerous. When he died, he was sent back, no choice. When he survived the Desolation, he was supposed to go back as well. Back to that place that he dreaded. Back to that place of pain and fire. What if he just decided . . . not to go?

Perilous thoughts, perhaps traitorous thoughts. He hastened on his way.

The place of meeting was in the shadow of a large rock formation, a spire rising into the sky. As always, the ten of them had decided upon it before the battle. The survivors would make their way here. Oddly, only one of the others was waiting for him. Jezrien. Had the other eight all died? It was possible. The battle had been so furious this time, one of the worst. The enemy was growing increasingly tenacious.

But no. Kalak frowned as he stepped up to the base of the spire. Seven magnificent swords stood proudly here, driven point-first into the stone ground. Each was a masterly work of art, flowing in design, inscribed with glyphs and patterns. He recognized each one. If their masters had died, the Blades would have vanished.

These Blades were weapons of power beyond even Shardblades. These were unique. Precious. Jezrien stood outside the ring of swords, looking eastward.

"Jezrien?"

The figure in white and blue glanced toward him. Even after all these centuries, Jezrien looked young, like a man barely into his thirtieth year. His short black beard was neatly trimmed, though his once-fine clothing was scorched and stained with blood. He folded his arms behind his back as he turned to Kalak.

"What is this, Jezrien?" Kalak asked. "Where are the others?"

"Departed." Jezrien's voice was calm, deep, regal. Though he hadn't worn a crown in centuries, his royal manner lingered. He always seemed to know what to do. "You might call it a miracle. Only one of us died this time."

[2]

"Talenel," Kalak said. His was the only Blade unaccounted for.

"Yes. He died holding that passage by the northern waterway."

Kalak nodded. Taln had a tendency to choose seemingly hopeless fights and win them. He also had a tendency to die in the process. He would be back now, in the place where they went between Desolations. The place of nightmares.

Kalak found himself shaking. When had he become so weak? "Jezrien, I can't return this time." Kalak whispered the words, stepping up and gripping the other man's arm. "I *can't.*"

Kalak felt something within him break at the admission. How long had it been? Centuries, perhaps millennia, of torture. It was so hard to keep track. Those fires, those hooks, digging into his flesh anew each day. Searing the skin off his arm, then burning the fat, then driving to the bone. He could smell it. Almighty, he could *smell* it!

"Leave your sword," Jezrien said.

"What?"

Jezrien nodded to the ring of weapons. "I was chosen to wait for you. We weren't certain if you had survived. A . . . a decision has been made. It is time for the Oathpact to end."

Kalak felt a sharp stab of horror. "What will that do?"

"Ishar believes that so long as there is one of us still bound to the Oathpact, it may be enough. There is a chance we might end the cycle of Desolations."

Kalak looked into the immortal king's eyes. Black smoke rose from a small patch to their left. Groans of the dying haunted them from behind. There, in Jezrien's eyes, Kalak saw anguish and grief. Perhaps even cowardice. This was a man hanging from a cliff by a thread.

Almighty above, Kalak thought. *You're broken too, aren't you?* They all were.

Kalak turned and walked to the side, where a low ridge overlooked part of the battlefield.

There were so many corpses, and among them walked the living. Men in primitive wraps, carrying spears topped by bronze heads. Juxtaposed between them were others in gleaming plate armor. One group walked past, four men in their ragged tanned skins or shoddy leather joining a powerful figure in beautiful silver plate, amazingly intricate. Such a contrast.

Jezrien stepped up beside him.

"They see us as divinities," Kalak whispered. "They rely upon us, Jezrien. We're all that they have."

"They have the Radiants. That will be enough."

Kalak shook his head. "He will not remain bound by this. The enemy. He will find a way around it. You know he will."

"Perhaps." The king of Heralds offered no further explanation.

"And Taln?" Kalak asked. *The flesh burning. The fires. The pain over and over and over . . .*

"Better that one man should suffer than ten," Jezrien whispered. He seemed so cold. Like a shadow caused by heat and light falling on someone honorable and true, casting this black imitation behind.

Jezrien walked back to the ring of swords. His own Blade formed in his hands, appearing from mist, wet with condensation. "It has been decided, Kalak. We will go our ways, and we will not seek out one another. Our Blades must be left. The Oathpact ends now." He lifted his sword and rammed it into the stone with the other seven.

Jezrien hesitated, looking at the sword, then bowed his head and turned away. As if ashamed. "We chose this burden willingly. Well, we can choose to drop it if we wish."

"What do we tell the people, Jezrien?" Kalak asked. "What will they say of this day?"

"It's simple," Jezrien said, walking away. "We tell them that they finally won. It's an easy enough lie. Who knows? Maybe it will turn out to be true."

Kalak watched Jezrien depart across the burned landscape. Finally, he summoned his own Blade and slammed it into the stone beside the other eight. He turned and walked in the direction opposite from Jezrien.

And yet, he could not help glancing back at the ring of

swords and the single open spot. The place where the tenth sword should have gone.

The one of them who was lost. The one they had abandoned.

Forgive us, Kalak thought, then left.

BOOK

ONE

⬧⬧⬧

THE WAY OF KINGS

4,500 Years Later

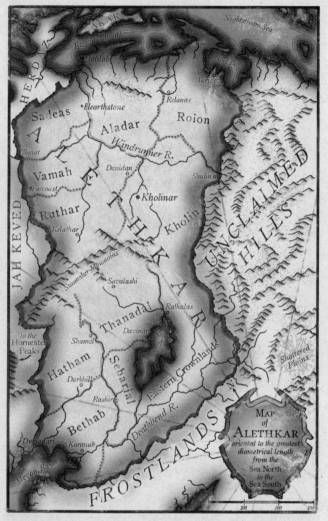

Map of Alethkar and surroundings, created by His Majesty Gavilar Kholin's royal surveyors, circa 1167.

"The love of men is a frigid thing, a mountain stream only three steps from the ice. We are his. Oh Stormfather . . . we are his. It is but a thousand days, and the Everstorm comes."

—Collected on the first day of the week Palah of the month Shash of the year 1171, thirty-one seconds before death. Subject was a darkeyed pregnant woman of middle years. The child did not survive.

Szeth-son-son-Vallano, Truthless of Shinovar, wore white on the day he was to kill a king. The white clothing was a Parshendi tradition, foreign to him. But he did as his masters required and did not ask for an explanation.

He sat in a large stone room, baked by enormous firepits that cast a garish light upon the revelers, causing beads of sweat to form on their skin as they danced, and drank, and yelled, and sang, and clapped. Some fell to the ground red-faced, the revelry too much for them, their stomachs proving to be inferior wineskins. They looked as if they were dead, at least until their friends carried them out of the feast hall to waiting beds.

Szeth did not sway to the drums, drink the sapphire wine, or stand to dance. He sat on a bench at the back, a still servant in white robes. Few at the treaty-signing celebration noticed him. He was just a servant, and Shin were easy to ignore. Most out here in the East thought Szeth's kind were docile and harmless. They were generally right.

The drummers began a new rhythm. The beats shook Szeth like a quartet of thumping hearts, pumping waves of invisible blood through the room. Szeth's masters—who were dismissed as savages by those in more civilized kingdoms—sat at their own tables. They were men with skin of black marbled with red. Parshendi, they were named—cousins to the more docile servant peoples known as parshmen in most of the world. An oddity. They did not call themselves Parshendi; this was the Alethi name for them. It meant, roughly, "parshmen who can think." Neither side seemed to see that as an insult.

The Parshendi had brought the musicians. At first, the Alethi lighteyes had been hesitant. To them, drums were base instruments of the common, darkeyed people. But wine was the great assassin of both tradition and propriety, and now the Alethi elite danced with abandon.

Szeth stood and began to pick his way through the room. The revelry had lasted long; even the king had retired hours ago. But many still celebrated. As he walked, Szeth was forced to step around Dalinar Kholin—the king's own brother—who slumped drunken at a small table. The aging but powerfully built man kept waving away those who tried to encourage him to bed. Where was Jasnah, the king's daughter? Elhokar, the king's son and heir, sat at the high table, ruling the feast in his father's absence. He was in conversation with two men, a dark-skinned Azish man who had an odd patch of pale skin on his cheek and a thinner, Alethi-looking man who kept glancing over his shoulder.

The heir's feasting companions were unimportant. Szeth stayed far from the heir, skirting the sides of the room, passing the drummers. Musicspren zipped through the air around them, the tiny spirits taking the form of spinning translucent ribbons. As Szeth passed the drummers, they noted him. They would withdraw soon, along with all of the other Parshendi.

They did not seem offended. They did not seem angry. And yet they were going to break their treaty of only a few hours. It made no sense. But Szeth did not ask questions.

At the edge of the room, he passed rows of unwavering azure lights that bulged out where wall met floor. They held sapphires infused with Stormlight. Profane. How could the men of these lands use something so sacred for mere illumination? Worse, the Alethi scholars were said to be close to creating new Shardblades. Szeth hoped that was just wishful boasting. For if it *did* happen, the world would be changed. Likely in a way that ended with people in all countries—from distant Thaylenah to towering Jah Keved—speaking Alethi to their children.

They were a grand people, these Alethi. Even drunk, there was a natural nobility to them. Tall and well made, the men dressed in dark silk coats that buttoned down the sides of the chest and were elaborately embroidered in silver or gold. Each one looked a general on the field.

The women were even more splendid. They wore grand silk dresses, tightly fitted, the bright colors a contrast to the dark tones favored by the men. The left sleeve of each dress was longer than the right one, covering the hand. Alethi had an odd sense of propriety.

Their pure black hair was pinned up atop their heads, either in intricate weavings of braids or in loose piles. It was often woven with gold ribbons or ornaments, along with gems that glowed with Stormlight. Beautiful. Profane, but beautiful.

Szeth left the feasting chamber behind. Just outside, he passed the doorway into the Beggars' Feast. It was an Alethi tradition, a room where some of the poorest men and women in the city were given a feast complementing that of the king and his guests. A man with a long grey and black beard slumped in the doorway, smiling foolishly—though whether from wine or a weak mind, Szeth could not tell.

"Have you seen me?" the man asked with slurred speech. He laughed, then began to speak in gibberish, reaching for a wineskin. So it was drink after all. Szeth brushed by, continuing past a line of statues depicting the Ten Heralds from ancient Vorin theology. Jezerezeh, Ishi, Kelek, Talenelat. He counted off each one, and realized there were only nine here. One was conspicuously missing. Why had Shalash's statue been removed? King Gavilar was said to be very devout in his Vorin worship. Too devout, by some people's standards.

The hallway here curved to the right, running around the perimeter of the domed palace. They were on the king's floor, two levels up, surrounded by rock walls, ceiling, and floor. That was profane. Stone was not to be trod upon. But what was he to do? He was Truthless. He did as his masters demanded.

Today, that included wearing white. Loose white trousers tied at the waist with a rope, and over them a filmy shirt with long sleeves, open at the front. White clothing for a killer was a tradition among the Parshendi. Although Szeth had not asked, his masters had explained why.

White to be bold. White to not blend into the night. White to give warning.

For if you were going to assassinate a man, he was entitled to see you coming.

Szeth turned right, taking the hallway directly toward the king's chambers. Torches burned on the walls, their light unsatisfying to him, a meal of thin broth after a long fast. Flamespren danced around them, like large insects made solely of congealed light. The torches were useless to him. He reached for his pouch and the spheres it contained, but then hesitated when he saw more of the blue lights ahead: a pair of Stormlight lamps hanging on the wall, brilliant sapphires glowing at their hearts. Szeth walked up to one of these, holding out his hand to cup it around the glass-shrouded gemstone.

"You there!" a voice called in Alethi. There were two guards at the intersection. Double guard, for there were savages abroad in Kholinar this night. True, those savages were supposed to be allies now. But alliances could be shallow things indeed.

This one wouldn't last the hour.

Szeth looked as the two guards approached. They carried spears; they weren't lighteyes, and were therefore forbidden the sword. Their painted blue breastplates were ornate, however, as were their helms. They might be darkeyed, but they were high-ranking citizens with honored positions in the royal guard.

Stopping a few feet away, the guard at the front gestured with his spear. "Go on, now. This is no place for you." He had tan Alethi skin and a thin mustache that ran all the way around his mouth, becoming a beard at the bottom.

Szeth didn't move.

"Well?" the guard said. "What are you waiting for?"

Szeth breathed in deeply, drawing forth the Stormlight. It streamed into him, siphoned from the twin sapphire lamps on the walls, sucked in as if by his deep inhalation. The Stormlight raged inside of him, and the hallway suddenly grew darker, falling into shade like a hilltop cut off from the sun by a transient cloud.

Szeth could feel the Light's warmth, its fury, like a tempest that had been injected directly into his veins. The power of it was invigorating but dangerous. It pushed him to act. To move. To strike.

Holding his breath, he clung to the Stormlight. He could still feel it leaking out. Stormlight could be held for only a short time, a few minutes at most. It leaked away, the human body too porous a container. He had heard that the Voidbringers could hold it in perfectly. But, then, did they even exist? His punishment declared that they didn't. His honor demanded that they did.

Afire with holy energy, Szeth turned to the guards. They could see that he was leaking Stormlight, wisps of it curling from his skin like luminescent smoke. The lead guard squinted, frowning. Szeth was sure the man had never seen anything like it before. As far as he knew, Szeth had killed every stonewalker who had ever seen what he could do.

"What . . . what are you?" The guard's voice had lost its certainty. "Spirit or man?"

"What am I?" Szeth whispered, a bit of Light leaking from his lips as he looked past the man down the long hallway. "I'm . . . sorry."

Szeth blinked, Lashing himself to that distant point down the hallway. Stormlight raged from him in a flash, chilling his skin, and the ground immediately stopped pulling him downward. Instead, he was pulled toward that distant point—it was as if, to him, that direction had suddenly become *down*.

This was a Basic Lashing, first of his three kinds of Lashings. It gave him the ability to manipulate whatever force, spren, or god it was that held men to the ground. With this Lashing, he could bind people or objects to different surfaces or in different directions.

From Szeth's perspective, the hallway was now a deep shaft down which he was falling, and the two guards stood on one of the sides. They were shocked when Szeth's feet hit them, one for each face, throwing them over. Szeth shifted his view and Lashed himself to the floor. Light leaked from him. The floor of the hallway again became *down*, and he landed between the two guards, clothes crackling and dropping flakes of frost. He rose, beginning the process of summoning his Shardblade.

One of the guards fumbled for his spear. Szeth reached down, touching the soldier's shoulder while looking up. He focused on a point above him while willing the Light out of his body and into the guard, Lashing the poor man to the ceiling.

The guard yelped in shock as *up* became *down* for him. Light trailing from his form, he crashed into the ceiling and dropped his spear. It was not Lashed directly, and clattered back down to the floor near Szeth.

To kill. It was the greatest of sins. And yet here Szeth stood, Truthless, profanely walking on stones used for building. And it would not end. As Truthless, there was only one life he was forbidden to take.

And that was his own.

At the tenth beat of his heart, his Shardblade dropped into his waiting hand. It formed as if condensing from mist, water beading along the metal length. His Shardblade was long and thin, edged on both sides, smaller than most others. Szeth swept it out, carving a line in the stone floor and passing through the second guard's neck.

As always, the Shardblade killed oddly; though it cut easily through stone, steel, or anything inanimate, the metal fuzzed when it touched living skin. It traveled through the guard's neck without leaving a mark, but once it did, the man's eyes smoked and burned. They blackened, shriveling up in his head, and he slumped forward, dead. A Shardblade did not cut living flesh; it severed the soul itself.

Above, the first guard gasped. He'd managed to get to his feet, even though they were planted on the ceiling of the hallway. "Shardbearer!" he shouted. "A Shardbearer assaults the king's hall! To arms!"

Finally, Szeth thought. Szeth's use of Stormlight was unfamiliar to the guards, but they knew a Shardblade when they saw one.

Szeth bent down and picked up the spear that had fallen from above. As he did so, he released the breath he'd been holding since drawing in the Stormlight. It sustained him while he held it, but those two lanterns hadn't contained much of it, so he would need to breathe again soon. The Light began to leak away more quickly, now that he wasn't holding his breath.

Szeth set the spear's butt against the stone floor, then looked upward. The guard above stopped shouting, eyes opening wide as the tails of his shirt began to slip downward, the earth below reasserting its dominance. The Light steaming off his body dwindled.

He looked down at Szeth. Down at the spear tip pointing directly at his heart. Violet fearspren crawled out of the stone ceiling around him.

The Light ran out. The guard fell.

He screamed as he hit, the spear impaling him through the chest. Szeth let the spear fall away, carried to the ground with a muffled thump by the body twitching on its end. Shardblade in hand, he turned down a side corridor, following the map he'd memorized. He ducked around a corner and flattened himself against the wall just as a troop of guards reached the dead men. The newcomers began shouting immediately, continuing the alarm.

His instructions were clear. Kill the king, but be seen doing it. Let the Alethi know he was coming and what he was doing. Why? Why did the Parshendi agree to this treaty, only to send an assassin the very night of its signing?

More gemstones glowed on the walls of the hallway here. King Gavilar liked lavish display, and he couldn't know that he was leaving sources of power for Szeth to use in his Lashings. The things Szeth did hadn't been seen for millennia. Histories from those times were all but nonexistent, and the legends were horribly inaccurate.

Szeth peeked back out into the corridor. One of the guards at the intersection saw him, pointing and yelling. Szeth made sure they got a good look, then ducked away. He took a deep breath as he ran, drawing in Stormlight from the lanterns. His body came alive with it, and his speed increased, his muscles bursting with energy. Light became a storm inside of him; his blood thundered in his ears. It was terrible and wonderful at the same time.

Two corridors down, one to the side. He threw open the door of a storage room, then hesitated a moment—just long enough for a guard to round the corner and see him—before dashing into the room. Preparing for a Full Lashing, he raised his arm and commanded the Stormlight to pool there, causing the skin to burst alight with radiance. Then he flung his hand out toward the doorframe, spraying white luminescence across it like paint. He slammed the door just as the guards arrived.

The Stormlight held the door in the frame with the strength of a hundred arms. A Full Lashing bound objects together, holding them fast until the Stormlight ran out. It took longer to create—and drained Stormlight far more quickly—than a Basic Lashing. The door handle shook, and then the wood began to crack as the guards threw their weight against it, one man calling for an axe.

Szeth crossed the room in rapid strides, weaving around the shrouded furniture that had been stored here. It was of red cloth and deep expensive woods. He reached the far wall and—preparing himself for yet another blasphemy—he raised his Shardblade and slashed horizontally through the dark grey stone. The rock sliced easily; a Shardblade could cut any inanimate object. Two vertical slashes followed, then one across the bottom, cutting a large square block. He pressed his hand against it, willing Stormlight into the stone.

Behind him the room's door began to crack. He looked over his shoulder and focused on the shaking door, Lashing the block in that direction. Frost crystallized on his clothing—Lashing something so large required a great deal of Stormlight. The tempest within him stilled, like a storm reduced to a drizzle.

He stepped aside. The large stone block shuddered, sliding into the room. Normally, moving the block would have been impossible. Its own weight would have held it against the stones below. Yet now, that same weight pulled it free; for the block, the direction of the room's door was *down*. With a deep grinding sound, the block slid free of the wall and tumbled through the air, smashing furniture.

The soldiers finally broke through the door, staggering into the room just as the enormous block crashed into them.

Szeth turned his back on the terrible sound of the screams, the splintering of wood, the breaking of bones. He ducked and stepped through his new hole, entering the hallway outside.

He walked slowly, drawing Stormlight from the lamps he passed, siphoning it to him and stoking anew the tempest within. As the lamps dimmed, the corridor darkened. A thick wooden door stood at the end, and as he approached, small fearspren—shaped like globs of purple goo—began to wriggle from the masonry, pointing toward the doorway. They were drawn by the terror being felt on the other side.

Szeth pushed the door open, entering the last corridor leading to the king's chambers. Tall, red ceramic vases lined the pathway, and they were interspersed with nervous soldiers. They flanked a long, narrow rug. It was red, like a river of blood.

The spearmen in front didn't wait for him to get close. They broke into a trot, lifting their short throwing spears. Szeth slammed his hand to the side, pushing Stormlight into the doorframe, using the third and final type of Lashing, a Reverse Lashing. This one worked differently from the other two. It did not make the doorframe emit Stormlight; indeed, it seemed to pull nearby light *into* it, giving it a strange penumbra.

The spearmen threw, and Szeth stood still, hand on the doorframe. A Reverse Lashing required his constant touch, but took comparatively little Stormlight. During one, anything that approached him—particularly lighter objects—was instead pulled toward the Lashing itself.

The spears veered in the air, splitting around him and slamming into the wooden frame. As he felt them hit, Szeth leaped into the air and Lashed himself to the right wall, his feet hitting the stone with a slap.

He immediately reoriented his perspective. To his eyes, he wasn't standing on the wall, the soldiers were, the blood-red carpet streaming between them like a long tapestry. Szeth bolted down the hallway, striking with his Shardblade, shearing through the necks of two men who had thrown spears at him. Their eyes burned, and they collapsed.

The other guards in the hallway began to panic. Some tried to attack him, others yelled for more help, still others cringed away from him. The attackers had trouble—they were disoriented by the oddity of striking at someone who hung on the wall. Szeth cut down a few, then flipped into the air, tucking into a roll, and Lashed himself back to the floor.

He hit the ground in the midst of the soldiers. Completely surrounded, but holding a Shardblade.

According to legend, the Shardblades were first carried by the Knights Radiant uncounted ages ago. Gifts of their god, granted to allow them to fight horrors of rock and flame, dozens of feet tall, foes whose eyes burned with hatred. The

Voidbringers. When your foe had skin as hard as stone itself, steel was useless. Something supernal was required.

Szeth rose from his crouch, loose white clothes rippling, jaw clenched against his sins. He struck out, his weapon flashing with reflected torchlight. Elegant, wide swings. Three of them, one after another. He could neither close his ears to the screams that followed nor avoid seeing the men fall. They dropped round him like toys knocked over by a child's careless kick. If the Blade touched a man's spine, he died, eyes burning. If it cut through the core of a limb, it killed that limb. One soldier stumbled away from Szeth, arm flopping uselessly on his shoulder. He would never be able to feel it or use it again.

Szeth lowered his Shardblade, standing among the cinder-eyed corpses. Here, in Alethkar, men often spoke of the legends—of mankind's hard-won victory over the Voidbringers. But when weapons created to fight nightmares were turned against common soldiers, the lives of men became cheap things indeed.

Szeth turned and continued on his way, slippered feet falling on the soft red rug. The Shardblade, as always, glistened silver and clean. When one killed with a Blade, there was no blood. That seemed like a sign. The Shardblade was just a tool; it could not be blamed for the murders.

The door at the end of the hallway burst open. Szeth froze as a small group of soldiers rushed out, ushering a man in regal robes, his head ducked as if to avoid arrows. The soldiers wore deep blue, the color of the King's Guard, and the corpses didn't make them stop and gawk. They were prepared for what a Shardbearer could do. They opened a side door and shoved their ward through, several leveling spears at Szeth as they backed out.

Another figure stepped from the king's quarters; he wore glistening blue armor made of smoothly interlocking plates. Unlike common plate armor, however, this armor had no leather or mail visible at the joints—just smaller plates, fitting together with intricate precision. The armor was beautiful, the blue inlaid with golden bands around the edges of each piece of plate, the helm ornamented with three waves of small, hornlike wings.

Shardplate, the customary complement to a Shardblade. The newcomer carried a sword as well, an enormous Shardblade six feet long with a design along the blade like burning flames, a weapon of silvery metal that gleamed and almost seemed to glow. A weapon designed to slay dark gods, a larger counterpart to the one Szeth carried.

Szeth hesitated. He didn't recognize the armor; he had not been warned that he would be set at this task, and hadn't been given proper time to memorize the various suits of Plate or Blades owned by the Alethi. But a Shardbearer would have to be dealt with before he chased the king; he could not leave such a foe behind.

Besides, perhaps a Shardbearer could defeat him, kill him and end his miserable life. His Lashings wouldn't work directly on someone in Shardplate, and the armor would enhance the man, strengthen him. Szeth's honor would not allow him to betray his mission or seek death. But if that death occurred, he *would* welcome it.

The Shardbearer struck, and Szeth Lashed himself to the side of the hallway, leaping with a twist and landing on the wall. He danced backward, Blade held at the ready. The Shardbearer fell into an aggressive posture, using one of the swordplay stances favored here in the East. He moved far more nimbly than one would expect for a man in such bulky armor. Shardplate was special, as ancient and magical as the Blades it complemented.

The Shardbearer struck. Szeth skipped to the side and Lashed himself to the ceiling as the Shardbearer's Blade sliced into the wall. Feeling a thrill at the contest, Szeth dashed forward and attacked downward with an overhand blow, trying to hit the Shardbearer's helm. The man ducked, going down on one knee, letting Szeth's Blade cleave empty air.

Szeth leaped backward as the Shardbearer swung upward with his Blade, slicing into the ceiling. Szeth didn't own a set of Plate himself, and didn't care to. His Lashings interfered with the gemstones that powered Shardplate, and he had to choose one or the other.

As the Shardbearer turned, Szeth sprinted forward across the ceiling. As expected, the Shardbearer swung again, and Szeth leaped to the side, rolling. He came up from his roll and flipped, Lashing himself to the floor again. He spun to land on the ground behind the Shardbearer. He slammed his Blade into his opponent's open back.

Unfortunately, there was one major advantage Plate offered: It could block a Shardblade. Szeth's weapon hit solidly, causing a web of glowing lines to spread out across the back of the armor, and Stormlight began to leak free from them. Shardplate didn't dent or bend like common metal. Szeth would have to hit the Shardbearer in the same location at least once more to break through.

Szeth danced out of range as the Shardbearer swung in anger, trying to cut at Szeth's knees. The tempest within Szeth gave him many advantages—including the ability to quickly recover from small wounds. But it would not restore limbs killed by a Shardblade.

He rounded the Shardbearer, then picked a moment and dashed forward. The Shardbearer swung again, but Szeth briefly Lashed himself to the ceiling for lift. He shot into the air, cresting over the swing, then immediately Lashed himself back to the floor. He struck as he landed, but the Shardbearer recovered quickly and executed a perfect follow-through stroke, coming within a finger of hitting Szeth.

The man was dangerously skilled with that Blade. Many Shardbearers depended too much on the power of their weapon and armor. This man was different.

Szeth jumped to the wall and struck at the Shardbearer with quick, terse attacks, like a snapping eel. The Shardbearer fended him off with wide, sweeping counters. His Blade's length kept Szeth at bay.

This is taking too long! Szeth thought. If the king slipped away into hiding, Szeth would fail in his mission no matter how many people he killed. He ducked in for another strike, but the Shardbearer forced him back. Each second this fight lasted was another for the king's escape.

It was time to be reckless. Szeth launched into the air, Lashing himself to the other end of the hallway and falling feet-first toward his adversary. The Shardbearer didn't hesitate to swing, but Szeth Lashed himself down at an angle, dropping immediately. The Shardblade swished through the air above him.

He landed in a crouch, using his momentum to throw himself forward, and swung at the Shardbearer's side, where the Plate had cracked. He hit with a powerful blow. That piece of the Plate shattered, bits of molten metal streaking away. The Shardbearer grunted, dropping to one knee, raising a hand to his side. Szeth raised a foot to the man's side and shoved him backward with a Stormlight-enhanced kick.

The heavy Shardbearer crashed into the door of the king's quarters, smashing it and falling partway into the room beyond. Szeth left him, ducking instead through the doorway to the right, following the way the king had gone. The hallway here had the same red carpet, and Stormlight lamps on the walls gave Szeth a chance to recharge the tempest within.

Energy blazed within him again, and he sped up. If he could get far enough ahead, he could deal with the king, then turn back to fight off the Shardbearer. It wouldn't be easy. A Full Lashing on a doorway wouldn't stop a Shardbearer, and that Plate would let the man run supernaturally fast. Szeth glanced over his shoulder.

The Shardbearer wasn't following. The man sat up in his armor, looking dazed. Szeth could just barely see him, sitting in the doorway, surrounded by broken bits of wood. Perhaps Szeth had wounded him more than he'd thought.

Or maybe . . .

Szeth froze. He thought of the ducked head of the man who'd been rushed out, face obscured. The Shardbearer *still* wasn't following. He was so skilled. It was said that few men could rival Gavilar Kholin's swordsmanship. Could it be?

Szeth turned and dashed back, trusting his instincts. As soon as the Shardbearer saw him, he climbed to his feet with alacrity. Szeth ran faster. What was the safest place for your king? In the hands of some guards, fleeing? Or protected in a suit of Shardplate, left behind, dismissed as a bodyguard?

Clever, Szeth thought as the formerly sluggish Shardbearer fell into another battle stance. Szeth attacked with renewed vigor, swinging his Blade in a flurry of strikes. The Shardbearer—the king—aggressively struck out with broad, sweeping blows. Szeth pulled away from one of these, feeling the wind of the weapon passing just inches before him. He timed his next move, then dashed forward, ducking underneath the king's follow-through.

The king, expecting another strike at his side, twisted with his arm held protectively to block the hole in his Plate. That gave Szeth the room to run past him and into the king's chambers.

The king spun around to follow, but Szeth ran through the lavishly furnished chamber, flinging out his hand, touching pieces of furniture he passed. He infused them with Stormlight, Lashing them to a point behind the king. The furniture tumbled as if the room had been turned on its side, couches, chairs, and tables dropping toward the surprised king. Gavilar made the mistake of chopping at them with his Shardblade. The weapon easily sheared through a large couch, but the pieces still crashed into him, making him stumble. A footstool hit him next, throwing him to the ground.

Gavilar rolled out of the way of the furniture and charged forward, Plate leaking streams of Light from the cracked sections. Szeth gathered himself, then leaped into the air, Lashing himself backward and to the right as the king arrived. He zipped out of the way of the king's blow, then Lashed himself forward with two Basic Lashings in a row. Stormlight flashed out of him, clothing freezing, as he was pulled toward the king at twice the speed of a normal fall.

The king's posture indicated surprise as Szeth lurched in midair, then spun toward him, swinging. He slammed his Blade into the king's helm, then immediately Lashed himself to the ceiling and fell upward, slamming into the stone roof above. He'd Lashed himself in too many directions too quickly, and his body had lost track, making it difficult to land gracefully. He stumbled back to his feet.

Below, the king stepped back, trying to get into position to swing up at Szeth. The man's helm was cracked, leaking Stormlight, and he stood protectively, defending the side with the broken plate. The king used a one-handed swing, reaching for the ceiling. Szeth immediately Lashed himself downward, judging that the king's attack would leave him unable to get his sword back in time.

Szeth underestimated his opponent. The king stepped into Szeth's attack, trusting his helm to absorb the blow. Just as Szeth hit the helm a second time—shattering it—Gavilar punched with his off hand, slamming his gauntleted fist into Szeth's face.

Blinding light flashed in Szeth's eyes, a counterpoint to the sudden agony that crashed across his face. Everything blurred, his vision fading.

Pain. So much *pain*!

He screamed, Stormlight leaving him in a rush, and he slammed back into something hard. The balcony doors. More pain broke out across his shoulders, as if someone had stabbed him with a hundred daggers, and he hit the ground and rolled to a stop, muscles trembling. The blow would have killed an ordinary man.

No time for pain. No time for pain. No time for pain!

He blinked, shaking his head, the world blurry and dark. Was he blind? No. It was dark outside. He was on the wooden balcony; the force of the blow had thrown him through the doors. Something was thumping. Heavy footfalls. The Shardbearer!

Szeth stumbled to his feet, vision swimming. Blood streamed from the side of his face, and Stormlight rose from his skin, blinding his left eye. The Light. It would heal him, if it could. His jaw felt unhinged. Broken? He'd dropped his Shardblade.

A lumbering shadow moved in front of him; the Shardbearer's armor had leaked enough Stormlight that the king was having trouble walking. But he was coming.

Szeth screamed, kneeling, infusing Stormlight into the wooden balcony, Lashing it downward. The air frosted around him. The tempest roared, traveling down his arms into the wood. He Lashed it downward, then did it again. He Lashed a fourth time as Gavilar stepped onto the balcony. It lurched under the extra weight. The wood cracked, straining.

The Shardbearer hesitated.

Szeth Lashed the balcony downward a fifth time. The balcony supports shattered and the entire structure broke free from the building. Szeth screamed through a broken jaw and used his final bit of Stormlight to Lash himself to the side of the building. He fell to the side, passing the shocked Shardbearer, then hit the wall and rolled.

The balcony dropped away, the king looking up with shock as he lost his footing. The fall was brief. In the moonlight, Szeth watched solemnly—vision still fuzzy, blinded in one eye—as the structure crashed to the stone ground below. The wall of the palace trembled, and the crash of broken wood echoed from the nearby buildings.

Still lying on the side of the wall, Szeth groaned, climbing to his feet. He felt weak; he'd used up his Stormlight too quickly, straining his body. He stumbled down the side of the building, approaching the wreckage, barely able to remain standing.

The king was still moving. Shardplate would protect a man from such a fall, but a large length of bloodied wood stuck up through Gavilar's side, piercing him where Szeth had broken the Plate earlier. Szeth knelt down, inspecting the man's pain-wracked face. Strong features, square chin, black beard flecked with white, striking pale green eyes. Gavilar Kholin.

"I . . . expected you . . . to come," the king said between gasps.

Szeth reached underneath the front of the man's breastplate, tapping the straps there. They unfastened, and he pulled the front of the breastplate free, exposing the gemstones on its interior. Two had been cracked and burned out. Three still glowed. Numb, Szeth breathed in sharply, absorbing the Light.

The storm began to rage again. More Light rose from the side of his face, repairing his damaged skin and bones. The pain was still great; Stormlight healing was far from instantaneous. It would be hours before he recovered.

The king coughed. "You can tell . . . Thaidakar . . . that he's too late. . . ."

"I don't know who that is," Szeth said, standing, his words slurring from his broken jaw. He held his hand to the side, resummoning his Shardblade.

The king frowned. "Then who . . . ? Restares? Sadeas? I never thought . . ."

"My masters are the Parshendi," Szeth said. Ten heartbeats passed, and his Blade dropped into his hand, wet with condensation.

"The Parshendi? That makes no sense." Gavilar coughed, hand quivering, reaching toward his chest and fumbling at a pocket. He pulled out a small crystalline sphere tied to a chain. "You must take this. They must not get it." He seemed dazed. "Tell . . . tell my brother . . . he must find the most important words a man can say. . . ."

Gavilar fell still.

Szeth hesitated, then knelt down and took the sphere. It was odd, unlike any he'd seen before. Though it was completely dark, it seemed to glow somehow. With a light that was black.

The Parshendi? Gavilar had said. *That makes no sense.*

"Nothing makes sense anymore," Szeth whispered, tucking the strange sphere away. "It's all unraveling. I am sorry, King of the Alethi. I doubt that you care. Not anymore, at least." He stood up. "At least you won't have to watch the world ending with the rest of us."

Beside the king's body, his Shardblade materialized from mist, clattering to the stones now that its master was dead. It was worth a fortune; kingdoms had fallen as men vied to possess a single Shardblade.

Shouts of alarm came from inside the palace. Szeth needed to go. But . . .

Tell my brother . . .

To Szeth's people, a dying request was sacred. He took the king's hand, dipping it in the man's own blood, then used it to scrawl on the wood, *Brother. You must find the most important words a man can say.*

With that, Szeth escaped into the night. He left the king's Shardblade; he had no use for it. The Blade Szeth already carried was curse enough.

PART
ONE

Above Silence

KALADIN • SHALLAN

"You've killed me. Bastards, you've killed me! While the sun is still hot, I die!"

—Collected on the fifth day of the week Chach of the month Betab of the year 1171, ten seconds before death. Subject was a darkeyed soldier thirty-one years of age. Sample is considered questionable.

FIVE YEARS LATER

I'm going to die, aren't I?" Cenn asked.

The weathered veteran beside Cenn turned and inspected him. The veteran wore a full beard, cut short. At the sides, the black hairs were starting to give way to grey.

I'm going to die, Cenn thought, clutching his spear—the shaft slick with sweat. *I'm going to die. Oh, Stormfather. I'm going to die. . . .*

"How old are you, son?" the veteran asked. Cenn didn't remember the man's name. It was hard to recall anything while watching that other army form lines across the rocky battlefield. That lining up seemed so civil. Neat, organized. Shortspears in the front ranks, longspears and javelins next, archers at the sides. The darkeyed spearmen wore equipment like Cenn's: leather jerkin and knee-length skirt with a simple steel cap and a matching breastplate.

Many of the lighteyes had full suits of armor. They sat astride horses, their honor guards clustering around them with breastplates that gleamed burgundy and deep forest green. Were there Shardbearers among them? Brightlord Amaram wasn't a Shardbearer. Were any of his men? What if Cenn had to fight one? Ordinary men didn't kill Shardbearers. It had happened so infrequently that each occurrence was now legendary.

It's really happening, he thought with mounting terror. This wasn't a drill in the camp. This wasn't training out in the fields, swinging sticks. This was *real*. Facing that fact— his heart pounding like a frightened animal in his chest, his legs unsteady—Cenn suddenly realized that he was a coward. He shouldn't have left the herds! He should never have—

"Son?" the veteran said, voice firm. "How old are you?"

"Fifteen, sir."

"And what's your name?"

"Cenn, sir."

The mountainous, bearded man nodded. "I'm Dallet."

"Dallet," Cenn repeated, still staring out at the other army. There were so many of them! Thousands. "I'm going to die, aren't I?"

"*No.*" Dallet had a gruff voice, but somehow that was comforting. "You're going to be just fine. Keep your head on straight. Stay with the squad."

"But I've barely had three months' training!" He swore he could hear faint clangs from the enemy's armor or shields. "I can barely hold this spear! Stormfather, I'm *dead*. I can't—"

"Son," Dallet interrupted, soft but firm. He raised a hand and placed it on Cenn's shoulder. The rim of Dallet's large round shield reflected the light from where it hung on his back. "You are *going* to be *fine*."

"How can you know?" It came out as a plea.

"Because, lad. You're in Kaladin Stormblessed's squad." The other soldiers nearby nodded in agreement.

Behind them, waves and waves of soldiers were lining up—thousands of them. Cenn was right at the front, with Kaladin's squad of about thirty other men. Why had Cenn been moved to a new squad at the last moment? It had something to do with camp politics.

Why was this squad at the very front, where casualties were bound to be the greatest? Small fearspren—like globs of purplish goo—began to climb up out of the ground and gather around his feet. In a moment of sheer panic, he nearly dropped his spear and scrambled away. Dallet's hand tightened on his shoulder. Looking up into Dallet's confident black eyes, Cenn hesitated.

"Did you piss before we formed ranks?" Dallet asked.

"I didn't have time to—"

"Go now."

"*Here?*"

"If you don't, you'll end up with it running down your leg in battle, distracting you, maybe killing you. Do it."

Embarrassed, Cenn handed Dallet his spear and relieved himself onto the stones. When he finished, he shot glances at those next to him. None of Kaladin's soldiers smirked. They stood steady, spears to their sides, shields on their backs.

The enemy army was almost finished. The field between the two forces was bare, flat slickrock, remarkably even and smooth, broken only by occasional rockbuds. It would have made a good pasture. The warm wind blew in Cenn's face, thick with the watery scents of last night's highstorm.

"Dallet!" a voice said.

A man walked up through the ranks, carrying a short-spear that had two leather knife sheaths strapped to the haft. The newcomer was a young man—perhaps four years older than Cenn's fifteen—but he was taller by several fingers than even Dallet. He wore the common leathers of a spearman, but under them was a pair of dark trousers. That wasn't supposed to be allowed.

His black Alethi hair was shoulder-length and wavy, his eyes a dark brown. He also had knots of white cord on the shoulders of his jerkin, marking him as a squadleader.

The thirty men around Cenn snapped to attention, raising their spears in salute. *This is Kaladin Stormblessed?* Cenn thought incredulously. *This youth?*

"Dallet, we're soon going to have a new recruit," Kaladin said. He had a strong voice. "I need you to . . ." He trailed off as he noticed Cenn.

"He found his way here just a few minutes ago, sir," Dallet said with a smile. "I've been gettin' him ready."

"Well done," Kaladin said. "I paid good money to get that boy away from Gare. That man's so incompetent he might as well be fighting for the other side."

What? Cenn thought. *Why would anyone* pay *to get me?*

"What do you think about the field?" Kaladin asked. Several of the other spearmen nearby raised hands to shade from the sun, scanning the rocks.

"That dip next to the two boulders on the far right?" Dallet asked.

Kaladin shook his head. "Footing's too rough."

"Aye. Perhaps it is. What about the short hill over there? Far enough to avoid the first fall, close enough to not get too far ahead."

Kaladin nodded, though Cenn couldn't see what they were looking at. "Looks good."

"The rest of you louts hear that?" Dallet shouted.

The men raised their spears high.

"Keep an eye on the new boy, Dallet," Kaladin said. "He won't know the signs."

"Of course," Dallet said, smiling. Smiling! How could the man smile? The enemy army was blowing horns. Did that mean they were ready? Even though Cenn had just relieved himself, he felt a trickle of urine run down his leg.

"Stay firm," Kaladin said, then trotted down the front line to talk to the next squadleader over. Behind Cenn and the others, the dozens of ranks were still growing. The archers on the sides prepared to fire.

"Don't worry, son," Dallet said. "We'll be fine. Squadleader Kaladin is lucky."

The soldier on the other side of Cenn nodded. He was a

lanky, red-haired Veden, with darker tan skin than the Alethi. Why was he fighting in an Alethi army? "That's right. Kaladin, he's stormblessed, right sure he is. We only lost . . . what, one man last battle?"

"But someone *did* die," Cenn said.

Dallet shrugged. "People always die. Our squad loses the fewest. You'll see."

Kaladin finished conferring with the other squadleader, then jogged back to his team. Though he carried a shortspear—meant to be wielded one-handed with a shield in the other hand—his was a hand longer than those held by the other men.

"At the ready, men!" Dallet called. Unlike the other squadleaders, Kaladin didn't fall into rank, but stood out in front of his squad.

The men around Cenn shuffled, excited. The sounds were repeated through the vast army, the stillness giving way before eagerness. Hundreds of feet shuffling, shields slapping, clasps clanking. Kaladin remained motionless, staring down the other army. "Steady, men," he said without turning.

Behind, a lighteyed officer passed on horseback. "Be ready to fight! I want their blood, men. Fight and kill!"

"Steady," Kaladin said again, after the man passed.

"Be ready to run," Dallet said to Cenn.

"Run? But we've been trained to march in formation! To stay in our line!"

"Sure," Dallet said. "But most of the men don't have much more training than you. Those who can fight well end up getting sent to the Shattered Plains to battle the Parshendi. Kaladin's trying to get us into shape to go there, to fight for the king." Dallet nodded down the line. "Most of these here will break and charge; the lighteyes aren't good enough commanders to keep them in formation. So stay with us and run."

"Should I have my shield out?" Around Kaladin's team, the other ranks were unhooking their shields. But Kaladin's squad left their shields on their backs.

Before Dallet could answer, a horn blew from behind.

"Go!" Dallet said.

Cenn didn't have much choice. The entire army started moving in a clamor of marching boots. As Dallet had predicted, the steady march didn't last long. Some men began yelling, the roar taken up by others. Lighteyes called for them to go, run, fight. The line disintegrated.

As soon as that happened, Kaladin's squad broke into a dash, running out into the front at full speed. Cenn scrambled to keep up, panicked and terrified. The ground wasn't as smooth as it had seemed, and he nearly tripped on a hidden rockbud, vines withdrawn into its shell.

He righted himself and kept going, holding his spear in one hand, his shield clapping against his back. The distant army was in motion as well, their soldiers charging down the field. There was no semblance of a battle formation or a careful line. This wasn't anything like the training had claimed it would be.

Cenn didn't even know who the enemy was. A landlord was encroaching on Brightlord Amaram's territory—the land owned, ultimately, by Highprince Sadeas. It was a border skirmish, and Cenn thought it was with another Alethi princedom. Why were they fighting each other? Perhaps the king would have put a stop to it, but he was on the Shattered Plains, seeking vengeance for the murder of King Gavilar five years before.

The enemy had a lot of archers. Cenn's panic climbed to a peak as the first wave of arrows flew into the air. He stumbled again, itching to take out his shield. But Dallet grabbed his arm and yanked him forward.

Hundreds of arrows split the sky, dimming the sun. They arced and fell, dropping like skyeels upon their prey. Amaram's soldiers raised shields. But not Kaladin's squad. No shields for them.

Cenn screamed.

And the arrows slammed into the middle ranks of Amaram's army, behind him. Cenn glanced over his shoulder, still running. The arrows fell *behind* him. Soldiers screamed, arrows broke against shields; only a few straggling arrows landed anywhere near the front ranks.

"Why?" he yelled at Dallet. "How did you know?"

"They want the arrows to hit where the men are most crowded," the large man replied. "Where they'll have the greatest chance of finding a body."

Several other groups in the van left their shields lowered, but most ran awkwardly with their shields angled up to the sky, worried about arrows that wouldn't hit them. That slowed them, and they risked getting trampled by the men behind who *were* getting hit. Cenn itched to raise his shield anyway; it felt so wrong to run without it.

The second volley hit, and men screamed in pain. Kaladin's squad barreled toward the enemy soldiers, some of whom were dying to arrows from Amaram's archers. Cenn could hear the enemy soldiers bellowing war cries, could make out individual faces. Suddenly, Kaladin's squad pulled to a halt, forming a tight group. They'd reached the small incline that Kaladin and Dallet had chosen earlier.

Dallet grabbed Cenn and shoved him to the very center of the formation. Kaladin's men lowered spears, pulling out shields as the enemy bore down on them. The charging foe used no careful formation; they didn't keep the ranks of long-spears in back and shortspears in front. They all just ran forward, yelling in a frenzy.

Cenn scrambled to get his shield unlatched from his back. Clashing spears rang in the air as squads engaged one an-other. A group of enemy spearmen rushed up to Kaladin's squad, perhaps coveting the higher ground. The three dozen attackers had some cohesion, though they weren't in as tight a formation as Kaladin's squad was.

The enemy seemed determined to make up for it in pas-sion; they bellowed and screamed in fury, rushing Kaladin's line. Kaladin's team held rank, defending Cenn as if he were some lighteyes and they were his honor guard. The two forces met with a crash of metal on wood, shields slamming together. Cenn cringed back.

It was over in a few eyeblinks. The enemy squad pulled back, leaving two dead on the stone. Kaladin's team hadn't lost anyone. They held their bristling V formation, though one man stepped back and pulled out a bandage to wrap a thigh wound. The rest of the men closed in to fill the spot. The wounded man was hulking and thick-armed; he cursed, but the wound didn't look bad. He was on his feet in a moment, but didn't return to the place where he'd been. Instead, he moved down to one end of the V formation, a more protected spot.

The battlefield was chaos. The two armies mingled indistinguishably; sounds of clanging, crunching, and screaming churned in the air. Many of the squads broke apart, members rushing from one encounter to another. They moved like hunters, groups of three or four seeking lone individuals, then brutally falling on them.

Kaladin's team held its ground, engaging only enemy squads that got too close. Was this what a battle really was? Cenn's practice had trained him for long ranks of men, shoulder to shoulder. Not this frenzied intermixing, this brutal pandemonium. Why didn't more hold formation?

The real soldiers are all gone, Cenn thought. *Off fighting in a real battle at the Shattered Plains. No wonder Kaladin wants to get his squad there.*

Spears flashed on all sides; it was difficult to tell friend from foe, despite the emblems on breastplates and colored paint on shields. The battlefield broke down into hundreds of small groups, like a thousand different wars happening at the same time.

After the first few exchanges, Dallet took Cenn by the shoulder and placed him in the rank at the very bottom of the V pattern. Cenn, however, was worthless. When Kaladin's team engaged enemy squads, all of his training fled him. It took everything he had to just remain there, holding his spear outward and trying to look threatening.

For the better part of an hour, Kaladin's squad held their small hill, working as a team, shoulder to shoulder. Kaladin often left his position at the front, rushing this way and that, banging his spear on his shield in a strange rhythm.

Those are signals, Cenn realized as Kaladin's squad moved

from the V shape into a ring. With the screams of the dying and the thousands of men calling to others, it was nearly impossible to hear a single person's voice. But the sharp clang of the spear against the metal plate on Kaladin's shield was clear. Each time they changed formations, Dallet grabbed Cenn by the shoulder and steered him.

Kaladin's team didn't chase down stragglers. They remained on the defensive. And, while several of the men in Kaladin's team took wounds, none of them fell. Their squad was too intimidating for the smaller groups, and larger enemy units retreated after a few exchanges, seeking easier foes.

Eventually something changed. Kaladin turned, watching the tides of the battle with discerning brown eyes. He raised his spear and smacked his shield in a quick rhythm he hadn't used before. Dallet grabbed Cenn by the arm and pulled him away from the small hill. Why abandon it now?

Just then, the larger body of Amaram's force broke, the men scattering. Cenn hadn't realized how poorly the battle in this quarter had been going for his side. As Kaladin's team retreated, they passed many wounded and dying, and Cenn grew nauseated. Soldiers were sliced open, their insides spilling out.

He didn't have time for horror; the retreat quickly turned into a rout. Dallet cursed, and Kaladin beat his shield again. The squad changed direction, heading eastward. There, Cenn saw, a larger group of Amaram's soldiers was holding.

But the enemy had seen the ranks break, and that made them bold. They rushed forward in clusters, like wild axehounds hunting stray hogs. Before Kaladin's team was halfway across the field of dead and dying, a large group of enemy soldiers intercepted them. Kaladin reluctantly banged his shield; his squad slowed.

Cenn felt his heart begin to thump faster and faster. Nearby, a squad of Amaram's soldiers was consumed; men stumbled and fell, screaming, trying to get away. The enemies used their spears like skewers, killing men on the ground like cremlings.

Kaladin's men met the enemy in a crash of spears and

shields. Bodies shoved on all sides, and Cenn was spun about. In the jumble of friend and foe, dying and killing, Cenn grew overwhelmed. So many men running in so many directions!

He panicked, scrambling for safety. A group of soldiers nearby wore Alethi uniforms. Kaladin's squad. Cenn ran for them, but when some turned toward him, Cenn was terrified to realize he didn't recognize them. This *wasn't* Kaladin's squad, but a small group of unfamiliar soldiers holding an uneven, broken line. Wounded and terrified, they scattered as soon as an enemy squad got close.

Cenn froze, holding his spear in a sweaty hand. The enemy soldiers charged right for him. His instincts urged him to flee, yet he had seen so many men picked off one at a time. He had to stand! He had to face them! He couldn't run, he couldn't—

He yelled, stabbing his spear at the lead soldier. The man casually knocked the weapon aside with his shield, then drove his shortspear into Cenn's thigh. The pain was hot, so hot that the blood squirting out on his leg felt cold by comparison. Cenn gasped.

The soldier yanked the weapon free. Cenn stumbled backward, dropping his spear and shield. He fell to the rocky ground, splashing in someone else's blood. His foe raised a spear high, a looming silhouette against the stark blue sky, ready to ram it into Cenn's heart.

And then *he* was there.

Squadleader. Stormblessed. Kaladin's spear came as if out of nowhere, narrowly deflecting the blow that was to have killed Cenn. Kaladin set himself in front of Cenn, alone, facing down six spearmen. He didn't flinch. He *charged*.

It happened so quickly. Kaladin swept the feet from beneath the man who had stabbed Cenn. Even as that man fell, Kaladin reached up and flipped a knife from one of the sheaths tied about his spear. His hand snapped, knife flashing and hitting the thigh of a second foe. That man fell to one knee, screaming.

A third man froze, looking at his fallen allies. Kaladin shoved past a wounded enemy and slammed his spear into the gut of the third man. A fourth man fell with a knife to the eye. When had Kaladin grabbed that knife? He spun between the last two, his spear a blur, wielding it like a quarterstaff. For a moment, Cenn thought he could see something surrounding the squadleader. A warping of the air, like the wind itself become visible.

I've lost a lot of blood. It's flowing out so quickly. . . .

Kaladin spun, knocking aside attacks, and the last two spearmen fell with gurgles that Cenn thought sounded surprised. Foes all down, Kaladin turned and knelt beside Cenn. The squadleader set aside his spear and whipped a white strip of cloth from his pocket, then efficiently wrapped it tight around Cenn's leg. Kaladin worked with the ease of one who had bound wounds dozens of times before.

"Kaladin, sir!" Cenn said, pointing at one of the soldiers Kaladin had wounded. The enemy man held his leg as he stumbled to his feet. In a second, however, mountainous Dallet was there, shoving the foe with his shield. Dallet didn't kill the wounded man, but let him stumble away, unarmed.

The rest of the squad arrived and formed a ring around Kaladin, Dallet, and Cenn. Kaladin stood up, raising his spear to his shoulder; Dallet handed him back his knives, retrieved from the fallen foes.

"Had me worried there, sir," Dallet said. "Running off like that."

"I knew you'd follow," Kaladin said. "Raise the red banner. Cyn, Korater, you're going back with the boy. Dallet, hold here. Amaram's line is bulging in this direction. We should be safe soon."

"And you, sir?" Dallet asked.

Kaladin looked across the field. A pocket had opened in the enemy forces, and a man rode there on a white horse, swinging about him with a wicked mace. He wore full plate armor, polished and gleaming silver.

"A Shardbearer," Cenn said.

Dallet snorted. "No, thank the Stormfather. Just a light-eyed officer. Shardbearers are far too valuable to waste on a minor border dispute."

Kaladin watched the lighteyes with a seething hatred. It was the same hatred Cenn's father had shown when he'd spoken of chull rustlers, or the hatred Cenn's mother would display when someone mentioned Kusiri, who had run off with the cobbler's son.

"Sir?" Dallet said hesitantly.

"Subsquads Two and Three, pincer pattern," Kaladin said, his voice hard. "We're taking a brightlord off his throne."

"You sure that's wise, sir? We've got wounded."

Kaladin turned toward Dallet. "That's one of Hallaw's officers. He might be the one."

"You don't know that, sir."

"Regardless, he's a battalionlord. If we kill an officer that high, we're all but guaranteed to be in the next group sent to the Shattered Plains. We're taking him." His eyes grew distant. "Imagine it, Dallet. Real soldiers. A warcamp with discipline and lighteyes with integrity. A place where our fighting will *mean* something."

Dallet sighed, but nodded. Kaladin waved to a group of his soldiers; then they raced across the field. A smaller group of soldiers, including Dallet, waited behind with the wounded. One of those—a thin man with black Alethi hair speckled with a handful of blond hairs, marking some foreign blood— pulled a long red ribbon from his pocket and attached it to his spear. He held the spear aloft, letting the ribbon flap in the wind.

"It's a call for runners to carry our wounded off the field," Dallet said to Cenn. "We'll have you out of here soon. You were brave, standing against those six."

"Fleeing seemed stupid," Cenn said, trying to take his mind off his throbbing leg. "With so many wounded on the field, how can we think that the runners'll come for us?"

"Squadleader Kaladin bribes them," Dallet said. "They usually only carry off lighteyes, but there are more runners than there are wounded lighteyes. The squadleader puts most of his pay into the bribes."

"This squad *is* different," Cenn said, feeling light-headed.

"Told you."

"Not because of luck. Because of training."

"That's part of it. Part of it is because we know if we get hurt, Kaladin will get us off the battlefield." He paused, looking over his shoulder. As Kaladin had predicted, Amaram's line was surging back, recovering.

The mounted enemy lighteyes from before was energetically laying about with his mace. A group of his honor guard moved to one side, engaging Kaladin's subsquads. The lighteyes turned his horse. He wore an open-fronted helm that had sloping sides and a large set of plumes on the top. Cenn couldn't make out his eye color, but he knew it would be blue or green, maybe yellow or light grey. He was a brightlord, chosen at birth by the Heralds, marked for rule.

He impassively regarded those who fought nearby. Then one of Kaladin's knives took him in the right eye.

The brightlord screamed, falling back off the saddle as Kaladin somehow slipped through the lines and leaped upon him, spear raised.

"Aye, it's part training," Dallet said, shaking his head. "But it's mostly him. He fights like a storm, that one, and thinks twice as fast as other men. The way he moves sometimes . . ."

"He bound my leg," Cenn said, realizing he was beginning to speak nonsense due to the blood loss. Why point out the bound leg? It was a simple thing.

Dallet just nodded. "He knows a lot about wounds. He can read glyphs too. He's a strange man, for a lowly darkeyed spearman, our squadleader is." He turned to Cenn. "But you should save your strength, son. The squadleader won't be pleased if we lose you, not after what he paid to get you."

"Why?" Cenn asked. The battlefield was growing quieter, as if many of the dying men had already yelled themselves hoarse. Almost everyone around them was an ally, but Dallet still watched to make sure no enemy soldiers tried to strike at Kaladin's wounded.

"Why, Dallet?" Cenn repeated, feeling urgent. "Why bring me into his squad? Why *me*?"

Dallet shook his head. "It's just how he is. Hates the thought of young kids like you, barely trained, going to battle.

Every now and again, he grabs one and brings him into his squad. A good half dozen of our men were once like you." Dallet's eyes got a far-off look. "I think you all remind him of someone."

Cenn glanced at his leg. Painspren—like small orange hands with overly long fingers—were crawling around him, reacting to his agony. They began turning away, scurrying in other directions, seeking other wounded. His pain was fading, his leg—his whole body—feeling numb.

He leaned back, staring up at the sky. He could hear faint thunder. That was odd. The sky was cloudless.

Dallet cursed.

Cenn turned, shocked out of his stupor. Galloping directly toward them was a massive black horse bearing a rider in gleaming armor that seemed to radiate light. That armor was seamless—no chain underneath, just smaller plates, incredibly intricate. The figure wore an unornamented full helm, and the plate was gilded. He carried a massive sword in one hand, fully as long as a man was tall. It wasn't a simple, straight sword—it was curved, and the side that wasn't sharp was ridged, like flowing waves. Etchings covered its length.

It was beautiful. Like a work of art. Cenn had never seen a Shardbearer, but he knew immediately what this was. How could he ever have mistaken a simple armored lighteyes for one of *these* majestic creatures?

Hadn't Dallet claimed there would be no Shardbearers on this battlefield? Dallet scrambled to his feet, calling for the subsquad to form up. Cenn just sat where he was. He couldn't have stood, not with that leg wound.

He felt so light-headed. How much blood had he lost? He could barely think.

Either way, he couldn't fight. You didn't fight something like this. Sun gleamed against that plate armor. And that gorgeous, intricate, sinuous sword. It was like . . . like the Almighty himself had taken form to walk the battlefield.

And why would you want to fight the Almighty?

Cenn closed his eyes.

"Ten orders. We were loved, once. Why have you forsaken us, Almighty! Shard of my soul, where have you gone?"

—Collected on the second day of Kakash, year 1171, five seconds before death. Subject was a lighteyed woman in her third decade.

EIGHT MONTHS LATER

Kaladin's stomach growled as he reached through the bars and accepted the bowl of slop. He pulled the small bowl—more a cup—between the bars, sniffed it, then grimaced as the caged wagon began to roll again. The sludgy grey slop was made from overcooked tallew grain, and this batch was flecked with crusted bits of yesterday's meal.

Revolting though it was, it was all he would get. He began to eat, legs hanging out between the bars, watching the scenery pass. The other slaves in his cage clutched their bowls protectively, afraid that someone might steal from them. One of them tried to steal Kaladin's food on the first day. He'd nearly broken the man's arm. Now everyone left him alone.

Suited him just fine.

He ate with his fingers, careless of the dirt. He'd stopped noticing dirt months ago. He hated that he felt some of that same paranoia that the others showed. How could he not, after eight months of beatings, deprivation, and brutality?

He fought down the paranoia. He *wouldn't* become like them. Even if he'd given up everything else—even if all had been taken from him, even if there was no longer hope of escape. This one thing he would retain. He was a slave. But he didn't need to think like one.

He finished the slop quickly. Nearby, one of the other slaves began to cough weakly. There were ten slaves in the wagon, all men, scraggly-bearded and dirty. It was one of three wagons in their caravan through the Unclaimed Hills.

The sun blazed reddish white on the horizon, like the hottest part of a smith's fire. It lit the framing clouds with a spray of color, paint thrown carelessly on a canvas. Covered in tall, monotonously green grass, the hills seemed endless. On a nearby mound, a small figure flitted around the plants, dancing like a fluttering insect. The figure was amorphous, vaguely translucent. Windspren were devious spirits who had a penchant for staying where they weren't wanted. He'd hoped that this one had gotten bored and left, but as Kaladin tried to toss his wooden bowl aside, he found that it stuck to his fingers.

The windspren laughed, zipping by, nothing more than a ribbon of light without form. He cursed, tugging on the bowl. Windspren often played pranks like that. He pried at the bowl, and it eventually came free. Grumbling, he tossed it to one of the other slaves. The man quickly began to lick at the remnants of the slop.

"Hey," a voice whispered.

Kaladin looked to the side. A slave with dark skin and matted hair was crawling up to him, timid, as if expecting Kaladin to be angry. "You're not like the others." The slave's black eyes glanced upward, toward Kaladin's forehead, which bore three brands. The first two made a glyphpair, given to him eight months ago, on his last day in Amaram's army.

The third was fresh, given to him by his most recent master. *Shash*, the last glyph read. Dangerous.

The slave had his hand hidden behind his rags. A knife? No, that was ridiculous. None of these slaves could have hidden a weapon; the leaves hidden in Kaladin's belt were as close as one could get. But old instincts could not be banished easily, so Kaladin watched that hand.

"I heard the guards talking," the slave continued, shuffling a little closer. He had a twitch that made him blink too frequently. "You've tried to escape before, they said. You *have* escaped before."

Kaladin made no reply.

"Look," the slave said, moving his hand out from behind his rags and revealing his bowl of slop. It was half full. "Take me with you next time," he whispered. "I'll give you this. Half my food from now until we get away. Please." As he spoke, he attracted a few hungerspren. They looked like brown flies that flitted around the man's head, almost too small to see.

Kaladin turned away, looking out at the endless hills and their shifting, moving grasses. He rested one arm across the bars and placed his head against it, legs still hanging out.

"Well?" the slave asked.

"You're an idiot. If you gave me half your food, you'd be too weak to escape if I *were* to flee. Which I won't. It doesn't work."

"But—"

"Ten times," Kaladin whispered. "Ten escape attempts in eight months, fleeing from five different masters. And how many of them worked?"

"Well . . . I mean . . . you're still here. . . ."

Eight months. Eight months as a slave, eight months of slop and beatings. It might as well have been an eternity. He barely remembered the army anymore. "You can't hide as a slave," Kaladin said. "Not with that brand on your forehead. Oh, I got away a few times. But they always found me. And then back I went."

Once, men had called him lucky. Stormblessed. Those had been lies—if anything, Kaladin had *bad* luck. Soldiers were a superstitious sort, and though he'd initially resisted that way of thinking, it was growing harder and harder. Every person he had ever tried to protect had ended up dead. Time and time again. And now, here he was, in an even worse situation than where he'd begun. It was better not to resist. This was his lot, and he was resigned to it.

There was a certain power in that, a freedom. The freedom of not having to care.

The slave eventually realized Kaladin wasn't going to say anything further, and so he retreated, eating his slop. The wagons continued to roll, fields of green extending in all directions. The area around the rattling wagons was bare, however. When they approached, the grass pulled away, each individual stalk withdrawing into a pinprick hole in the stone. After the wagons moved on, the grass timidly poked back out and stretched its blades toward the air. And so, the cages moved along what appeared to be an open rock highway, cleared just for them.

This far into the Unclaimed Hills, the highstorms were incredibly powerful. The plants had learned to survive. That's what you had to do, learn to survive. Brace yourself, weather the storm.

Kaladin caught a whiff of another sweaty, unwashed body and heard the sound of shuffling feet. He looked suspiciously to the side, expecting that same slave to be back.

It was a different man this time, though. He had a long black beard stuck with bits of food and snarled with dirt. Kaladin kept his own beard shorter, allowing Tvlakv's mercenaries to hack it down periodically. Like Kaladin, the slave wore the remains of a brown sack tied with a rag, and he was darkeyed, of course—perhaps a deep dark green, though with darkeyes it was hard to tell. They all looked brown or black unless you caught them in the right light.

The newcomer cringed away, raising his hands. He had a rash on one hand, the skin just faintly discolored. He'd likely approached because he'd seen Kaladin respond to that other man. The slaves had been frightened of him since the first day, but they were also obviously curious.

Kaladin sighed and turned away. The slave hesitantly sat down. "Mind if I ask how you became a slave, friend? Can't help wondering. We're all wondering."

Judging by the accent and the dark hair, the man was Alethi, like Kaladin. Most of the slaves were. Kaladin didn't reply to the question.

"Me, I stole a herd of chull," the man said. He had a raspy voice, like sheets of paper rubbing together. "If I'd taken one chull, they might have just beaten me. But a whole herd. Seventeen head . . ." He chuckled to himself, admiring his own audacity.

In the far corner of the wagon, someone coughed again. They were a sorry lot, even for slaves. Weak, sickly, underfed. Some, like Kaladin, were repeat runaways—though Kaladin was the only one with a *shash* brand. They were the most worthless of a worthless caste, purchased at a steep discount. They were probably being taken for resale in a remote place where men were desperate for labor. There were plenty of small, independent cities along the coast of the Unclaimed Hills, places where Vorin rules governing the use of slaves were just a distant rumor.

Coming this way was dangerous. These lands were ruled by nobody, and by cutting across open land and staying away from established trade routes, Tvlakv could easily run afoul of unemployed mercenaries. Men who had no honor and no fear of slaughtering a slavemaster and his slaves in order to steal a few chulls and wagons.

Men who had no honor. Were there men who *had* honor?

No, Kaladin thought. *Honor died eight months ago.*

"So?" asked the scraggly-bearded man. "What did you do to get made a slave?"

Kaladin raised his arm against the bars again. "How did you get caught?"

"Odd thing, that," the man said. Kaladin hadn't answered his question, but he *had* replied. That seemed enough. "It was a woman, of course. Should have known she'd sell me."

"Shouldn't have stolen chulls. Too slow. Horses would have been better."

The man laughed riotously. "Horses? What do you think me, a madman? If I'd been caught stealing *those,* I'd have been hanged. Chulls, at least, only earned me a slave's brand."

Kaladin glanced to the side. This man's forehead brand was older than Kaladin's, the skin around the scar faded to white. What was that glyphpair? "*Sas morom,*" Kaladin said. It was the highlord's district where the man had originally been branded.

The man looked up with shock. "Hey! You know glyphs?" Several of the slaves nearby stirred at this oddity. "You must have an even better story than I thought, friend."

Kaladin stared out over those grasses blowing in the mild breeze. Whenever the wind picked up, the more sensitive of the grass stalks shrank down into their burrows, leaving the landscape patchy, like the coat of a sickly horse. That windspren was still there, moving between patches of grass. How long had it been following him? At least a couple of months now. That was downright odd. Maybe it wasn't the same one. They were impossible to tell apart.

"Well?" the man prodded. "Why are you here?"

"There are many reasons why I'm here," Kaladin said. "Failures. Crimes. Betrayals. Probably the same for most every one of us."

Around him, several of the men grunted in agreement; one of those grunts then degenerated into a hacking cough. *Persistent coughing,* a part of Kaladin's mind thought, *accompanied by an excess of phlegm and fevered mumbling at night. Sounds like the grindings.*

"Well," the talkative man said, "perhaps I should ask a different question. Be more specific, that's what my mother always said. Say what you mean and ask for what you want. What's the story of you getting that first brand of yours?"

Kaladin sat, feeling the wagon thump and roll beneath him. "I killed a lighteyes."

His unnamed companion whistled again, this time even more appreciative than before. "I'm surprised they let you live."

"Killing the lighteyes isn't why I was made a slave," Kaladin said. "It's the one I *didn't* kill that's the problem."

"How's that?"

Kaladin shook his head, then stopped answering the talkative man's questions. The man eventually wandered to the front of the wagon's cage and sat down, staring at his bare feet.

.•.

Hours later, Kaladin still sat in his place, idly fingering the glyphs on his forehead. This was his life, day in and day out, riding in these cursed wagons.

His first brands had healed long ago, but the skin around the *shash* brand was red, irritated, and crusted with scabs. It throbbed, almost like a second heart. It hurt even worse than the burn had when he grabbed the heated handle of a cooking pot as a child.

Lessons drilled into Kaladin by his father whispered in the back of his brain, giving the proper way to care for a burn. Apply a salve to prevent infection, wash once daily. Those memories weren't a comfort; they were an annoyance. He didn't *have* fourleaf sap or lister's oil; he didn't even have water for the washing.

The parts of the wound that had scabbed over pulled at his skin, making his forehead feel tight. He could barely pass a few minutes without scrunching up his brow and irritating the wound. He'd grown accustomed to reaching up and wiping away the streaks of blood that trickled from the cracks; his right forearm was smeared with it. If he'd had a mirror, he could probably have spotted tiny red rotspren gathering around the wound.

The sun set in the west, but the wagons kept rolling. Violet Salas peeked over the horizon to the east, seeming hesitant at first, as if making sure the sun had vanished. It was a clear night, and the stars shivered high above. Taln's Scar—a swath of deep red stars that stood out vibrantly from the twinkling white ones—was high in the sky this season.

That slave who'd been coughing earlier was at it again. A

ragged, wet cough. Once, Kaladin would have been quick to go help, but something within him had changed. So many people he'd tried to help were now dead. It seemed to him— irrationally—that the man would be better off without his interference. After failing Tien, then Dallet and his team, then ten successive groups of slaves, it was hard to find the will to try again.

Two hours past First Moon, Tvlakv finally called a halt. His two brutish mercenaries climbed from their places atop their wagons, then moved to build a small fire. Lanky Taran— the serving boy—tended the chulls. The large crustaceans were nearly as big as wagons themselves. They settled down, pulling into their shells for the night with clawfuls of grain. Soon they were nothing more than three lumps in the darkness, barely distinguishable from boulders. Finally, Tvlakv began checking on the slaves one at a time, giving each a ladle of water, making certain his investments were healthy. Or, at least, as healthy as could be expected for this poor lot.

Tvlakv started with the first wagon, and Kaladin—still sitting—pushed his fingers into his makeshift belt, checking on the leaves he'd hidden there. They crackled satisfactorily, the stiff, dried husks rough against his skin. He still wasn't certain what he was going to do with them. He'd grabbed them on a whim during one of the sessions when he'd been allowed out of the wagon to stretch his legs. He doubted anyone else in the caravan knew how to recognize blackbane—narrow leaves on a trefoil prong—so it hadn't been too much of a risk.

Absently, he took the leaves out and rubbed them between forefinger and palm. They had to dry before reaching their potency. Why did he carry them? Did he mean to give them to Tvlakv and get revenge? Or were they a contingency, to be retained in case things got too bad, too unbearable?

Surely I haven't fallen that far, he thought. It was just more likely his instinct of securing a weapon when he saw one, no matter how unusual. The landscape was dark. Salas was the smallest and dimmest of the moons, and while her violet coloring had inspired countless poets, she didn't do much to help you see your hand in front of your face.

"Oh!" a soft, feminine voice said. "What's that?"

A translucent figure—just a handspan tall—peeked up from over the edge of the floor near Kaladin. She climbed up and into the wagon, as if scaling some high plateau. The windspren had taken the shape of a young woman—larger spren could change shapes and sizes—with an angular face and long, flowing hair that faded into mist behind her head. She—Kaladin couldn't help but think of the windspren as a she—was formed of pale blues and whites and wore a simple, flowing white dress of a girlish cut that came down to midcalf. Like the hair, it faded to mist at the very bottom. Her feet, hands, and face were crisply distinct, and she had the hips and bust of a slender woman.

Kaladin frowned at the spirit. Spren were all around; you just ignored them most of the time. But this one was an oddity. The windspren walked upward, as if climbing an invisible staircase. She reached a height where she could stare at Kaladin's hand, so he closed his fingers around the black leaves. She walked around his fist in a circle. Although she glowed like an afterimage from looking at the sun, her form provided no real illumination.

She bent down, looking at his hand from different angles, like a child expecting to find a hidden piece of candy. "What is it?" Her voice was like a whisper. "You can show me. I won't tell anyone. Is it a treasure? Have you cut off a piece of the night's cloak and tucked it away? Is it the heart of a beetle, so tiny yet powerful?"

He said nothing, causing the spren to pout. She floated up, hovering though she had no wings, and looked him in the eyes. "Kaladin, why must you ignore me?"

Kaladin started. "What did you say?"

She smiled mischievously, then sprang away, her figure blurring into a long white ribbon of blue-white light. She shot between the bars—twisting and warping in the air, like a strip of cloth caught in the wind—and darted beneath the wagon.

"Storm you!" Kaladin said, leaping to his feet. "Spirit! What did you say? Repeat that!" Spren didn't use people's names. Spren weren't intelligent. The larger ones—like windspren or riverspren—could mimic voices and expressions, but they didn't actually think. They didn't . . .

"Did any of you hear that?" Kaladin asked, turning to the cage's other occupants. The roof was just high enough to let Kaladin stand. The others were lying back, waiting to get their ladle of water. He got no response beyond a few mutters to be quiet and some coughs from the sick man in the corner. Even Kaladin's "friend" from earlier ignored him. The man had fallen into a stupor, staring at his feet, wiggling his toes periodically.

Maybe they hadn't seen the spren. Many of the larger ones were invisible except to the person they were tormenting. Kaladin sat back down on the floor of the wagon, hanging his legs outside. The windspren *had* said his name, but undoubtedly she'd just repeated what she'd heard before. But . . . none of the men in the cage knew his name.

Maybe I'm going mad, Kaladin thought. *Seeing things that aren't there. Hearing voices.*

He took a deep breath, then opened his hand. His grip had cracked and broken the leaves. He'd need to tuck them away to prevent further—

"Those leaves look interesting," said that same feminine voice. "You like them a lot, don't you?"

Kaladin jumped, twisting to the side. The windspren stood in the air just beside his head, white dress rippling in a wind Kaladin couldn't feel.

"How do you know my name?" he demanded.

The windspren didn't answer. She walked on air over to the bars, then poked her head out, watching Tvlakv the slaver administer drinks to the last few slaves in the first wagon. She looked back at Kaladin. "Why don't you fight? You did before. Now you've stopped."

"Why do you care, spirit?"

She cocked her head. "I don't know," she said, as if surprised at herself. "But I do. Isn't that odd?"

It was more than odd. What did he make of a spren that not only used his name, but seemed to *remember* things he had done weeks ago?

"People don't eat leaves, you know, Kaladin," she said, folding translucent arms. Then she cocked her head. "Or do you? I can't remember. You're so strange, stuffing some things into your mouths, leaking out other things when you don't think anyone is looking."

"How do you know my name?" he whispered.

"How do *you* know it?"

"I know it because . . . because it's mine. My parents told it to me. I don't know."

"Well I don't either," she said, nodding as if she'd just won some grand argument.

"Fine," he said. "But why are you *using* my name?"

"Because it's polite. And you are *im*polite."

"Spren don't know what that means!"

"See, there," she said, pointing at him. "Impolite."

Kaladin blinked. Well, he was far from where he'd grown up, walking foreign stone and eating foreign food. Perhaps the spren who lived here were different from those back home.

"So why don't you fight?" she asked, flitting down to rest on his legs, looking up at his face. She had no weight that he could feel.

"I can't fight," he said softly.

"You did before."

He closed his eyes and rested his head forward against the bars. "I'm so tired." He didn't mean the physical fatigue, though eight months eating leftovers had stolen much of the lean strength he'd cultivated while at war. He *felt* tired. Even when he got enough sleep. Even on those rare days when he wasn't hungry, cold, or stiff from a beating. So tired . . .

"You have been tired before."

"I've failed, spirit," he replied, squeezing his eyes shut. "Must you torment me so?"

They were all dead. Cenn and Dallet, and before that Tukks and the Takers. Before that, Tien. Before that, blood on his hands and the corpse of a young girl with pale skin.

Some of the slaves nearby muttered, likely thinking he was mad. Anyone could end up drawing a spren, but you learned early that talking to one was pointless. *Was* he mad? Perhaps he should wish for that—madness was an escape from the pain. Instead, it terrified him.

He opened his eyes. Tvlakv was finally waddling up to Kaladin's wagon with his bucket of water. The portly, brown-eyed man walked with a very faint limp; the result of a broken leg, perhaps. He was Thaylen, and all Thaylen men had the same stark white beards—regardless of their age or the color of the hair on their heads—and white eyebrows. Those eyebrows grew very long, and the Thaylen wore them pushed back over the ears. That made him appear to have two white streaks in his otherwise black hair.

His clothing—striped trousers of black and red with a dark blue sweater that matched the color of his knit cap—had once been fine, but it was now growing ragged. Had he once been something other than a slaver? This life—the casual buying and selling of human flesh—seemed to have an effect on men. It wearied the soul, even if it did fill one's money pouch.

Tvlakv kept his distance from Kaladin, carrying his oil lantern over to inspect the coughing slave at the front of the cage. Tvlakv called to his mercenaries. Bluth—Kaladin didn't know why he'd bothered to learn their names—wandered over. Tvlakv spoke quietly, pointing at the slave. Bluth nodded, slablike face shadowed in the lanternlight, and pulled the cudgel free from his belt.

The windspren took the form of a white ribbon, then zipped over toward the sick man. She spun and twisted a few times before landing on the floor, becoming a girl again. She leaned in to inspect the man. Like a curious child.

Kaladin turned away and closed his eyes, but he could still hear the coughing. Inside his mind, his father's voice responded. *To cure the grinding coughs,* said the careful, precise tone, *administer two handfuls of bloodivy, crushed to a powder, each day. If you don't have that, be certain to give the patient plenty of liquids, preferably with sugar stirred in. As long as the patient stays hydrated, he will most likely survive. The disease sounds far worse than it is.*

Most likely survive . . .

Those coughs continued. Someone unlatched the cage door. Would they know how to help the man? Such an easy solution. Give him water, and he would live.

It didn't matter. Best not to get involved.

Men dying on the battlefield. A youthful face, so familiar and dear, looking to Kaladin for salvation. A sword wound slicing open the side of a neck. A Shardbearer charging through Amaram's ranks.

Blood. Death. Failure. Pain.

And his father's voice. *Can you really leave him, son? Let him die when you could have helped?*

Storm it!

"Stop!" Kaladin yelled, standing.

The other slaves scrambled back. Bluth jumped up, slamming the cage door closed and holding up his cudgel. Tvlakv shied behind the mercenary, using him as cover.

Kaladin took a deep breath, closing his hand around the leaves and then raising the other to his head, wiping away a smear of blood. He crossed the small cage, bare feet thumping on the wood. Bluth glared as Kaladin knelt beside the sick man. The flickering light illuminated a long, drawn face and nearly bloodless lips. The man had coughed up phlegm; it was greenish and solid. Kaladin felt the man's neck for swelling, then checked his dark brown eyes.

"It's called the grinding coughs," Kaladin said. "He will live, if you give him an extra ladle of water every two hours for five days or so. You'll have to force it down his throat. Mix in sugar, if you have any."

Bluth scratched at his ample chin, then glanced at the shorter slaver.

"Pull him out," Tvlakv said.

The wounded slave awoke as Bluth unlocked the cage. The mercenary waved Kaladin back with his cudgel, and Kaladin reluctantly withdrew. After putting away his cudgel, Bluth grabbed the slave under the arms and dragged him out, all the while trying to keep a nervous eye on Kaladin. Kaladin's last failed escape attempt had involved twenty armed slaves.

His master should have executed him for that, but he had claimed Kaladin was "intriguing" and branded him with *shash*, then sold him for a pittance.

There always seemed to be a reason Kaladin survived when those he'd tried to help died. Some men might have seen that as a blessing, but he saw it as an ironic kind of torment. He'd spent some time under his previous master speaking with a slave from the West, a Selay man who had spoken of the Old Magic from their legends and its ability to curse people. Could that be what was happening to Kaladin?

Don't be foolish, he told himself.

The cage door snapped back in place, locking. The cages were necessary—Tvlakv had to protect his fragile investment from the highstorms. The cages had wooden sides that could be pulled up and locked into place during the furious gales.

Bluth dragged the slave over to the fire, beside the unpacked water barrel. Kaladin felt himself relax. *There,* he told himself. *Perhaps you can still help. Perhaps there's a reason to care.*

Kaladin opened his hand and looked down at the crumbled black leaves in his palm. He didn't need these. Sneaking them into Tvlakv's drink would not only be difficult, but pointless. Did he really want the slaver dead? What would that accomplish?

A low crack rang in the air, followed by a second one, duller, like someone dropping a bag of grain. Kaladin snapped his head up, looking to where Bluth had deposited the sick slave. The mercenary raised his cudgel one more time, then snapped it down, the weapon making a cracking sound as it hit the slave's skull.

The slave hadn't uttered a cry of pain or protest. His corpse slumped over in the darkness; Bluth casually picked it up and slung it over his shoulder.

"No!" Kaladin yelled, leaping across the cage and slamming his hands against the bars.

Tvlakv stood warming himself by the fire.

"Storm you!" Kaladin screamed. "He could have lived, you bastard!"

Tvlakv glanced at him. Then, leisurely, the slaver walked over, straightening his deep blue knit cap. "He would have gotten you all sick, you see." His voice was lightly accented, smashing words together, not giving the proper syllables emphasis. Thaylens always sounded to Kaladin like they were mumbling. "I would not lose an entire wagon for one man."

"He's past the spreading stage!" Kaladin said, slamming his hands against the bars again. "If any of us were going to catch it, we'd have done so by now."

"Hope that you don't. I think he was past saving."

"I told you otherwise!"

"And I should believe you, deserter?" Tvlakv said, amused. "A man with eyes that smolder and hate? You would kill me." He shrugged. "I care not. So long as you are strong when it is time for sales. You should bless me for saving you from that man's sickness."

"I'll bless your cairn when I pile it up myself," Kaladin replied.

Tvlakv smiled, walking back toward the fire. "Keep that fury, deserter, and that strength. It will pay me well on our arrival."

Not if you don't live that long, Kaladin thought. Tvlakv always warmed the last of the water from the bucket he used for the slaves. He'd make himself tea from it, hanging it over the fire. If Kaladin made sure he was watered last, then powdered the leaves and dropped them into the—

Kaladin froze, then looked down at his hands. In his haste, he'd forgotten that he'd been holding the blackbane. He'd dropped the flakes as he slammed his hands against the bars. Only a few bits stuck to his palms, not enough to be potent.

He spun to look backward; the floor of the cage was dirty and covered with grime. If the flakes had fallen there, there was no way to collect them. The wind gathered suddenly, blowing dust, crumbs, and dirt out of the wagon and into the night.

Even in this, Kaladin failed.

He sank down, his back to the bars, and bowed his head. Defeated. That cursed windspren kept darting around him, looking confused.

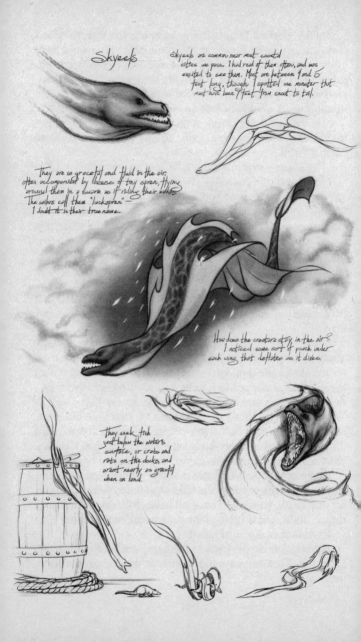

Skyeels

Skyeels are common near most coastal cities we pass. I had read of them often, and was excited to see them. Most are between 1 and 5 feet long, though I spotted one monster that must have been 9 feet from snout to tail.

They are so graceful and fluid in the air, often accompanied by dozens of tiny spren, flying around them in a swarm as if riding their wakes. The sailors call them "luckspren" — I doubt it is their true name.

How does the creature stay in the air? I noticed some sort of pouch under each wing, that deflates as it dives.

They seek fish just below the waters surface, or crabs and rats on the docks, and arent nearly as graceful when on land.

3

CITY OF BELLS

"A man stood on a cliffside and watched his homeland fall into dust. The waters surged beneath, so far beneath. And he heard a child crying. They were his own tears."

—Collected on the 4th of Tanates, year 1171, thirty seconds before death. Subject was a cobbler of some renown.

Kharbranth, City of Bells, was not a place that Shallan had ever imagined she would visit. Though she'd often dreamed of traveling, she'd expected to spend her early life sequestered in her family's manor, only escaping through the books of her father's library. She'd expected to marry one of her father's allies, then spend the rest of her life sequestered in *his* manor.

But expectations were like fine pottery. The harder you held them, the more likely they were to crack.

She found herself breathless, clutching her leather-bound drawing pad to her chest as longshoremen pulled the ship into the dock. Kharbranth was enormous. Built up the side of a steep incline, the city was wedge-shaped, as if it were built into a wide crack, with the open side toward the ocean. The buildings were blocky, with square windows, and appeared to have been constructed of some kind of mud or daub. Crem, perhaps? They were painted bright colors, reds and oranges most often, but occasional blues and yellows too.

She could hear the bells already, tinkling in the wind, ringing with pure voices. She had to strain her neck to look up toward the city's loftiest rim; Kharbranth was like a mountain towering over her. How many people lived in a place like this? Thousands? Tens of thousands? She shivered again— daunted yet excited—then blinked pointedly, fixing the image of the city in her memory.

Sailors rushed about. The *Wind's Pleasure* was a narrow, single-masted vessel, barely large enough for her, the captain, his wife, and the half-dozen crew. It had seemed so small at first, but Captain Tozbek was a calm and cautious man, an excellent sailor, even if he was a pagan. He'd guided the ship with care along the coast, always finding a sheltered cove to ride out highstorms.

The captain oversaw the work as the men secured the mooring. Tozbek was a short man, even-shouldered with Shallan, and he wore his long white Thaylen eyebrows up in a curious spiked pattern. It was like he had two waving fans above his eyes, a foot long each. He wore a simple knit cap and a silver-buttoned black coat. She'd imagined him getting that scar on his jaw in a furious sea battle with pirates. The day before, she'd been disappointed to hear it had been caused by loose tackle during rough weather.

His wife, Ashlv, was already walking down the gangplank to register their vessel. The captain saw Shallan inspecting him, and so walked over. He was a business connection of her family's, long trusted by her father. That was good, since the plan she and her brothers had concocted had contained no place for her bringing along a lady-in-waiting or nurse.

That plan made Shallan nervous. Very, *very* nervous. She hated being duplicitous. But the financial state of her house . . . They either needed a spectacular infusion of wealth or some other edge in local Veden house politics. Otherwise, they wouldn't last the year.

First things first, Shallan thought, forcing herself to be calm. *Find Jasnah Kholin. Assuming she hasn't moved off without you again.*

"I've sent a lad on your behalf, Brightness," Tozbek said. "If the princess is still here, we shall soon know."

Shallan nodded gratefully, still clutching her drawing pad. Out in the city, there were people *everywhere*. Some wore familiar clothing—trousers and shirts that laced up the front for the men, skirts and colorful blouses for the women. Those could have been from her homeland, Jah Keved. But Kharbranth was a free city. A small, politically fragile city-state, it held little territory but had docks open to all ships that passed, and it asked no questions about nationality or status. People flowed to it.

That meant many of the people she saw were exotic. Those single-sheet wraps would mark a man or woman from Tashikk, far to the west. The long coats, enveloping down to the ankles, but open in the front like cloaks . . . where were those from? She'd rarely seen so many parshmen as she noted working the docks, carrying cargo on their backs. Like the parshmen her father had owned, these were stout and thick of limb, with their odd marbled skin—some parts pale or black, others a deep crimson. The mottled pattern was unique to each individual.

After chasing Jasnah Kholin from town to town for the better part of six months, Shallan was beginning to think she'd never catch the woman. Was the princess avoiding her? No, that didn't seem likely—Shallan just wasn't important enough to wait for. Brightness Jasnah Kholin was one of the most powerful women in the world. And one of the most infamous. She was the only member of a faithful royal house who was a professed heretic.

Shallan tried not to grow anxious. Most likely, they'd discover that Jasnah had moved on again. The *Wind's Pleasure* would dock for the night, and Shallan would negotiate a price with the captain—steeply discounted, because of her family's investments in Tozbek's shipping business—to take her to the next port.

Already, they were months past the time when Tozbek had expected to be rid of her. She'd never sensed resentment from him; his honor and loyalty kept him agreeing to her requests. However, his patience wouldn't last forever, and neither would her money. She'd already used over half the spheres she'd brought with her. He wouldn't abandon her in an unfamiliar city, of course, but he might regretfully insist on taking her back to Vedenar.

"Captain!" a sailor said, rushing up the gangplank. He wore only a vest and loose, baggy trousers, and had the darkly tanned skin of one who worked in the sun. "No message, sir. Dock registrar says that Jasnah hasn't left yet."

"Ha!" the captain said, turning to Shallan. "The hunt is over!"

"Bless the Heralds," Shallan said softly.

The captain smiled, flamboyant eyebrows looking like streaks of light coming from his eyes. "It must be your beautiful face that brought us this favorable wind! The windspren themselves were entranced by you, Brightness Shallan, and led us here!"

Shallan blushed, considering a response that wasn't particularly proper.

"Ah!" the captain said, pointing at her. "I can see you have a reply—I see it in your eyes, young miss! Spit it out. Words aren't meant to be kept inside, you see. They are free creatures, and if locked away will unsettle the stomach."

"It's not polite," Shallan protested.

Tozbek bellowed a laugh. "Months of travel, and still you claim that! I keep telling you that we're sailors! We forgot how to be polite the moment we set first foot on a ship; we're far beyond redemption now."

She smiled. She'd been trained by stern nurses and tutors to hold her tongue—unfortunately, her brothers had been even more determined in encouraging her to do the opposite. She'd made a habit of entertaining them with witty comments when nobody else was near. She thought fondly of hours spent by the crackling greatroom hearth, the younger three of her four brothers huddled around her, listening as she made sport of their father's newest sycophant or a traveling ardent. She'd often fabricated silly versions of conversations to fill the mouths of people they could see, but not hear.

That had established in her what her nurses had referred to as an "insolent streak." And the sailors were even more appreciative of a witty comment than her brothers had been.

"Well," Shallan said to the captain, blushing but still eager to speak, "I was just thinking this: You say that my beauty coaxed the winds to deliver us to Kharbranth with haste. But wouldn't that imply that on other trips, my lack of beauty was to blame for us arriving late?"

"Well ... er ..."

"So in reality," Shallan said, "you're telling me I'm beautiful precisely one-sixth of the time."

"Nonsense! Young miss, you're like a morning sunrise, you are!"

"Like a sunrise? By that you mean entirely too crimson"—she pulled at her long red hair—"and prone to making men grouchy when they see me?"

He laughed, and several of the sailors nearby joined in. "All right then," Captain Tozbek said, "you're like a flower."

She grimaced. "I'm allergic to flowers."

He raised an eyebrow.

"No, really," she admitted. "I think they're quite captivating. But if you were to give me a bouquet, you'd soon find me in a fit so energetic that it would have you searching the walls for stray freckles I might have blown free with the force of my sneezes."

"Well, be that true, I still say you're as *pretty* as a flower."

"If I am, then young men my age must be afflicted with the same allergy—for they keep their distance from me noticeably." She winced. "Now, see, I told you this wasn't polite. Young women should not act in such an irritable way."

"Ah, young miss," the captain said, tipping his knit cap toward her. "The lads and I will miss your clever tongue. I'm not sure what we'll do without you."

"Sail, likely," she said. "And eat, and sing, and watch the waves. All the things you do now, only you shall have rather *more* time to accomplish all of it, as you won't be stumbling across a youthful girl as she sits on your deck sketching and mumbling to herself. But you have my thanks, Captain, for a trip that was wonderful—if somewhat exaggerated in length."

He tipped his cap to her in acknowledgment.

Shallan grinned—she hadn't expected being out on her own to be so liberating. Her brothers had worried that she'd be frightened. They saw her as timid because she didn't like to argue and remained quiet when large groups were talking. And perhaps she *was* timid—being away from Jah Keved was daunting. But it was also wonderful. She'd filled three sketchbooks with pictures of the creatures and people she'd seen, and while her worry over her house's finances was a perpetual cloud, it was balanced by the sheer delight of experience.

Tozbek began making dock arrangements for his ship. He was a good man. As for his praise of her supposed beauty, she took that for what it was. A kind, if overstated, mark of affection. She was pale-skinned in an era when Alethi tan was seen as the mark of true beauty, and though she had light blue eyes, her impure family line was manifest in her auburn-red hair. Not a single lock of proper black. Her freckles had faded as she reached young womanhood—Heralds be blessed—but there were still some visible, dusting her cheeks and nose.

"Young miss," the captain said to her after conferring with his men, "Your Brightness Jasnah, she'll undoubtedly be at the Conclave, you see."

"Oh, where the Palanaeum is?"

"Yes, yes. And the king lives there too. It's the center of the city, so to speak. Except it's on the top." He scratched his chin. "Well, anyway, Brightness Jasnah Kholin is sister to a king; she will stay nowhere else, not in Kharbranth. Yalb here will show you the way. We can deliver your trunk later."

"Many thanks, Captain," she said. "*Shaylor mkabat nour.*" *The winds have brought us safely.* A phrase of thanks in the Thaylen language.

The captain smiled broadly. "*Mkai bade fortenthis!*"

She had no idea what that meant. Her Thaylen was quite

good when she was reading, but hearing it spoken was something else entirely. She smiled at him, which seemed the proper response, for he laughed, gesturing to one of his sailors.

"We'll wait here in this dock for two days," he told her. "There is a highstorm coming tomorrow, you see, so we cannot leave. If the situation with the Brightness Jasnah does not proceed as hoped, we'll take you back to Jah Keved."

"Thank you again."

"'Tis nothing, young miss," he said. "Nothing but what we'd be doing anyway. We can take on goods here and all. Besides, that's a right nice likeness of my wife you gave me for my cabin. Right nice."

He strode over to Yalb, giving him instructions. Shallan waited, putting her drawing pad back into her leather portfolio. Yalb. The name was difficult for her Veden tongue to pronounce. Why were the Thaylens so fond of mashing letters together, without proper vowels?

Yalb waved for her. She moved to follow.

"Be careful with yourself, lass," the captain warned as she passed. "Even a safe city like Kharbranth hides dangers. Keep your wits about you."

"I should think I'd prefer my wits inside my skull, Captain," she replied, carefully stepping onto the gangplank. "If I keep them 'about me' instead, then someone has gotten entirely too close to my head with a cudgel."

The captain laughed, waving her farewell as she made her way down the gangplank, holding the railing with her freehand. Like all Vorin women, she kept her left hand—her safehand—covered, exposing only her freehand. Common darkeyed women would wear a glove, but a woman of her rank was expected to show more modesty than that. In her case, she kept her safehand covered by the oversized cuff of her left sleeve, which was buttoned closed.

The dress was of a traditional Vorin cut, formfitting through the bust, shoulders, and waist, with a flowing skirt below. It was blue silk with chull-shell buttons up the sides, and she carried her satchel by pressing it to her chest with her safehand while holding the railing with her freehand.

She stepped off the gangplank into the furious activity of the docks, messengers running this way and that, women in red coats tracking cargos on ledgers. Kharbranth was a Vorin kingdom, like Alethkar and like Shallan's own Jah Keved. They weren't pagans here, and writing was a feminine art; men learned only glyphs, leaving letters and reading to their wives and sisters.

She hadn't asked, but she was certain Captain Tozbek could read. She'd seen him holding books; it had made her uncomfortable. Reading was an unseemly trait in a man. At least, men who weren't ardents.

"You wanna ride?" Yalb asked her, his rural Thaylen dialect so thick she could barely make out the words.

"Yes, please."

He nodded and rushed off, leaving her on the docks, surrounded by a group of parshmen who were laboriously moving wooden crates from one pier to another. Parshmen were thick-witted, but they made excellent workers. Never complaining, always doing as they were told. Her father had preferred them to ordinary slaves.

Were the Alethi really fighting *parshmen* out on the Shattered Plains? That seemed so odd to Shallan. Parshmen didn't fight. They were docile and practically mute. Of course, from what she'd heard, the ones out on the Shattered Plains—the Parshendi, they were called—were physically different from normal parshmen. Stronger, taller, keener of mind. Perhaps they weren't really parshmen at all, but distant relatives of some kind.

To her surprise, she could see signs of animal life all around the docks. A few skyeels undulated through the air, searching for rats or fish. Tiny crabs hid between cracks in the dock's boards, and a cluster of haspers clung to the dock's thick logs. In a street inland of the docks, a prowling mink skulked in the shadows, watching for morsels that might be dropped.

She couldn't resist pulling open her portfolio and beginning a sketch of a pouncing skyeel. Wasn't it afraid of all the people? She held her sketchpad with her safehand, hidden

fingers wrapping around the top as she used a charcoal pencil to draw. Before she was finished, her guide returned with
a man pulling a curious contraption with two large wheels
and a canopy-covered seat. She hesitantly lowered her sketchpad. She'd expected a palanquin.

The man pulling the machine was short and dark-skinned,
with a wide smile and full lips. He gestured for Shallan to sit,
and she did so with the modest grace her nurses had drilled
into her. The driver asked her a question in a clipped, terse-
sounding language she didn't recognize.

"What was that?" she asked Yalb.

"He wants to know if you'd like to be pulled the long way
or the short way." Yalb scratched his head. "I'm not right sure
what the difference is."

"I suspect one takes longer," Shallan said.

"Oh, you *are* a clever one." Yalb said something to the
porter in that same clipped language, and the man responded.

"The long way gives a good view of the city," Yalb said.
"The short way goes straight up to the Conclave. Not many
good views, he says. I guess he noticed you were new to the
city."

"Do I stand out that much?" Shallan asked, flushing.

"Eh, no, of course not, Brightness."

"And by that you mean that I'm as obvious as a wart on
a queen's nose."

Yalb laughed. "Afraid so. But you can't go someplace a
second time until you been there a first time, I reckon. Everyone has to stand out sometime, so you might as well do it in a
pretty way like yourself!"

She'd had to get used to gentle flirtation from the sailors.
They were never too forward, and she suspected the captain's
wife had spoken to them sternly when she'd noticed how it
made Shallan blush. Back at her father's manor, servants—
even those who had been full citizens—had been afraid to
step out of their places.

The porter was still waiting for an answer. "The short way,
please," she told Yalb, though she longed to take the scenic
path. She was finally in a *real* city and she took the direct

route? But Brightness Jasnah had proven to be as elusive as a wild songling. Best to be quick.

The main roadway cut up the hillside in switchbacks, and so even the short way gave her time to see much of the city. It proved intoxicatingly rich with strange people, sights, and ringing bells. Shallan sat back and took it all in. Buildings were grouped by color, and that color seemed to indicate purpose. Shops selling the same items would be painted the same shades—violet for clothing, green for foods. Homes had their own pattern, though Shallan couldn't interpret it. The colors were soft, with a washed-out, subdued tonality.

Yalb walked alongside her cart, and the porter began to talk back toward her. Yalb translated, hands in the pockets of his vest. "He says that the city is special because of the lait here."

Shallan nodded. Many cities were built in laits—areas protected from the highstorms by nearby rock formations.

"Kharbranth is one of the most sheltered major cities in the world," Yalb continued, translating, "and the bells are a symbol of that. It's said they were first erected to warn that a highstorm was blowing, since the winds were so soft that people didn't always notice." Yalb hesitated. "He's just saying things because he wants a big tip, Brightness. I've heard that story, but I think it's blustering ridiculous. If the winds blew strong enough to move bells, then people'd notice. Besides, people didn't notice it was *raining* on their blustering heads?"

Shallan smiled. "It's all right. He can continue."

The porter chatted on in his clipped voice—what language *was* that, anyway? Shallan listened to Yalb's translation, drinking in the sights, sounds, and—unfortunately—scents. She'd grown up accustomed to the crisp smell of freshly dusted furniture and flatbread baking in the kitchens. Her ocean journey had taught her new scents, of brine and clean sea air.

There was nothing clean in what she smelled here. Each passing alleyway had its own unique array of revolting stenches. These alternated with the spicy scents of street vendors and their foods, and the juxtaposition was even more nauseating. Fortunately, her porter moved into the central part of the roadway, and the stenches abated, though it did slow them as they had to contend with thicker traffic. She gawked at those they passed. Those men with gloved hands and faintly bluish skin were from Natanatan. But who were those tall, stately people dressed in robes of black? And the men with their beards bound in cords, making them rodlike?

The sounds put Shallan in mind of the competing choruses of wild songlings near her home, only multiplied in variety and volume. A hundred voices called to one another, mingling with doors slamming, wheels rolling on stone, occasional skyeels crying. The ever-present bells tinkled in the background, louder when the wind blew. They were displayed in the windows of shops, hung from rafters. Each lantern pole along the street had a bell hung under the lamp, and her cart had a small silvery one at the very tip of its canopy. When she was about halfway up the hillside, a rolling wave of loud clock bells rang the hour. The varied, unsynchronized chimes made a clangorous din.

The crowds thinned as they reached the upper quarter of the city, and eventually her porter pulled her to a massive building at the very apex of the city. Painted white, it was carved from the rock face itself, rather than built of bricks or clay. The pillars out front grew seamlessly from the stone, and the back side of the building melded smoothly into the cliff. The outcroppings of roof had squat domes atop them, and were painted in metallic colors. Lighteyed women passed in and out, carrying scribing utensils and wearing dresses like Shallan's, their left hands properly cuffed. The men entering or leaving the building wore military-style Vorin coats and stiff trousers, buttons up the sides and ending in a stiff collar that wrapped the entire neck. Many carried swords at their waists, the belts wrapping around the knee-length coats.

The porter stopped and made a comment to Yalb. The sailor began arguing with him, hands on hips. Shallan smiled at his stern expression, and she blinked pointedly, affixing the scene in her memory for later sketching.

"He's offering to split the difference with me if I let him

inflate the price of the trip," Yalb said, shaking his head and offering a hand to help Shallan from the cart. She stepped down, looking at the porter, who shrugged, smiling like a child who had been caught sneaking sweets.

She clutched her satchel with her cuffed arm, searching through it with her freehand for her money pouch. "How much should I actually give him?"

"Two clearchips should be more than enough. I'd have offered one. The thief wanted to ask for *five*."

Before this trip, she'd never used money; she'd just admired the spheres for their beauty. Each one was composed of a glass bead a little larger than a person's thumbnail with a much smaller gemstone set at the center. The gemstones could absorb Stormlight, and that made the spheres glow. When she opened the money pouch, shards of ruby, emerald, diamond, and sapphire shone out on her face. She fished out three diamond chips, the smallest denomination. Emeralds were the most valuable, for they could be used by Soulcasters to create food.

The glass part of most spheres was the same size; the size of the gemstone at the center determined the denomination. The three chips, for instance, each had only a tiny splinter of diamond inside. Even that was enough to glow with Stormlight, far fainter than a lamp, but still visible. A mark—the medium denomination of sphere—was a little less bright than a candle, and it took five chips to make a mark.

She'd brought only infused spheres, as she'd heard that dun ones were considered suspect, and sometimes a moneylender would have to be brought in to judge the authenticity of the gemstone. She kept the most valuable spheres she had in her safepouch, of course, which was buttoned to the inside of her left sleeve.

She handed the three chips to Yalb, who cocked his head. She nodded at the porter, blushing, realizing that she'd reflexively used Yalb like a master-servant intermediary. Would he be offended?

He laughed and stood up stiffly, as if imitating a master-servant, paying the porter with a mock stern expression. The porter laughed, bowed to Shallan, then pulled his cart away.

"This is for you," Shallan said, taking out a ruby mark and handing it to Yalb.

"Brightness, this is too much!"

"It's partially out of thanks," she said, "but is also to pay you to stay here and wait for a few hours, in case I return."

"Wait a few hours for a firemark? That's wages for a week's sailing!"

"Then it should be enough to make certain you don't wander off."

"I'll be right here!" Yalb said, giving her an elaborate bow that was surprisingly well-executed.

Shallan took a deep breath and strode up the steps toward the Conclave's imposing entrance. The carved rock really was remarkable—the artist in her wanted to linger and study it, but she didn't dare. Entering the large building was like being swallowed. The hallway inside was lined with Stormlight lamps that shone with white light. Diamond broams were probably set inside them; most buildings of fine construction used Stormlight to provide illumination. A broam—the highest denomination of sphere—glowed with about the same light as several candles.

Their light shone evenly and softly on the many attendants, scribes, and lighteyes moving through the hallway. The building appeared to be constructed as one broad, high, and long tunnel, burrowed into the rock. Grand chambers lined the sides, and subsidiary corridors branched off the central grand promenade. She felt far more comfortable than she had outdoors. This place—with its bustling servants, its lesser brightlords and brightladies—was familiar.

She raised her freehand in a sign of need, and sure enough, a master-servant in a crisp white shirt and black trousers hurried over to her. "Brightness?" he asked, speaking her native Veden, likely because of the color of her hair.

"I seek Jasnah Kholin," Shallan said. "I have word that she is within these walls."

The master-servant bowed crisply. Most master-servants prided themselves on their refined service—the very same air that Yalb had been mocking moments ago. "I shall return, Brightness." He would be of the second nahn, a darkeyed citizen of very high rank. In Vorin belief, one's Calling—the task to which one dedicated one's life—was of vital importance. Choosing a good profession and working hard at it was the best way to ensure good placement in the afterlife. The specific devotary that one visited for worship often had to do with the nature of one's chosen Calling.

Shallan folded her arms, waiting. She had thought long about her own Calling. The obvious choice was her art, and she did so love sketching. But it was more than just the drawing that attracted her—it was the *study*, the questions raised by observation. Why weren't the skyeels afraid of people? What did haspers feed on? Why did a rat population thrive in one area, but fail in another? So she'd chosen natural history instead.

She longed to be a true scholar, to receive real instruction, to spend time on deep research and study. Was that part of why she'd suggested this daring plan of seeking out Jasnah and becoming her ward? Perhaps. However, she needed to remain focused. Becoming Jasnah's ward—and therefore student—was only one step.

She considered this as she idly walked up to a pillar, using her freehand to feel the polished stone. Like much of Roshar—save for certain coastal regions—Kharbranth was built on raw, unbroken stone. The buildings outside had been set directly on the rock, and this one sliced into it. The pillar was granite, she guessed, though her geological knowledge was sketchy.

The floor was covered with long, burnt-orange rugs. The material was dense, designed to look rich but bear heavy traffic. The broad, rectangular hallway had an *old* feel to it. One book she'd read claimed that Kharbranth had been founded way back into the shadowdays, years before the Last Desolation. That would make it old indeed. Thousands of years old, created before the terrors of the Hierocracy, long before—

even—the Recreance. Back when Voidbringers with bodies of stone were said to have stalked the land.

"Brightness?" a voice asked.

Shallan turned to find that the servant had returned.

"This way, Brightness."

She nodded to the servant, and he led her quickly down the busy hallway. She went over how to present herself to Jasnah. The woman was a legend. Even Shallan—living in the remote estates of Jah Keved—had heard of the Alethi king's brilliant, heretic sister. Jasnah was only thirty-four years old, yet many felt she would already have obtained the cap of a master scholar if it weren't for her vocal denunciations of religion. Most specifically, she denounced the devotaries, the various religious congregations that proper Vorin people joined.

Improper quips would not serve Shallan well here. She would have to be proper. Wardship to a woman of great renown was the best way to be schooled in the feminine arts: music, painting, writing, logic, and science. It was much like how a young man would train in the honor guard of a brightlord he respected.

Shallan had originally written to Jasnah requesting a wardship in desperation; she hadn't actually expected the woman to reply in the affirmative. When she had—via a letter commanding Shallan to attend her in Dumadari in two weeks—Shallan had been shocked. She'd been chasing the woman ever since.

Jasnah was a heretic. Would she demand that Shallan renounce her faith? She doubted she could do such a thing. Vorin teachings regarding one's Glory and Calling had been one of her few refuges during the difficult days, when her father had been at his worst.

They turned into a narrower hallway, entering corridors increasingly far from the main cavern. Finally, the master-servant stopped at a corner and gestured for Shallan to continue. There were voices coming from the corridor to the right.

Shallan hesitated. Sometimes, she wondered how it had come to this. She was the quiet one, the timid one, the youngest of five siblings and the only girl. Sheltered, protected all her life. And now the hopes of her entire house rested on her shoulders.

Their father was dead. And it was vital that remain a secret.

She didn't like to think of that day—she all but blocked it from her mind, and trained herself to think of other things. But the effects of his loss could not be ignored. He had made many promises—some business deals, some bribes, some of the latter disguised as the former. House Davar owed great amounts of money to a great number of people, and without her father to keep them all appeased, the creditors would soon begin making demands.

There was nobody to turn to. Her family, mostly because of her father, was loathed even by its allies. Highprince Valam—the brightlord to whom her family gave fealty—was ailing, and no longer offered them the protection he once had. When it became known that her father was dead and her family bankrupt, that would be the end of House Davar. They'd be consumed and subjugated to another house.

They'd be worked to the bone as punishment—in fact, they might even face assassination by disgruntled creditors. Preventing that depended on Shallan, and the first step came with Jasnah Kholin.

Shallan took a deep breath, then strode around the corner.

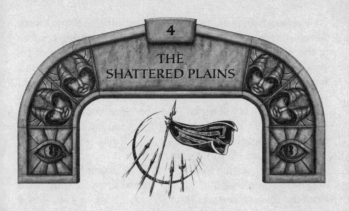

4

THE SHATTERED PLAINS

"I'm dying, aren't I? Healer, why do you take my blood? Who is that beside you, with his head of lines? I can see a distant sun, dark and cold, shining in a black sky."

—Collected on the 3rd of Jesnan, 1172, 11 seconds pre-death. Subject was a Reshi chull trainer. Sample is of particular note.

W hy don't you cry?" the windspren asked.

Kaladin sat with his back to the corner of the cage, looking down. The floor planks in front of him were splintered, as if someone had dug at them with nothing but his fingernails. The splintered section was stained dark where the dry grey wood had soaked up blood. A futile, delusional attempt at escape.

The wagon continued to roll. The same routine each day. Wake up sore and aching from a fitful night spent without mattress or blanket. One wagon at a time, the slaves were let out and hobbled with leg irons and given time to shuffle around and relieve themselves. Then they were packed away and given morning slop, and the wagons rolled until afternoon slop. More rolling. Evening slop, then a ladle of water before sleep.

Kaladin's *shash* brand was still cracked and bleeding. At least the cage's top gave shade from the sun.

The windspren shifted to mist, floating like a tiny cloud. She moved in close to Kaladin, the motion outlining her face at the front of the cloud, as if blowing back the fog and revealing something more substantial underneath. Vaporous, feminine, and angular. With such curious eyes. Like no other spren he'd seen.

"The others cry at night," she said. "But you don't."

"Why cry?" he said, leaning his head back against the bars. "What would it change?"

"I don't know. Why *do* men cry?"

He smiled, closing his eyes. "Ask the Almighty why men cry, little spren. Not me." His forehead dripped with sweat from the Eastern summer humidity, and it stung as it seeped into his wound. Hopefully, they'd have some weeks of spring again soon. Weather and seasons were unpredictable. You never knew how long they would go on, though typically each would last a few weeks.

The wagon rolled on. After a time, he felt sunlight on his face. He opened his eyes. The sun shone in through the upper side of the cage. Two or three hours past noon, then. What of afternoon slop? Kaladin stood, pulling himself up with one hand on the steel bars. He couldn't make out Tvlakv driving the wagon up ahead, only flat-faced Bluth behind. The mercenary had on a dirty shirt that laced up the front and wore a wide-brimmed hat against the sun, his spear and cudgel riding on the wagon bench beside him. He didn't carry a sword—not even Tvlakv did that, not near Alethi land.

The grass continued to part for the wagons, vanishing just in front, then creeping out after the wagons passed. The landscape here was dotted with strange shrubs that Kaladin didn't recognize. They had thick stalks and stems and spiny green needles. Whenever the wagons grew too close, the needles pulled into the stalks, leaving behind twisted, wormlike trunks with knotted branches. They dotted the hilly landscape, rising from the grass-covered rocks like diminutive sentries.

The wagons just kept on going, well past noon. *Why aren't we stopping for slop?*

The lead wagon finally pulled to a stop. The other two

lurched to a halt behind it, the red-carapaced chulls fidgeted, their antennae waving back and forth. The box-shaped animals had bulging, stony shells and thick, trunklike red legs. From what Kaladin had heard, their claws could snap a man's arm. But chulls were docile, particularly domesticated ones, and he'd never known anyone in the army to get more than a halfhearted pinch from one.

Bluth and Tag climbed down from their wagons and walked up to meet Tvlakv. The slavemaster stood on his wagon's seat, shading his eyes against the white sunlight and holding a sheet of paper in his hand. An argument ensued. Tvlakv kept waving in the direction they had been going, then pointing at his sheet of paper.

"Lost, Tvlakv?" Kaladin called. "Perhaps you should pray to the Almighty for guidance. I hear he has a fondness for slavers. Keeps a special room in Damnation just for you."

To Kaladin's left, one of the slaves—the long-bearded man who had talked to him a few days back—sidled away, not wanting to stand close to a person who was provoking the slaver.

Tvlakv hesitated, then waved curtly to his mercenaries, silencing them. The portly man hopped down from his wagon and walked over to Kaladin. "You," he said. "Deserter. Alethi armies travel these lands for their war. Do you know anything of the area?"

"Let me see the map," Kaladin said. Tvlakv hesitated, then held it up for Kaladin.

Kaladin reached through the bars and snatched the paper. Then, without reading it, Kaladin ripped it in two. In seconds he'd shredded it into a hundred pieces in front of Tvlakv's horrified eyes.

Tvlakv called for the mercenaries, but by the time they arrived, Kaladin had a double handful of confetti to toss out at them. "Happy Middlefest, you bastards," Kaladin said as the flakes of paper fluttered around them. He turned and walked to the other side of the cage and sat down, facing them.

Tvlakv stood, speechless. Then, red-faced, he pointed at Kaladin and hissed something at the mercenaries. Bluth took a step toward the cage, but then thought better of it. He glanced at Tvlakv, then shrugged and walked away. Tvlakv turned to Tag, but the other mercenary just shook his head, saying something soft.

After a few minutes of stewing at the cowardly mercenaries, Tvlakv rounded the cage and approached where Kaladin was sitting. Surprisingly, when he spoke, his voice was calm. "I see you are clever, deserter. You have made yourself invaluable. My other slaves, they aren't from this area, and I have never come this way. You can bargain. What is it you wish in exchange for leading us? I can promise you an extra meal each day, should you please me."

"You want me to lead the caravan?"

"Instructions will be acceptable."

"All right. First, find a cliff."

"That, it will give you a vantage to see the area?"

"No," Kaladin said. "It will give me something to throw you off of."

Tvlakv adjusted his cap in annoyance, brushing back one of his long white eyebrows. "You hate me. That is good. Hatred will keep you strong, make you sell for much. But you will not find vengeance on me unless I have a chance to take you to market. I will not let you escape. But perhaps someone else would. You want to be sold, you see?"

"I don't want vengeance," Kaladin said. The windspren came back—she'd darted off for a time to inspect one of the strange shrubs. She landed in the air and began walking around Tvlakv's face, inspecting him. He didn't seem to be able to see her.

Tvlakv frowned. "No vengeance?"

"It doesn't work," Kaladin said. "I learned that lesson long ago."

"Long ago? You cannot be older than eighteen years, deserter."

It was a good guess. He was nineteen. Had it really only been four years since he'd joined Amaram's army? Kaladin felt as if he'd aged a dozen.

"You are young," Tvlakv continued. "You could escape

this fate of yours. Men have been known to live beyond the slave's brand—you could pay off your slave price, you see? Or convince one of your masters to give you your freedom. You could become a free man again. It is not so unlikely."

Kaladin snorted. "I'll never be free of these brands, Tvlakv. You must know that I've tried—and failed—to escape ten times over. It's more than these glyphs on my head that makes your mercenaries wary."

"Past failure does not prove that there is not chance in the future, yes?"

"I'm finished. I don't care." He eyed the slaver. "Besides, you don't actually believe what you're saying. I doubt a man like you would be able to sleep at night if he thought the slaves he sold would be free to seek him out one day."

Tvlakv laughed. "Perhaps, deserter. Perhaps you are right. Or perhaps I simply think that if you *were* to get free, you would hunt down the first man who sold you to slavery, you see? Highlord Amaram, was it not? His death would give me warning so I can run."

How had he known? How had he heard about Amaram? *I'll find him,* Kaladin thought. *I'll gut him with my own hands. I'll twist his head right off his neck, I'll—*

"Yes," Tvlakv said, studying Kaladin's face, "so you were not so honest when you said you do not thirst for vengeance. I see."

"How do you know about Amaram?" Kaladin said, scowling. "I've changed hands a half-dozen times since then."

"Men talk. Slavers more than most. We must be friends with one another, you see, for nobody else will stomach us."

"Then you know that I didn't get this brand for deserting."

"Ah, but it is what we must pretend, you see? Men guilty of high crimes, they do not sell so well. With that *shash* glyph on your head, it will be difficult enough to get a good price for you. If I cannot sell you, then you . . . well, you will not wish for that status. So we will play a game together. I will say you are a deserter. And you will say nothing. It is an easy game, I think."

"It's illegal."

"We are not in Alethkar," Tvlakv said, "so there is no law. Besides, desertion was the official reason for your sale. Claim otherwise, and you will gain nothing but a reputation for dishonesty."

"Nothing besides a headache for you."

"But you just said you have no desire for vengeance against me."

"I could learn."

Tvlakv laughed. "Ah, if you have not learned that already, then you probably never will! Besides, did you not threaten to throw me off a cliff? I think you have learned already. But now, we *must* discuss how to proceed. My map has met with an untimely demise, you see."

Kaladin hesitated, then sighed. "I don't know," he said honestly. "I've never been this way either."

Tvlakv frowned. He leaned closer to the cage, inspecting Kaladin, though he still kept his distance. After a moment, Tvlakv shook his head. "I believe you, deserter. A pity. Well, I shall trust my memory. The map was poorly rendered anyway. I am almost glad you ripped it, for I was tempted to do the same myself. If I should happen across any portraits of my former wives, I shall see that they cross your path and take advantage of your unique talents." He strolled away.

Kaladin watched him go, then cursed to himself.

"What was that for?" the windspren said, walking up to him, head cocked.

"I almost find myself liking him," Kaladin said, pounding his head back against the cage.

"But . . . after what he did . . ."

Kaladin shrugged. "I didn't say Tvlakv isn't a bastard. He's just a likable bastard." He hesitated, then grimaced. "Those are the worst kind. When you kill them, you end up feeling guilty for it."

❖

The wagon leaked during highstorms. That wasn't surprising; Kaladin suspected that Tvlakv had been driven to slaving by ill fortune. He would rather be trading other goods, but something—lack of funds, a need to leave his previous environs with haste—had forced him to pick up this least reputable of careers.

Men like him couldn't afford luxury, or even quality. They could barely stay ahead of their debts. In this case, that meant wagons which leaked. The boarded sides were strong enough to withstand highstorm winds, but they weren't comfortable.

Tvlakv had almost missed getting ready for this highstorm. Apparently, the map Kaladin had torn up had also included a list of highstorm dates purchased from a roving stormwarden. The storms could be predicted mathematically; Kaladin's father had made a hobby of it. He'd been able to pick the right day eight times out of ten.

The boards rattled against the cage's bars as wind buffeted the vehicle, shaking it, making it lurch like a clumsy giant's plaything. The wood groaned and spurts of icy rainwater sprayed through cracks. Flashes of lightning leaked through as well, accompanied by thunder. That was the only light they got.

Occasionally, light would flash without the thunder. The slaves would groan in terror at this, thinking about the Stormfather, the shades of the Lost Radiants, or the Voidbringers—all of which were said to haunt the most violent highstorms. They huddled together on the far side of the wagon, sharing warmth. Kaladin left them to it, sitting alone with his back to the bars.

Kaladin didn't fear stories of things that walked the storms. In the army, he'd been forced to weather a highstorm or two beneath the lip of a protective stone overhang or other bit of impromptu shelter. Nobody liked to be out during a storm, but sometimes you couldn't avoid it. The things that walked the storms—perhaps even the Stormfather himself—weren't nearly so deadly as the rocks and branches cast up into the air. In fact, the storm's initial tempest of water and wind—the stormwall—was the most dangerous part. The longer one endured after that, the weaker the storm grew, until the trailing edge was nothing more than sprinkling rain.

No, he wasn't worried about Voidbringers looking for

flesh to feast upon. He was worried that something would happen to Tvlakv. The slavemaster waited out the storm in a cramped wooden enclosure built into the bottom of his wagon. That was ostensibly the safest place in the caravan, but an unlucky twist of fate—a tempest-thrown boulder, the collapse of the wagon—could leave him dead. In that case, Kaladin could see Bluth and Tag running off, leaving everyone in their cages, wooden sides locked up. The slaves would die a slow death by starvation and dehydration, baking under the sun in these boxes.

The storm continued to blow, shaking the wagon. Those winds felt like live things at times. And who was to say they weren't? Were windspren attracted *to* gusts of wind, or *were* they the gusts of wind? The souls of the force that now wanted so badly to destroy Kaladin's wagon?

That force—sentient or not—failed. The wagons were chained to nearby boulders with their wheels locked. The blasts of wind grew more lethargic. Lightning stopped flashing, and the maddening drumming of rain became a quiet tapping instead. Only once during their journey had a wagon toppled during a highstorm. Both it and the slaves inside had survived with a few dents and bruises.

The wooden side to Kaladin's right shook suddenly, then fell open as Bluth undid its clasps. The mercenary wore his leather coat against the wet, streams of water falling from the brim of his hat as he exposed the bars—and the occupants—to the rain. It was cold, though not as piercingly so as during the height of the storm. It sprayed across Kaladin and the huddled slaves. Tvlakv always ordered the wagons uncovered before the rain stopped; he said it was the only way to wash away the slaves' stink.

Bluth slid the wooden side into place beneath the wagon, then opened the other two sides. Only the wall at the front of the wagon—just behind the driver's seat—couldn't be brought down.

"Little early to be taking down the sides, Bluth," Kaladin said. It wasn't quite the riddens yet—the period near the end of a highstorm when the rain sprinkled softly. This rain was still heavy, the wind still gusting on occasion.

"The master wants you plenty clean today."

"Why?" Kaladin asked, rising, water streaming from his ragged brown clothing.

Bluth ignored him. *Perhaps we're nearing our destination*, Kaladin thought as he scanned the landscape.

Over the last few days, the hills had given way to uneven rock formations—places where weathering winds had left behind crumbling cliffs and jagged shapes. Grass grew up the rocky sides that saw the most sun, and other plants were plentiful in the shade. The time right after a highstorm was when the land was most alive. Rockbud polyps split and sent out their vines. Other kinds of vine crept from crevices, licking up water. Leaves unfolded from shrubs and trees. Cremlings of all kinds slithered through puddles, enjoying the banquet. Insects buzzed into the air; larger crustaceans—crabs and leggers—left their hiding places. The very rocks seemed to come to life.

Kaladin noted a half-dozen windspren flitting overhead, their translucent forms chasing after—or perhaps cruising along with—the highstorm's last gusts. Tiny lights rose around the plants. Lifespren. They looked like motes of glowing green dust or swarms of tiny translucent insects.

A legger—its hairlike spines lifted to the air to give warning of changes in the wind—climbed along the side of the cart, its long body lined with dozens of pairs of legs. That was familiar enough, but he'd never seen a legger with such a deep purple carapace. Where was Tvlakv taking the caravan? Those uncultivated hillsides were perfect for farming. You could spread stumpweight sap on them—mixed with lavis seeds— during seasons of weaker storms following the Weeping. In four months, you'd have polyps larger than a man's head growing all along the hill, ready to break open for the grain inside.

The chulls lumbered about, feasting on rockbuds, slugs, and smaller crustaceans that had appeared after the storm.

Tag and Bluth quietly hitched the beasts to their harnesses as a grumpy-looking Tvlakv crawled out of his waterproof refuge. The slavemaster pulled on a cap and deep black cloak against the rain. He rarely came out until the storm had passed completely; he was *very* eager to get to their destination. Were they that close to the coast? That was one of the only places where they'd find cities in the Unclaimed Hills.

Within minutes, the wagons were rolling again across the uneven ground. Kaladin settled back as the sky cleared, the highstorm a smudge of blackness on the western horizon. The sun brought welcome warmth, and the slaves basked in the light, streams of water dripping from their clothing and running out the back of the rocking wagon.

Presently, a translucent ribbon of light zipped up to Kaladin. He was coming to take the windspren's presence for granted. She had gone out during the storm, but she'd come back. As always.

"I saw others of your kind," Kaladin said idly.

"Others?" she asked, taking the form of a young woman. She began to step around him in the air, spinning occasionally, dancing to some unheard beat.

"Windspren," Kaladin said. "Chasing after the storm. Are you certain you don't want to go with them?"

She glanced westward, longingly. "No," she finally said, continuing her dance. "I like it here."

Kaladin shrugged. She'd ceased playing as many pranks as she once had, and so he'd stopped letting her presence annoy him.

"There are others near," she said. "Others like you."

"Slaves?"

"I don't know. People. Not the ones here. Other ones."

"Where?"

She turned a translucent white finger, pointing eastward. "There. Many of them. Lots and lots."

Kaladin stood up. He couldn't imagine that a spren had a good handle on how to measure distance and numbers. *Yes . . .* Kaladin squinted, studying the horizon. *That's smoke. From chimneys?* He caught a gust of it on the wind; if not for the rain, he'd probably have smelled it sooner.

Should he care? It didn't matter where he was a slave; he'd still be a slave. He'd accepted this life. That was his way now. Don't care, don't bother.

Still, he watched with curiosity as his wagon climbed the side of a hill and gave the slaves inside a good vantage of what was ahead. It wasn't a city. It was something grander, something larger. An enormous army encampment.

"Great Father of Storms . . ." Kaladin whispered.

Ten masses of troops bivouacked in familiar Alethi patterns—circular, by company rank, with camp followers on the outskirts, mercenaries in a ring just inside them, citizen soldiers near the middle, lighteyed officers at the very center. They were camped in a series of enormous craterlike rock formations, only the sides were more irregular, more jagged. Like broken eggshells.

Kaladin had left an army much like this eight months ago, though Amaram's force had been much smaller. This one covered miles of stone, stretching far both north and south. A thousand banners bearing a thousand different family glyphpairs flapped proudly in the air. There were some tents—mainly on the outside of the armies—but most of the troops were housed in large stone barracks. That meant Soulcasters.

That encampment directly ahead of them flew a banner Kaladin had seen in books. Deep blue with white glyphs—*khokh* and *linil*, stylized and painted as a sword standing before a crown. House Kholin. The king's house.

Daunted, Kaladin looked beyond the armies. The landscape to the east was as he'd heard it described in a dozen different stories detailing the king's campaign against the Parshendi betrayers. It was an enormous riven plain of rock—so wide he couldn't see the other side—that was split and cut by sheer chasms, crevasses twenty or thirty feet wide. They were so deep that they disappeared into darkness and formed a jagged mosaic of uneven plateaus. Some large, others tiny. The expansive plain looked like a platter that had been broken, its pieces then reassembled with small gaps between the fragments.

"The Shattered Plains," Kaladin whispered.

"What?" the windspren asked. "What's wrong?"

Kaladin shook his head, bemused. "I spent years trying to get to this place. It's what Tien wanted, in the end at least. To come here, fight in the king's army . . ."

And now Kaladin was here. Finally. *Accidentally.* He felt like laughing at the absurdity. *I should have realized,* he thought. *I should have known. We weren't ever heading toward the coast and its cities. We were heading here. To war.*

This place would be subject to Alethi law and rules. He'd expected that Tvlakv would want to avoid such things. But here, he'd probably also find the best prices.

"The Shattered Plains?" one of the slaves said. "Really?"

Others crowded around, peering out. In their sudden excitement, they seemed to forget their fear of Kaladin.

"It *is* the Shattered Plains!" another man said. "That's the king's army!"

"Perhaps we'll find justice here," another said.

"I hear the king's household servants live as well as the finest merchants," said another. "His slaves have to be better off too. We'll be in Vorin lands; we'll even make wages!"

That much was true. When worked, slaves had to be paid a small wage—half what a nonslave would be paid, which was already often less than a full citizen would make for the same work. But it was something, and Alethi law required it. Only ardents—who couldn't own anything anyway—didn't have to be paid. Well, them and parshmen. But parshmen were more animal than anything else.

A slave could apply his earnings to his slave debt and, after years of labor, earn his freedom. Theoretically. The others continued to chatter as the wagons rolled down the incline, but Kaladin withdrew to the back of the wagon. He suspected that the option to pay off a slave's price was a sham, intended to keep slaves docile. The debt was enormous, far more than a slave sold for, and virtually impossible to earn out.

Under previous masters, he'd demanded his wages be given

to him. They had always found ways to cheat him—charging him for his housing, his food. That's how lighteyes were. Roshone, Amaram, Katarotam . . . Each lighteyes Kaladin had known, whether as a slave or a free man, had shown himself to be corrupt to the core, for all his outward poise and beauty. They were like rotting corpses clothed in beautiful silk.

The other slaves kept talking about the king's army, and about justice. *Justice?* Kaladin thought, resting back against the bars. *I'm not convinced there is such a thing as justice.* Still, he found himself wondering. That was the king's army—the armies of all ten highprinces—come to fulfill the Vengeance Pact.

If there was one thing he still let himself long for, it was the chance to hold a spear. To fight again, to try and find his way back to the man he had been. A man who had cared.

If he would find that anywhere, he'd find it here.

"I have seen the end, and have heard it named. The Night of Sorrows, the True Desolation. The Everstorm."

—Collected on the 1st of Nanes, 1172, 15 seconds pre-death. Subject was a darkeyed youth of unknown origin.

S hallan had not expected Jasnah Kholin to be so beautiful. It was a stately, mature beauty—as one might find in the portrait of some historical scholar. Shallan realized that she'd naively been expecting Jasnah to be an ugly spinster, like the stern matrons who had tutored her years ago. How else could one picture a heretic well into her mid-thirties and still unmarried?

Jasnah was nothing like that. She was tall and slender, with clear skin, narrow black eyebrows, and thick, deep onyx hair. She wore part of it up, wrapped around a small, scroll-shaped golden ornament with two long hairpins holding it in place. The rest tumbled down behind her neck in small, tight curls. Even twisted and curled as it was, it came down to Jasnah's shoulders—if left unbound, it would be as long as Shallan's hair, reaching past the middle of her back.

She had a squarish face and discriminating pale violet eyes. She was listening to a man dressed in robes of burnt orange and white, the Kharbranthian royal colors. Brightness

Kholin was several fingers taller than the man—apparently, the Alethi reputation for height was no exaggeration. Jasnah glanced at Shallan, noting her, then returned to her conversation.

Stormfather! This woman *was* the sister of a king. Reserved, statuesque, dressed immaculately in blue and silver. Like Shallan's dress, Jasnah's buttoned up the sides and had a high collar, though Jasnah had a much fuller chest than Shallan. The skirts were loose below the waist, falling generously to the floor. Her sleeves were long and stately, and the left one was buttoned up to hide her safehand.

On her freehand was a distinctive piece of jewelry: two rings and a bracelet connected by several chains, holding a triangular group of gemstones across the back of the hand. A Soulcaster—the word was used for both the people who performed the process and the fabrial that made it possible.

Shallan edged into the room, trying to get a better look at the large, glowing gemstones. Her heart began to beat a little faster. The Soulcaster looked identical to the one she and her brothers had found in the inside pocket of her father's coat.

Jasnah and the man in robes began walking in Shallan's direction, still talking. How would Jasnah react, now that her ward had finally caught up to her? Would she be angry because of Shallan's tardiness? Shallan couldn't be blamed for that, but people often expect irrational things from their inferiors.

Like the grand cavern outside, this hallway was cut from the rock, but it was more richly furbished, with ornate hanging chandeliers made with Stormlit gemstones. Most were deep violet garnets, which were among the less valuable stones. Even so, the sheer number hanging there glistening with violet light would make the chandelier worth a small fortune. More than that, however, Shallan was impressed with the symmetry of the design and the beauty of the pattern of crystals hanging at the sides of the chandelier.

As Jasnah grew near, Shallan could hear some of what she was saying.

". . . realize that this action might prompt an unfavorable

reaction from the devotaries?" the woman said, speaking in Alethi. It was very near to Shallan's native Veden, and she'd been taught to speak it well during her childhood.

"Yes, Brightness," said the robed man. He was elderly, with a wispy white beard, and had pale grey eyes. His open, kindly face seemed very concerned, and he wore a squat, cylindrical hat that matched the orange and white of his robes. Rich robes. Was this some kind of royal steward, perhaps?

No. Those gemstones on his fingers, the way he carried himself, the way other lighteyed attendants deferred to him . . . *Stormfather!* Shallan thought. *This has to be the king himself!* Not Jasnah's brother, Elhokar, but the king of Kharbranth. Taravangian.

Shallan hastily performed an appropriate curtsy, which Jasnah noted.

"The ardents have much sway here, Your Majesty," Jasnah said with a smooth voice.

"As do I," the king said. "You needn't worry about me."

"Very well," Jasnah said. "Your terms are agreeable. Lead me to the location, and I shall see what can be done. If you will excuse me as we walk, however, I have someone to attend to." Jasnah made a curt motion toward Shallan, waving her to join them.

"Of course, Brightness," the king said. He seemed to defer to Jasnah. Kharbranth was a very small kingdom—just a single city—while Alethkar was one of the world's most powerful. An Alethi princess might well outrank a Kharbranthian king in real terms, however protocol would have it.

Shallan hurried to catch up to Jasnah, who walked a little behind the king as he began to speak to his attendants. "Brightness," Shallan said. "I am Shallan Davar, whom you asked to meet you. I deeply regret not being able to get to you in Dumadari."

"The fault was not yours," Jasnah said with a wave of the fingers. "I didn't expect that you would make it in time. I wasn't certain where I would be going after Dumadari when I sent you that note, however."

Jasnah wasn't angry; that was a good sign. Shallan felt some of her anxiety recede.

"I am impressed by your tenacity, child," Jasnah continued. "I honestly didn't expect you to follow me this far. After Kharbranth, I was going to forgo leaving you notes, as I'd presumed that you'd have given up. Most do so after the first few stops."

Most? Then it was a *test* of some sort? And Shallan had passed?

"Yes indeed," Jasnah continued, voice musing. "Perhaps I will actually allow you to petition me for a place as my ward."

Shallan almost stumbled in shock. *Petition* her? Wasn't that what she'd already done? "Brightness," Shallan said, "I thought that . . . Well, your letter . . ."

Jasnah eyed her. "I gave you leave to *meet* me, Miss Davar. I did not promise to take you on. The training and care of a ward is a distraction for which I have little tolerance or time at the present. But you have traveled far. I will entertain your request, though understand that my requirements are strict."

Shallan covered a grimace.

"No tantrum," Jasnah noted. "That is a good sign."

"Tantrum, Brightness? From a lighteyed woman?"

"You'd be surprised," Jasnah said dryly. "But attitude alone will not earn your place. Tell me, how extensive is your education?"

"Extensive in some areas," Shallan said. Then she hesitantly added, "Extensively lacking in others."

"Very well," Jasnah said. Ahead, the king seemed to be in a hurry, but he was old enough that even an urgent walk was still slow. "Then we shall do an evaluation. Answer truthfully and do not exaggerate, as I will soon discover your lies. Feign no false modesty, either. I haven't the patience for a simperer."

"Yes, Brightness."

"We shall begin with music. How would you judge your skill?"

"I have a good ear, Brightness," Shallan said honestly. "I'm best with voice, though I have been trained on the zither and the pipes. I would be far from the best you'd heard, but I'd also be far from the worst. I know most historical ballads by heart."

"Give me the refrain from 'Lilting Adrene.'"

"Here?"

"I'm not fond of repeating myself, child."

Shallan blushed, but began to sing. It wasn't her finest performance, but her tone was pure and she didn't stumble over any of the words.

"Good," Jasnah said as Shallan paused for a breath. "Languages?"

Shallan fumbled for a moment, bringing her attention away from frantically trying to remember the next verse. Languages? "I can speak your native Alethi, obviously," Shallan said. "I have a passable reading knowledge of Thaylen and good spoken Azish. I can make myself understood in Selay, but not read it."

Jasnah made no comment either way. Shallan began to grow nervous.

"Writing?" Jasnah asked.

"I know all of the major, minor, and topical glyphs and can paint them calligraphically."

"So can most children."

"The glyphwards that I paint are regarded by those who know me as quite impressive."

"Glyphwards?" Jasnah said. "I had reason to believe you wanted to be a scholar, not a purveyor of superstitious nonsense."

"I have kept a journal since I was a child," Shallan continued, "in order to practice my writing skills."

"Congratulations," Jasnah said. "Should I need someone to write a treatise on their stuffed pony or give an account of an interesting pebble they discovered, I shall send for you. Is there nothing you can offer that shows you have true skill?"

Shallan blushed. "With all due respect, Brightness, you have a letter from me yourself, and it was persuasive enough to make you grant me this audience."

"A valid point," Jasnah said, nodding. "It took you long

enough to make it. How is your training in logic and its related arts?"

"I am accomplished in basic mathematics," Shallan said, still flustered, "and I often helped with minor accounts for my father. I have read through the complete works of Tormas, Nashan, Niali the Just, and—of course—Nohadon."

"Placini?"

Who? "No."

"Gabrathin, Yustara, Manaline, Syasikk, Shauka-daughter-Hasweth?"

Shallan cringed and shook her head again. That last name was obviously Shin. Did the Shin people even *have* logic-masters? Did Jasnah really expect her wards to have studied such obscure texts?

"I see," Jasnah said. "Well, what of history?"

History. Shallan shrank down even further. "I . . . This is one of the areas where I'm obviously deficient, Brightness. My father was never able to find a suitable tutor for me. I read the history books he owned. . . ."

"Which were?"

"The entire set of Barlesha Lhan's *Topics*, mostly."

Jasnah waved her freehand dismissively. "Barely worth the time spent scribing them. A popular survey of historical events at best."

"I apologize, Brightness."

"This is an embarrassing hole. History is *the* most important of the literary subarts. One would think that your parents would have taken specific care in this area, if they'd hoped to submit you to study under a historian like myself."

"My circumstances are unusual, Brightness."

"Ignorance is hardly unusual, Miss Davar. The longer I live, the more I come to realize that it is the natural state of the human mind. There are many who will strive to defend its sanctity and then expect you to be impressed with their efforts."

Shallan blushed again. She'd realized she had some deficiencies, but Jasnah had unreasonable expectations. She said nothing, continuing to walk beside the taller woman. How long was this hallway, anyway? She was so flustered she didn't even look at the paintings they passed. They turned a corner, walking deeper into the mountainside.

"Well, let us move on to science, then," Jasnah said, tone displeased. "What can you say of yourself there?"

"I have the reasonable foundation in the sciences you might expect of a young woman my age," Shallan said, more stiffly than she would have liked.

"Which means?"

"I can speak with skill about geography, geology, physics, and chemistry. I've made particular study of biology and botany, as I was able to pursue them with a reasonable level of independence on my father's estates. But if you expect me to be able to solve Fabrisan's Conundrum with a wave of my hand, I suspect you shall be disappointed."

"Have I not a right to make reasonable demands of my potential students, Miss Davar?"

"Reasonable? Your demands are about as *reasonable* as the ones made of the Ten Heralds on Proving Day! With all due respect, Brightness, you seem to want potential wards to be master scholars already. I may be able to find a pair of eighty-year-old ardents in the city who *might* fit your requirements. They could interview for the position, though they may have trouble hearing well enough to answer your questions."

"I see," Jasnah replied. "And do you speak with such pique to your parents as well?"

Shallan winced. Her time spent with the sailors had loosened her tongue far too much. Had she traveled all this way only to offend Jasnah? She thought of her brothers, destitute, keeping up a tenuous facade back home. Would she have to return to them in defeat, having squandered this opportunity? "I did not speak to them this way, Brightness. Nor should I to you. I apologize."

"Well, at least you are humble enough to admit fault. Still, I am disappointed. How is it that your mother considered you ready for a wardship?"

"My mother passed away when I was just a child, Brightness."

"And your father soon remarried. Malise Gevelmar, I believe."

Shallan started at her knowledge. House Davar was ancient, but only of middling power and importance. The fact that Jasnah knew the name of Shallan's stepmother said a lot about her. "My stepmother passed away recently. She didn't send me to be your ward. I took this initiative upon myself."

"My condolences," Jasnah said. "Perhaps you should be with your father, seeing to his estates and comforting him, rather than wasting my time."

The men walking ahead turned down another side passage. Jasnah and Shallan followed, entering a smaller corridor with an ornate red and yellow rug, mirrors hanging on the walls.

Shallan turned to Jasnah. "My father has no need of me." Well, that was true. "But I have great need of you, as this interview itself has proven. If ignorance galls you so much, can you in good conscience pass up the opportunity to rid me of mine?"

"I've done so before, Miss Davar. You are the twelfth young woman to ask me for a wardship this year."

Twelve? Shallan thought. *In one year?* And she'd assumed that women would stay away from Jasnah because of her antagonism toward the devotaries.

The group reached the end of the narrow hallway, turning a corner to find—to Shallan's surprise—a place where a large chunk of rock had fallen from the ceiling. A dozen or so attendants stood here, some looking anxious. What was going on?

Much of the rubble had evidently been cleared away, though the gouge in the ceiling gaped ominously. It didn't look out on the sky; they had been progressing downward, and were probably far underground. A massive stone, taller than a man, had fallen into a doorway on the left. There was no getting past it into the room beyond. Shallan thought she heard sounds on the other side. The king stepped up to the stone, speaking in a comforting voice. He pulled a handkerchief out of his pocket and wiped his aged brow.

"The dangers of living in a building cut directly into the rock," Jasnah said, striding forward. "When did this happen?" Apparently she hadn't been summoned to the city specifically for this purpose; the king was simply taking advantage of her presence.

"During the recent highstorm, Brightness," the king said. He shook his head, making his drooping, thin white mustache tremble. "The palace architects might be able to cut a way into the room, but it would take time, and the next highstorm is scheduled to hit in just a few days. Beyond that, breaking in might bring down more of the ceiling."

"I thought Kharbranth was protected from the highstorms, Your Majesty," Shallan said, causing Jasnah to shoot her a glance.

"The city is sheltered, young woman," the king said. "But the stone mountain behind us is buffeted quite strongly. Sometimes it causes avalanches on that side, and that can cause the entire mountainside to shake." He glanced at the ceiling. "Cave-ins are very rare, and we thought this area was quite safe, but . . ."

"But it is rock," Jasnah said, "and there is no telling if a weak vein lurks just beyond the surface." She inspected the monolith that had fallen from the ceiling. "This will be difficult. I will probably lose a very valuable focal stone."

"I—" the king began, wiping his brow again. "If only we had a Shardblade—"

Jasnah cut him off with a wave of the hand. "I was not seeking to renegotiate our bargain, Your Majesty. Access to the Palanaeum is worth the cost. You will want to send someone for wet rags. Have the majority of the servants move down to the other end of the hallway. You may wish to wait there yourself."

"I will stay here," the king said, causing his attendants to object, including a large man wearing a black leather cuirass, probably his bodyguard. The king silenced them by raising his wrinkled hand. "I will not hide like a coward when my granddaughter is trapped."

No wonder he was so anxious. Jasnah didn't argue further, and Shallan could see from her eyes that it was of no consequence to her if the king risked his life. The same apparently went for Shallan, for Jasnah didn't order her away. Servants approached with wetted cloths and distributed them. Jasnah refused hers. The king and his bodyguard raised theirs to their faces, covering mouth and nose.

Shallan took hers. What was the point of it? A couple of servants passed some wet cloths through a space between the rock and the wall to those inside. Then all of the servants rushed away down the hallway.

Jasnah picked and prodded at the boulder. "Miss Davar," she said, "what method would you use to ascertain the mass of this stone?"

Shallan blinked. "Well, I suppose I'd ask His Majesty. His architects probably calculated it."

Jasnah cocked her head. "An elegant response. Did they do that, Your Majesty?"

"Yes, Brightness Kholin," the king said. "It's roughly fifteen thousand kavals."

Jasnah eyed Shallan. "A point in your favor, Miss Davar. A scholar knows not to waste time rediscovering information already known. It's a lesson I sometimes forget."

Shallan felt herself swell at the words. She already had an inkling that Jasnah did not give such praise lightly. Did this mean that the woman was still considering her as a ward?

Jasnah held up her freehand, Soulcaster glistening against the skin. Shallan felt her heartbeat speed up. She'd never seen Soulcasting done in person. The ardents were very secretive in using their fabrials, and she hadn't even known that her father had one until they'd found it on him. Of course, his no longer worked. That was one of the main reasons she was here.

The gemstones set into Jasnah's Soulcaster were enormous, some of the largest that Shallan had ever seen, worth many spheres each. One was smokestone, a pure glassy black gemstone. The second was a diamond. The third was a ruby. All three were cut—a cut stone could hold more Stormlight—into glistening, many-faceted oval shapes.

Jasnah closed her eyes, pressing her hand against the fallen boulder. She raised her head, inhaling slowly. The stones on the back of her hand began to glow more fiercely, the smokestone in particular growing so bright it was difficult to look at.

Shallan held her breath. The only thing she dared do was blink, committing the scene to memory. For a long, extended moment, nothing happened.

And then, briefly, Shallan heard a sound. A low thrumming, like a distant group of voices, humming together a single, pure note.

Jasnah's hand *sank* into the rock.

The stone vanished.

A burst of dense black smoke exploded into the hallway. Enough to blind Shallan; it seemed the output of a thousand fires, and smelled of burned wood. Shallan hastily raised the wet rag to her face, dropping to her knees. Oddly, her ears felt stopped up, as if she'd climbed down from a great height. She had to swallow to pop them.

She shut her eyes tightly as they began to water, and she held her breath. Her ears filled with a rushing sound.

It passed. She blinked open her eyes to find the king and his bodyguard huddled against the wall beside her. Smoke still pooled at the ceiling; the hallway smelled strongly of it. Jasnah stood, eyes still closed, oblivious of the smoke—though grime now dusted her face and clothing. It had left marks on the walls too.

Shallan had read of this, but she was still in awe. Jasnah had transformed the boulder into smoke, and since smoke was far less dense than stone, the change had pushed the smoke away in an explosive outburst.

It was true; Jasnah really *did* have a functioning Soulcaster. And a powerful one too. Nine out of ten Soulcasters were capable of a few limited transformations: creating water or grain from stone; forming bland, single-roomed rock buildings out of air or cloth. A greater one, like Jasnah's, could effectuate any transformation. Literally turn any substance into any other one. How it must grate on the ardents that such a powerful, holy relic was in the hands of someone outside the ardentia. And a heretic no less!

Shallan stumbled to her feet, leaving the cloth at her mouth, breathing humid but dust-free air. She swallowed, her ears popping again as the hall's pressure returned to normal. A moment later, the king rushed into the now-accessible room. A small girl—along with several nursemaids and other palace servants—sat on the other side, coughing. The king pulled the girl into his arms. She was too young to have a modesty sleeve.

Jasnah opened her eyes, blinking, as if momentarily confused by her location. She took a deep breath, and didn't cough. Indeed, she actually *smiled*, as if enjoying the scent of the smoke.

Jasnah turned to Shallan, focusing on her. "You are still waiting for a response. I'm afraid you will not like what I say."

"But you haven't finished your testing of me yet," Shallan said, forcing herself to be bold. "Surely you won't give judgment until you have."

"I haven't finished?" Jasnah asked, frowning.

"You didn't ask me about all of the feminine arts. You left out painting and drawing."

"I have never had much use for them."

"But *they* are of the arts," Shallan said, feeling desperate. This was where she was most accomplished! "Many consider the visual arts the most refined of them all. I brought my portfolio. I would show you what I can do."

Jasnah pursed her lips. "The visual arts are frivolity. I have weighed the facts, child, and I cannot accept you. I'm sorry."

Shallan's heart sank.

"Your Majesty," Jasnah said to the king, "I would like to go to the Palanaeum."

"Now?" the king said, cradling his granddaughter. "But we are going to have a feast—"

"I appreciate the offer," Jasnah said, "but I find myself with an abundance of everything *but* time."

"Of course," the king said. "I will take you personally. Thank you for what you've done. When I heard that you had requested entrance . . ." He continued to babble at Jasnah, who followed him wordlessly down the hallway, leaving Shallan behind.

She clutched her satchel to her chest, lowering the cloth from her mouth. Six months of chasing, for this. She gripped the rag in frustration, squeezing sooty water between her fingers. She wanted to cry. That was what she probably would have done if she'd been that same child she had been six months ago.

But things had changed. *She* had changed. If she failed, House Davar would fall. Shallan felt her determination redouble, though she wasn't able to stop a few tears of frustration from squeezing out of the corners of her eyes. She was not going to give up until Jasnah was forced to truss her up in chains and have the authorities drag her away.

Her step surprisingly firm, she walked in the direction Jasnah had gone. Six months ago, she had explained a desperate plan to her brothers. She would apprentice herself to Jasnah Kholin, scholar, heretic. Not for the education. Not for the prestige. But in order to learn where she kept her Soulcaster.

And then Shallan would steal it.

Charcoal rubbing of a map of Sadeas's warcamp as used by a common spearman. It was scratched on the back of a palm-size cremling shell. Rubbing labeled in ink by an anonymous Alethi scholar, circa 1173.

BRIDGE FOUR

*"I'm cold. Mother, I'm cold. Mother? Why can I still hear
the rain? Will it stop?"*

—Collected on Vevishes, 1172, 32 seconds pre-death. Subject
was a lighteyed female child, approximately six years old.

Tvlakv released all of the slaves from their cages at once.
This time, he didn't fear runaways or a slave rebellion—
not with nothing but wilderness behind them and over a
hundred thousand armed soldiers just ahead.

Kaladin stepped down from the wagon. They were inside
one of the craterlike formations, its jagged stone wall rising
just to the east. The ground had been cleared of plant life, and
the rock was slick beneath his unshod feet. Pools of rainwater
had gathered in depressions. The air was crisp and clean, and
the sun strong overhead, though with this Eastern humidity,
he always felt damp.

Around them spread the signs of an army long settled;
this war had been going on since the old king's death, nearly
six years ago. Everyone told stories of that night, the night
when Parshendi tribesmen had murdered King Gavilar.

Squads of soldiers marched by, following directions indicated by painted circles at each intersection. The camp was
packed with long stone bunkers, and there were more tents

than Kaladin had discerned from above. Soulcasters couldn't be used to create every shelter. After the stink of the slave caravan, the place smelled good, brimming with familiar scents like treated leather and oiled weapons. However, many of the soldiers had a disorderly look. They weren't dirty, but they didn't seem particularly disciplined either. They roamed the camp in packs with coats undone. Some pointed and jeered at the slaves. This was the army of a highprince? The elite force that fought for Alethkar's honor? This was what Kaladin had aspired to join?

Bluth and Tag watched carefully as Kaladin lined up with the other slaves, but he didn't try anything. Now was not the time to provoke them—Kaladin had seen how mercenaries acted when around commissioned troops. Bluth and Tag played their part, walking with their chests out and hands on their weapons. They shoved a few of the slaves into place, ramming a cudgel into one man's belly and cursing him gruffly.

They stayed clear of Kaladin.

"The king's army," said the slave next to him. It was the dark-skinned man who had talked to Kaladin about escaping. "I thought we were meant for mine work. Why, this won't be so bad at all. We'll be cleaning latrines or maintaining roads."

Odd, to look forward to latrine work or labor in the hot sun. Kaladin hoped for something else. Hoped. Yes, he'd discovered that he could still hope. A spear in his hands. An enemy to face. He could live like that.

Tvlakv spoke with an important-looking lighteyed woman. She wore her dark hair up in a complex weave, sparkling with infused amethysts, and her dress was a deep crimson. She looked much as Laral had, at the end. She was probably of the fourth or fifth dahn, wife and scribe to one of the camp's officers.

Tvlakv began to brag about his wares, but the woman raised a delicate hand. "I can see what I am purchasing, slaver," she said in a smooth, aristocratic accent. "I will inspect them myself."

She began to walk down the line, accompanied by several soldiers. Her dress was cut in the Alethi noble fashion—a solid swath of silk, tight and formfitting through the top with sleek skirts below. It buttoned up the sides of the torso from waist to neck, where it was topped by a small, gold-embroidered collar. The longer left cuff hid her safehand. Kaladin's mother had always just worn a glove, which seemed far more practical to him.

Judging by her face, she was not particularly impressed with what she saw. "These men are half-starved and sickly," she said, taking a thin rod from a young female attendant. She used it to lift the hair from one man's forehead, inspecting his brand. "You are asking two emerald broams a head?"

Tvlakv began to sweat. "Perhaps one and a half?"

"And what would I use them for? I wouldn't trust men this filthy near food, and we have parshmen to do most other work."

"If Your Ladyship is not pleased, I could approach other highprinces. . . ."

"No," she said, smacking the slave she'd been regarding as he shied away from her. "One and a quarter. They can help cut timber for us in the northern forests. . . ." She trailed off as she noticed Kaladin. "Here now. This is far better stock than the others."

"I thought that you might like this one," Tvlakv said, stepping up to her. "He *is* quite—"

She raised the rod and silenced Tvlakv. She had a small sore on one lip. Some ground cussweed root could help with that.

"Remove your top, slave," she commanded.

Kaladin stared her right in her blue eyes and felt an almost irresistible urge to spit at her. No. No, he couldn't afford that. Not when there was a chance. He pulled his arms out of the sacklike clothing, letting it fall to his waist, exposing his chest.

Despite eight months as a slave, he was far better muscled than the others. "A large number of scars for one so young," the noblewoman said thoughtfully. "You are a military man?"

"Yes." His windspren zipped up to the woman, inspecting her face.

"Mercenary?"

"Amaram's army," Kaladin said. "A citizen, second nahn."

"*Once* a citizen," Tvlakv put in quickly. "He was—"

She silenced Tvlakv again with her rod, glaring at him. Then she used the rod to push aside Kaladin's hair and inspect his forehead.

"*Shash* glyph," she said, clicking her tongue. Several of the soldiers nearby stepped closer, hands on their swords. "Where I come from, slaves who deserve these are simply executed."

"They are fortunate," Kaladin said.

"And how did you end up here?"

"I killed someone," Kaladin said, preparing his lies carefully. *Please,* he thought to the Heralds. *Please.* It had been a long time since he had prayed for anything.

The woman raised an eyebrow.

"I'm a murderer, Brightness," Kaladin said. "Got drunk, made some mistakes. But I can use a spear as well as any man. Put me in your brightlord's army. Let me fight again." It was a strange lie to make, but the woman would never let Kaladin fight if she thought he was a deserter. In this case, better to be known as an accidental murderer.

Please . . . he thought. To be a soldier again. It seemed, in one moment, the most glorious thing he could ever have wanted. How much better it would be to die on the battlefield than waste away emptying chamber pots.

To the side, Tvlakv stepped up beside the lighteyed woman. He glanced at Kaladin, then sighed. "He's a deserter, Brightness. Don't listen to him."

No! Kaladin felt a blazing burst of anger consume his hope. He raised hands toward Tvlakv. He'd strangle the rat, and—

Something cracked him across the back. He grunted, stumbling and falling to one knee. The noblewoman stepped back, raising her safehand to her breast in alarm. One of the army soldiers grabbed Kaladin and towed him back to his feet.

"Well," she finally said. "That is unfortunate."

"I *can* fight," Kaladin growled against the pain. "Give me a spear. Let me—"

She raised her rod, cutting him off.

"Brightness," Tvlakv said, not meeting Kaladin's eyes. "I would not trust him with a weapon. It is true that he is a murderer, but he is also known to disobey and lead rebellions against his masters. I couldn't sell him to you as a bonded soldier. My conscience, it would not allow it." He hesitated. "The men in his wagon, he might have corrupted them all with talk of escape. My honor demands that I tell you this."

Kaladin gritted his teeth. He was tempted to try to take down the soldier behind him, grab that spear and spend his last moments ramming it through Tvlakv's portly gut. Why? What did it matter to Tvlakv how Kaladin was treated by this army?

I should never have ripped up the map, Kaladin thought. *Bitterness is repaid more often than kindness.* One of his father's sayings.

The woman nodded, moving on. "Show me which ones," she said. "I'll still take them, because of your honesty. We need some new bridgemen."

Tvlakv nodded eagerly. Before moving on, he paused and leaned in to Kaladin. "I cannot trust that you will behave. The people in this army, they will blame a merchant for not revealing all he knew. I . . . am sorry." With that, the merchant scuttled away.

Kaladin growled in the back of his throat, and then pulled himself free of the soldiers, but remained in line. So be it. Cutting down trees, building bridges, fighting in the army. None of it mattered. He would just keep living. They'd taken his freedom, his family, his friends, and—most dear of all—his dreams. They could do nothing more to him.

After her inspection, the noblewoman took a writing board from her assistant and made a few quick notations on its paper. Tvlakv gave her a ledger detailing how much each slave had paid down on their slave debt. Kaladin caught a glimpse; it said that not a single one of the men had paid anything. Perhaps Tvlakv lied about the figures. Not unlikely.

Kaladin would probably just let all of his wages go to his debt this time. Let them squirm as they saw him actually call their bluff. What would they do if he got close to earning out his debt? He'd probably never find out—depending on what these bridgemen earned, it could take anything from ten to fifty years to get there.

The lighteyed woman assigned most of the slaves to forest duty. A half-dozen of the more spindly ones were sent to work the mess halls, despite what she'd said before. "Those ten," the noblewoman said, raising her rod to point at Kaladin and the others from his wagon. "Take them to the bridge crews. Tell Lamaril and Gaz that the tall one is to be given special treatment."

The soldiers laughed, and one began shoving Kaladin's group along the pathway. Kaladin endured it; these men had no reason to be gentle, and he wouldn't give them a reason to be rougher. If there was a group citizen soldiers hated more than mercenaries, it was deserters.

As he walked, he couldn't help noticing the banner flying above the camp. It bore the same symbol emblazoned on the soldiers' uniform coats: a yellow glyphpair in the shape of a tower and a hammer on a field of deep green. That was the banner of Highprince Sadeas, ultimate ruler of Kaladin's own home district. Was it irony or fate that had landed Kaladin here?

Soldiers lounged idly, even those who appeared to be on duty, and the camp streets were littered with refuse. Camp followers were plentiful: whores, worker women, coopers, chandlers, and wranglers. There were even children running through the streets of what was half city, half warcamp.

There were also parshmen. Carrying water, working on trenches, lifting sacks. That surprised him. Weren't they fighting parshmen? Weren't they worried that these would rise up? Apparently not. The parshmen here worked with the same docility as the ones back in Hearthstone. Perhaps it made sense. Alethi had fought against Alethi back in his armies at home, so why shouldn't there be parshmen on both sides of this conflict?

The soldiers took Kaladin all the way around to the northeastern quarter of the camp, a hike that took some time. Though the Soulcast stone barracks each looked exactly the same, the rim of the camp was broken distinctively, like ragged mountains. Old habits made him memorize the route. Here, the towering circular wall had been worn away by countless highstorms, giving a clear view eastward. That open patch of ground would make a good staging area for an army to gather on before marching down the incline to the Shattered Plains themselves.

The northern edge of the field contained a subcamp filled with several dozen barracks, and at their center a lumberyard filled with carpenters. They were breaking down some of the stout trees Kaladin had seen on the plains outside: stripping off their stringy bark, sawing them into planks. Another group of carpenters assembled the planks into large contraptions.

"We're to be woodworkers?" Kaladin asked.

One of the soldiers laughed roughly. "You're joining the bridge crews." He pointed to where a group of sorry-looking men sat on the stones in the shade of a barrack, scooping food out of wooden bowls with their fingers. It looked depressingly similar to the slop that Tvlakv had fed them.

One of the soldiers shoved Kaladin forward again, and he stumbled down the shallow incline and crossed the grounds. The other nine slaves followed, herded by the soldiers. None of the men sitting around the barracks so much as glanced at them. They wore leather vests and simple trousers, some with dirty laced shirts, others bare-chested. The grim, sorry lot weren't much better than the slaves, though they did look to be in slightly better physical condition.

"New recruits, Gaz," one of the soldiers called.

A man lounged in the shade a distance from the eating men. He turned, revealing a face that was so scarred his beard grew in patches. He was missing one eye—the other was brown—and didn't bother with an eye patch. White knots at his shoulders marked him as a sergeant, and he had the lean toughness Kaladin had learned to associate with someone who knew his way around a battlefield.

"These spindly things?" Gaz said, chewing on something as he walked over. "They'll barely stop an arrow."

The soldier beside Kaladin shrugged, shoving him forward once more for good measure. "Brightness Hashal said to do something special with this one. The rest are up to you." The soldier nodded to his companions, and they began to trot away.

Gaz looked the slaves over. He focused on Kaladin last.

"I have military training," Kaladin said. "In the army of Highlord Amaram."

"I don't really care," Gaz cut in, spitting something dark to the side.

Kaladin hesitated. "When Amaram—"

"You keep mentioning that name," Gaz snapped. "Served under some unimportant landlord, did you? Expect me to be impressed?"

Kaladin sighed. He'd met this kind of man before, a lesser sergeant with no hope of advancement. His only pleasure in life came from his authority over those even sorrier than himself. Well, so be it.

"You have a slave's mark," Gaz said, snorting. "I doubt you ever held a spear. Either way, you'll have to condescend to join us now, Lordship."

Kaladin's windspren flitted down and inspected Gaz, then closed one of her eyes, imitating him. For some reason, seeing her made Kaladin smile. Gaz misinterpreted the smile. The man scowled and stepped forward, pointing.

At that moment, a loud chorus of horns echoed through the camp. Carpenters glanced up, and the soldiers who had guided Kaladin dashed back toward the center of camp. The slaves behind Kaladin looked around anxiously.

"Stormfather!" Gaz cursed. "Bridgemen! Up, up, you louts!" He began kicking at some of the men who were eating. They scattered their bowls, scrambling to their feet. They wore simple sandals instead of proper boots.

"You, Lordship," Gaz said, pointing at Kaladin.

"I didn't say—"

"I don't care what in Damnation you said! You're in Bridge

Four." He pointed at a group of departing bridgemen. "The rest of you, go wait over there. I'll divide you up later. Get moving, or I'll see you strung up by your heels."

Kaladin shrugged and jogged after the group of bridgemen. It was one of many teams of such men pouring out of barracks or picking themselves up out of alleys. There seemed to be quite a lot of them. Around fifty barracks, with—perhaps—twenty or thirty men in each . . . that would make nearly as many bridgemen in this army as there had been soldiers in Amaram's entire force.

Kaladin's team crossed the grounds, weaving between boards and piles of sawdust, approaching a large wooden contraption. It had obviously weathered a few highstorms and some battles. The dents and holes scattered along its length looked like places where arrows had struck. The bridge in bridgeman, perhaps?

Yes, Kaladin thought. It was a wooden bridge, over thirty feet long, eight feet wide. It sloped down at the front and back, and had no railings. The wood was thick, with the largest boards for support through the center. There were some forty or fifty bridges lined up here. Perhaps one for each barrack, making one crew for each bridge? About twenty bridge crews were gathering at this point.

Gaz had found himself a wooden shield and a gleaming mace, but there were none for anyone else. He quickly inspected each team. He stopped beside Bridge Four and hesitated. "Where's your bridgeleader?" he demanded.

"Dead," one of the bridgemen said. "Tossed himself down the Honor Chasm last night."

Gaz cursed. "Can't you keep a bridgeleader for even a week? Storm it! Line up; I'll run near you. Listen for my commands. We'll sort out another bridgeleader after we see who survives." Gaz pointed at Kaladin. "You're at the back, lordling. The rest of you, get moving! Storm you, I won't suffer another reprimand because of you fools! Move, move!"

The others were lifting. Kaladin had no choice but to go to the open slot at the tail of the bridge. He'd been a little low in his assessment; looked like about thirty-five to forty men per bridge. There was room for five men across—three under the bridge and one on each side—and eight deep, though this crew didn't have a man for each position.

He helped lift the bridge into the air. They were probably using a very light wood for the bridges, but the thing was still storms-cursed heavy. Kaladin grunted as he struggled with the weight, hoisting the bridge up high and then stepping underneath. Men dashed in to fill the middle slots down the length of the structure, and slowly they all set the bridge down on their shoulders. At least there were rods on the bottom to use as handholds.

The other men had pads on the shoulders of their vests to cushion the weight and adjust their height to fit the supports. Kaladin hadn't been given a vest, so the wooden supports dug directly into his skin. He couldn't see a thing; there was an indentation for his head, but wood cut off his view to all sides. The men at the edges had better views; he suspected those spots were more coveted.

The wood smelled of oil and sweat.

"Go!" Gaz said from outside, voice muffled.

Kaladin grunted as the crew broke into a jog. He couldn't see where he was going, and struggled to keep from tripping as the bridge crew marched down the eastern slope to the Shattered Plains. Soon, Kaladin was sweating and cursing under his breath, the wood rubbing and digging into the skin on his shoulders. He was already starting to bleed.

"Poor fool," a voice said from the side.

Kaladin glanced to the right, but the wooden handholds obstructed his view. "Are you . . ." Kaladin puffed. "Are you talking to me?"

"You shouldn't have insulted Gaz," the man said. His voice sounded hollow. "He sometimes lets new men run in an outside row. Sometimes."

Kaladin tried to respond, but he was already gasping for breath. He'd thought himself in better shape than this, but he'd spent eight months being fed slop, being beaten, and waiting out highstorms in leaking cellars, muddy barns, or cages. He was hardly the same man anymore.

"Breathe in and out deeply," said the muffled voice. "Focus on the steps. Count them. It helps."

Kaladin followed the advice. He could hear other bridge crews running nearby. Behind them came the familiar sounds of men marching and hoofbeats on the stone. They were being followed by an army.

Below, rockbuds and small shalebark ridges grew from the stone, tripping him. The landscape of the Shattered Plains appeared to be broken, uneven, and rent, covered with outcroppings and shelves of rock. That explained why they didn't use wheels on the bridges—porters were probably much faster over such rough terrain.

Soon, his feet were ragged and battered. Couldn't they have given him shoes? He set his jaw against the agony and kept on going. Just another job. He would continue, and he would survive.

A thumping sound. His feet fell on wood. A bridge, a permanent one, crossing a chasm between plateaus on the Shattered Plains. In seconds the bridge crew was across it, and his feet fell on stone again.

"Move, move!" Gaz bellowed. "Storm you, keep going!"

They continued jogging as the army crossed the bridge behind them, hundreds of boots resounding on the wood. Before too long, blood ran down Kaladin's shoulders. His breathing was torturous, his side aching painfully. He could hear others gasping, the sounds carrying through the confined space beneath the bridge. So he wasn't the only one. Hopefully, they would arrive at their destination quickly.

He hoped in vain.

The next hour was torture. It was worse than any beating he'd suffered as a slave, worse than any wound on the battlefield. There seemed to be no end to the march. Kaladin vaguely remembered seeing the permanent bridges, back when he'd looked down on the plains from the slave cart. They connected the plateaus where the chasms were easiest to span, not where it would be most efficient for those traveling. That often meant detours north or south before they could continue eastward.

The bridgemen grumbled, cursed, groaned, then fell silent.

They crossed bridge after bridge, plateau after plateau. Kaladin never got a good look at one of the chasms. He just kept running. And running. He couldn't feel his feet any longer. He kept running. He knew, somehow, that if he stopped, he'd be beaten. He felt as if his shoulders had been rubbed to the bone. He tried counting steps, but was too exhausted even for that.

But he didn't stop running.

Finally, mercifully, Gaz called for them to halt. Kaladin blinked, stumbling to a stop and nearly collapsing.

"Lift!" Gaz bellowed.

The men lifted, Kaladin's arms straining at the motion after so much time holding the bridge in one place.

"Drop!"

They stepped aside, the bridgemen underneath taking handholds at the sides. It was awkward and difficult, but these men had practice, apparently. They kept the bridge from toppling as they set it on the ground.

"Push!"

Kaladin stumbled back in confusion as the men pushed at their handholds on the side or back of the bridge. They were at the edge of a chasm lacking a permanent bridge. To the sides, the other bridge crews were pushing their own bridges forward.

Kaladin glanced over his shoulder. The army was two thousand men in forest green and pure white. Twelve hundred darkeyed spearmen, several hundred cavalry atop rare, precious horses. Behind them, a large group of heavy foot, lighteyed men in thick armor and carrying large maces and square steel shields.

It seemed that they'd intentionally chosen a point where the chasm was narrow and the first plateau was a little higher than the second. The bridge was twice as long as the chasm's width here. Gaz cursed at him, so Kaladin joined the others, shoving the bridge across the rough ground with a scraping sound. When the bridge thumped into place on the other side of the chasm, the bridge crew drew back to let the cavalry trot across.

He was too exhausted to watch. He collapsed to the stones and lay back, listening to sounds of foot soldiers tromping across the bridge. He rolled his head to the side. The other bridgemen had lain down as well. Gaz walked among the various crews, shaking his head, his shield on his back as he muttered about their worthlessness.

Kaladin longed to lie there, staring at the sky, oblivious of the world. His training, however, warned that might cause him to cramp up. That would make the return trip even worse. That training . . . it belonged to another man, from another time. Almost from the shadowdays. But while Kaladin might not *be* him any longer, he could still *heed* him.

And so, with a groan, Kaladin forced himself to sit up and begin rubbing his muscles. Soldiers crossed the bridge four across, spears held high, shields forward. Gaz watched them with obvious envy, and Kaladin's windspren danced around the man's head. Despite his fatigue, Kaladin felt a moment of jealousy. Why was she bothering that blowhard instead of Kaladin?

After a few minutes, Gaz noticed Kaladin and scowled at him.

"He's wondering why you aren't lying down," said a familiar voice. The man who had been running beside Kaladin lay on the ground a short distance away, staring up at the sky. He was older, with greying hair, and he had a long, leathery face to complement his kindly voice. He looked as exhausted as Kaladin felt.

Kaladin kept rubbing his legs, pointedly ignoring Gaz. Then he ripped off some portions of his sacklike clothing and bound his feet and shoulders. Fortunately, he was accustomed to walking barefoot as a slave, so the damage wasn't too bad.

As he finished, the last of the foot soldiers passed over the bridge. They were followed by several mounted lighteyes in gleaming armor. At their center rode a man in majestic, burnished red Shardplate. It was distinct from the one other Kaladin had seen—each suit was said to be an individual work of art—but it had the same *feel*. Ornate, interlocking, topped by a beautiful helm with an open visor.

The armor felt *alien* somehow. It had been crafted in another epoch, a time when gods had walked Roshar.

"Is that the king?" Kaladin asked.

The leathery bridgeman laughed tiredly. "We could only wish."

Kaladin turned toward him, frowning.

"If that were the king," the bridgeman said, "then that would mean we were in Brightlord Dalinar's army."

The name was vaguely familiar to Kaladin. "He's a highprince, right? The king's uncle?"

"Aye. The best of men, the most honorable Shardbearer in the king's army. They say he's never broken his word."

Kaladin sniffed in disdain. Much the same had been said about Amaram.

"You should wish to be in Highprince Dalinar's force, lad," the older man said. "He doesn't use bridge crews. Not like these, at least."

"All right, you cremlings!" Gaz bellowed. "On your feet!"

The bridgemen groaned, stumbling upright. Kaladin sighed. The brief rest had been just enough to show how exhausted he was. "I'll be glad to get back," he muttered.

"Back?" the leathery bridgeman said.

"We aren't turning around?"

His friend chuckled wryly. "Lad, we aren't *nearly* there yet. Be glad we aren't. Arriving is the worst part."

And so the nightmare began its second phase. They crossed the bridge, pulled it over behind them, then lifted it up on sore shoulders once more. They jogged across the plateau. At the other side, they lowered the bridge again to span another chasm. The army crossed, then it was back to carrying the bridge again.

They repeated this a good dozen times. They did get to rest between carries, but Kaladin was so sore and overworked that the brief respites weren't enough. He barely caught his breath each time before being forced to pick up the bridge again.

They were expected to be quick about it. The bridgemen got to rest while the army crossed, but they had to make up the time by jogging across the plateaus—passing the ranks of soldiers—so that they could arrive at the next chasm before the army. At one point, his leathery-faced friend warned him that if they didn't have their bridge in place quickly enough, they'd be punished with whippings when they returned to camp.

Gaz gave orders, cursing the bridgemen, kicking them when they moved too slowly, never doing any real work. It didn't take long for Kaladin to nurture a seething hatred of the scrawny, scar-faced man. That was odd; he hadn't felt hatred for his other sergeants. It was their *job* to curse at the men and keep them motivated.

That wasn't what burned Kaladin. Gaz had sent him on this trip without sandals or a vest. Despite his bandages, Kaladin would bear scars from his work this day. He'd be so bruised and stiff in the morning that he'd be unable to walk.

What Gaz had done was the mark of a petty bully. He risked the mission by losing a carrier, all because of a hasty grudge.

Storming man, Kaladin thought, using his hatred of Gaz to sustain him through the ordeal. Several times after pushing the bridge into place, Kaladin collapsed, feeling sure he'd never be able to stand again. But when Gaz called for them to rise, Kaladin somehow struggled to his feet. It was either that or let Gaz win.

Why were they going through all of this? What was the point? Why were they running so much? They had to protect their bridge, the precious weight, the cargo. They had to hold up the sky and run, they had to . . .

He was growing delirious. Feet, running. One, two, one, two, one, two.

"Stop!"

He stopped.

"Lift!"

He raised his hands up.

"Drop!"

He stepped back, then lowered the bridge.

"Push!"

He pushed the bridge.

Die.

That last command was his own, added each time. He fell back to the stone, a rockbud hastily withdrawing its vines as he touched them. He closed his eyes, no longer able to care about cramps. He entered a trance, a kind of half sleep, for what seemed like one heartbeat.

"Rise!"

He stood, stumbling on bloody feet.

"Cross!"

He crossed, not bothering to look at the deadly drop on either side.

"Pull!"

He grabbed a handhold and pulled the bridge across the chasm after him.

"Switch!"

Kaladin stood up dumbly. He didn't understand that command; Gaz had never given it before. The troops were forming ranks, moving with that mixture of skittishness and forced relaxation that men often went through before a battle. A few anticipationspren—like red streamers, growing from the ground and whipping in the wind—began to sprout from the rock and wave among the soldiers.

A battle?

Gaz grabbed Kaladin's shoulder and shoved him to the front of the bridge. "Newcomers get to go first at this part, Your Lordship." The sergeant smiled wickedly.

Kaladin dumbly picked up the bridge with the others, raising it over his head. The handholds were the same here, but this front row had a notched opening before his face, allowing him to see out. All of the bridgemen had changed positions; the men who had been running in the front moved to the back, and those at the back—including Kaladin and the leathery-faced bridgeman—moved to the front.

Kaladin didn't ask the point of it. He didn't care. He liked the front, though; jogging was easier now that he could see ahead of him.

The landscape on the plateaus was that of rough stormlands; there were scattered patches of grass, but the stone here was too hard for their seeds to fully burrow into. Rockbuds were more common, growing like bubbles across the entire plateau, imitating rocks about the size of a man's head. Many of the buds were split, trailing out their vines like thick green tongues. A few were even in bloom.

After so many hours breathing in the stuffy confines beneath the bridge, running in the front was almost relaxing. Why had they given such a wonderful position to a newcomer?

"Talenelat'Elin, bearer of all agonies," said the man to his right, voice horrified. "It's going to be a bad one. They're already lined up! It's going to be a bad one!"

Kaladin blinked, focusing on the approaching chasm. On the other side of the rift stood a rank of men with marbled crimson and black skin. They were wearing a strange rusty orange armor that covered their forearms, chests, heads, and legs. It took his numbed mind a moment to understand.

The Parshendi.

They weren't like common parshman workers. They were far more muscular, far more *solid*. They had the bulky build of soldiers, and each one carried a weapon strapped to his back. Some wore dark red and black beards tied with bits of rock, while others were clean-shaven.

As Kaladin watched, the front row of Parshendi knelt down. They held shortbows, arrows nocked. Not longbows intended to launch arrows high and far. Short, recurve bows to fire straight and quick and strong. An excellent bow to use for killing a group of bridgemen before they could lay their bridge.

Arriving is the worst part. . . .

Now, finally, the *real* nightmare began.

Gaz hung back, bellowing at the bridge crews to keep going. Kaladin's instincts screamed at him to get out of the line of fire, but the momentum of the bridge forced him forward. Forced him down the throat of the beast itself, its teeth poised to snap closed.

Kaladin's exhaustion and pain fled. He was shocked alert. The bridges charged forward, the men beneath them screaming as they ran. Ran toward death.

The archers released.

The first wave killed Kaladin's leathery-faced friend, dropping him with three separate arrows. The man to Kaladin's left fell as well—Kaladin hadn't even seen his face. That man cried out as he dropped, not dead immediately, but the bridge crew trampled him. The bridge got noticeably heavier as men died.

The Parshendi calmly drew a second volley and launched. To the side, Kaladin barely noticed another of the bridge crews floundering. The Parshendi seemed to focus their fire on certain crews. That one got a full wave of arrows from dozens of archers, and the first three rows of bridgemen dropped and tripped those behind them. Their bridge lurched, skidding on the ground and making a sickening crunch as the mass of bodies fell over one another.

Arrows zipped past Kaladin, killing the other two men in the front line with him. Several other arrows smacked into the wood around him, one slicing open the skin of his cheek.

He screamed. In horror, in shock, in pain, in sheer bewilderment. Never before had he felt so powerless in a battle. He'd charged enemy fortifications, he'd run beneath waves of arrows, but he'd always felt a measure of control. He'd had his spear, he'd had his shield, he could fight back.

Not this time. The bridge crews were like hogs running to the slaughter.

A third volley flew, and another of the twenty bridge crews fell. Waves of arrows came from the Alethi side as well, falling and striking the Parshendi. Kaladin's bridge was almost to the chasm. He could see the black eyes of the Parshendi on the other side, could make out the features of their lean marbled faces. All around him, bridgemen were screaming in pain, arrows cutting them out from underneath their bridges.

There was a crashing sound as another bridge dropped, its bridgemen slaughtered.

Behind, Gaz called out. "Lift and down, you fools!"

The bridge crew lurched to a stop as the Parshendi launched another volley. Men behind Kaladin screamed. The Parshendi firing was interrupted by a return volley from the Alethi army. Though he was shocked senseless, Kaladin's reflexes knew what do to. Drop the bridge, get into position to push.

This exposed the bridgemen who had been safe in the back ranks. The Parshendi archers obviously knew this was coming; they prepared and launched one final volley. Arrows struck the bridge in a wave, dropping a half-dozen men, spraying blood across the dark wood. Fearspren—wiggling and violet—sprang up through the wood and wriggled in the air. The bridge lurched, growing much harder to push as they suddenly lost those men.

Kaladin stumbled, hands slipping. He fell to his knees and pitched out, leaning over the chasm. He barely managed to catch himself.

He teetered, one hand dangling above the void, the other gripping the edge. His overextended mind wavered with vertigo as he stared down that sheer cliff, down into darkness. The height was beautiful; he'd always loved climbing high rock formations with Tien.

By reflex, he shoved himself back onto the plateau, scrambling backward. A group of foot soldiers, protected by shields, had taken up positions pushing the bridge. The army's archers exchanged arrows with the Parshendi as the soldiers pushed the bridge into place and heavy cavalry thundered across, smashing into the Parshendi. Four bridges had fallen, but sixteen had been placed in a row, allowing for an effective charge.

Kaladin tried to move, tried to crawl away from the bridge. But he just collapsed where he was, his body refusing to obey. He couldn't even roll over onto his stomach.

I should go . . . he thought in exhaustion. *See if that leathery-faced man is still alive. . . . Bind his wounds. . . . Save. . . .*

But he couldn't. He couldn't move. Couldn't think. To his shame, he just let himself close his eyes and gave himself over to unconsciousness.

∴

"Kaladin."

He didn't want to open his eyes. To wake meant returning to that awful world of pain. A world where defenseless, exhausted men were made to charge lines of archers.

That world was the nightmare.

"Kaladin!" The feminine voice was soft, like a whisper, yet still urgent. "They're going to leave you. Get up! You'll die!"

I can't . . . I can't go back. . . .

Let me go.

Something snapped against his face, a slight *slap* of energy with a sting to it. He cringed. It was nothing compared with his other pains, but somehow it was far more demanding. He raised a hand, swatting. The motion was enough to drive away the last vestiges of stupor.

He tried to open his eyes. One refused, blood from a cut on his cheek having run down and crusted around the eyelid. The sun had moved. Hours had passed. He groaned—sitting up, rubbing the dried blood from his eye. The ground near him was littered with bodies. The air smelled of blood and worse.

A pair of sorry bridgemen were shaking each man in turn, checking for life, then pulling the vests and sandals off their bodies, shooing away the cremlings feeding on the bodies. The men would never have checked on Kaladin. He didn't have anything for them to take. They'd have left him with the corpses, stranded on the plateau.

Kaladin's windspren flitted through the air above him, moving anxiously. He rubbed his jaw where she'd struck him. Large spren like her could move small objects and give little pinches of energy. That made them all the more annoying.

This time, it had probably saved Kaladin's life. He groaned

at all the places where he hurt. "Do you have a name, spirit?" he asked, forcing himself to his battered feet.

On the plateau the army had crossed to, soldiers were picking through the corpses of the dead Parshendi, looking for something. Harvesting equipment, maybe? It appeared that Sadeas's force had won. At least, there didn't seem to be any Parshendi still alive. They'd either been killed or had fled.

The plateau they'd fought on seemed exactly like the others they'd crossed. The only thing that was different here was that there was a large lump of . . . something in the center of the plateau. It looked like an enormous rockbud, perhaps some kind of chrysalis or shell, a good twenty feet tall. One side had been hacked open, exposing slimy innards. He hadn't noticed it on the initial charge; the archers had demanded all of his attention.

"A name," the windspren said, her voice distant. "Yes. I *do* have a name." She seemed surprised as she looked at Kaladin. "Why do I have a name?"

"How should I know?" Kaladin said, forcing himself to move. His feet blazed with pain. He could barely limp.

The nearby bridgemen looked to him with surprise, but he ignored them, limping across the plateau until he found the corpse of a bridgeman who still had his vest and shoes. It was the leathery-faced man who had been so kind to him, dead with an arrow through the neck. Kaladin ignored those shocked eyes, staring blankly into the sky, and harvested the man's clothing—leather vest, leather sandals, lacing shirt stained red with blood. Kaladin felt disgusted with himself, but he wasn't going to count on Gaz giving him clothing.

Kaladin sat down and used the cleaner parts of the shirt to change his improvised bandages, then put on the vest and sandals, trying to keep from moving too much. A breeze now blew, carrying away the scents of blood and the sounds of soldiers calling to one another. The cavalry was already forming up, as if eager to return.

"A name," the windspren said, walking through the air to

stand beside his face. She was in the shape of a young woman, complete with flowing skirt and delicate feet. "Sylphrena."

"Sylphrena," Kaladin repeated, tying on the sandals.

"Syl," the spirit said. She cocked her head. "That's amusing. It appears that I have a nickname."

"Congratulations." Kaladin stood up again, wobbling.

To the side, Gaz stood with hands on hips, shield tied to his back. "You," he said, pointing at Kaladin. He then gestured to the bridge.

"You've got to be kidding," Kaladin said, looking as the remnants of the bridge crew—fewer than half of their previous number remained—gathered around the bridge.

"Either carry or stay behind," Gaz said. He seemed angry about something.

I was supposed to die, Kaladin realized. *That's why he didn't care if I had a vest or sandals. I was at the front.* Kaladin was the only one on the first row who had lived.

Kaladin nearly sat down and let them leave him. But dying of thirst on a lonely plateau was not the way he'd choose to go. He stumbled over to the bridge.

"Don't worry," said one of the other bridgemen. "They'll let us go slow this time, take lots of breaks. And we'll have a few soldiers to help—takes at least twenty-five men to lift a bridge."

Kaladin sighed, getting into place as some unfortunate soldiers joined them. Together, they heaved the bridge into the air. It was terribly heavy, but they managed it, somehow.

Kaladin walked, feeling numb. He'd thought that there was nothing more life could do to him, nothing worse than the slave's brand with a *shash*, nothing worse than losing all he had to the war, nothing more terrible than failing those he'd sworn to protect.

It appeared that he'd been wrong. There *had* been something more they could do to him. One final torment the world had reserved just for Kaladin.

And it was called Bridge Four.

*"They are aflame. They burn. They bring the darkness
when they come, and so all you can see is that their skin is
aflame. Burn, burn, burn. . . ."*

—Collected on Palahishev, 1172, 21 seconds pre-death. Subject
was a baker's apprentice.

Shallan hurried down the hallway with its burnt-orange
colorings, the ceiling and upper walls now stained by the
passing of black smoke from Jasnah's Soulcasting. Hopefully, the paintings on the walls hadn't been ruined.

Ahead, a small group of parshmen arrived, bearing rags,
buckets, and stepladders to use in wiping off the soot. They
bowed to her as she passed, uttering no words. Parshmen
could speak, but they rarely did so. Many seemed mute. As a
child, she'd found the patterns of their marbled skin beautiful. That had been before her father forbade her to spend any
time with the parshmen.

She turned her mind to her task. How was she going to
convince Jasnah Kholin, one of the most powerful women in
the world, to change her mind about taking Shallan as a ward?
The woman was obviously stubborn; she had spent years resisting the devotaries' attempts at reconciliation.

She reentered the broad main cavern, with its lofty stone

ceiling and bustling, well-dressed occupants. She felt daunted, but that brief glimpse of the Soulcaster seduced her. Her family, House Davar, had prospered in recent years, coming out of obscurity. This had primarily been because of her father's skill in politics—he had been hated by many, but his ruthlessness had carried him far. So had the wealth lent by the discovery of several important new marble deposits on Davar lands.

Shallan had never known enough to be suspicious of that wealth's origins. Every time the family had exhausted one of its quarries, her father had gone out with his surveyor and discovered a new one. Only after interrogating the surveyor had Shallan and her brothers discovered the truth: Her father, using his forbidden Soulcaster, had been *creating* new deposits at a careful rate. Not enough to be suspicious. Just enough to give him the money he needed to further his political goals.

Nobody knew where he'd gotten the fabrial, which she now carried in her safepouch. It was unusable, damaged on the same disastrous evening that her father had died. *Don't think about that,* she told herself forcefully.

They'd had a jeweler repair the broken Soulcaster, but it no longer worked. Their house steward—one of her father's close confidants, an advisor named Luesh—had been trained to use the device, and he could no longer make it function.

Her father's debts and promises were outrageous. Their choices were limited. Her family had some time—perhaps as long as a year—before the missed payments became egregious, and before her father's absence became obvious. For once, her family's isolated, backcountry estates were an advantage, providing a reason that communications were being delayed. Her brothers were scrambling, writing letters in her father's name, making a few appearances and spreading rumors that Brightlord Davar was planning something big.

All to give her time to make good on her bold plan. Find Jasnah Kholin. Become her ward. Learn where she kept her Soulcaster. Then replace it with the nonfunctional one.

With the fabrial, they'd be able to make new quarries and restore their wealth. They'd be able to make food to feed their house soldiers. With enough wealth in hand to pay off debts and make bribes, they could announce their father's death and not suffer destruction.

Shallan hesitated in the main hallway, considering her next move. What she planned to do was very risky. She'd have to escape without implicating herself in the theft. Though she'd devoted much thought to that, she still didn't know how she'd manage it. But Jasnah was known to have many enemies. There had to be a way to pin the fabrial's "breaking" on them instead.

That step would come later. For now, Shallan *had* to convince Jasnah to accept her as a ward. All other results were unacceptable.

Nervously, Shallan held her arms in the sign of need, covered safehand bent across her chest and touching the elbow of her freehand, which was raised with fingers outspread. A woman approached, wearing the well-starched white laced shirt and black skirt that were the universal sign of a masterservant.

The stout woman curtsied. "Brightness?"

"The Palanaeum," Shallan said.

The woman bowed and led Shallan farther into the depths of the long hallway. Most of the women here—servants included—wore their hair bound, and Shallan felt conspicuous with hers loose. The deep red color made her stand out even more.

Soon, the grand hallway began to slope down steeply. But when the half-hour arrived, she could still hear distant bells ring behind her. Perhaps that was why the people here liked them so much; even in the depths of the Conclave, one could hear the outside world.

The servant led Shallan to a pair of grand steel doors. The servant bowed and Shallan dismissed her with a nod.

Shallan couldn't help but admire the beauty of the doors; their exterior was carved in an intricate geometric pattern with circles and lines and glyphs. It was some kind of chart, half on each door. There was no time to study the details, unfortunately, and she passed them by.

Beyond the doors was a breathtakingly large room. The sides were of smooth rock and they stretched high; the dim illumination made it impossible to tell just how high, but she saw flickers of distant light. Set into the walls were dozens of small balconies, much like the private box seats of a theater. Soft light shone from many of these. The only sounds were turning pages and faint whispers. Shallan raised her safehand to her breast, feeling dwarfed by the magnificent chamber.

"Brightness?" a young male master-servant said, approaching. "What do you need?"

"A new sense of perspective, apparently," Shallan said absently. "How . . ."

"This room is called the Veil," the servant explained softly. "That which comes before the Palanaeum itself. Both were here when the city was founded. Some think these chambers might have been cut by the Dawnsingers themselves."

"Where are the books?"

"The Palanaeum proper is this way." The servant gestured, leading her to a set of doors on the other side of the room. Through them, she entered a smaller chamber that was partitioned with walls of thick crystal. Shallan approached the nearest one, feeling it. The crystal's surface was rough like hewn rock.

"Soulcast?" she asked.

The servant nodded. Behind him, another servant passed leading an elderly ardent. Like most ardents, the aged man had a shaved head and a long beard. His simple grey robes were tied with a brown sash. The servant led him around a corner, and Shallan could vaguely make out their shapes on the other side, shadows swimming through the crystal.

She took a step forward, but her servant cleared his throat. "I will need your chit of admittance, Brightness."

"How much does one cost?" Shallan asked hesitantly.

"A thousand sapphire broams."

"So much?"

"The king's many hospitals require much upkeep," the man said apologetically. "The only things Kharbranth has to sell are fish, bells, and information. The first two are hardly unique to us. But the third . . . well, the Palanaeum has the finest collection of tomes and scrolls on Roshar. More, even, than the Holy Enclave in Valath. At last count, there were over seven hundred thousand separate texts in our archive."

Her father had owned exactly eighty-seven books. Shallan had read them all several times over. How much could be contained in *seven hundred thousand* books? The weight of that much information dazzled her. She found herself hungering to look through those hidden shelves. She could spend months just reading their titles.

But no. Perhaps once she'd made certain her brothers were safe—once her house's finances were restored—she could return. Perhaps.

She felt like she was starving, yet leaving a warm fruit pie uneaten. "Where might I wait?" she asked. "If someone I know is inside."

"You may use one of the reading alcoves," the servant said, relaxing. Perhaps he'd feared that she would make a scene. "No chit is required to sit in one. There are parshman porters who will raise you to the higher levels, if that is what you wish."

"Thank you," Shallan said, turning her back on the Palanaeum. She felt like a child again, locked in her room, not allowed to run through the gardens because of her father's paranoid fears. "Does Brightness Jasnah have an alcove yet?"

"I can ask," the servant said, leading the way back into the Veil, with its distant, unseen ceiling. He hurried off to speak with some others, leaving Shallan standing beside the doorway to the Palanaeum.

She could run in. Sneak through—

No. Her brothers teased her for being too timid, but it was not timidity that held her back. There would undoubtedly be guards; bursting in would not only be futile, it would ruin any chance she had of changing Jasnah's mind.

Change Jasnah's mind, prove herself. Considering it made her sick. She *hated* confrontation. During her youth, she'd felt like a piece of delicate crystalware, locked in a cabinet to be displayed but never touched. The only daughter, the last memory of Brightlord Davar's beloved wife. It still felt odd to her that *she* been the one to take charge after . . . After the incident . . . After . . .

Memories attacked her. Nan Balat bruised, his coat torn. A long, silvery sword in her hand, sharp enough to cut stones as if they were water.

No, Shallan thought, her back to the stone wall, clutching her satchel. *No. Don't think of the past.*

She sought solace in drawing, raising fingers to her satchel and reaching for her paper and pencils. The servant came back before she had a chance to get them out, however. "Brightness Jasnah Kholin has indeed asked that a reading alcove be set aside for her," he said. "You may wait there for her, if you wish it."

"I do," Shallan said. "Thank you."

The servant led her to a shadowed enclosure, inside of which four parshmen stood upon a sturdy wooden platform. The servant and Shallan stepped onto the platform, and the parshmen pulled ropes that were strung into a pulley above, raising the platform up the stone shaft. The only lights were broam spheres set at each corner of the lift's ceiling. Amethysts, which had a soft violet light.

She needed a plan. Jasnah Kholin did not seem the type to change her mind easily. Shallan would have to surprise her, impress her.

They reached a level about forty feet or so off the ground, and the servant waved for the porters to stop. Shallan followed the master-servant down a dark hallway to one of the small balconies that extended out over the Veil. It was round, like a turret, and had a waist-high stone rim with a wooden railing above that. Other occupied alcoves glowed with different colors from the spheres being used to light them; the darkness of the huge space made them seem to hover in the air.

This alcove had a long, curving stone desk joined directly into the rim of the balcony. There was a single chair and a gobletlike crystal bowl. Shallan nodded in thanks to the servant, who withdrew, then she pulled out a handful of spheres and dropped them into the bowl, lighting the alcove.

She sighed, sitting down in the chair and laying her satchel on the desk. She undid the laces on her satchel, busying herself as she tried to think of something—anything—that would persuade Jasnah.

First, she decided, *I need to clear my mind.*

From her satchel she removed a sheaf of thick drawing paper, a set of charcoal pencils of different widths, some brushes and steel pens, ink, and watercolors. Finally, she took out her smaller notebook, bound in codex form, which contained the nature sketches she'd done during her weeks aboard the *Wind's Pleasure.*

These were simple things, really, but worth more to her than a chest full of spheres. She took a sheet off the stack, then selected a fine-pointed charcoal pencil, rolling it between her fingers. She closed her eyes and fixed an image in her mind: Kharbranth as she'd memorized it in that moment soon after landing on the docks. Waves surging against the wooden posts, a salty scent to the air, men climbing rigging calling one another with excitement. And the city itself, rising up the hillside, homes stacked atop homes, not a speck of land wasted. Bells, distant, tinkling softly in the air.

She opened her eyes and began to draw. Her fingers moved on their own, sketching broad lines first. The cracklike valley the city was situated in. The port. Here, squares to be homes, there a slash to mark a switchback of the grand roadway that led up to the Conclave. Slowly, bit by bit, she added detail. Shadows as windows. Lines to fill out the roadways. Hints of people and carts to show the chaos of the thoroughfares.

She had read of how sculptors worked. Many would take a blank stone block and work it into a vague shape first. Then, they'd work it over again, carving more detail with each pass. It was the same for her in drawing. Broad lines first, then some details, then more, then down to the finest of lines. She had no formal training in pencils; she simply did what felt right.

The city took shape beneath her fingers. She coaxed it free, line by line, scratch by scratch. What would she do without this? Tension bled from her body, as if released from her fingertips into the pencil.

She lost track of time as she worked. Sometimes she felt like she was entering a trance, everything else fading. Her fingers almost seemed to draw of their own accord. It was so much easier to think while drawing.

Before too long, she had copied her Memory onto the page. She held up the sheet, satisfied, relaxed, her mind clear. The memorized image of Kharbranth was gone from her head; she'd released it into her sketch. There was a sense of relaxation to that too. As if her mind was put under tension holding Memories until they could be used.

She did Yalb next, standing shirtless in his vest and gesturing to the short porter who had pulled her up to the Conclave. She smiled as she worked, remembering Yalb's affable voice. He'd likely returned to the *Wind's Pleasure* by now. Had it been two hours? Probably.

She was always more excited by drawing animals and people than she was by drawing things. There was something energizing about putting a living creature onto the page. A city was lines and boxes, but a person was circles and curves. Could she get that smirk on Yalb's face right? Could she show his lazy contentedness, the way he would flirt with a woman far above his station? And the porter, with his thin fingers and sandaled feet, his long coat and baggy pants. His strange language, his keen eyes, his plan to increase his tip by offering not just a ride, but a tour.

When she drew, she didn't feel as if she worked with only charcoal and paper. In drawing a portrait, her medium was the soul itself. There were plants from which one could remove a tiny cutting—a leaf, or a bit of stem—then plant it and grow a duplicate. When she collected a Memory of a person, she was snipping free a bud of their soul, and she cultivated and grew it on the page. Charcoal for sinew, paper pulp for bone, ink for blood, the paper's texture for skin. She fell into a rhythm, a cadence, the scratching of her pencil like the sound of breathing from those she depicted.

Creationspren began to gather around her pad, looking at her work. Like other spren, they were said to always be around, but usually invisible. Sometimes you attracted them. Sometimes you didn't. With drawing, skill seemed to make a difference.

Creationspren were of medium size, as tall as one of her fingers, and they glowed with a faint silvery light. They transformed perpetually, taking new shapes. Usually the shapes were things they had seen recently. An urn, a person, a table, a wheel, a nail. Always of the same silvery color, always the same diminutive height. They imitated shapes exactly, but moved them in strange ways. A table would roll like a wheel, an urn would shatter and repair itself.

Her drawing gathered about a half-dozen of them, pulling them by her act of creation just as a bright fire would draw flamespren. She'd learned to ignore them. They weren't substantial—if she moved her arm through one, its figure would smear like scattered sand, then re-form. She never felt a thing when touching one.

Eventually, she held up the page, satisfied. It depicted Yalb and the porter in detail, with hints of the busy city behind. She'd gotten their eyes right. That was the most important. Each of the Ten Essences had an analogous part of the human body—blood for liquid, hair for wood, and so forth. The eyes were associated with crystal and glass. The windows into a person's mind and spirit.

She set the page aside. Some men collected trophies. Others collected weapons or shields. Many collected spheres.

Shallan collected people. People, and interesting creatures. Perhaps it was because she'd spent so much of her youth in a virtual prison. She'd developed the habit of memorizing faces, then drawing them later, after her father had discovered her sketching the gardeners. His daughter? Drawing pictures of darkeyes? He'd been furious with her—one of the infrequent times he'd directed his infamous temper at his daughter.

After that, she'd done drawings of people only when in private, instead using her open drawing times to sketch the insects, crustaceans, and plants of the manor gardens. Her father hadn't minded this—zoology and botany were proper feminine pursuits—and had encouraged her to choose natural history as her Calling.

She took out a third blank sheet. It seemed to beg her to fill it. A blank page was nothing but potential, pointless until it was used. Like a fully infused sphere cloistered inside a pouch, prevented from making its light useful.

Fill me.

The creationspren gathered around the page. They were still, as if curious, anticipatory. Shallan closed her eyes and imagined Jasnah Kholin, standing before the blocked door, the Soulcaster glowing on her hand. The hallway hushed, save for a child's sniffles. Attendants holding their breath. An anxious king. A still reverence.

Shallan opened her eyes and began to draw with vigor, intentionally losing herself. The less she was in the *now* and the more she was in the *then*, the better the sketch would be. The other two pictures had been warm-ups; this was the day's masterpiece. With the paper bound onto the board—safehand holding that—her freehand flew across the page, occasionally switching to other pencils. Soft charcoal for deep, thick blackness, like Jasnah's beautiful hair. Hard charcoal for light greys, like the powerful waves of light coming from the Soulcaster's gems.

For a few extended moments, Shallan was back in that hallway again, watching something that should not be: a heretic wielding one of the most sacred powers in all the world. The power of change itself, the power by which the Almighty had created Roshar. He had another name, allowed to pass only the lips of ardents. *Elithanathile.* He Who Transforms.

Shallan could smell the musty hallway. She could hear the child whimpering. She could feel her own heart beating in anticipation. The boulder would soon change. Sucking away the Stormlight in Jasnah's gemstone, it would give up its essence, becoming something new. Shallan's breath caught in her throat.

And then the memory faded, returning her to the quiet, dim alcove. The page now held a perfect rendition of the scene, worked in blacks and greys. The princess's proud figure regarded the fallen stone, demanding that it give way before her will. It *was* her. Shallan knew, with the intuitive certainty of an artist, that this was one of the finest pieces she had ever done. In a very small way, she had captured Jasnah Kholin, something the devotaries had never managed. That gave her a euphoric thrill. Even if this woman rejected Shallan again, one fact would not change. Jasnah Kholin had joined Shallan's collection.

Shallan wiped her fingers on her cleaning cloth, then lifted the paper. She noted absently that she'd attracted some two dozen creationspren now. She would have to lacquer the page with plytree sap to set the charcoal and protect it from smudges. She had some in her satchel. First she wanted to study the page and the figure it contained. Who *was* Jasnah Kholin? Not one to be cowed, certainly. She was a woman to the bone, master of the feminine arts, but not by any means delicate.

Such a woman would appreciate Shallan's determination. She *would* listen to another request for wardship, assuming it was presented properly.

Jasnah was also a rationalist, a woman with the audacity to deny the existence of the Almighty himself based on her own reasoning. Jasnah would appreciate strength, but only if it was shaped by logic.

Shallan nodded to herself, taking out a fourth sheet of paper and a fine-tipped brushpen, then shaking and opening her jar of ink. Jasnah had demanded proof of Shallan's logical and writing skills. Well, what better way to do that than to supplicate the woman with words?

Brightness Jasnah Kholin, Shallan wrote, painting the letters as neatly and beautifully as she could. She could have used a reed instead, but a brushpen was for works of art. She intended this page to be just that. *You have rejected my petition. I accept that. Yet, as anyone trained in formal inquiry knows, no supposition should be treated as axiomatic.* The actual argument usually read "no supposition—save for the existence of the Almighty himself—should be held as axiomatic." But this wording would appeal to Jasnah.

A scientist must be willing to change her theories if experiment disproves them. I hold to the hope that you treat decisions in a like manner: as preliminary results pending further information.

From our brief interaction, I can see that you appreciate tenacity. You complimented me on continuing to seek you out. Therefore, I presume that you will not find this letter a breach of good taste. Take it as proof of my ardor to be your ward, and not as disdain for your expressed decision.

Shallan raised the end of her brushpen to her lips as she considered her next step. The creationspren slowly faded away, vanishing. There were said to be logicspren—in the form of tiny stormclouds—who were attracted to great arguments, but Shallan had never seen them.

You expect proof of my worthiness, Shallan continued. *I wish I could demonstrate that my schooling is more complete than our interview revealed. Unfortunately, I haven't the grounds for such an argument. I have weaknesses in my understanding. That is plain and not subject to reasonable dispute.*

But the lives of men and women are more than logical puzzles; the context of their experiences is invaluable in making good decisions. My study in logic does not rise to your standards, but even I know that the rationalists have a rule: One cannot apply logic as an absolute where human beings are concerned. We are not beings of thought only.

Therefore, the soul of my argument here is to give perspective on my ignorance. Not by way of excuse, but of explanation. You expressed displeasure that one such as I should be trained so inadequately. What of my stepmother? What of my tutors? Why was my education handled so poorly?

The facts are embarrassing. I have had few tutors and virtually no education. My stepmother tried, but she had no education herself. It is a carefully guarded secret, but many of the rural Veden houses ignore the proper training of their women.

I had three different tutors when I was very young, but each left after a few months, citing my father's temper or rudeness as her reason. I was left to my own devices in education. I have learned what I could through reading, filling in the gaps by taking advantage of my own curious nature. But I will not be capable of matching knowledge with someone who has been given the benefit of a formal—and expensive—education.

Why is this an argument that you should accept me? Because everything I have learned has come by way of great personal struggle. What others were handed, I had to hunt. I believe that because of this, my education—limited though it is—has extra worth and merit. I respect your decisions, but I do ask you to reconsider. Which would you rather have? A ward who is able to repeat the correct answers because an overpriced tutor drilled them into her, or a ward who had to struggle and fight for everything she has learned?

I assure you that one of those two will prize your teachings far more than the other.

She raised her brush. Her arguments seemed imperfect now that she considered them. She exposed her ignorance, then expected Jasnah to welcome her? Still, it seemed the right thing to do, for all the fact that this letter was a lie. A lie built of truths. She hadn't truly come to partake of Jasnah's knowledge. She had come as a thief.

That made her conscience itch, and she nearly reached out and crumpled the page. Steps in the hallway outside made her freeze. She leaped to her feet, spinning, safehand held to her breast. She fumbled for words to explain her presence to Jasnah Kholin.

Light and shadows flickered in the hallway, then a figure hesitantly looked into the alcove, a single white sphere cupped in one hand for light. It was *not* Jasnah. It was a man in his early twenties wearing simple grey robes. An ardent. Shallan relaxed.

The young man noticed her. His face was narrow, his blue eyes keen. His beard was trimmed short and square, his head shaved. When he spoke, his voice had a cultured tone. "Ah, excuse me, Brightness. I thought this was the alcove of Jasnah Kholin."

"It is," Shallan said.

"Oh. You're waiting for her too?"

"Yes."

"Would you mind terribly if I waited with you?" He had a faint Herdazian accent.

"Of course not, Ardent." She nodded her head in respect, then gathered up her things in haste, preparing the seat for him.

"I can't take your seat, Brightness! I'll fetch another for myself."

She raised a hand in protest, but he had already retreated. He returned a few moments later, carrying a chair from another alcove. He was tall and lean, and—she decided with slight discomfort—rather handsome. Her father had owned only three ardents, all elderly men. They had traveled his lands and visited the villages, ministering to the people, helping them reach Points in their Glories and Callings. She had their faces in her collection of portraits.

The ardent set down his chair. He hesitated before sitting, glancing at the table. "My, my," he said in surprise.

For a moment, Shallan thought he was reading her letter, and she felt an irrational surge of panic. The ardent, however, was regarding the three drawings that lay at the head of the table, awaiting lacquer.

"You did these, Brightness?" he said.

"Yes, Ardent," Shallan said, lowering her eyes.

"No need to be so formal!" the ardent said, leaning down and adjusting his spectacles as he studied her work. "Please, I am Brother Kabsal, or just Kabsal. Really, it's fine. And you are?"

"Shallan Davar."

"By Vedeledev's golden keys, Brightness!" Brother Kabsal said, seating himself. "Did Jasnah Kholin teach you this skill with the pencil?"

"No, Ardent," she said, still standing.

"Still so formal," he said, smiling at her. "Tell me, am I so intimidating as that?"

"I have been brought up to show respect to ardents."

"Well, I myself find that respect is like manure. Use it where needed, and growth will flourish. Spread it on too thick, and things just start to smell." His eyes twinkled.

Had an *ardent*—a servant of the Almighty—just spoken of *manure*? "An ardent is a representative of the Almighty himself," she said. "To show you lack of respect would be to show it to the Almighty."

"I see. And this is how you'd respond if the Almighty himself appeared to you here? All of this formality and bowing?"

She hesitated. "Well, no."

"Ah, and how *would* you react?"

"I suspect with screams of pain," she said, letting her thought slip out too easily. "As it is written that the Almighty's glory is such that any who look upon him would immediately be burned to ash."

The ardent laughed at that. "Wisely spoken indeed. Please, do sit, though."

She did so, hesitant.

"You still appear conflicted," he said, holding up her portrait of Jasnah. "What must I do to put you at ease? Shall I step up onto this desk here and do a jig?"

She blinked in surprise.

"No objection?" Brother Kabsal said. "Well, then . . ." He set down the portrait and began to climb up on his chair.

"No, please!" Shallan said, holding out her freehand.

"Are you certain?" he glanced at the desk appraisingly.

"Yes," Shallan said, imagining the ardent teetering and making a misstep, then falling off the balcony and plunging dozens of feet to the ground below. "Please, I promise not to respect you any longer!"

He chuckled, hopping down and seating himself. He leaned closer to her, as if conspiratorially. "The table jig threat almost always works. I've only ever had to go through with it once, due to a lost bet against Brother Lhanin. The master ardent of our monastery nearly keeled over in shock."

Shallan found herself smiling. "You're an ardent; you're forbidden to have possessions. What did you bet?"

"Two deep breaths of a winter rose's fragrance," said Brother Kabsal, "and the sunlight's warmth on your skin." He smiled. "We can be rather creative at times. Years spent marinating in a monastery can do that to a man. Now, you were about to explain to me where you learned such skill with a pencil."

"Practice," Shallan said. "I should suspect that is how everyone learns, eventually."

"Wise words again. I am beginning to wonder which of us is the ardent. But surely you had a master to teach you."

"Dandos the Oilsworn."

"Ah, a true master of pencils if there ever was one. Now, not that I doubt your word, Brightness, but I'm rather intrigued how Dandos Heraldin could have trained you in arts, as—last I checked—he's suffering a rather terminal and perpetual ailment. Namely, that of being *dead*. For three hundred years."

Shallan blushed. "My father had a book of his instruction."

"You learned this," Kabsal said, lifting up her drawing of Jasnah, "from a *book*."

"Er . . . yes?"

He looked back at the picture. "I need to read more."

Shallan found herself laughing at the ardent's expression, and she took a Memory of him sitting there, admiration and perplexity blending on his face as he studied the picture, rubbing his bearded chin with one finger.

He smiled pleasantly, setting down the picture. "You have lacquer?"

"I do," she said, getting it out of her satchel. It was contained in a bulb sprayer of the type often used for perfume.

He accepted the small jar and twisted the clasp on the

front, then gave the bottle a shake and tested the lacquer on the back of his hand. He nodded in satisfaction and reached for the drawing. "A piece such as this should not be allowed to risk smudging."

"I can lacquer it," Shallan said. "No need to trouble yourself."

"It is no trouble; it's an honor. Besides, I am an ardent. We don't know what to do with ourselves when we aren't busying about, doing things others could do for themselves. It is best just to humor me." He began to apply the lacquer, dusting the page with careful puffs.

She had trouble keeping herself from reaching to snatch the sketch away. Fortunately, his hands were careful, and the lacquer went on evenly. He'd obviously done this before.

"You are from Jah Keved, I presume?" he asked.

"From the hair?" she asked, raising a hand to her red locks. "Or from the accent?"

"From the way you treat ardents. The Veden Church is by far the most traditional. I have visited your lovely country on two occasions; while your food sits well in my stomach, the amount of bowing and scraping you show ardents made me uncomfortable."

"Perhaps you should have danced on a few tables."

"I considered it," he said, "but my brother and sister ardents from your country would likely have dropped dead of embarrassment. I would hate to have that on my conscience. The Almighty is not kind toward those who kill his priests."

"I should think that killing in general would be frowned upon," she responded, still watching him apply the lacquer. It felt odd to let someone else work on her art.

"What does Brightness Jasnah think of your skill?" he asked as he worked.

"I don't think she cares," Shallan said, grimacing and remembering her conversation with the woman. "She doesn't seem terribly appreciative of the visual arts."

"So I have heard. It's one of her few faults, unfortunately."

"Another being that little matter of her heresy?"

"Indeed," Kabsal said, smiling. "I must admit, I stepped

in here expecting indifference, not deference. How did you come to be part of her entourage?"

Shallan started, realizing for the first time that Brother Kabsal must have assumed her to be one of the Brightlady Kholin's attendants. Perhaps a ward.

"Bother," she said to herself.

"Hum?"

"It appears I've inadvertently misled you, Brother Kabsal. I'm not associated with Brightness Jasnah. Not yet, anyway. I've been trying to get her to take me on as a ward."

"Ah," he said, finishing his lacquering.

"I'm sorry."

"For what? You did nothing wrong." He blew on the picture, then turned it for her to see. It was perfectly lacquered, without any smears. "If you would do me a favor, child?" he said, setting the page aside.

"Anything."

He raised an eyebrow at that.

"Anything reasonable," she corrected.

"By whose reason?"

"Mine, I guess."

"Pity," he said, standing. "Then I will limit myself. If you would kindly let Brightness Jasnah know that I called upon her?"

"She knows you?" What business had a Herdazian ardent with Jasnah, a confirmed atheist?

"Oh, I wouldn't say that," he replied. "I'd hope she's heard my name, though, since I've requested an audience with her several times."

Shallan nodded, rising. "You want to try to convert her, I presume?"

"She presents a unique challenge. I don't think I could live with myself if I didn't at least *try* to persuade her."

"And we wouldn't want you to be unable to live with yourself," Shallan noted, "as the alternative harks back to your nasty habit of almost killing ardents."

"Exactly. Anyway, I think a personal message from you might help where written requests have been ignored."

"I . . . doubt that."

"Well, if she refuses, it only means that I'll be back." He smiled. "That would mean—hopefully—that we shall meet each other again. So I look forward to it."

"I as well. And I'm sorry again about the misunderstanding."

"Brightness! Please. Don't take responsibility for *my* assumptions."

She smiled. "I should hesitate to take responsibility for you in *any* manner or regard, Brother Kabsal. But I still feel bad."

"It will pass," he noted, blue eyes twinkling. "But I'll do my best to make you feel well again. Is there anything you're fond of? Other than respecting ardents and drawing amazing pictures, that is?"

"Jam."

He cocked his head.

"I like it," she said, shrugging. "You asked what I was fond of. Jam."

"So it shall be." He withdrew into the dark corridor, fishing in his robe pocket for his sphere to give him light. In moments, he was gone.

Why didn't he wait for Jasnah to return himself? Shallan shook her head, then lacquered her other two pictures. She had just finished letting them dry—packing them in her satchel—when she heard footsteps in the hallway again and recognized Jasnah's voice speaking.

Shallan hurriedly gathered her things, leaving the letter on the desk, then stepped up to the side of the alcove to wait. Jasnah Kholin entered a moment later, accompanied by a small group of servants.

She did not look pleased.

*"Victory! We stand atop the mount! We scatter them be-
fore us! Their homes become our dens, their lands are now
our farms! And they shall burn, as we once did, in a place
that is hollow and forlorn."*

—Collected on Ishashan, 1172, 18 seconds pre-death. Subject
was a lighteyed spinster of the eighth dahn.

Shallan's fears were confirmed as Jasnah looked straight at
her, then lowered her safehand to her side in a mark of
frustration. "So you *are* here."

Shallan cringed. "The servants told you, then?"

"You didn't think that they would leave someone in my
alcove and not warn me?" Behind Jasnah, a small group of
parshmen hesitated in the hallway, each carrying an armload
of books.

"Brightness Kholin," Shallan said. "I just—"

"I have wasted enough time on you already," Jasnah said,
eyes furious. "You will withdraw, Miss Davar. And I will not
see you again during my time here. Am I *understood*?"

Shallan's hopes crumbled. She shrank back. There was a
gravity to Jasnah Kholin. One did not disobey her. One need
only look into those eyes to understand.

"I'm sorry to have bothered you," Shallan whispered,

clutching her satchel and leaving with as much dignity as she could manage. She barely kept the tears of embarrassment and disappointment from her eyes as she hastened down the hallway, feeling like a complete fool.

She reached the porter's shaft, though they had already returned below after bringing up Jasnah. Shallan didn't pull the bell to summon them. Instead she placed her back to the wall and sank down to the floor, knees up against her chest, satchel in her lap. She wrapped her arms around her legs, free-hand clasping her safehand through the fabric of her cuff, breathing quietly.

Angry people unsettled her. She couldn't help but think of her father in one of his tirades, couldn't help but hear screams, bellows, and whimpers. Was she weak because confrontation unsettled her so? She felt that she was.

Foolish, idiot girl, she thought, a few painspren crawling out of the wall near her head. *What made you think you could do this? You've only set foot off your family grounds a half-dozen times during your life. Idiot, idiot,* idiot*!*

She had persuaded her brothers to trust her, to put hope in her ridiculous plan. And now what had she done? Wasted six months during which their enemies circled closer.

"Brightness Davar?" asked a hesitant voice.

Shallan looked up, realizing she'd been so wrapped in her misery that she hadn't seen the servant approach. He was a younger man, wearing an all black uniform, no emblem on the breast. Not a master-servant, but perhaps one in training.

"Brightness Kholin would like to speak with you." The young man gestured back down the hallway.

To berate me further? Shallan thought with a grimace. But a highlady like Jasnah got what she wanted. Shallan forced herself to stop shaking, then stood. At least she'd been able to keep the tears away; she hadn't ruined her makeup. She followed the servant back to the lit alcove, satchel clutched before her like a shield on the battlefield.

Jasnah Kholin sat in the chair Shallan had been using, stacks of books on the table. Jasnah was rubbing her forehead with her freehand. The Soulcaster rested against the back of her skin, the smokestone dark and cracked. Though Jasnah looked fatigued, she sat with perfect posture, her fine silk dress covering her feet, her safehand held across her lap.

Jasnah focused on Shallan, lowering her freehand. "I should not have treated you with such anger, Miss Davar," she said in a tired voice. "You were simply showing persistence, a trait I normally encourage. Storms alight, I've oft been guilty of stubbornness myself. Sometimes we find it hardest to accept in others that which we cling to in ourselves. My only excuse can be that I have put myself under an unusual amount of strain lately."

Shallan nodded in gratitude, though she felt terribly awkward.

Jasnah turned to look out of the balcony into the dark space of the Veil. "I know what people say of me. I should hope that I am not as harsh as some say, though a woman could have far worse than a reputation for sternness. It can serve one well."

Shallan had to forcibly keep herself from fidgeting. Should she withdraw?

Jasnah shook her head to herself, though Shallan could not guess what thoughts had caused the unconscious gesture. Finally, she turned back to Shallan and waved toward the large, gobletlike bowl on the desk. It held a dozen of Shallan's spheres.

Shallan raised her freehand to her lips in shock. She'd completely forgotten the money. She bowed to Jasnah in thanks, then hurriedly collected the spheres. "Brightness, lest I forget, I should mention that an ardent—Brother Kabsal—came to see you while I waited here. He wished me to pass on his desire to speak with you."

"Not surprising," Jasnah said. "You seem surprised about the spheres, Miss Davar. I assumed that you were waiting outside to recover them. Is that not why you were so close?"

"No, Brightness. I was just settling my nerves."

"Ah."

Shallan bit her lip. The princess appeared to have gotten

past her initial tirade. Perhaps . . . "Brightness," Shallan said, cringing at her brashness, "what did you think of my letter?"

"Letter?"

"I . . ." Shallan glanced at the desk. "Beneath that stack of books, Brightness."

A servant quickly moved aside the stack of books; the parshman must have set it on the paper without noticing. Jasnah picked up the letter, raising an eyebrow, and Shallan hurriedly undid her satchel and placed the spheres in her money pouch. Then she cursed herself for being so quick, as now she had nothing to do but stand and wait for Jasnah to finish reading.

"This is true?" Jasnah looking up from the paper. "You are self-trained?"

"Yes, Brightness."

"That is remarkable."

"Thank you, Brightness."

"And this letter was a clever maneuver. You correctly assumed that I would respond to a written plea. This shows me your skill with words, and the rhetoric of the letter gives proof that you can think logically and make a good argument."

"Thank you, Brightness," Shallan said, feeling another surge of hope, mixed with fatigue. Her emotions had been jerked back and forth like a rope being used for a tugging contest.

"You should have left the note for me, and withdrawn before I returned."

"But then the note would have been lost beneath that stack of books."

Jasnah raised an eyebrow at her, as if to show that she did not appreciate being corrected. "Very well. The context of a person's life *is* important. Your circumstances do not excuse your lack of education in history and philosophy, but leniency is in order. I will allow you to petition me again at a later date, a privilege I have never given any aspiring ward. Once you have a sufficient groundwork in those two subjects, come to me again. If you have improved suitably, I will accept you."

Shallan's emotions sank. Jasnah's offer *was* kindly, but it would take years of study to accomplish what she asked. House Davar would have fallen by then, her family's lands divided among its creditors, her brothers and herself stripped of title and perhaps enslaved.

"Thank you, Brightness," Shallan said, bowing her head.

Jasnah nodded, as if considering the matter closed. Shallan withdrew, walking quietly down the hallway and pulling the cord to ring for the porters.

Jasnah had all but promised to accept her at a later date. For most, that would be a great victory. Being trained by Jasnah Kholin—thought by some to be the finest living scholar—would have ensured a bright future. Shallan would have married extremely well, likely to the son of a highprince, and would have found new social circles open to her. Indeed, if Shallan had possessed the time to train under Jasnah, the sheer prestige of a Kholin affiliation might have been enough to save her house.

If only.

Eventually, Shallan made her way out of the Conclave; there were no gates on the front, just pillars set before the open maw. She was surprised to discover how dim it was outside. She trailed down the large steps, then took a smaller, more cultivated side path where she would be out of the way. Small shelves of ornamental shalebark had been grown along this walkway, and several species had let out fanlike tendrils to wave in the evening breeze. A few lazy lifespren—like specks of glowing green dust—flitted from one frond to the next.

Shallan leaned back against the stonelike plant, the tendrils pulling in and hiding. From this vantage, she could look down at Kharbranth, lights glowing beneath her like a cascade of fire streaming down the cliff face. The only other option for her and her brothers was to run. To abandon the family estates in Jah Keved and seek asylum. But where? Were there old allies her father *hadn't* alienated?

There was that matter of the strange collection of maps they'd found in his study. What did they mean? He'd rarely spoken of his plans to his children. Even her father's advisors knew very little. Helaran—her eldest brother—had known more, but he had vanished over a year ago, and her father had proclaimed him dead.

As always, thinking of her father made her feel ill, and the pain started to constrict her chest. She raised her freehand to her head, suddenly overwhelmed by the weight of House Davar's situation, her part in it, and the secret she now carried, hidden ten heartbeats away.

"Ho, young miss!" a voice called. She turned, shocked to see Yalb standing up on a rocky shelf a short distance from the Conclave entrance. A group of men in guard uniforms sat on the rock around him.

"Yalb?" she said, aghast. He should have returned to his ship hours ago. She hurried over to stand below the short stone outcropping. "Why are you still here?"

"Oh," he said, grinning, "I found myself a game of kabers here with these fine, upstanding gentlemen of the city guard. Figured officers of the law were right unlikely to cheat me, so we entered into a friendly-type game while I waited."

"But you didn't *need* to wait."

"Didn't need to win eighty chips off these fellows neither," Yalb said with a laugh. "But I did both!"

The men sitting around him looked far less enthusiastic. Their uniforms were orange tabards tied about the middle with white sashes.

"Well, I suppose I should be leading you back to the ship, then," Yalb said, reluctantly gathering up the spheres in the pile at his feet. They glowed with a variety of hues. Their light was small—each was only a chip—but it was impressive winnings.

Shallan stepped back as Yalb hopped off the rock shelf. His companions protested his departure, but he gestured to Shallan. "You'd have me leave a lighteyed woman of her stature to walk back to the ship on her own? I figured you for men of honor!"

That quieted their protests.

Yalb chuckled to himself, bowing to Shallan and leading

her away down the path. He had a twinkle to his eyes. "Stormfather, but it's fun to win against lawmen. I'll have free drinks at the docks once this gets around."

"You shouldn't gamble," Shallan said. "You shouldn't try to guess the future. I didn't give you that sphere so you could waste it on such practices."

Yalb laughed. "It ain't gambling if you know you're going to win, young miss."

"You *cheated*?" she hissed, horrified. She glanced back at the guardsmen, who had settled down to continue their game, lit by the spheres on the stones before them.

"Not so loud!" Yalb said in a low voice. However, he seemed very pleased with himself. "Cheating four guardsmen, now that's a trick. Hardly believe I managed it!"

"I'm disappointed in you. This is *not* proper behavior."

"It is if you're a sailor, young miss." He shrugged. "It's what they right expected from me. Watched me like handlers of poisonous skyeels, they did. The game wasn't about the cards—it was about them trying to figure how I was cheating and me trying to figure how to keep them from hauling me off. I think I might not have managed to walk away with my skin if you hadn't arrived!" That didn't seem to worry him much.

The roadway down to the docks was not nearly as busy as it had been earlier, but there were still a surprisingly large number of people about. The street was lit by oil lanterns—spheres would just have ended up in someone's pouch—but many of the people about carried sphere lanterns, casting a rainbow of colored light on the roadway. The people were almost like spren, each a different hue, moving this way or that.

"So, young miss," Yalb said, leading her carefully through the traffic. "You really want to go back? I just said what I did so I could extract myself from that game there."

"Yes, I do want to go back, please."

"And your princess?"

Shallan grimaced. "The meeting was . . . unproductive."

"She didn't take you? What's wrong with her?"

"Chronic competence, I should guess. She's been so successful in life that she has unrealistic expectations of others."

Yalb frowned, guiding Shallan around a group of revelers stumbling drunkenly up the roadway. Wasn't it a little early for that sort of thing? Yalb got a few steps ahead, turning and walking backward, looking at her. "That doesn't make sense, young miss. What more could she want than you?"

"Much more, apparently."

"But you're perfect! Pardon my forwardness."

"You're walking backward."

"Pardon my backwardness, then. You look good from any side, young miss, that you do."

She found herself smiling. Tozbek's sailors had far too high an opinion of her.

"You'd make an ideal ward," he continued. "Genteel, pretty, refined and such. Don't much like your opinion on gambling, but that's to be expected. Wouldn't be right for a proper woman not to scold a fellow for gambling. It'd be like the sun refusing to rise or the sea turning white."

"Or Jasnah Kholin smiling."

"Exactly! Anyway, you're perfect."

"It's kind of you to say so."

"Well, it's true," he said, putting hands on hips, stopping. "So that's it? You're going to give up?"

She gave him a perplexed stare. He stood there on the busy roadway, lit from above by a lantern burning yellow-orange, hands on his hips, white Thaylen eyebrows drooping along the sides of his face, bare-chested under his open vest. That was a posture no citizen, no matter how high ranked, had ever taken at her father's mansion.

"I *did* try to persuade her," Shallan said, blushing. "I went to her a second time, and she rejected me again."

"Two times, eh? In cards, you always got to try a third hand. It wins the most often."

Shallan frowned. "But that's not really true. The laws of probability and statistics—"

"Don't know much blustering math," Yalb said, folding his arms. "But I do know the Passions. You win when you need it most, you see."

The Passions. Pagan superstition. Of course, Jasnah had

referred to glyphwards as superstition too, so perhaps it all came down to perspective.

Try a third time . . . Shallan shivered to consider Jasnah's wrath if Shallan bothered her yet again. She'd surely withdraw the offer to come study with her in the future.

But Shallan would never get to take that offer. It was like a glass sphere with no gemstone at the center. Pretty, but worthless. Was it not better to take one last chance at getting the position she needed *now*?

It wouldn't work. Jasnah had made it quite clear that Shallan was not yet educated enough.

Not yet educated enough . . .

An idea sparked in Shallan's head. She raised her safehand to her breast, standing on that roadway, considering the audacity of it. She'd likely get herself thrown from the city at Jasnah's demand.

Yet if she returned home without trying every avenue, could she face her brothers? They depended on her. For once in her life, someone *needed* Shallan. That responsibility excited her. And terrified her.

"I need a book merchant," she found herself saying, voice wavering slightly.

Yalb raised an eyebrow at her.

"Third hand wins the most. Do you think you can find me a book merchant who is open at this hour?"

"Kharbranth is a major port, young miss," he said with a laugh. "Stores stay open late. Just wait here." He dashed off into the evening crowd, leaving her with an anxious protest on her lips.

She sighed, then seated herself in a demure posture on the stone base of a lantern pole. It should be safe. She saw other lighteyed women passing on the street, though they were often carried in palanquins or those small, hand-pulled vehicles. She even saw the occasional real carriage, though only the very wealthy could afford to keep horses.

A few minutes later, Yalb popped out of the crowd as if from nowhere and waved for her to follow. She rose and hurried to him.

"Should we get a porter?" she asked as he led her to a large side street that ran laterally across the city's hill. She stepped carefully; her skirt was long enough that she worried about tearing the hem on the stone. The strip at the bottom was designed to be easily replaced, but Shallan could hardly afford to waste spheres on such things.

"Nah," Yalb said. "It's right here." He pointed along another cross street. This one had a row of shops climbing up the steep slope, each with a sign hanging out front bearing the glyphpair for *book*, and those glyphs were often styled into the shape of a book. Illiterate servants who might be sent to a shop had to be able to recognize them.

"Merchants of the same type like to clump together," Yalb said, rubbing his chin. "Seems dumb to me, but I guess merchants are like fish. Where you find one, you'll find others."

"The same could be said of ideas," Shallan said, counting. Six different shops. All were lit with Stormlight in the windows, cool and even.

"Third one on the left," Yalb said, pointing. "Merchant's name is Artmyrn. My sources say he's the best." It was a Thaylen name. Likely Yalb had asked others from his homeland, and they had pointed him here.

She nodded to Yalb and they climbed up the steep stone street to the shop. Yalb didn't enter with her; she'd noticed that many men were uncomfortable around books and reading, even those who weren't Vorin.

She pushed through the door—stout wood set with two crystal panels—and stepped into a warm room, uncertain what to expect. She'd never gone into a store to purchase anything; she'd either sent servants, or the merchants had come to her.

The room inside looked very inviting, with large, comfortable easy chairs beside a hearth. Flamespren danced on burning logs there, and the floor was wood. Seamless wood; it had probably been Soulcast that way directly from the stone beneath. Lavish indeed.

A woman stood behind a counter at the back of the room. She wore an embroidered skirt and blouse, rather than the sleek, silk, one-piece havah that Shallan wore. She was dark-eyed, but she was obviously affluent. In Vorin kingdoms, she'd likely be of the first or second nahn. Thaylens had their own system of ranks. At least they weren't completely pagan—they respected eye color, and the woman wore a glove on her safehand.

There weren't many books in the place. A few on the counter, one on a stand beside the chairs. A clock ticked on the wall, its underside hung with a dozen shimmering silver bells. This looked more like a person's home than a shop.

The woman slid a marker into her book, smiling at Shallan. It was a smooth, eager smile. Almost predatory. "Please, Brightness, sit," she said, waving toward the chairs. The woman had curled her long, white Thaylen eyebrows so they hung down the sides of her face like locks from her bangs.

Shallan sat hesitantly as the woman rang a bell on the underside of the counter. Soon, a portly man waddled into the room wearing a vest that seemed ready to burst from the stress of holding in his girth. His hair was greying, and he kept his eyebrows combed back, over his ears.

"Ah," he said, clapping ample hands, "dear young woman. Are you in the market for a nice novel? Some leisure reading to pass the cruel hours while you are separated from a lost love? Or perhaps a book on geography, with details of exotic locations?" He had a slightly condescending tone and spoke in her native Veden.

"I— No, thank you. I need an extensive set of books on history and three on philosophy." She thought back, trying to recall the names Jasnah had used. "Something by Placini, Gabrathin, Yustara, Manaline, or Shauka-daughter-Hasweth."

"Heavy reading for one so young," the man said, nodding to the woman, who was probably his wife. She ducked into the back room. He'd use her for reading; even if he could read himself, he wouldn't want to offend customers by doing so in their presence. He would handle the money; commerce was a masculine art in most situations.

"Now, why is a young flower like yourself bothering herself with such topics?" the merchant said, easing himself down into the chair across from her. "Can't I interest you in a nice romantic novel? They are my specialty, you see. Young women from across the city come to me, and I always carry the best."

His tone set her on edge. It was galling enough to *know* she was a sheltered child. Was it really necessary to remind her of it? "A romantic novel," she said, holding her satchel close to her chest. "Yes, perhaps that would be nice. Do you by chance have a copy of *Nearer the Flame*?"

The merchant blinked. *Nearer the Flame* was written from the viewpoint of a man who slowly descended into madness after watching his children starve.

"Are you certain you want something so, er, ambitious?" the man asked.

"Is ambition such an unseemly attribute in a young woman?"

"Well, no, I suppose not." He smiled again—the thick, toothy smile of a merchant trying to put someone at ease. "I can see you are a woman of discriminating taste."

"I am," Shallan said, voice firm though her heart fluttered. Was she destined to get into an argument with everyone she met? "I *do* like my meals prepared very carefully, as my palate is quite delicate."

"Pardon. I meant that you have discriminating taste *in books*."

"I've never eaten one, actually."

"Brightness, I believe you are having sport with me."

"Not yet I'm not. I haven't even really begun."

"I—"

"Now," she said, "you were right to compare the mind and the stomach."

"But—"

"Too many of us," she said, "take great pains with what we ingest through our mouths, and far less with what we partake of through our ears and eyes. Wouldn't you say?"

He nodded, perhaps not trusting her to let him speak

without interrupting. Shallan knew, somewhere in the back of her mind, that she was letting herself go too far—that she was tense and frustrated after her interactions with Jasnah.

She didn't care at the moment. "Discriminating," she said, testing the world. "I'm not certain I agree with your choice of words. To discriminate is to maintain prejudice against. To be exclusive. Can a person afford to be exclusive with what they ingest? Whether we speak of food or of thoughts?"

"I think they must be," the merchant said. "Isn't that what you just said?"

"I said we should take thought for what we read or eat. Not that we should be exclusive. Tell me, what do you think would happen to a person who ate only sweets?"

"I know well," the man said. "I have a sister-in-law who periodically upsets her stomach by doing that."

"See, she was *too* discriminating. The body needs many different foods to remain healthy. And the mind needs many different ideas to remain sharp. Wouldn't you agree? And so if I were to read only these silly romances you presume that my ambition can handle, my mind would grow sick as surely as your sister-in-law's stomach. Yes, I should think that the metaphor is a solid one. You are quite clever, Master Artmyrn."

His smile returned.

"Of course," she noted, not smiling back, "being talked down to upsets both the mind *and* the stomach. So nice of you to give a poignant object lesson to accompany your brilliant metaphor. Do you treat all of your customers this way?"

"Brightness . . . I believe you stray into sarcasm."

"Funny. I thought I'd run straight into it, screaming at the top of my lungs."

He blushed and stood. "I'll go help my wife." He hurriedly withdrew.

She sat back, and realized she was annoyed at herself for letting her frustration boil out. It was just what her nurses had warned her about. A young woman had to mind her words. Her father's intemperate tongue had earned their house a regrettable reputation; would she add to it?

She calmed herself, enjoying the warmth and watching the dancing flamespren until the merchant and his wife returned, bearing several stacks of books. The merchant took his seat again, and his wife pulled over a stool, setting the tomes on the floor and then showing them one at a time as her husband spoke.

"For history, we have two choices," the merchant said, condescension—and friendliness—gone. "*Times and Passage,* by Rencalt, is a single volume survey of Rosharan history since the Hierocracy." His wife held up a red, cloth-bound volume. "I told my wife that you would likely be insulted by such a shallow option, but she insisted."

"Thank you," Shallan said. "I am not insulted, but I do require something more detailed."

"Then perhaps *Eternathis* will serve you," he said as his wife held up a blue-grey set of four volumes. "It is a philosophical work which examines the same time period by focusing only on the interactions of the five Vorin kingdoms. As you can see, the treatment is exhaustive."

The four volumes were thick. The *five* Vorin kingdoms? She'd thought there were four. Jah Keved, Alethkar, Kharbranth, and Natanatan. United by religion, they had been strong allies during the years following the Recreance. What was the fifth kingdom?

The volumes intrigued her. "I will take them."

"Excellent," the merchant said, a bit of the gleam returning to his eye. "Of the philosophical works you listed, we didn't have anything by Yustara. We have one each of works by Placini and Manaline; both are collections of excerpts from their most famous writings. I've had the Placini book read to me; it's quite good."

Shallan nodded.

"As for Gabrathin," he said, "we have four different volumes. My, but he was a prolific one! Oh, and we have a single book by Shauka-daughter-Hasweth." The wife held up a thin green volume. "I have to admit, I've never had any of her work read to me. I didn't realize that there were any Shin philosophers of note."

Shallan looked at the four books by Gabrathin. She had no idea which one she should take, so she avoided the question, pointing at the two collections he had mentioned first and the single volume by Shauka-daughter-Hasweth. A philosopher from distant Shin, where people lived in mud and worshipped rocks? The man who had killed Jasnah's father nearly six years before—prompting the war against the Parshendi in Natanatan—had been Shin. The Assassin in White, they called him.

"I will take those three," Shallan said, "along with the histories."

"Excellent!" the merchant repeated. "For buying so many, I will give you a fair discount. Let us say, ten emerald broams?"

Shallan nearly choked. An emerald broam was the largest denomination of sphere, worth a thousand diamond chips. Ten of them was more than her trip to Kharbranth had cost by several magnitudes!

She opened her satchel, looking in at her money pouch. She had around eight emerald broams left. She'd have to take fewer of the books, obviously, but which ones?

Suddenly, the door slammed open. Shallan jumped and was surprised to see Yalb standing there, holding his cap in his hands, nervous. He rushed to her chair, going down on one knee. She was too stunned to say anything. Why was he so worried?

"Brightness," he said, bowing his head. "My master bids you return. He's reconsidered his offer. Truly, we can take the price you offered."

Shallan opened her mouth, but found herself stupefied.

Yalb glanced at the merchant. "Brightness, don't buy from this man. He's a liar and a cheat. My master will sell you much finer books at a better price."

"Now, what's this?" Artmyrn said, standing. "How dare you! Who is your master?"

"Barmest," Yalb said defensively.

"That rat. He sends a boy into *my* shop trying to steal *my* customer? Outrageous!"

"She came to our shop first!" Yalb said.

Shallan finally recovered her wits. *Stormfather! He's quite the actor.* "You had your chance," she said to Yalb. "Run along and tell your master that I refuse to be swindled. I will visit every bookshop in the city if that is what it takes to find someone reasonable."

"Artmyrn isn't reasonable," Yalb said, spitting to the side. The merchant's eyes opened wide with rage.

"We shall see," Shallan said.

"Brightness," Artmyrn said, red-faced. "Surely you don't believe these allegations!"

"And how much were you going to charge her?" Yalb asked.

"Ten emerald broams," Shallan said. "For those seven books."

Yalb laughed. "And you didn't stand up and walk right out! You practically had my master's ears, and he offered you a better deal than that! Please, Brightness, return with me. We're ready to—"

"Ten was just an opening figure," Artmyrn said. "I didn't expect her to take them." He looked at Shallan. "Of course, *eight. . . .*"

Yalb laughed again. "I'm sure we have those same books, Brightness. I'll bet my master gives them to you for two."

Artmyrn grew more red-faced, muttering. "Brightness, surely you wouldn't patronize someone so *crass* as to send a servant into someone else's shop to steal his customers!"

"Perhaps I would," Shallan said. "At least he didn't insult my intelligence."

Artmyrn's wife glared at her husband, and the man grew even more red in the face. "Two emerald, three sapphire. That is as low as I can go. If you want cheaper than that, then buy from that scoundrel Barmest. The books will probably be missing pages, though."

Shallan hesitated, glancing at Yalb; he was caught up in his role, bowing and scraping. She caught his eyes, and he just kind of gave a shrug.

"I'll do it," she said to Artmyrn, prompting a groan from Yalb. He slunk away with a curse from Artmyrn's wife. Shallan rose and counted out the spheres; the emerald broams she retrieved from her safepouch.

Soon, she walked from the shop bearing a heavy canvas bag. She walked down the steep street, and found Yalb lounging beside a lamppost. She smiled as he took the bag from her. "How did you know what a fair price for a book was?" she asked.

"Fair price?" he said, slinging the bag over his shoulder. "For a book? I've no idea. I just figured he'd be trying to take you for as much as he could. That's why I asked around for who his biggest rival was and came back to help get him to be more reasonable."

"It was that obvious I'd let myself be swindled?" she asked with a blush, the two of them walking out of the side street.

Yalb chuckled. "Just a little. Anyway, conning men like him is almost as much fun as cheating guards. You probably could have gotten him down further by actually leaving with me, then coming back later to give him another chance."

"That sounds complicated."

"Merchants is like mercenaries, my gammer always said. Only difference is that merchants will take your head off, then pretend to be your friend all the same."

This from a man who had just spent the evening cheating a group of guards at cards. "Well, you have my thanks, anyway."

"Wasn't nothing. It was fun, though I can't believe you paid what you did. It's just a bunch of wood. I could find some driftwood and put some funny marks on it. Would you pay me pure spheres for that too?"

"I can't offer that," she said, fishing in her satchel. She took out the picture she'd drawn of Yalb and the porter. "But please, take this, with my thanks."

Yalb took the picture and stepped up beneath a nearby lantern to get a look. He laughed, cocking his head, smiling broadly. "Stormfather! Ain't that something? Looks like I'm seeing myself in a polished plate, it does. I can't take this, Brightness!"

"Please. I insist." She did, however, blink her eyes, taking a Memory of him standing there, one hand on his chin as he studied the picture of himself. She'd redraw him later. After what he'd done for her, she dearly wanted him in her collection.

Yalb carefully tucked the picture between the pages of a book, then hefted the bag and continued. They stepped back onto the main roadway. Nomon—the middle moon—had begun to rise, bathing the city in pale blue light. Staying up this late had been a rare privilege for her in her father's house, but these city people around them barely seemed to notice the late hour. What a strange place this city was.

"Back to the ship now?" Yalb asked.

"No," Shallan said, taking a deep breath. "Back to the Conclave."

He raised an eyebrow, but led her back. Once there, she bid Yalb farewell, reminding him to take his picture. He did so, wishing her luck before hastening from the Conclave, probably worried about meeting the guardsmen he'd cheated earlier.

Shallan had a servant carry her books, and made her way down the hallway back to the Veil. Just inside the ornate iron doors, she caught the attention of a master-servant.

"Yes, Brightness?" the man asked. Most of the alcoves were now dim, and patient servants were returning tomes to their safe place beyond the crystal walls.

Shaking off her fatigue, Shallan counted up the rows. There was still a light in Jasnah's alcove. "I'd like to use the alcove there," she said, pointing to the next balcony over.

"Do you have a chit of admittance?"

"I'm afraid not."

"Then you'll have to rent the space if you wish to use it regularly. Two skymarks."

Wincing at the price, Shallan dug out the proper spheres and paid. Her money pouches were looking depressingly flat. She let the parshman porters haul her up to the appropriate level, then she quietly walked to her alcove. There, she used all her remaining spheres to fill the oversized goblet lamp. To get enough light, she was forced to use spheres of all nine colors and all three sizes, so the illumination was patchy and varied.

Shallan peeked over the side of her alcove, out at the next balcony over. Jasnah sat studying, heedless of the hour, her goblet filled to the brim with pure diamond broams. They were best for light, but less useful in Soulcasting, so weren't as valuable.

Shallan ducked back around. There was a place at the very edge of the alcove's table where she could sit, hidden by the wall from Jasnah, so she sat there. Perhaps she should have chosen an alcove on another level, but she wanted to keep an eye on the woman. Hopefully Jasnah would spend weeks here studying. Enough time for Shallan to dedicate herself to some fierce cramming. Her ability to memorize pictures and scenes didn't work as well on text, but she could learn lists and facts at a rate that her tutors had found remarkable.

She settled herself in the chair, pulling out the books and arranging them. She rubbed her eyes. It was really quite late, but there wasn't time to waste. Jasnah had said that Shallan could make another petition when the gaps in her knowledge were filled. Well, Shallan intended to fill those gaps in record time, then present herself again. She'd do it when Jasnah was ready to leave Kharbranth.

It was a last, desperate hope, so frail that a strong gust of circumstance seemed likely to topple it. Taking a deep breath, Shallan opened the first of the history books.

"I'm never going to be rid of you, am I?" a soft, feminine voice asked.

Shallan jumped up, nearly knocking over her books as she spun toward the doorway. Jasnah Kholin stood there, deep blue dress embroidered in silver, its silken sheen reflecting the light of Shallan's spheres. The Soulcaster was covered by a fingerless black glove to block the bright gemstones.

"Brightness," Shallan said, rising and curtsying in an awkward rush. "I didn't mean to disturb you. I—"

Jasnah quieted her with a wave of the hand. She stepped aside as a parshman entered Shallan's alcove, carrying a chair. He placed it beside Shallan's desk, and Jasnah glided over and sat.

Shallan tried to judge Jasnah's mood, but the older woman's emotions were impossible to read. "I honestly didn't want to disturb you."

"I bribed the servants to tell me if you returned to the Veil," Jasnah said idly, picking up one of Shallan's tomes, reading the title. "I didn't want to be interrupted again."

"I—" Shallan looked down, blushing furiously.

"Don't bother apologizing," Jasnah said. She looked tired; more tired than Shallan felt. Jasnah picked through the books. "A fine selection. You chose well."

"It wasn't really much of a choice," Shallan said. "It was just about all the merchant had."

"You intended to study their contents quickly, I assume?" Jasnah said musingly. "Try to impress me one last time before I left Kharbranth?"

Shallan hesitated, then nodded.

"A clever ploy. I should have put a time restriction on your reapplication." She looked at Shallan, glancing her over. "You are very determined. That is good. And I know why you wish so desperately to be my ward."

Shallan started. She *knew*?

"Your house has many enemies," Jasnah continued, "and your father is reclusive. It will be difficult for you to marry well without a tactically sound alliance."

Shallan relaxed, though she tried to keep it from showing.

"Let me see your satchel," Jasnah said.

Shallan frowned, resisting the urge to pull it close. "Brightness?"

Jasnah held out her hand. "You recall what I said about repeating myself?"

Reluctantly, Shallan handed it over. Jasnah carefully removed its contents, neatly lining up the brushes, pencils, pens, jar of lacquer, ink, and solvent. She placed the stacks of paper, the notebooks, and the finished pictures in a line.

Then she got out Shallan's money pouches, noting their emptiness. She glanced at the goblet lamp, counting its contents. She raised an eyebrow.

Next, she began to look through Shallan's pictures. First the loose-leaf ones, where she lingered on Shallan's picture of Jasnah herself. Shallan watched the woman's face. Was she pleased? Surprised? Displeased at how much time Shallan spent sketching sailors and serving women?

Finally, Jasnah moved on to the sketchbook filled with drawings of plants and animals Shallan had observed during her trip. Jasnah spent the longest on this, reading through each notation. "Why have you made these sketches?" Jasnah asked at the end.

"Why, Brightness? Well, because I wanted to." She grimaced. Should she have said something profound instead?

Jasnah nodded slowly. Then she rose. "I have rooms in the Conclave, granted to me by the king. Gather your things and go there. You look exhausted."

"Brightness?" Shallan asked, rising, a thrill of excitement running through her.

Jasnah hesitated at the doorway. "At first meeting, I took you for a rural opportunist, seeking only to ride my name to greater wealth."

"You've changed your mind?"

"No," Jasnah said, "there is undoubtedly some of that in you. But we are each many different people, and you can tell much about a person by what they carry with them. If that notebook is any indication, you pursue scholarship in your free time for its own sake. That is encouraging. It is, perhaps, the best argument you could make on your own behalf.

"If I cannot be rid of you, then I might as well make use of you. Go and sleep. Tomorrow we will begin early, and you will divide your time between your education and helping me with my studies."

With that, Jasnah withdrew.

Shallan sat, bemused, blinking tired eyes. She got out a sheet of paper and wrote a quick prayer of thanks, which she'd burn later. Then she hurriedly gathered up her books and went looking for a servant to send to the *Wind's Pleasure* for her trunk.

It had been a very, *very* long day. But she'd won. The first step had been completed.

Now her real task began.

Chulls

Chulls are everywhere, of course, and they come in a variety of shapes and sizes. There must be far more breeds of the animals than I'd originally assumed. I've seen them pulling carts, towing boxes, carrying jugs of water in racks on their sides.

I even saw a man riding one for transportation, though it seems that walking would be far faster.

The shells aren't nearly as heavy as they look.

In the wild, plants grow in the crevices, and a sleeping chull looks much like a boulder.

Apparently, the beasts aren't hurt if the shell is cracked, or even shaped. Some people sand flat places on top to ride, and many carts are hooked to fittings drilled directly into the shell.

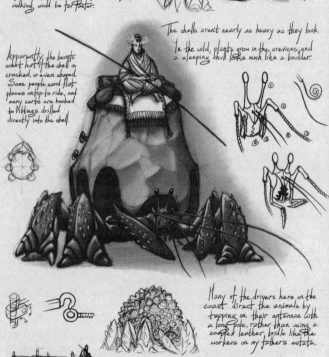

Many of the drivers here on the coast direct the animals by tapping on their antennae with a long pole, rather than using a complex leather bridle like the workers on my father's estate.

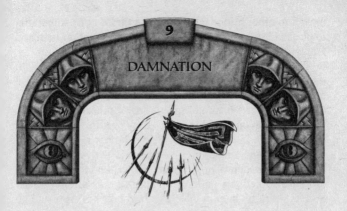

DAMNATION

"Ten people, with Shardblades alight, standing before a wall of black and white and red."

—Collected: Jesachev, 1173, 12 seconds pre-death. Subject: one of our own ardents, overheard during his last moments.

Kaladin had not been assigned to Bridge Four by chance. Out of all the bridge crews, Bridge Four had the highest casualty rate. That was particularly notable, considering that average bridge crews often lost one-third to one-half of their number on a single run.

Kaladin sat outside, back to the barrack wall, a sprinkle of rain falling on him. It wasn't a highstorm. Just an ordinary spring rain. Soft. A timid cousin to the great storms.

Syl sat on Kaladin's shoulder. Or hovered on it. Whatever. She didn't seem to have any weight. Kaladin sat slumped, chin against his chest, staring at a dip in the stone, which was slowly collecting rainwater.

He should have moved inside Bridge Four's barrack. It was cold and unfurnished, but it would keep off the rain. But he just . . . couldn't care. How long had he been with Bridge Four now? Two weeks? Three? An eternity?

Of the twenty-five men who had survived his first bridge deployment, twenty-three were now dead. Two had been moved to other bridge crews because they'd done something to please Gaz, but they'd died there. Only one other man and Kaladin remained. Two out of nearly forty.

The bridge crew's numbers had been replenished with more unfortunates, and most of those had died too. They had been replaced. Many of those had died. Bridgeleader after bridgeleader had been chosen. It was supposed to be a favored position on a bridge crew, always getting to run in the best places. It didn't matter for Bridge Four.

Some bridge runs weren't as bad. If the Alethi arrived before the Parshendi, no bridgemen died. And if they arrived too late, sometimes another highprince was already there. Sadeas wouldn't help in that case; he'd take his army and go back to camp. Even in a bad run, the Parshendi would often choose to focus their arrows on certain crews, trying to bring them down one at a time. Sometimes, dozens of bridgemen would fall, but not a single one from Bridge Four.

That was rare. For some reason, Bridge Four always seemed to get targeted. Kaladin didn't bother to learn the names of his companions. None of the bridgemen did. What was the point? Learn a man's name, and one of you would be dead before the week was out. Odds were, you'd both be dead. Maybe he *should* learn names. Then he'd have someone to talk to in Damnation. They could reminisce about how terrible Bridge Four had been, and agree that eternal fires were much more pleasant.

He smirked dully, still staring at the rock in front of him. Gaz would come for them soon, send them to work. Scrubbing latrines, cleaning streets, mucking stables, gathering rocks. Something to keep their minds off their fate.

He still didn't know why they fought on those blustering plateaus. Something about those large chrysalises. They had gemstones at their hearts, apparently. But what did that have to do with the Vengeance Pact?

Another bridgeman—a youthful Veden with reddish-blond hair—lay nearby, staring up into the spitting sky. Rainwater pooled in the corners of his brown eyes, then ran down his face. He didn't blink.

They couldn't run. The warcamp might as well have been

a prison. The bridgemen could go to the merchants and spend their meager earnings on cheap wine or whores, but they couldn't leave the warcamp. The perimeter was secure. Partially, this was to keep out soldiers from the other camps—there was always rivalry where armies met. But mostly it was so bridgemen and slaves could not flee.

Why? Why did this all have to be so horrible? None of it made *sense*. Why not let a few bridgemen run out in front of the bridges with shields to block arrows? He'd asked, and had been told that would slow them down too much. He'd asked again, and had been told he'd be strung up if he didn't shut his mouth.

The lighteyes acted as if this entire mess were some kind of grand game. If it was, the rules were hidden from bridgemen, just as pieces on a board had no inkling what the player's strategy might be.

"Kaladin?" Syl asked, floating down and landing on his leg, holding the girlish form with the long dress flowing into mist. "Kaladin? You haven't spoken in days."

He kept staring, slumped. There *was* a way out. Bridgemen could visit the chasm nearest the camp. There were rules forbidding it, but the sentries ignored them. It was seen as the one mercy that could be given the bridgemen.

Bridgemen who took that path never returned.

"Kaladin?" Syl said, voice soft, worried.

"My father used to say that there are two kinds of people in the world," Kaladin whispered, voice raspy. "He said there are those who take lives. And there are those who save lives."

Syl frowned, cocking her head. This kind of conversation confused her; she wasn't good with abstractions.

"I used to think he was wrong. I thought there was a third group. People who killed in order to save." He shook his head. "I was a fool. There *is* a third group, a big one, but it isn't what I thought."

"What group?" she said, sitting down on his knee, brow scrunched up.

"The people who exist to be saved or to be killed. The group in the middle. The ones who can't do anything but die or be protected. The victims. That's all I am."

He looked up across the wet lumberyard. The carpenters had retreated, throwing tarps over untreated wood and bearing away tools that could rust. The bridgeman barracks ran around the west and north sides of the yard. Bridge Four's was set off a little from the others, as if bad luck were a disease that could be caught. Contagious by proximity, as Kaladin's father would say.

"We exist to be killed," Kaladin said. He blinked, glancing at the other few members of Bridge Four sitting apathetically in the rain. "If we're not dead already."

⁕⁎

"I hate seeing you like this," Syl said, buzzing about Kaladin's head as his team of bridgemen dragged a log down into the lumberyard. The Parshendi often set fire to the outermost permanent bridges, so Highprince Sadeas's engineers and carpenters were always busy.

The old Kaladin might have wondered why the armies didn't work harder to defend the bridges. *There's something wrong here!* a voice inside him said. *You're missing part of the puzzle. They waste resources and bridgeman lives. They don't seem to care about pushing inward and assaulting the Parshendi. They just fight pitched battles on plateaus, then come back to the camps and celebrate. Why? WHY?*

He ignored that voice. It belonged to the man he had been.

"You used to be vibrant," Syl said. "So many looked up to you, Kaladin. Your squad of soldiers. The enemies you fought. The other slaves. Even some lighteyes."

Lunch would come soon. Then he could sleep until their bridgeleader kicked him awake for afternoon duty.

"I used to watch you fight," Syl said. "I can barely remember it. My memories of then are fuzzy. Like looking at you through a rainstorm."

Wait. That was odd. Syl hadn't started following him until after his fall from the army. And she'd acted just like an ordinary windspren back then. He hesitated, earning a curse and a lash on his back from a taskmaster's whip.

He started pulling again. Bridgemen who were laggard in

work were whipped, and bridgemen who were laggard on runs were executed. The army was very serious about that. Refuse to charge the Parshendi, try to lag behind the other bridges, and you'd be beheaded. They reserved that fate for that specific crime, in fact.

There were lots of ways to get punished as a bridgeman. You could earn extra work detail, get whipped, have your pay docked. If you did something really bad, they'd string you up for the Stormfather's judgment, leaving you tied to a post or a wall to face a highstorm. But the only thing you could do to be executed directly was refuse to run at the Parshendi.

The message was clear. Charging with your bridge *might* get you killed, but refusing to do so *would* get you killed.

Kaladin and his crew lifted their log into a pile with others, then unhooked their dragging lines. They walked back toward the edge of the lumberyard, where more logs waited.

"Gaz!" a voice called. A tall, yellow-and-black-haired soldier stood at the edge of the bridge grounds, a group of miserable men huddled behind him. That was Laresh, one of the soldiers who worked the duty tent. He brought new bridgemen to replace those who'd been killed.

The day was bright, without a hint of clouds, and the sun was hot on Kaladin's back. Gaz hustled up to meet the new recruits, and Kaladin and the others happened to be walking in that direction to pick up a log.

"What a sorry lot," Gaz said, looking over the recruits. "Of course, if they weren't, they wouldn't be sent *here*."

"That's the truth," Laresh said. "These ten at the front were caught smuggling. You know what to do."

New bridgemen were constantly needed, but there were always enough bodies. Slaves were common, but so were thieves or other lawbreakers from among the camp followers. Never parshmen. They were too valuable, and besides, the Parshendi were some kind of cousins to the parshmen. Better not to give the parshman workers in camp the sight of their kind fighting.

Sometimes a soldier would be thrown into a bridge crew. That only happened if he'd done something extremely bad, like striking an officer. Acts that would earn a hanging in many armies meant being sent to the bridge crews here. Supposedly, if you survived a hundred bridge runs, you'd be released. It had happened once or twice, the stories said. It was probably just a myth, intended to give the bridgemen some tiny hope for survival.

Kaladin and the others walked past the newcomers, gazes down, and began hooking their ropes to the next log.

"Bridge Four needs some men," Gaz said, rubbing his chin.

"Four always needs men," Laresh said. "Don't worry. I brought a special batch for it." He nodded toward a second group of recruits, much more ragtag, walking up behind.

Kaladin slowly stood upright. One of the prisoners in that group was a boy of barely fourteen or fifteen. Short, spindly, with a round face. "Tien?" he whispered, taking a step forward.

He stopped, shaking himself. Tien was dead. But this newcomer looked so familiar, with those frightened black eyes. It made Kaladin want to shelter the boy. Protect him.

But . . . he'd failed. Everyone he'd tried to protect—from Tien to Cenn—had ended up dead. What was the point?

He turned back to dragging the log.

"Kaladin," Syl said, landing on the log, "I'm going to leave."

He blinked in shock. Syl. Leave? But . . . she was the last thing he had left. "No," he whispered. It came out as a croak.

"I'll try to come back," she said. "But I don't know what will happen when I leave you. Things are strange. I have odd memories. No, most of them aren't even memories. Instincts. One of those tells me that if I leave you, I might lose myself."

"Then don't go," he said, growing terrified.

"I have to," she said, cringing. "I can't watch this anymore. I'll try to return." She looked sorrowful. "Goodbye." And with that, she zipped away into the air, adopting the form of a tiny group of tumbling, translucent leaves.

Kaladin watched her go, numb.

Then he turned back to hauling the log. What else could he do?

The youth, the one that reminded him of Tien, died during the very next bridge run.

It was a bad one. The Parshendi were in position, waiting for Sadeas. Kaladin charged the chasm, not even flinching as men were slaughtered around him. It wasn't bravery that drove him; it wasn't even a wish that those arrows would take him and end it all. He ran. That was what he did. Like a boulder rolled down a hill, or like rain fell from the sky. They didn't have a choice. Neither did he. He wasn't a man; he was a thing, and things just did what they did.

The bridgemen laid their bridges in a tight line. Four crews had fallen. Kaladin's own team had lost nearly enough to stop them.

Bridge placed, Kaladin turned away, the army charging across the wood to start the real battle. He stumbled back across the plateau. After a few moments, he found what he was looking for. The boy's body.

Kaladin stood, wind whipping at his hair, looking down at the corpse. It lay faceup in a small hollow in the stone. Kaladin remembered lying in a similar hollow, holding a similar corpse.

Another bridgeman had fallen nearby, bristling with arrows. It was the man who'd lived through Kaladin's first bridge run all those weeks back. His body slumped to the side, lying on a stone outcropping a foot or so above the corpse of the boy. Blood dripped from the tip of an arrow sticking out his back. It fell, one ruby drop at a time, splattering on the boy's open, lifeless eye. A little trail of red ran from the eye down the side of his face. Like crimson tears.

That night, Kaladin huddled in the barrack, listening to a highstorm buffet the wall. He curled against the cold stone. Thunder shattered the sky outside.

I can't keep going like this, he thought. *I'm dead inside, as sure as if I'd taken a spear through the neck.*

The storm continued its tirade. And for the first time in over eight months, Kaladin found himself crying.

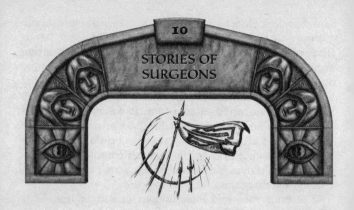

NINE YEARS AGO

Kal stumbled into the surgery room, the open door letting in bright white sunlight. At ten years old, he was already showing signs that he would be tall and lanky. He'd always preferred Kal to his full name, Kaladin. The shorter name made him fit in better. Kaladin sounded like a lighteyes's name.

"I'm sorry, Father," he said.

Kal's father, Lirin, carefully tightened the strap around the arm of the young woman who was tied onto the narrow operating table. Her eyes were closed; Kal had missed the administration of the drug. "We will discuss your tardiness later," Lirin said, securing the woman's other hand. "Close the door."

Kal cringed and closed the door. The windows were dark, shutters firmly in place, and so the only light was that of the Stormlight shining from a large globe filled with spheres. Each of those spheres was a broam, in total an incredible sum that was on permanent loan from Hearthstone's landlord. Lanterns flickered, but Stormlight was always true. That could save lives, Kal's father said.

Kal approached the table, anxious. The young woman,

Sani, had sleek black hair, not tinged with even a single strand of brown or blond. She was fifteen, and her freehand was wrapped with a bloody, ragged bandage. Kal grimaced at the clumsy bandaging job—it looked like the cloth had been ripped from someone's shirt and tied in haste.

Sani's head rolled to the side, and she mumbled, drugged. She wore only a white cotton shift, her safehand exposed. Older boys in the town sniggered about the chances they'd had—or *claimed* to have had—at seeing girls in their shifts, but Kal didn't understand what the excitement was all about. He *was* worried about Sani, though. He always worried when someone was wounded.

Fortunately, the wound didn't look terrible. If it had been life-threatening, his father would have already begun working on it, using Kal's mother—Hesina—as an assistant.

Lirin walked to the side of the room and gathered up a few small, clear bottles. He was a short man, balding despite his relative youth. He wore his spectacles, which he called the most precious gift he'd ever been given. He rarely got them out except for surgery, as they were too valuable to risk just wearing about. What if they were scratched or broken? Hearthstone was a large town, but its remote location in northern Alethkar would make replacing the spectacles difficult.

The room was kept neat, the shelves and table washed clean each morning, everything in its place. Lirin said you could tell a lot about a man from how he kept his workspace. Was it sloppy or orderly? Did he respect his tools or did he leave them casually about? The town's only fabrial clock sat here on the counter. The small device bore a single dial at the center and a glowing Smokestone at its heart; it had to be infused to keep the time. Nobody else in the town cared about minutes and hours as Lirin did.

Kal pulled over a stool to get a better vantage. Soon he wouldn't need the stool; he was growing taller by the day. He inspected Sani's hand. *She'll be all right,* he told himself, as his father had trained him. *A surgeon needs to be calm. Worry just wastes time.*

It was hard advice to follow.

"Hands," Lirin said, not turning away from gathering his tools.

Kal sighed, hopping off his stool and hurrying over to the basin of warm, soapy water by the door. "Why does it matter?" He wanted to be at work, helping Sani.

"Wisdom of the Heralds," Lirin said absently, repeating a lecture he'd given many times before. "Deathspren and rotspren hate water. It will keep them away."

"Hammie says that's silly," Kal said. "He says deathspren are mighty good at killing folk, so why should they be afraid of a little water?"

"The Heralds were wise beyond our understanding."

Kal grimaced. "But they're *demons*, father. I heard it off that ardent who came teaching last spring."

"That's the Radiants he spoke of," Lirin said sharply. "You're mixing them again."

Kal sighed.

"The Heralds were sent to teach mankind," Lirin said. "They led us against the Voidbringers after we were cast from heaven. The Radiants were the orders of knights they founded."

"Who were demons."

"Who betrayed us," Lirin said, "once the Heralds left." Lirin raised a finger. "They were not demons, they were just men who had too much power and not enough sense. Either way, you are *always* to wash your hands. You can see the effect it has on rotspren with your own eyes, even if deathspren cannot be seen."

Kal sighed again, but did as he was told. Lirin walked over to the table again, bearing a tray lined with knives and little glass bottles. His ways were odd—though Lirin made certain that his son didn't mix up the Heralds and the Lost Radiants, Kal had heard his father say that he thought the Voidbringers weren't real. Ridiculous. Who else could be blamed when things went missing in the night, or when a crop got infected with diggerworms?

The others in town thought Lirin spent too much time with books and sick people, and that made him strange. They were uncomfortable around him, and with Kal by association. Kal was only just beginning to realize how painful it could feel to be different.

Hands washed, he hopped back up onto the stool. He began to feel nervous again, hoping that nothing would go wrong. His father used a mirror to focus the spheres' light onto Sani's hand. Gingerly, he cut off the makeshift bandage with a surgeon's knife. The wound wasn't life-threatening, but the hand *was* pretty badly mangled. When his father had started training Kal two years before, sights like this had sickened him. Now he was used to torn flesh.

That was good. Kal figured this would be useful when he went to war someday, to fight for his highprince and the lighteyes.

Sani had three broken fingers and the skin on her hand was scraped and gouged, the wound cluttered with sticks and dirt. The third finger was the worst, shattered and twisted nastily, splinters of bone protruding through the skin. Kal felt its length, noting the fractured bones, the blackness on the skin. He carefully wiped away dried blood and dirt with a wet cloth, picking out rocks and sticks as his father cut thread for sewing.

"The third finger will have to go, won't it?" Kal said, tying a bandage around the base of the finger to keep it from bleeding.

His father nodded, a hint of a smile on his face. He'd hoped Kal would discern that. Lirin often said that a wise surgeon must know what to remove and what to save. If that third finger had been set properly at first . . . but no, it was beyond recovery. Sewing it back together would mean leaving it to fester and die.

His father did the actual amputation. He had such careful, precise hands. Training as a surgeon took over ten years, and it would be some time yet before Lirin let Kal hold the knife. Instead, Kal wiped away blood, handed his father knives, and held the sinew to keep it from tangling as his father sewed. They repaired the hand so far as they could, working with deliberate speed.

Kal's father finished the final suture, obviously pleased at having been able to save four of the fingers. That wasn't how Sani's parents would see it. They'd be disappointed that their beautiful daughter would now have a disfigured hand. It almost always happened that way—terror at the initial wound, then anger at Lirin's inability to work wonders. Lirin said it was because the townsfolk had grown accustomed to having a surgeon. To them, the healing had become an expectation, rather than a privilege.

But Sani's parents were good people. They'd make a small donation, and Kal's family—his parents, him, and his younger brother Tien—would continue to be able to eat. Odd, how they survived because of others' misfortune. Maybe that was part of what made the townsfolk resent them.

Lirin finished by using a small heated rod to cauterize where he felt the stitches wouldn't be enough. Finally, he spread pungent lister's oil across the hand to prevent infection—the oil frightened away rotspren even better than soap and water. Kal wrapped on clean bandages, careful not to disturb the splints.

Lirin disposed of the finger, and Kal began to relax. She'd be all right.

"You still need to work on those nerves of yours, son," Lirin said softly, washing blood from his hands.

Kal looked down.

"It is good to care," Lirin said. "But caring—like anything else—can be a problem if it interferes with your ability to perform surgery."

Caring too much can be a problem? Kal thought back at his father. *And what about being so selfless that you never charge for your work?* He didn't dare say the words.

Cleaning the room came next. It seemed like half of Kal's life was spent cleaning, but Lirin wouldn't let him go until they were done with it. At least he opened the shutters, letting sunlight stream in. Sani continued to doze; the winterwort would keep her unconscious for hours yet.

"So where were you?" Lirin asked, bottles of oil and alcohol clinking as he returned them to their places.

"With Jam."

"Jam is two years your senior," Lirin said. "I doubt he has much fondness for spending his time with those much younger than he."

"His father started training him in the quarterstaff," Kal said in a rush. "Tien and I went to see what he's learned." Kal cringed, waiting for the lecture.

His father just continued, wiping down each of his surgeon's knives with alcohol, then oil, as the old traditions dictated. He didn't turn toward Kal.

"Jam's father was a soldier in Brightlord Amaram's army," Kal said tentatively. Brightlord Amaram! The noble lighteyed general who watched over northern Alethkar. Kal wanted so much to see a *real* lighteyes, not stuffy old Wistiow. A soldier, like everyone talked about, like the stories were about.

"I know about Jam's father," Lirin said. "I've had to operate on that lame leg of his three times now. A gift of his glorious time as a soldier."

"We *need* soldiers, father. You'd have our borders violated by the Thaylens?"

"Thaylenah is an island kingdom," Lirin said calmly. "They don't share a border with us."

"Well, then, they could attack from the sea!"

"They're mostly tradesmen and merchants. Every one I've met has tried to swindle me, but that's hardly the same thing as invading."

All the boys liked to tell stories about far-off places. It was hard to remember that Kal's father—the only man of second nahn in the town—had traveled all the way to Kharbranth during his youth.

"Well, we fight with *someone*," Kal continued, moving to scrub the floor.

"Yes," his father said after a pause. "King Gavilar always finds people for us to fight. That much is true."

"So we need soldiers, like I said."

"We need surgeons more." Lirin sighed audibly, turning away from his cabinet. "Son, you nearly cry each time someone is brought to us; you grind your teeth anxiously during even simple procedures. What makes you think you could actually *hurt* someone?"

"I'll get stronger."

"That's foolishness. Who's put these ideas in your head? *Why* would you want to learn to hit other boys with a stick?"

"For honor, Father," Kal said. "Who tells stories about *surgeons*, for the Heralds' sake!"

"The children of the men and women whose lives we save," Lirin said evenly, meeting Kal's gaze. "That's who tell stories of surgeons."

Kal blushed and shrank back, then finally returned to his scrubbing.

"There are two kinds of people in this world, son," his father said sternly. "Those who save lives. And those who take lives."

"And what of those who protect and defend? The ones who save lives *by* taking lives?"

His father snorted. "That's like trying to stop a storm by blowing harder. Ridiculous. You can't protect by killing."

Kal kept scrubbing.

Finally, his father sighed, walking over and kneeling down beside him, helping with the scrubbing. "What are the properties of winterwort?"

"Bitter taste," Kal said immediately, "which makes it safer to keep, since people won't eat it by accident. Crush it to powder, mix it with oil, use one spoonful per ten brickweight of the person you're drugging. Induces a deep sleep for about five hours."

"And how can you tell if someone has the fiddlepox?"

"Nervous energy," Kal said, "thirst, trouble sleeping, and swelling on the undersides of the arms."

"You've got such a good mind, son," Lirin said softly. "It took me years to learn what you've done in months. I've been saving. I'd like to send you to Kharbranth when you turn sixteen, to train with real surgeons."

Kal felt a spike of excitement. Kharbranth? That was in an entirely different kingdom! Kal's father had traveled there as a courier, but he hadn't trained there as a surgeon. He'd learned from old Vathe in Shorsebroon, the nearest town of any size.

"You have a gift from the Heralds themselves," Lirin said, resting a hand on Kal's shoulder. "You could be ten times the surgeon I am. Don't dream the small dreams of other men. Our grandfathers bought and worked us to the second nahn so that we could have full citizenship and the right of travel. Don't waste that on killing."

Kal hesitated, but soon found himself nodding.

DROPLETS

"Three of sixteen ruled, but now the Broken One reigns."

—Collected: Chachanan, 1173, 84 seconds pre-death. Subject: a cutpurse with the wasting sickness, of partial Iriali descent.

The highstorm eventually subsided. It was the dusk of the day the boy had died, the day Syl had left him. Kaladin slid on his sandals—the same ones he'd taken from the leathery-faced man on that first day—and stood up. He walked through the crowded barrack.

There were no beds, just one thin blanket per bridgeman. One had to choose whether to use it for cushioning or warmth. You could freeze or you could ache. Those were a bridgeman's options, though several of the bridgemen had found a third use for the blankets. They wrapped them around their heads, as if to block out sight, sound, and smell. To hide from the world.

The world would find them anyway. It was good at these kinds of games.

Rain fell in sheets outside, the wind still stiff. Flashes lit the western horizon, where the center of the storm flew onward. This was an hour or so before the riddens, and was as early as one would want to go out in a highstorm.

Well, one never *wanted* to go out in a highstorm. But this was about as early as it was *safe* to go out. The lightning had passed; the winds were manageable.

He passed through the dim lumberyard, hunched against the wind. Branches lay scattered about like bones in a whitespine's lair. Leaves were plastered by rainwater to the rough sides of barracks. Kaladin splashed through puddles that chilled and numbed his feet. That felt good; they were still sore from the bridge run earlier.

Waves of icy rain blew across him, wetting his hair, dripping down his face and into his scruffy beard. He hated having a beard, particularly the way the whiskers itched at the corners of his mouth. Beards were like axehound pups. Boys dreamed of the day they'd get one, never realizing how annoying they could be.

"Out for a stroll, Your Lordship?" a voice said.

Kaladin looked up to find Gaz huddled in a nearby hollow between two of the barracks. Why was he out in the rain?

Ah. Gaz had fastened a small metal basket on the leeward wall of one of the barracks, and a soft glowing light came from within. He left his spheres out in the storm, then had come out early to retrieve them.

It was a risk. Even a sheltered basket could get torn free. Some people believed that the shades of the Lost Radiants haunted the storms, stealing spheres. Perhaps that was true. But during his time in the army, Kaladin had known more than one man who had been wounded sneaking around during full storm, looking for spheres. No doubt the superstition was due to more worldly thieves.

There were safer ways to infuse spheres. Moneychangers would exchange dun spheres for infused ones, or you could pay them to infuse yours in one of their safely guarded nests.

"What are you doing?" Gaz demanded. The short, one-eyed man clutched the basket to his chest. "I'll have you strung up if you've stolen anyone's spheres."

Kaladin turned away from him.

"Storm you! I'll have you strung up anyway! Don't think you can run away; there are still sentries. You—"

"I'm going to the Honor Chasm," Kaladin said quietly. His voice would barely be audible over the storm.

Gaz shut up. The Honor Chasm. He lowered his metal basket and made no further objections. There was a certain deference given to men who took that road.

Kaladin continued to cross the courtyard.

"Lordling," Gaz called.

Kaladin turned.

"Leave the sandals and vest," Gaz said. "I don't want to have to send someone down to fetch them."

Kaladin pulled the leather vest over his head and dropped it to the ground with a splash, then left the sandals in a puddle. That left him in a dirty shirt and stiff brown trousers, both taken off a dead man.

Kaladin walked through the storm to the east side of the lumberyard. A low thundering rumbled from the west. The pathway down to the Shattered Plains was familiar to him now. He'd run this way a dozen times with the bridge crews. There wasn't a battle every day—perhaps one in every two or three—and not every bridge crew had to go on every run. But many of the runs were so draining, so horrific, that they left the bridgemen stunned, almost unresponsive, for the days between.

Many bridgemen had trouble making decisions. The same happened to men who were shocked by battle. Kaladin felt those effects in himself. Even deciding to come to the chasm had been difficult.

But the bleeding eyes of that unnamed boy haunted him. He wouldn't make himself go through something like that again. He *couldn't*.

He reached the base of the slope, wind-driven rain pelting his face as if trying to shove him back toward the camp. He kept on, walking up to the nearest chasm. The Honor Chasm, the bridgemen called it, for it was the place where they could make the one decision left to them. The "honorable" decision. Death.

They weren't natural, these chasms. This one started narrow, but as it ran toward the east, it grew wider—and deeper—

incredibly quickly. At only ten feet long, the crack was already wide enough that it would be difficult to jump. A group of six rope ladders with wooden rungs hung here, affixed to spikes in the rock, used by bridgemen sent down to salvage from corpses that had fallen into the chasms during bridge runs.

Kaladin looked out over the plains. He couldn't see much through the darkness and rain. No, this place wasn't natural. The land had been broken. And now it broke the people who came to it. Kaladin walked past the ladders, a little farther along the edge of the chasm. Then he sat down, legs over the side, looking down as the rain fell around him, the droplets plunging into the dark depths.

To his sides, the more adventurous cremlings had already left their lairs, scuttling about, feeding on plants that lapped up the rainwater. Lirin had once explained that highstorm rains were rich with nutrients. Stormwardens in Kholinar and Vedenar had proven that plants given storm water did better than those given lake or river water. Why was it that scientists were so excited to discover facts that farmers had known for generations and generations?

Kaladin watched the drops of water streaking down toward oblivion in the crevasse. Little suicidal jumpers. Thousands upon thousands of them. Millions upon millions. Who knew what awaited them in that darkness? You couldn't see it, couldn't know it, until you joined them. Leaping off into the void and letting the wind bear you down . . .

"You were right, Father," Kaladin whispered. "You can't stop a storm by blowing harder. You can't save men by killing others. We should all become surgeons. Every last one of us. . . ."

He was rambling. But, oddly, his mind felt clearer now than it had in weeks. Perhaps it was the clarity of perspective. Most men spent their entire lives wondering about the future. Well, his future was empty now. So he turned backward, thinking about his father, about Tien, about decisions.

Once, his life had seemed simple. That was before he'd lost his brother, before he'd been betrayed in Amaram's army.

Would Kaladin go back to those innocent days, if he could? Would he prefer to pretend everything was simple?

No. He'd had no easy fall, like those drops. He'd earned his scars. He'd bounced off walls, bashed his face and hands. He'd killed innocent men by accident. He'd walked beside those with hearts like blackened coals, adoring them. He'd scrambled and climbed and fallen and stumbled.

And now here he was. At the end of it all. Understanding so much more, but somehow feeling no wiser. He climbed to his feet on the lip of that chasm, and could feel his father's disappointment looming over him, like the thunderheads above.

He put one foot out over the void.

"Kaladin!"

He froze at the soft but piercing voice. A translucent form bobbed in the air, approaching through the weakening rain. The figure lunged forward, then sank, then surged higher again, like it was bearing something heavy. Kaladin brought his foot back and held out his hand. Syl unceremoniously alighted upon it, shaped like a skyeel clutching something dark in its mouth.

She switched to the familiar form of a young woman, dress fluttering around her legs. She held in her hands a narrow, dark green leaf with a point divided in three. Blackbane.

"What is this?" Kaladin asked.

She looked exhausted. "These things are heavy!" She lifted the leaf. "I brought it for you!"

He took the leaf between two fingers. Blackbane. Poison. "Why did you bring this to me?" he said harshly.

"I thought . . ." Syl said, shying back. "Well, you kept those other leaves so carefully. Then you lost them when you tried to help that man in the slave cages. I thought it would make you happy to have another one."

Kaladin almost laughed. She had no concept of what she'd done, fetching him a leaf of one of Roshar's most deadly natural poisons because she'd wanted to make him happy. It was ridiculous. And sweet.

"Everything seemed to go wrong when you lost that leaf," Syl said in a soft voice. "Before that, you fought."

"I failed."

She cowered down, kneeling on his palm, misty skirt around her legs, drops of rainwater passing through her and rippling her form. "You don't like it then? I flew so far . . . I almost forgot myself. But I came back. I came *back*, Kaladin."

"Why?" he pled. "Why do you care?"

"Because I do," she said, cocking her head. "I watched you, you know. Back in that army. You'd always find the young, untrained men and protect them, even though it put you into danger. I can remember. Just barely, but I do."

"I failed them. They're dead now."

"They would have died more quickly without you. You made it so they had a family in the army. I remember their gratitude. It's what drew me in the first place. You helped them."

"No," he said, clutching the blackbane in his fingers. "Everything I touch withers and dies." He teetered on the ledge. Thunder rumbled in the distance.

"Those men in the bridge crew," Syl whispered. "You could help them."

"Too late." He closed his eyes, thinking of the dead boy earlier in the day. "It's too late. I've failed. They're dead. They're all going to die, and there's no way out."

"What is one more try, then?" Her voice was soft, yet somehow stronger than the storm. "What could it hurt?"

He paused.

"You can't fail this time, Kaladin. You've said it. They're all going to die anyway."

He thought of Tien, and his dead eyes staring upward.

"I don't know what you mean most of the time when you speak," she said. "My mind is so cloudy. But it seems that if you're worried about hurting people, you shouldn't be afraid to help the bridgemen. What more could you do to them?"

"I . . ."

"One more try, Kaladin," Syl whispered. "Please."

One more try. . . .

The men huddled in the barrack with barely a blanket to

call their own. Frightened of the storm. Frightened of each other. Frightened of what the next day would bring.

One more try. . . .

He thought of himself, crying at the death of a boy he hadn't known. A boy he hadn't even tried to help.

One more try.

Kaladin opened his eyes. He was cold and wet, but he felt a tiny, warm candle flame of determination come alight inside him. He clenched his hand, crushing the blackbane leaf inside, then dropped it over the side of the chasm. He lowered the other hand, which had been holding Syl.

She zipped up into the air, anxious. "Kaladin?"

He stalked away from the chasm, bare feet splashing in puddles and stepping heedlessly on rockbud vines. The incline he'd come down was covered with flat, slatelike plants that had opened like books to the rain, ruffled lacy red and green leaves connecting the two halves. Lifespren—little green blips of light, brighter than Syl but small as spores—danced among the plants, dodging raindrops.

Kaladin strode up, water streaming past him in tiny rivers. At the top, he returned to the bridge yard. It was still empty save for Gaz, who was tying a ripped tarp back into place.

Kaladin had crossed most of the distance to the man before Gaz noticed him. The wiry sergeant scowled. "Too cowardly to go through with it, Your Lordship? Well, if you think I'm giving back—"

He cut off with a gagging noise as Kaladin lunged forward, grabbing Gaz by the neck. Gaz lifted an arm in surprise, but Kaladin batted it away and swept the man's legs out from under him, slamming him down to the rocky ground, throwing up a splash of water. Gaz's eye opened wide with shock and pain, and he began to strangle under the pressure of Kaladin's grip on his throat.

"The world just changed, Gaz," Kaladin said, leaning in close. "I died down at that chasm. Now you've got my vengeful spirit to deal with."

Squirming, Gaz looked about frantically for help that wasn't there. Kaladin didn't have trouble holding him down.

There was one thing about running bridges: If you survived long enough, it built up the muscles.

Kaladin let up slightly on Gaz's neck, allowing him a gasping breath. Then Kaladin leaned down further. "We're going to start over new, you and I. Clean. And I want you to understand something from the start. I'm *already* dead. You can't hurt me. Understand?"

Gaz nodded slowly and Kaladin gave him another breath of frigid, humid air.

"Bridge Four is mine," Kaladin said. "You can assign us tasks, but I'm bridgeleader. The other one died today, so you have to pick a new leader anyway. Understand?"

Gaz nodded again.

"You learn quickly," Kaladin said, letting the man breathe freely. He stepped back, and Gaz hesitantly got to his feet. There was hatred in his eyes, but it was veiled. He seemed worried about something—something more than Kaladin's threats.

"I want to stop paying down my slave debt," Kaladin said. "How much do bridgemen make?"

"Two clearmarks a day," Gaz said, scowling at him and rubbing his neck.

So a slave would make half that. One diamond mark. A pittance, but Kaladin would need it. He'd also need to keep Gaz in line. "I'll start taking my wages," Kaladin said, "but you get to keep one mark in five."

Gaz started, glancing at him in the dim, overcast light.

"For your efforts," Kaladin said.

"For what efforts?"

Kaladin stepped up to him. "Your efforts in staying the *Damnation* out of my way. Understood?"

Gaz nodded again. Kaladin walked away. He hated to waste money on a bribe, but Gaz needed a consistent, re-petitive reminder of why he should avoid getting Kaladin killed. One mark every five days wasn't much of a reminder—but for a man who was willing to risk going out in the middle of a highstorm to protect his spheres, it might be enough.

Kaladin walked back to Bridge Four's small barrack, pulling open the thick wooden door. The men huddled inside, just as he'd left them. But something had changed. Had they always looked that pathetic?

Yes. They had. Kaladin was the one who had changed, not they. He felt a strange dislocation, as if he'd allowed himself to forget—if only in part—the last nine months. He reached back across time, studying the man he had been. The man who'd still fought, and fought well.

He couldn't be that man again—he couldn't erase the scars—but he could *learn* from that man, as a new squad-leader learned from the victorious generals of the past. Kaladin Stormblessed was dead, but Kaladin Bridgeman was of the same blood. A descendant with potential.

Kaladin walked to the first huddled figure. The man wasn't sleeping—who could sleep through a highstorm? The man cringed as Kaladin knelt beside him.

"What's your name?" Kaladin asked, Syl flitting down and studying the man's face. He wouldn't be able to see her.

The man was older, with drooping cheeks, brown eyes, and close-cropped, white-salted hair. His beard was short and he didn't have a slave mark.

"Your name?" Kaladin repeated firmly.

"Storm off," the man said, rolling over.

Kaladin hesitated, then leaned in, speaking in a low voice. "Look, friend. You can either tell me your name, or I'll keep pestering you. Continue refusing, and I'll tow you out into that storm and hang you over the chasm by one leg until you tell me."

The man glanced back over his shoulder. Kaladin nodded slowly, holding the man's gaze.

"Teft," the man finally said. "My name's Teft."

"That wasn't so hard," Kaladin said, holding out his hand. "I'm Kaladin. Your bridgeleader."

The man hesitated, then took Kaladin's hand, wrinkling his brow in confusion. Kaladin vaguely remembered the man. He'd been in the crew for a while, a few weeks at least. Before that, he'd been on another bridge crew. One of the punishments for bridgemen who committed camp infractions was a transfer to Bridge Four.

"Get some rest," Kaladin said, releasing Teft's hand. "We're going to have a hard day tomorrow."

"How do you know?" Teft asked, rubbing his bearded chin.

"Because we're bridgemen," Kaladin said, standing. "*Every* day is hard."

Teft hesitated, then smiled faintly. "Kelek knows that's true."

Kaladin left him, moving down the line of huddled figures. He visited each man, prodding or threatening until the man gave his name. They each resisted. It was as if their names were the last things they owned, and wouldn't be given up cheaply, though they seemed surprised—perhaps even encouraged—that someone cared to ask.

He clutched to these names, repeating each one in his head, holding them like precious gemstones. The names mattered. The men mattered. Perhaps Kaladin would die in the next bridge run, or perhaps he would break under the strain, and give Amaram one final victory. But as he settled down on the ground to plan, he felt that tiny warmth burning steadily within him.

It was the warmth of decisions made and purpose seized. It was responsibility.

Syl alighted on his leg as he sat, whispering the names of the men to himself. She looked encouraged. Bright. Happy. He didn't feel any of that. He felt grim, tired, and wet. But he wrapped himself in the responsibility he had taken, the responsibility for these men. He held to it like a climber clung to his last handhold as he dangled from a cliff side.

He *would* find a way to protect them.

THE END OF

Part One

BRANDON SANDERSON

OTHER WORKS

Elantris

Fleet, fun, and full of surprises, this is a rare epic fantasy debut that doesn't recycle the classics. A city and people go from blessed to bewitched, but when the latest outcast arrives, he brings something new—hope.

Warbreaker

By using Breath and the color in everyday objects, miracles and mischief can be accomplished—and are. But it will take considerable quantities of each for two sisters and a Returned God as they face the challenges ahead.

The Rithmatist

While Joel's mind for figures would make him a genius with the magic of Rithmatics, he doesn't have the spark. But he could be the only one able to protect the other students when they start disappearing. A new favorite of YA readers, this fantasy has lively and feisty characters and an inventive and detailed magic system.

tor-forge.com

Sign up for author updates at: tor-forge.com/author/brandonsanderson

Note: Within series, books are best read in listed order.

PRAISE FOR BRANDON SANDERSON
AND MISTBORN

"*Mistborn* utilizes a well thought-out system of magic. It also has a great cast of believable characters, a plausible world, an intriguing political system, and despite being the first book of a trilogy, a very satisfying ending. Highly recommended to anyone hungry for a good read."

—Robin Hobb

"[Sanderson] has created a fascinating world here, one that deserves a sequel.   —*The Washington Post Book World*

"The characters in this book are amazingly believable. Vin is an eminently sympathetic protagonist whose development over the course of the book is beautifully and realistically delineated. The system of magic is exceedingly clever and well integrated into the complex and plausible world that Vin and Kelsier inhabit. While this is the first in a series, it's an exceedingly satisfying book on its own, and fans of the genre should waste no time picking it up."

—*Romantic Times BOOKreviews*

"Brandon Sanderson made a sensational debut with *Elantris* as another in the recent crop of fantasy writers who use familiar epic forms to produce far-from-generic results. . . . *Mistborn* examines the makings of hero and villain, legend and myth, as seemingly different stages of what may be the same process. . . . [It's an] enjoyable, adventurous read . . . [and] along the way to the grand finale, anyone who cares to can learn a great deal about the underside of power."   —Faren Miller, *Locus*

"Brandon Sanderson is the real thing—an exciting storyteller with a unique and powerful vision." —David Farland

"It's rare for a fiction writer to have much understanding of how leadership works, how communities form, and how love really takes root in the human heart. Sanderson is astonishingly wise."   —Orson Scott Card

Tor Books by Brandon Sanderson

THE STORMLIGHT ARCHIVE

The Way of Kings
Words of Radiance

THE MISTBORN SERIES

Mistborn
The Well of Ascension
The Hero of Ages
The Alloy of Law

Warbreaker
Elantris
The Rithmatist

MISTBORN

THE FINAL EMPIRE

BRANDON SANDERSON

TOR
fantasy

A TOM DOHERTY ASSOCIATES BOOK
NEW YORK

This is a work of fiction. All of the characters, organizations, and events portrayed in this novel are either products of the author's imagination or are used fictitiously.

MISTBORN: THE FINAL EMPIRE

Copyright © 2006 by Brandon Sanderson

Edited by Moshe Feder

Maps by Isaac Stewart

All rights reserved.

A Tor Book
Published by Tom Doherty Associates, LLC
175 Fifth Avenue
New York, NY 10010

www.tor-forge.com

Tor® is a registered trademark of Tom Doherty Associates, LLC.

Printed in the United States of America

FOR BETH SANDERSON,

Who's been reading fantasy
*   For longer than I've been alive,*
And fully deserves
*   To have a grandson as loony as she is.*

THE FINAL EMPIRE

1. Luthadel

THE ASHMOUNTS

2. Tyrian 3. Zerinah
4. Faleast 5. Doriel
6. Morag 7. Kalling 8. Torinost

9. Lake Tyrian
10. Lake Luthadel
11. The Black Lake
12. River Searan

13. North Searan
14. South Searan
15. The River Channerel

2005

LUTH

STEEL GATE

IRON GATE

BRONZE GATE

1. FOUNTAIN SQUARE
2. KREDIK SHAW
3. CANTON OF
ORTHODOXY HEADQUARTERS
4. CANTON OF
FINANCE HEADQUARTERS
5. LUTHADEL GARRISON
6. KEEP VENTURE
7. KEEP HASTING
8. KEEP LEKAL
9. KEEP ERIKELLER
10. CLUBS' SHOP
11. CAMON'S SAFEHOUSE
12. OLD WALL STREET
13. KENTON STREET
14. AHLSTROM SQUARE
15. 15TH CROSSROADS
16. CANAL STREET
17. SKAA MARKET
18. CANTON OF RESOURCE HEADQUARTERS
19. CANTON OF INQUISITION HEADQUARTERS

ADEL

TIN GATE

SOOTWARRENS

PEWTER GATE

BLOCKSTREET

ZINC GATE

INDUSTRIAL DISTRICT

WALL BRIDGE

CHANNEL

THE CRICKS

SOUTHBRIDGE

BRASSGATE

BRASS GATE

COPPER GATE

2003

MISTBORN

Sometimes, I worry that I'm not the hero everyone thinks I am.

The philosophers assure me that this is the time, that the signs have been met. But I still wonder if they have the wrong man. So many people depend on me. They say I will hold the future of the entire world on my arms.

What would they think if they knew that their champion—the Hero of Ages, their savior—doubted himself? Perhaps they wouldn't be shocked at all. In a way, this is what worries me most. Maybe, in their hearts, they wonder—just as I do.

When they see me, do they see a liar?

PROLOGUE

ASH FELL FROM THE SKY.

Lord Tresting frowned, glancing up at the ruddy midday sky as his servants scuttled forward, opening a parasol over Tresting and his distinguished guest. Ashfalls weren't that uncommon in the Final Empire, but Tresting had hoped to avoid getting soot stains on his fine new suit coat and red vest, which had just arrived via canal boat from Luthadel itself. Fortunately, there wasn't much wind; the parasol would likely be effective.

Tresting stood with his guest on a small hilltop patio that overlooked the fields. Hundreds of people in brown smocks worked in the falling ash, caring for the crops. There was a sluggishness to their efforts—but, of course, that was the way of the skaa. The peasants were an indolent, unproductive lot.

They didn't complain, of course; they knew better than that. Instead, they simply worked with bowed heads, moving about their work with quiet apathy. The passing whip of a taskmaster would force them into dedicated motion for a few moments, but as soon as the taskmaster passed, they would return to their languor.

Tresting turned to the man standing beside him on the hill. "One would think," Tresting noted, "that a thousand years of working in fields would have bred them to be a little more effective at it."

The obligator turned, raising an eyebrow—the motion done as if to highlight his most distinctive feature, the intricate tattoos that laced the skin around his eyes. The tattoos were enormous, reaching all the way across his brow and up the sides of his nose. This was a full prelan—a very important obligator indeed. Tresting had his own, personal obligators back at the manor, but they were only minor functionaries, with barely a few marks around their eyes. This man had arrived from Luthadel with the same canal boat that had brought Tresting's new suit.

"You should see city skaa, Tresting," the obligator said, turning back to watch the skaa workers. "These are actually quite diligent compared to those inside Luthadel. You have more . . . direct control over your skaa here. How many would you say you lose a month?"

"Oh, a half dozen or so," Tresting said. "Some to beatings, some to exhaustion."

"Runaways?"

"Never!" Tresting said. "When I first inherited this land from my father, I had a few runaways—but I executed their families. The rest quickly lost heart. I've never understood men who have trouble with their skaa—I find the creatures easy to control, if you show a properly firm hand."

The obligator nodded, standing quietly in his gray robes. He seemed pleased—which was a good thing. The skaa weren't actually Tresting's property. Like all skaa, they belonged to the Lord Ruler; Tresting only leased the workers from his God, much in the same way he paid for the services of His obligators.

The obligator looked down, checking his pocket watch, then glanced up at the sun. Despite the ashfall, the sun was bright this day, shining a brilliant crimson red behind the smoky blackness of the upper sky. Tresting removed a handkerchief and wiped his brow, thankful for the parasol's shade against the midday heat.

"Very well, Tresting," the obligator said. "I will carry your proposal to Lord Venture, as requested. He will have a favorable report from me on your operations here."

Tresting held in a sigh of relief. An obligator was required to witness any contract or business deal between noblemen. True, even a lowly obligator like the ones Tresting employed could serve as such a witness—but it meant so much more to impress Straff Venture's own obligator.

The obligator turned toward him. "I will leave back down the canal this afternoon."

"So soon?" Tresting asked. "Wouldn't you care to stay for supper?"

"No," the obligator replied. "Though there is another matter I wish to discuss with you. I came not only at the behest of Lord Venture, but to . . . look in on some matters for the Canton of Inquisition. Rumors say that you like to dally with your skaa women."

Tresting felt a chill.

The obligator smiled; he likely meant it to be disarming, but Tresting only found it eerie. "Don't worry yourself, Tresting," the obligator said. "If there had been any *real* worries about your actions, a Steel Inquisitor would have been sent here in my place."

Tresting nodded slowly. Inquisitor. He'd never seen one of the inhuman creatures, but he had heard . . . stories.

"I have been satisfied regarding your actions with the skaa women," the obligator said, looking back over the fields. "What I've seen and heard here indicate that you always clean up your messes. A man such as yourself—efficient, productive—could go far in Luthadel. A few more years of work, some inspired mercantile deals, and who knows?"

The obligator turned away, and Tresting found himself smiling. It wasn't a promise, or even an endorsement—for the

most part, obligators were more bureaucrats and witnesses than they were priests—but to hear such praise from one of the Lord Ruler's own servants . . . Tresting knew that some nobility considered the obligators to be unsettling—some men even considered them a bother—but at that moment, Tresting could have kissed his distinguished guest.

Tresting turned back toward the skaa, who worked quietly beneath the bloody sun and the lazy flakes of ash. Tresting had always been a country nobleman, living on his plantation, dreaming of perhaps moving into Luthadel itself. He had heard of the balls and the parties, the glamour and the intrigue, and it excited him to no end.

I'll have to celebrate tonight, he thought. There was that young girl in the fourteenth hovel that he'd been watching for some time. . . .

He smiled again. A few more years of work, the obligator had said. But could Tresting perhaps speed that up, if he worked a little harder? His skaa population had been growing lately. Perhaps if he pushed them a bit more, he could bring in an extra harvest this summer and fulfill his contract with Lord Venture in extra measure.

Tresting nodded as he watched the crowd of lazy skaa, some working with their hoes, others on hands and knees, pushing the ash away from the fledgling crops. They didn't complain. They didn't hope. They barely dared think. That was the way it should be, for they were skaa. They were—

Tresting froze as one of the skaa looked up. The man met Tresting's eyes, a spark—no, a fire—of defiance showing in his expression. Tresting had never seen anything like it, not in the face of a skaa. Tresting stepped backward reflexively, a chill running through him as the strange, straight-backed skaa held his eyes.

And smiled.

Tresting looked away. "Kurdon!" he snapped.

The burly taskmaster rushed up the incline. "Yes, my lord?"

Tresting turned, pointing at . . .

He frowned. Where had that skaa been standing? Working with their heads bowed, bodies stained by soot and sweat,

they were so hard to tell apart. Tresting paused, searching. He thought he knew the place . . . an empty spot, where nobody now stood.

But, no. That couldn't be it. The man couldn't have disappeared from the group so quickly. Where would he have gone? He must be in there, somewhere, working with his head now properly bowed. Still, his moment of apparent defiance was inexcusable.

"My lord?" Kurdon asked again.

The obligator stood at the side, watching curiously. It would not be wise to let the man know that one of the skaa had acted so brazenly.

"Work the skaa in that southern section a little harder," Tresting ordered, pointing. "I see them being sluggish, even for skaa. Beat a few of them."

Kurdon shrugged, but nodded. It wasn't much of a reason for a beating—but, then, he didn't need much of a reason to give the workers a beating.

They were, after all, only skaa.

Kelsier had heard stories.

He had heard whispers of times when once, long ago, the sun had not been red. Times when the sky hadn't been clogged by smoke and ash, when plants hadn't struggled to grow, and when skaa hadn't been slaves. Times before the Lord Ruler. Those days, however, were nearly forgotten. Even the legends were growing vague.

Kelsier watched the sun, his eyes following the giant red disk as it crept toward the western horizon. He stood quietly for a long moment, alone in the empty fields. The day's work was done; the skaa had been herded back to their hovels. Soon the mists would come.

Eventually, Kelsier sighed, then turned to pick his way across the furrows and pathways, weaving between large heaps of ash. He avoided stepping on the plants—though he wasn't sure why he bothered. The crops hardly seemed worth the effort. Wan, with wilted brown leaves, the plants seemed as depressed as the people who tended them.

The skaa hovels loomed in the waning light. Already, Kelsier could see the mists beginning to form, clouding the air, and giving the moundlike buildings a surreal, intangible look. The hovels stood unguarded; there was no need for watchers, for no skaa would venture outside once night arrived. Their fear of the mists was far too strong.

I'll have to cure them of that someday, Kelsier thought as he approached one of the larger buildings. *But, all things in their own time.* He pulled open the door and slipped inside.

Conversation stopped immediately. Kelsier closed the door, then turned with a smile to confront the room of about thirty skaa. A firepit burned weakly at the center, and the large cauldron beside it was filled with vegetable-dappled water—the beginnings of an evening meal. The soup would be bland, of course. Still, the smell was enticing.

"Good evening, everyone," Kelsier said with a smile, resting his pack beside his feet and leaning against the door. "How was your day?"

His words broke the silence, and the women returned to their dinner preparations. A group of men sitting at a crude table, however, continued to regard Kelsier with dissatisfied expressions.

"Our day was filled with work, traveler," said Tepper, one of the skaa elders. "Something you managed to avoid."

"Fieldwork hasn't ever really suited me," Kelsier said. "It's far too hard on my delicate skin." He smiled, holding up hands and arms that were lined with layers and layers of thin scars. They covered his skin, running lengthwise, as if some beast had repeatedly raked its claws up and down his arms.

Tepper snorted. He was young to be an elder, probably barely into his forties—at most, he might be five years Kelsier's senior. However, the scrawny man held himself with the air of one who liked to be in charge.

"This is no time for levity," Tepper said sternly. "When we harbor a traveler, we expect him to behave himself and avoid suspicion. When you ducked away from the fields this morning, you could have earned a whipping for the men around you."

"True," Kelsier said. "But those men could also have been

whipped for standing in the wrong place, for pausing too long, or for coughing when a taskmaster walked by. I once saw a man beaten because his master claimed that he had 'blinked inappropriately.'"

Tepper sat with narrow eyes and a stiff posture, his arm resting on the table. His expression was unyielding.

Kelsier sighed, rolling his eyes. "Fine. If you want me to go, I'll be off then." He slung his pack up on his shoulder and nonchalantly pulled open the door.

Thick mist immediately began to pour through the portal, drifting lazily across Kelsier's body, pooling on the floor and creeping across the dirt like a hesitant animal. Several people gasped in horror, though most of them were too stunned to make a sound. Kelsier stood for a moment, staring out into the dark mists, their shifting currents lit feebly by the cooking pit's coals.

"Close the door." Tepper's words were a plea, not a command.

Kelsier did as requested, pushing the door closed and stemming the flood of white mist. "The mist is not what you think. You fear it far too much."

"Men who venture into the mist lose their souls," a woman whispered. Her words raised a question. Had Kelsier walked in the mists? What, then, had happened to his soul?

If you only knew, Kelsier thought. "Well, I guess this means I'm staying." He waved for a boy to bring him a stool. "It's a good thing, too—it would have been a shame for me to leave before I shared my news."

More than one person perked up at the comment. This was the real reason they tolerated him—the reason even the timid peasants would harbor a man such as Kelsier, a skaa who defied the Lord Ruler's will by traveling from plantation to plantation. A renegade he might be—a danger to the entire community—but he brought news from the outside world.

"I come from the north," Kelsier said. "From lands where the Lord Ruler's touch is less noticeable." He spoke in a clear voice, and people leaned unconsciously toward him as they worked. On the next day, Kelsier's words would be repeated

to the several hundred people who lived in other hovels. The skaa might be subservient, but they were incurable gossips.

"Local lords rule in the West," Kelsier said, "and they are far from the iron grip of the Lord Ruler and his obligators. Some of these distant noblemen are finding that happy skaa make better workers than mistreated skaa. One man, Lord Renoux, has even ordered his taskmasters to stop unauthorized beatings. There are whispers that he's considering paying wages to his plantation skaa, like city craftsmen might earn."

"Nonsense," Tepper said.

"My apologies," Kelsier said. "I didn't realize that Goodman Tepper had been to Lord Renoux's estates recently. When you dined with him last, did he tell you something that he did not tell me?"

Tepper blushed: Skaa did not travel, and they certainly didn't dine with lords. "You think me a fool, traveler," Tepper said, "but I know what you're doing. You're the one they call the Survivor; those scars on your arms give you away. You're a troublemaker—you travel the plantations, stirring up discontent. You eat our food, telling your grand stories and your lies, then you disappear and leave people like me to deal with the false hopes you give our children."

Kelsier raised an eyebrow. "Now, now, Goodman Tepper," he said. "Your worries are completely unfounded. Why, I have no intention of eating your food. I brought my own." With that, Kelsier reached over and tossed his pack onto the earth before Tepper's table. The loose bag slumped to the side, dumping an array of foods to the ground. Fine breads, fruits, and even a few thick, cured sausages bounced free.

A summerfruit rolled across the packed earthen floor and bumped lightly against Tepper's foot. The middle-aged skaa regarded the fruit with stunned eyes. "That's nobleman's food!"

Kelsier snorted. "Barely. You know, for a man of renowned prestige and rank, your Lord Tresting has remarkably poor taste. His pantry is an embarrassment to his noble station."

Tepper paled even further. "That's where you went this afternoon," he whispered. "You went to the manor. You . . . *stole from the master!*"

"Indeed," Kelsier said. "And, might I add that while your lord's taste in food is deplorable, his eye for soldiers is far more impressive. Sneaking into his manor during the day was quite a challenge."

Tepper was still staring at the bag of food. "If the task-masters find this here . . ."

"Well, I suggest you make it disappear then," Kelsier said. "I'd be willing to bet that it tastes a fair bit better than watered-down farlet soup."

Two dozen sets of hungry eyes studied the food. If Tepper intended further arguments, he didn't make them quickly enough, for his silent pause was taken as agreement. Within a few minutes, the bag's contents had been inspected and distributed, and the pot of soup sat bubbling and ignored as the skaa feasted on a meal far more exotic.

Kelsier settled back, leaning against the hovel's wooden wall and watching the people devour their food. He had spoken correctly: The pantry's offerings had been depressingly mundane. However, this was a people who had been fed on nothing but soup and gruel since they were children. To them, breads and fruits were rare delicacies—usually eaten only as aging discards brought down by the house servants.

"Your storytelling was cut short, young man," an elderly skaa noted, hobbling over to sit on a stool beside Kelsier.

"Oh, I suspect there will be time for more later," Kelsier said. "Once all evidence of my thievery has been properly devoured. Don't you want any of it?"

"No need," the old man said. "The last time I tried lords' food, I had stomach pains for three days. New tastes are like new ideas, young man—the older you get, the more difficult they are for you to stomach."

Kelsier paused. The old man was hardly an imposing sight. His leathered skin and bald scalp made him look more frail than they did wise. Yet, he had to be stronger than he looked; few plantation skaa lived to such ages. Many lords didn't allow the elderly to remain home from daily work, and the frequent beatings that made up a skaa's life took a terrible toll on the elderly.

"What was your name again?" Kelsier asked.

"Mennis."

Kelsier glanced back at Tepper. "So, Goodman Mennis, tell me something. Why do you let him lead?"

Mennis shrugged. "When you get to be my age, you have to be very careful where you waste your energy. Some battles just aren't worth fighting." There was an implication in Mennis's eyes; he was referring to things greater than his own struggle with Tepper.

"You're satisfied with this, then?" Kelsier asked, nodding toward the hovel and its half-starved, overworked occupants. "You're content with a life full of beatings and endless drudgery?"

"At least it's a life," Mennis said. "I know what wages, malcontent, and rebellion bring. The eye of the Lord Ruler, and the ire of the Steel Ministry, can be far more terrible than a few whippings. Men like you preach change, but I wonder. Is this a battle we can really fight?"

"You're fighting it already, Goodman Mennis. You're just losing horribly." Kelsier shrugged. "But, what do I know? I'm just a traveling miscreant, here to eat your food and impress your youths."

Mennis shook his head. "You jest, but Tepper might have been right. I fear your visit will bring us grief."

Kelsier smiled. "That's why I didn't contradict him—at least, not on the troublemaker point." He paused, then smiled more deeply. "In fact, I'd say calling me a troublemaker is probably the only accurate thing Tepper has said since I got here."

"How do you do that?" Mennis asked, frowning.

"What?"

"Smile so much."

"Oh, I'm just a happy person."

Mennis glanced down at Kelsier's hands. "You know, I've only seen scars like those on one other person—and he was dead. His body was returned to Lord Tresting as proof that his punishment had been carried out." Mennis looked up at Kelsier. "He'd been caught speaking of rebellion. Tresting sent him to the Pits of Hathsin, where he had worked until he died. The lad lasted less than a month."

Kelsier glanced down at his hands and forearms. They still burned sometimes, though he was certain the pain was only in his mind. He looked up at Mennis and smiled. "You ask why I smile, Goodman Mennis? Well, the Lord Ruler thinks he has claimed laughter and joy for himself. I'm disinclined to let him do so. This is one battle that doesn't take very much effort to fight."

Mennis stared at Kelsier, and for a moment Kelsier thought the old man might smile in return. However, Mennis eventually just shook his head. "I don't know. I just don't—"

The scream cut him off. It came from outside, perhaps to the north, though the mists distorted sounds. The people in the hovel fell silent, listening to the faint, high-pitched yells. Despite the distance and the mist, Kelsier could hear the pain contained in those screams.

Kelsier burned tin.

It was simple for him now, after years of practice. The tin sat with other Allomantic metals within his stomach, swallowed earlier, waiting for him to draw upon them. He reached inside with his mind and touched the tin, tapping powers he still barely understood. The tin flared to life within him, burning his stomach like the sensation of a hot drink swallowed too quickly.

Allomantic power surged through his body, enhancing his senses. The room around him became crisp, the dull firepit flaring to near blinding brightness. He could feel the grain in the wood of the stool beneath him. He could still taste the remnants of the loaf of bread he'd snacked on earlier. Most importantly, he could hear the screams with supernatural ears. Two separate people were yelling. One was an older woman, the other a younger woman—perhaps a child. The younger screams were getting farther and farther away.

"Poor Jess," a nearby woman said, her voice booming in Kelsier's enhanced ears. "That child of hers was a curse. It's better for skaa not to have pretty daughters."

Tepper nodded. "Lord Tresting was sure to send for the girl sooner or later. We all knew it. Jess knew it."

"Still a shame, though," another man said.

The screams continued in the distance. Burning tin, Kelsier was able to judge the direction accurately. Her voice was moving toward the lord's manor. The sounds set something off within him, and he felt his face flush with anger.

Kelsier turned. "Does Lord Tresting ever return the girls after he's finished with them?"

Old Mennis shook his head. "Lord Tresting is a law-abiding nobleman—he has the girls killed after a few weeks. He doesn't want to catch the eye of the Inquisitors."

That was the Lord Ruler's command. He couldn't afford to have half-breed children running around—children who might possess powers that skaa weren't even supposed to know existed. . . .

The screams waned, but Kelsier's anger only built. The yells reminded him of other screams. A woman's screams from the past. He stood abruptly, stool toppling to the ground behind him.

"Careful, lad," Mennis said apprehensively. "Remember what I said about wasting energy. You'll never raise that rebellion of yours if you get yourself killed tonight."

Kelsier glanced toward the old man. Then, through the screams and the pain, he forced himself to smile. "I'm not here to lead a rebellion among you, Goodman Mennis. I just want to stir up a little trouble."

"What good could that do?"

Kelsier's smile deepened. "New days are coming. Survive a little longer, and you just might see great happenings in the Final Empire. I bid you all thanks for your hospitality."

With that, he pulled open the door and strode out into the mist.

Mennis lay awake in the early hours of morning. It seemed that the older he became, the more difficult it was for him to sleep. This was particularly true when he was troubled about something, such as the traveler's failure to return to the hovel.

Mennis hoped that Kelsier had come to his senses and decided to move on. However, that prospect seemed unlikely; Mennis had seen the fire in Kelsier's eyes. It seemed such a

shame that a man who had survived the Pits would instead find death here, on a random plantation, trying to protect a girl everyone else had given up for dead.

How would Lord Tresting react? He was said to be particularly harsh with anyone who interrupted his nighttime enjoyments. If Kelsier had managed to disturb the master's pleasures, Tresting might easily decide to punish the rest of his skaa by association.

Eventually, the other skaa began to awake. Mennis lay on the hard earth—bones aching, back complaining, muscles exhausted—trying to decide if it was worth rising. Each day, he nearly gave up. Each day, it was a little harder. One day, he would just stay in the hovel, waiting until the taskmasters came to kill those who were too sick or too elderly to work.

But not today. He could see too much fear in the eyes of the skaa—they knew that Kelsier's nighttime activities would bring trouble. They needed Mennis; they looked to him. He needed to get up.

And so he did. Once he started moving, the pains of age decreased slightly, and he was able to shuffle out of the hovel toward the fields, leaning on a younger man for support.

It was then that he caught a scent in the air. "What's that?" he asked. "Do you smell smoke?"

Shum—the lad upon whom Mennis leaned—paused. The last remnants of the night's mist had burned away, and the red sun was rising behind the sky's usual haze of blackish clouds.

"I always smell smoke, lately," Shum said. "The Ashmounts are violent this year."

"No," Mennis said, feeling increasingly apprehensive. "This is different." He turned to the north, toward where a group of skaa were gathering. He let go of Shum, shuffling toward the group, feet kicking up dust and ash as he moved.

At the center of the group of people, he found Jess. Her daughter, the one they all assumed had been taken by Lord Tresting, stood beside her. The young girl's eyes were red from lack of sleep, but she appeared unharmed.

"She came back not long after they took her," the woman was explaining. "She came and pounded on the door, crying in the mist. Flen was sure it was just a mistwraith impersonat-

ing her, but I had to let her in! I don't care what he says, I'm not giving her up. I brought her out in the sunlight, and she didn't disappear. That proves she's not a mistwraith!"

Mennis stumbled back from the growing crowd. Did none of them see it? No taskmasters came to break up the group. No soldiers came to make the morning population counts. Something was very wrong. Mennis continued to the north, moving frantically toward the manor house.

By the time he arrived, others had noticed the twisting line of smoke that was just barely visible in the morning light. Mennis wasn't the first to arrive at the edge of the short hilltop plateau, but the group made way for him when he did.

The manor house was gone. Only a blackened, smoldering scar remained.

"By the Lord Ruler!" Mennis whispered. "What happened here?"

"He killed them all."

Mennis turned. The speaker was Jess's girl. She stood looking down at the fallen house, a satisfied expression on her youthful face.

"They were dead when he brought me out," she said. "All of them—the soldiers, the taskmasters, the lords . . . dead. Even Lord Tresting and his obligators. The master had left me, going to investigate when the noises began. On the way out, I saw him lying in his own blood, stab wounds in his chest. The man who saved me threw a torch in the building as we left."

"This man," Mennis said. "He had scars on his hands and arms, reaching past the elbows?"

The girl nodded silently.

"What kind of demon was that man?" one of the skaa muttered uncomfortably.

"Mistwraith," another whispered, apparently forgetting that Kelsier had gone out during the day.

But he did go out into the mist, Mennis thought. *And, how did he accomplish a feat like this . . . ? Lord Tresting kept over two dozen soldiers! Did Kelsier have a hidden band of rebels, perhaps?*

Kelsier's words from the night before sounded in his ears. *New days are coming. . . .*

"But, what of us?" Tepper asked, terrified. "What will happen when the Lord Ruler hears this? He'll think that we did it! He'll send us to the Pits, or maybe just send his koloss to slaughter us outright! Why would that troublemaker do something like this? Doesn't he understand the damage he's done?"

"He understands," Mennis said. "He warned us, Tepper. He came to stir up trouble."

"But, why?"

"Because he knew we'd never rebel on our own, so he gave us no choice."

Tepper paled.

Lord Ruler, Mennis thought. *I can't do this. I can barely get up in the mornings—I can't save this people.*

But what other choice was there?

Mennis turned. "Gather the people, Tepper. We must flee before word of this disaster reaches the Lord Ruler."

"Where will we go?"

"The caves to the east," Mennis said. "Travelers say there are rebel skaa hiding in them. Perhaps they'll take us in."

Tepper paled further. "But . . . we'd have to travel for days. Spend nights *in the mist.*"

"We can do that," Mennis said, "or we can stay here and die."

Tepper stood frozen for a moment, and Mennis thought the shock of it all might have overwhelmed him. Eventually, however, the younger man scurried off to gather the others, as commanded.

Mennis sighed, looking up toward the trailing line of smoke, cursing the man Kelsier quietly in his mind.

New days indeed.

THE SURVIVOR
OF HATHSIN

I consider myself to be a man of principle. But, what man does not? Even the cutthroat, I have noticed, considers his actions "moral" after a fashion.

Perhaps another person, reading of my life, would name me a religious tyrant. He could call me arrogant. What is to make that man's opinion any less valid than my own?

I guess it all comes down to one fact: In the end, I'm the one with the armies.

1

ASH FELL FROM THE SKY.

Vin watched the downy flakes drift through the air. Leisurely. Careless. Free. The puffs of soot fell like black snowflakes, descending upon the dark city of Luthadel. They drifted in corners, blowing in the breeze and curling in tiny whirlwinds over the cobblestones. They seemed so uncaring. What would that be like?

Vin sat quietly in one of the crew's watch-holes—a hidden alcove built into the bricks on the side of the safe house. From within it, a crewmember could watch the street for signs of danger. Vin wasn't on duty; the watch-hole was simply one of the few places where she could find solitude.

And Vin liked solitude. *When you're alone, no one can betray you.* Reen's words. Her brother had taught her so many things, then had reinforced them by doing what he'd always

promised he would—by betraying her himself. *It's the only way you'll learn. Anyone will betray you, Vin. Anyone.*

The ash continued to fall. Sometimes, Vin imagined she was like the ash, or the wind, or the mist itself. A thing without thought, capable of simply *being*, not thinking, caring, or hurting. Then she could be . . . free.

She heard shuffling a short distance away, then the trapdoor at the back of the small chamber snapped open.

"Vin!" Ulef said, sticking his head into the room. "There you are! Camon's been searching for you for a half hour."

That's kind of why I hid in the first place.

"You should get going," Ulef said. "The job's almost ready to begin."

Ulef was a gangly boy. Nice, after his own fashion—naive, if one who had grown up in the underworld could ever really be called "naive." Of course, that didn't mean he wouldn't betray her. Betrayal had nothing to do with friendship; it was a simple fact of survival. Life was harsh on the streets, and if a skaa thief wanted to keep from being caught and executed, he had to be practical.

And ruthlessness was the very most practical of emotions. Another of Reen's sayings.

"Well?" Ulef asked. "You should go. Camon's mad."

When is he not? However, Vin nodded, scrambling out of the cramped—yet comforting—confines of the watch-hole. She brushed past Ulef and hopped out of the trapdoor, moving into a hallway, then a run-down pantry. The room was one of many at the back of the store that served as a front for the safe house. The crew's lair itself was hidden in a tunneled stone cavern beneath the building.

She left the building through a back door, Ulef trailing behind her. The job would happen a few blocks away, in a richer section of town. It was an intricate job—one of the most complex Vin had ever seen. Assuming Camon wasn't caught, the payoff would be great indeed. If he was caught . . . Well, scamming noblemen and obligators was a very dangerous profession—but it certainly beat working in the forges or the textile mills.

Vin exited the alleyway, moving out onto a dark, tenement-

lined street in one of the city's many skaa slums. Skaa too sick to work lay huddled in corners and gutters, ash drifting around them. Vin kept her head down and pulled up her cloak's hood against the still falling flakes.

Free. No, I'll never be free. Reen made certain of that when he left.

"There you are!" Camon lifted a squat, fat finger and jabbed it toward her face. "Where were you?"

Vin didn't let hatred or rebellion show in her eyes. She simply looked down, giving Camon what he expected to see. There were other ways to be strong. That lesson she had learned on her own.

Camon growled slightly, then raised his hand and backhanded her across the face. The force of the blow threw Vin back against the wall, and her cheek blazed with pain. She slumped against the wood, but bore the punishment silently. Just another bruise. She was strong enough to deal with it. She'd done so before.

"Listen," Camon hissed. "This is an important job. It's worth thousands of boxings—worth more than you a hundred times over. I won't have you fouling it up. Understand?"

Vin nodded.

Camon studied her for a moment, his pudgy face red with anger. Finally, he looked away, muttering to himself.

He was annoyed about something—something more than just Vin. Perhaps he had heard about the skaa rebellion several days to the north. One of the provincial lords, Themos Tresting, had apparently been murdered, his manor burned to the ground. Such disturbances were bad for business; they made the aristocracy more alert, and less gullible. That, in turn, could cut seriously into Camon's profits.

He's looking for someone to punish, Vin thought. *He always gets nervous before a job.* She looked up at Camon, tasting blood on her lip. She must have let some of her confidence show, because he glanced at her out of the corner of his eye, and his expression darkened. He raised his hand, as if to strike her again.

Vin used up a bit of her Luck.

She expended just a smidgen; she'd need the rest for the job. She directed the Luck at Camon, calming his nervousness. The crewleader paused—oblivious of Vin's touch, yet feeling its effects nonetheless. He stood for a moment; then he sighed, turning away and lowering his hand.

Vin wiped her lip as Camon waddled away. The thiefmaster looked very convincing in his nobleman's suit. It was as rich a costume as Vin had ever seen—it had a white shirt overlaid by a deep green vest with engraved gold buttons. The black suit coat was long, after the current fashion, and he wore a matching black hat. His fingers sparkled with rings, and he even carried a fine dueling cane. Indeed, Camon did an excellent job of imitating a nobleman; when it came to playing a role, there were few thieves more competent than Camon. Assuming he could keep his temper under control.

The room itself was less impressive. Vin pulled herself to her feet as Camon began to snap at some of the other crewmembers. They had rented one of the suites at the top of a local hotel. Not too lavish—but that was the idea. Camon was going to be playing the part of "Lord Jedue," a country nobleman who had hit upon hard financial times and come to Luthadel to get some final, desperate contracts.

The main room had been transformed into a sort of audience chamber, set with a large desk for Camon to sit behind, the walls decorated with cheap pieces of art. Two men stood beside the desk, dressed in formal stewards' clothing; they would play the part of Camon's manservants.

"What is this ruckus?" a man asked, entering the room. He was tall, dressed in a simple gray shirt and a pair of slacks, with a thin sword tied at his waist. Theron was the other crewleader—this particular scam was actually his. He'd brought in Camon as a partner; he'd needed someone to play Lord Jedue, and everyone knew that Camon was one of the best.

Camon looked up. "Hum? Ruckus? Oh, that was just a minor discipline problem. Don't bother yourself, Theron." Camon punctuated his remark with a dismissive wave of the hand—there was a reason he played such a good aristocrat.

He was arrogant enough that he could have been from one of the Great Houses.

Theron's eyes narrowed. Vin knew what the man was probably thinking: He was deciding how risky it would be to put a knife in Camon's fat back once the scam was over. Eventually, the taller crewleader looked away from Camon, glancing at Vin. "Who's this?" he asked.

"Just a member of my crew," Camon said.

"I thought we didn't need anyone else."

"Well, we need her," Camon said. "Ignore her. My end of the operation is none of your concern."

Theron eyed Vin, obviously noting her bloodied lip. She glanced away. Theron's eyes lingered on her, however, running down the length of her body. She wore a simple white buttoned shirt and a pair of overalls. Indeed, she was hardly enticing; scrawny with a youthful face, she supposedly didn't even look her sixteen years. Some men preferred such women, however.

She considered using a bit of Luck on him, but eventually he turned away. "The obligator is nearly here," Theron said. "Are you ready?"

Camon rolled his eyes, settling his bulk down into the chair behind the desk. "Everything is perfect. Leave me be, Theron! Go back to your room and wait."

Theron frowned, then spun and walked from the room, muttering to himself.

Vin scanned the room, studying the decor, the servants, the atmosphere. Finally, she made her way to Camon's desk. The crewleader sat riffling through a stack of papers, apparently trying to decide which ones to put out on the desktop.

"Camon," Vin said quietly, "the servants are too fine."

Camon frowned, looking up. "What is that you're babbling?"

"The servants," Vin repeated, still speaking in a soft whisper. "Lord Jedue is supposed to be desperate. He'd have rich clothing left over from before, but he wouldn't be able to afford such rich servants. He'd use skaa."

Camon glared at her, but he paused. Physically, there was little difference between noblemen and skaa. The servants Camon had appointed, however, were dressed as minor

noblemen—they were allowed to wear colorful vests, and they stood a little more confidently.

"The obligator has to think that you're nearly impoverished," Vin said. "Pack the room with a lot of skaa servants instead."

"What do you know?" Camon said, scowling at her.

"Enough." She immediately regretted the word; it sounded too rebellious. Camon raised a bejeweled hand, and Vin braced herself for another slap. She couldn't afford to use up any more Luck. She had precious little remaining anyway.

However, Camon didn't hit her. Instead, he sighed and rested a pudgy hand on her shoulder. "Why do you insist on provoking me, Vin? You know the debts your brother left when he ran away. Do you realize that a less merciful man than myself would have sold you to the whoremasters long ago? How would you like that, serving in some nobleman's bed until he grew tired of you and had you executed?"

Vin looked down at her feet.

Camon's grip grew tight, his fingers pinching her skin where neck met shoulder, and she gasped in pain despite herself. He grinned at the reaction.

"Honestly, I don't know why I keep you, Vin," he said, increasing the pressure of his grip. "I should have gotten rid of you months ago, when your brother betrayed me. I suppose I just have too kindly a heart."

He finally released her, then pointed for her to stand over by the side of the room, next to a tall indoor plant. She did as ordered, orienting herself so she had a good view of the entire room. As soon as Camon looked away, she rubbed her shoulder. *Just another pain. I can deal with pain.*

Camon sat for a few moments. Then, as expected, he waved to the two "servants" at his side.

"You two!" he said. "You're dressed too richly. Go put on something that makes you look like skaa servants instead—and bring back six more men with you when you come."

Soon, the room was filled as Vin had suggested. The obligator arrived a short time later.

Vin watched Prelan Laird step haughtily into the room. Shaved bald like all obligators, he wore a set of dark gray robes. The Ministry tattoos around his eyes identified him as

a prelan, a senior bureaucrat in the Ministry's Canton of Finance. A set of lesser obligators trailed behind him, their eye tattoos far less intricate.

Camon rose as the prelan entered, a sign of respect—something even the highest of Great House noblemen would show to an obligator of Laird's rank. Laird gave no bow or acknowledgment of his own, instead striding forward and taking the seat in front of Camon's desk. One of the crewmen impersonating a servant rushed forward, bringing chilled wine and fruit for the obligator.

Laird picked at the fruit, letting the servant stand obediently, holding the platter of food as if he were a piece of furniture. "Lord Jedue," Laird finally said. "I am glad we finally have the opportunity to meet."

"As am I, Your Grace," Camon said.

"Why is it, again, that you were unable to come to the Canton building, instead requiring that I visit you here?"

"My knees, Your Grace," Camon said. "My physicians recommend that I travel as little as possible."

And you were rightly apprehensive about being drawn into a Ministry stronghold, Vin thought.

"I see," Laird said. "Bad knees. An unfortunate attribute in a man who deals in transportation."

"I don't have to go on the trips, Your Grace," Camon said, bowing his head. "Just organize them."

Good, Vin thought. *Make sure you remain subservient, Camon. You need to seem desperate.*

Vin needed this scam to succeed. Camon threatened her and he beat her—but he considered her a good-luck charm. She wasn't sure if he knew why his plans went better when she was in the room, but he had apparently made the connection. That made her valuable—and Reen had always said that the surest way to stay alive in the underworld was to make yourself indispensable.

"I see," Laird said again. "Well, I fear that our meeting has come too late for your purposes. The Canton of Finance has already voted on your proposal."

"So soon?" Camon asked with genuine surprise.

"Yes," Laird replied, taking a sip of his wine, still not dis-

missing the servant. "We have decided not to accept your contract."

Camon sat for a moment, stunned. "I'm sorry to hear that, Your Grace."

Laird came to meet you, Vin thought. *That means he's still in a position to negotiate.*

"Indeed," Camon continued, seeing what Vin had. "That is especially unfortunate, as I was ready to make the Ministry an even better offer."

Laird raised a tattooed eyebrow. "I doubt it will matter. There is an element of the Council who feels that the Canton would receive better service if we found a more stable house to transport our people."

"That would be a grave mistake," Camon said smoothly. "Let us be frank, Your Grace. We both know that this contract is House Jedue's last chance. Now that we've lost the Farwan deal, we cannot afford to run our canal boats to Luthadel anymore. Without the Ministry's patronage, my house is financially doomed."

"This is doing very little to persuade me, Your Lordship," the obligator said.

"Isn't it?" Camon asked. "Ask yourself this, Your Grace— who will serve you better? Will it be the house that has dozens of contracts to divide its attention, or the house that views your contract as its last hope? The Canton of Finance will not find a more accommodating partner than a desperate one. Let my boats be the ones that bring your acolytes down from the north—let my soldiers escort them—and you will not be disappointed."

Good, Vin thought.

"I . . . see," the obligator said, now troubled.

"I would be willing to give you an extended contract, locked in at the price of fifty boxings a head per trip, Your Grace. Your acolytes would be able to travel our boats at their leisure, and would always have the escorts they need."

The obligator raised an eyebrow. "That's half the former fee."

"I told you," Camon said. "We're desperate. My house *needs* to keep its boats running. Fifty boxings will not make us a profit, but that doesn't matter. Once we have the Ministry

contract to bring us stability, we can find other contracts to fill our coffers."

Laird looked thoughtful. It was a fabulous deal—one that might ordinarily have been suspicious. However, Camon's presentation created the image of a house on the brink of financial collapse. The other crewleader, Theron, had spent five years building, scamming, and finagling to create this moment. The Ministry would be remiss not to consider the opportunity.

Laird was realizing just that. The Steel Ministry was not just the force of bureaucracy and legal authority in the Final Empire—it was like a noble house unto itself. The more wealth it had, the better its own mercantile contracts, the more leverage the various Ministry Cantons had with each other—and with the noble houses.

Laird was still obviously hesitant, however. Vin could see the look in his eyes, the suspicion she knew well. He was not going to take the contract.

Now, Vin thought, *It's my turn.*

Vin used her Luck on Laird. She reached out tentatively—not even really sure what she was doing, or why she could even do it. Yet her touch was instinctive, trained through years of subtle practice. She'd been ten years old before she'd realized that other people couldn't do what she could.

She pressed against Laird's emotions, dampening them. He became less suspicious, less afraid. Docile. His worries melted away, and Vin could see a calm sense of control begin to assert itself in his eyes.

Yet, Laird still seemed slightly uncertain. Vin pushed harder. He cocked his head, looking thoughtful. He opened his mouth to speak, but she pushed against him again, desperately using up her last pinch of Luck.

He paused again. "Very well," he finally said. "I will take this new proposal to the Council. Perhaps an agreement can still be reached."

If men read these words, let them know that power is a heavy burden. Seek not to be bound by its chains. The Terris prophecies say that I will have the power to save the world.

They hint, however, that I will have the power to destroy it as well.

2

IN KELSIER'S OPINION, THE CITY of Luthadel—seat of the Lord Ruler—was a gloomy sight. Most of the buildings had been built from stone blocks, with tile roofs for the wealthy, and simple, peaked wooden roofs for the rest. The structures were packed closely together, making them seem squat despite the fact that they were generally three stories high.

The tenements and shops were uniform in appearance; this was not a place to draw attention to oneself. Unless, of course, you were a member of the high nobility.

Interspersed throughout the city were a dozen or so monolithic keeps. Intricate, with rows of spearlike spires or deep archways, these were the homes of the high nobility. In fact, they were the *mark* of a high noble family: Any family who could afford to build a keep and maintain a high-profile presence in Luthadel was considered to be a Great House.

Most of the open ground in the city was around these keeps. The patches of space amid the tenements were like clearings in a forest, the keeps themselves like solitary mounts rising above the rest of the landscape. Black mountains. Like the rest of the city, the keeps were stained by countless years of ashfalls.

Every structure in Luthadel—virtually every structure Kelsier had ever seen—had been blackened to some degree. Even the city wall, upon which Kelsier now stood, was blackened by a patina of soot. Structures were generally darkest at

the top, where the ash gathered, but rainwaters and evening condensations had carried the stains over ledges and down walls. Like paint running down a canvas, the darkness seemed to creep down the sides of buildings in an uneven gradient.

The streets, of course, were completely black. Kelsier stood waiting, scanning the city as a group of skaa workers worked in the street below, clearing away the latest mounds of ash. They'd take it to the River Channerel, which ran through the center of the city, sending the piles of ash to be washed away, lest it pile up and eventually bury the city. Sometimes, Kelsier wondered why the entire empire wasn't just one big mound of ash. He supposed the ash must break down into soil eventually. Yet, it took a ridiculous amount of effort to keep cities and fields clear enough to be used.

Fortunately, there were always enough skaa to do the work. The workers below him wore simple coats and trousers, ash-stained and worn. Like the plantation workers he had left behind several weeks before, they worked with beaten-down, despondent motions. Other groups of skaa passed the workers, responding to the bells in the distance, chiming the hour and calling them to their morning's work at the forges or mills. Luthadel's main export was metal; the city was home to hundreds of forges and refineries. However, the surgings of the river provided excellent locations for mills, both to grind grains and make textiles.

The skaa continued to work. Kelsier turned away from them, looking up into the distance, toward the city center, where the Lord Ruler's palace loomed like some kind of massive, multi-spined insect. Kredik Shaw, the Hill of a Thousand Spires. The palace was several times the size of any nobleman's keep, and was by far the largest building in the city.

Another ashfall began as Kelsier stood contemplating the city, the flakes falling lightly down upon the streets and buildings. *A lot of ashfalls, lately,* he thought, glad for the excuse to pull up the hood on his cloak. *The Ashmounts must be active.*

It was unlikely that anyone in Luthadel would recognize him—it had been three years since his capture. Still, the hood was reassuring. If all went well, there would come a time

when Kelsier would want to be seen and recognized. For now, anonymity was probably better.

Eventually, a figure approached along the wall. The man, Dockson, was shorter than Kelsier, and he had a squarish face that seemed well suited to his moderately stocky build. A nondescript brown hooded cloak covered his black hair, and he wore the same short half beard that he'd sported since his face had first put forth whiskers some twenty years before.

He, like Kelsier, wore a nobleman's suit: colored vest, dark coat and trousers, and a thin cloak to keep off the ash. The clothing wasn't rich, but it was aristocratic—indicative of the Luthadel middle class. Most men of noble birth weren't wealthy enough to be considered part of a Great House—yet, in the Final Empire, nobility wasn't just about money. It was about lineage and history; the Lord Ruler was immortal, and he apparently still remembered the men who had supported him during the early years of his reign. The descendants of those men, no matter how poor they became, would always be favored.

The clothing would keep passing guard patrols from asking too many questions. In the cases of Kelsier and Dockson, of course, that clothing was a lie. Neither was actually noble— though, technically, Kelsier was a half-blood. In many ways, however, that was worse than being just a normal skaa.

Dockson strolled up next to Kelsier, then leaned against the battlement, resting a pair of stout arms on the stone. "You're a few days late, Kell."

"I decided to make a few extra stops in the plantations to the north."

"Ah," Dockson said. "So you *did* have something to do with Lord Tresting's death."

Kelsier smiled. "You could say that."

"His murder caused quite a stir among the local nobility."

"That was kind of the intention," Kelsier said. "Though, to be honest, I wasn't planning anything quite so dramatic. It was almost more of an accident than anything else."

Dockson raised an eyebrow. "How do you 'accidentally' kill a nobleman in his own mansion?"

"With a knife in the chest," Kelsier said lightly. "Or, rather, a pair of knives in the chest—it always pays to be careful."

Dockson rolled his eyes.

"His death isn't exactly a loss, Dox," Kelsier said. "Even among the nobility, Tresting had a reputation for cruelty."

"I don't care about Tresting," Dockson said. "I'm just considering the state of insanity that led me to plan another job with you. Attacking a provincial lord in his manor house, surrounded by guards . . . Honestly, Kell, I'd nearly forgotten how foolhardy you can be."

"Foolhardy?" Kelsier asked with a laugh. "That wasn't foolhardy—that was just a small diversion. You should see some of the things I'm *planning* to do!"

Dockson stood for a moment, then he laughed too. "By the Lord Ruler, it's good to have you back, Kell! I'm afraid I've grown rather boring during the last few years."

"We'll fix that," Kelsier promised. He took a deep breath, ash falling lightly around him. Skaa cleaning crews were already back at work on the streets below, brushing up the dark ash. Behind, a guard patrol passed, nodding to Kelsier and Dockson. They waited in silence for the men to pass.

"It's good to be back," Kelsier finally said. "There's something homey about Luthadel—even if it is a depressing, stark pit of a city. You have the meeting organized?"

Dockson nodded. "We can't start until this evening, though. How'd you get in, anyway? I had men watching the gates."

"Hmm? Oh, I snuck in last night."

"But how—" Dockson paused. "Oh, right. That's going to take some getting used to."

Kelsier shrugged. "I don't see why. You always work with Mistings."

"Yes, but this is different," Dockson said. He held up a hand to forestall further argument. "No need, Kell. I'm not hedging—I just said it would take some getting used to."

"Fine. Who's coming tonight?"

"Well, Breeze and Ham will be there, of course. They're very curious about this mystery job of ours—not to mention rather annoyed that I won't tell him what you've been up to these last few years."

"Good," Kelsier said with a smile. "Let them wonder. How about Trap?"

Dockson shook his head. "Trap's dead. The Ministry finally caught up with him a couple months ago. Didn't even bother sending him to the Pits—they beheaded him on the spot."

Kelsier closed his eyes, exhaling softly. It seemed that the Steel Ministry caught up with everyone eventually. Sometimes, Kelsier felt that a skaa Misting's life wasn't so much about surviving as it was about picking the right time to die.

"This leaves us without a Smoker," Kelsier finally said, opening his eyes. "You have any suggestions?"

"Ruddy," Dockson said.

Kelsier shook his head. "No. He's a good Smoker, but he's not a good enough man."

Dockson smiled. "Not a good enough man to be on a thieving crew . . . Kell, I *have* missed working with you. All right, who then?"

Kelsier thought for a moment. "Is Clubs still running that shop of his?"

"As far as I know," Dockson said slowly.

"He's supposed to be one of the best Smokers in the city."

"I suppose," Dockson said. "But . . . isn't he supposed to be kind of hard to work with?"

"He's not so bad," Kelsier said. "Not once you get used to him. Besides, I think he might be . . . amenable to this particular job."

"All right," Dockson said, shrugging. "I'll invite him. I think one of his relatives is a Tineye. Do you want me to invite him too?"

"Sounds good," Kelsier said.

"All right," Dockson said. "Well, beyond that, there's just Yeden. Assuming he's still interested . . ."

"He'll be there," Kelsier said.

"He'd better be," Dockson said. "He'll be the one paying us, after all."

Kelsier nodded, then frowned. "You didn't mention Marsh."

Dockson shrugged. "I warned you. Your brother never did approve of our methods, and now . . . well, you know Marsh. He won't even have anything to do with Yeden and the rebellion anymore, let alone with a bunch of criminals like us. I think

we'll have to find someone else to infiltrate the obligators."

"No," Kelsier said. "He'll do it. I'll just have to stop by to persuade him."

"If you say so." Dockson fell silent then, and the two stood for a moment, leaning against the railing and looking out over the ash-stained city.

Dockson finally shook his head. "This is insane, eh?"

Kelsier smiled. "Feels good, doesn't it?"

Dockson nodded. "Fantastic."

"It will be a job like no other," Kelsier said, looking north—across the city and toward the twisted building at its center.

Dockson stepped away from the wall. "We have a few hours before the meeting. There's something I want to show you. I think there's still time—if we hurry."

Kelsier turned with curious eyes. "Well, I *was* going to go and chastise my prude of a brother. But . . ."

"This will be worth your time," Dockson promised.

Vin sat in the corner of the safe house's main lair. She kept to the shadows, as usual; the more she stayed out of sight, the more the others would ignore her. She couldn't afford to expend Luck keeping the men's hands off of her. She'd barely had time to regenerate what she'd used a few days before, during the meeting with the obligator.

The usual rabble lounged at tables in the room, playing at dice or discussing minor jobs. Smoke from a dozen different pipes pooled at the top of the chamber, and the walls were stained dark from countless years of similar treatment. The floor was darkened with patches of ash. Like most thieving crews, Camon's group wasn't known for its tidiness.

There was a door at the back of the room, and beyond it lay a twisting stone stairway that led up to a false rain grate in an alleyway. This room, like so many others hidden in the imperial capital of Luthadel, wasn't supposed to exist.

Rough laughter came from the front of the chamber, where Camon sat with a half-dozen cronies enjoying a typical afternoon of ale and crass jokes. Camon's table sat beside the bar,

where the overpriced drinks were simply another way Camon exploited those who worked for him. The Luthadel criminal element had learned quite well from the lessons taught by the nobility.

Vin tried her best to remain invisible. Six months before, she wouldn't have believed that her life could actually get worse without Reen. Yet, despite her brother's abusive anger, he had kept the other crewmembers from having their way with Vin. There were relatively few women on thieving crews; generally, those women who got involved with the under-world ended up as whores. Reen had always told her that a girl needed to be tough—tougher, even, than a man—if she wanted to survive.

You think some crewleader is going to want a liability like you on his team? he had said. *I don't even want to have to work with you, and I'm your brother.*

Her back still throbbed; Camon had whipped her the day before. The blood would ruin her shirt, and she wouldn't be able to afford another one. Camon was already retaining her wages to pay the debts Reen had left behind.

But, I am strong, she thought.

That was the irony. The beatings almost didn't hurt any-more, for Reen's frequent abuses had left Vin resilient, while at the same time teaching her how to look pathetic and bro-ken. In a way, the beatings were self-defeating. Bruises and welts mended, but each new lashing left Vin more hardened. Stronger.

Camon stood up. He reached into his vest pocket and pulled out his golden pocket watch. He nodded to one of his companions, then he scanned the room, searching for . . . her.

His eyes locked on Vin. "It's time."

Vin frowned. *Time for what?*

The Ministry's Canton of Finance was an imposing structure—but, then, *everything* about the Steel Ministry tended to be im-posing.

Tall and blocky, the building had a massive rose window in the front, though the glass was dark from the outside. Two

large banners hung down beside the window, the soot-stained red cloth proclaiming praises to the Lord Ruler.

Camon studied the building with a critical eye. Vin could sense his apprehension. The Canton of Finance was hardly the most threatening of Ministry offices—the Canton of Inquisition, or even the Canton of Orthodoxy, had a far more ominous reputation. However, voluntarily entering any Ministry office . . . putting yourself in the power of the obligators . . . well, it was a thing to do only after serious consideration.

Camon took a deep breath, then strode forward, his dueling cane tapping against the stones as he walked. He wore his rich nobleman's suit, and he was accompanied by a half-dozen crewmembers—including Vin—to act as his "servants."

Vin followed Camon up the steps, then waited as one of the crewmembers jumped forward to pull the door open for his "master." Of the six attendants, only Vin seemed to have been told nothing of Camon's plan. Suspiciously, Theron— Camon's supposed partner in the Ministry scam—was nowhere to be seen.

Vin entered the Canton building. Vibrant red light, sparkled with lines of blue, fell from the rose window. A single obligator, with midlevel tattoos around his eyes, sat behind a desk at the end of the extended entryway.

Camon approached, his cane thumping against the carpet as he walked. "I am Lord Jedue," he said.

What are you doing, Camon? Vin thought. *You insisted to Theron that you wouldn't meet with Prelan Laird in his Canton office. Yet, now you're here.*

The obligator nodded, making a notation in his ledger. He waved to the side. "You may take one attendant with you into the waiting chamber. The rest must remain here."

Camon's huff of disdain indicated what he thought of that prohibition. The obligator, however, didn't look up from his ledger. Camon stood for a moment, and Vin couldn't tell if he was genuinely angry or just playing the part of an arrogant nobleman. Finally, he jabbed a finger at Vin.

"Come," he said, turning and waddling toward the indicated door.

The room beyond was lavish and plush, and several noble-

men lounged in various postures of waiting. Camon chose a chair and settled into it, then pointed toward a table set with wine and red-frosted cakes. Vin obediently fetched him a glass of wine and a plate of food, ignoring her own hunger.

Camon began to pick hungrily at the cakes, smacking quietly as he ate.

He's nervous. More nervous, even, than before.

"Once we get in, you will say nothing," Camon grumbled between bites.

"You're betraying Theron," Vin whispered.

Camon nodded.

"But, how? Why?" Theron's plan was complex in execution, but simple in concept. Every year, the Ministry transferred its new acolyte obligators from a northern training facility south to Luthadel for final instruction. Theron had discovered, however, that those acolytes and their overseers brought down with them large amounts of Ministry funds— disguised as baggage—to be strongholded in Luthadel.

Banditry was very difficult in the Final Empire, what with the constant patrols along canal routes. However, if one were running the very canal boats that the acolytes were sailing upon, a robbery could become possible. Arranged at just the right time . . . the guards turning on their passengers . . . a man could make quite a profit, then blame it all on banditry.

"Theron's crew is weak," Camon said quietly. "He expended too many resources on this job."

"But, the return he'll make—" Vin said.

"Will never happen if I take what I can now, then run," Camon said, smiling. "I'll talk the obligators into a down payment to get my caravan boats afloat, then disappear and leave Theron to deal with the disaster when the Ministry realizes that it's been scammed."

Vin stood back, slightly shocked. Setting up a scam like this would have cost Theron thousands upon thousands of boxings—if the deal fell through now, he would be ruined. And, with the Ministry hunting him, he wouldn't even have time to seek revenge. Camon would make a quick profit, as well as rid himself of one of his more powerful rivals.

Theron was a fool to bring Camon into this, she thought.

But, then, the amount Theron had promised to pay Camon was great; he probably assumed that Camon's greed would keep him honest until Theron himself could pull a double cross. Camon had simply worked faster than anyone, even Vin, had expected. How could Theron have known that Camon would undermine the job itself, rather than wait and try and steal the entire haul from the caravan boats?

Vin's stomach twisted. *It's just another betrayal*, she thought sickly. *Why does it still bother me so? Everyone betrays everyone else. That's the way life is. . . .*

She wanted to find a corner—someplace cramped and secluded—and hide. Alone.

Anyone will betray you. Anyone.

But there was no place to go. Eventually, a minor obligator entered and called for Lord Jedue. Vin followed Camon as they were ushered into an audience chamber.

The man who waited inside, sitting behind the audience desk, was not Prelan Laird.

Camon paused in the doorway. The room was austere, bearing only the desk and simple gray carpeting. The stone walls were unadorned, the only window barely a handspan wide. The obligator who waited for them had some of the most intricate tattoos around his eyes that Vin had ever seen. She wasn't even certain what rank they implied, but they extended all the way back to the obligator's ears and up over his forehead.

"Lord Jedue," the strange obligator said. Like Laird, he wore gray robes, but he was very different from the stern, bureaucratic men Camon had dealt with before. This man was lean in a muscular way, and his clean-shaven, triangular head gave him an almost predatory look.

"I was under the impression that I would be meeting with Prelan Laird," Camon said, still not moving into the room.

"Prelan Laird has been called away on other business. I am High Prelan Arriev—head of the board that was reviewing your proposal. You have a rare opportunity to address me directly. I normally don't hear cases in person, but Laird's absence has made it necessary for me to share in some of his work."

Vin's instincts made her tense. *We should go. Now.*

Camon stood for a long moment, and Vin could see him considering. Run now? Or, take a risk for the greater prize? Vin didn't care about prizes; she just wanted to live. Camon, however, had not become crewleader without the occasional gamble. He slowly moved into the room, eyes cautious as he took the seat opposite the obligator.

"Well, High Prelan Arriev," Camon said with a careful voice. "I assume that since I have been called back for another appointment, the board is considering my offer?"

"Indeed we are," the obligator said. "Though I must admit, there are some Council members who are apprehensive about dealing with a family that is so near to economic disaster. The Ministry generally prefers to be conservative in its financial operations."

"I see."

"But," Arriev said, "there are others on the board who are quite eager to take advantage of the savings you offered us."

"And with which group do you identify, Your Grace?"

"I, as of yet, have not made my decision." The obligator leaned forward. "Which is why I noted that you have a rare opportunity. Convince me, Lord Jedue, and you will have your contract."

"Surely Prelan Laird outlined the details of our offer," Camon said.

"Yes, but I would like to hear the arguments from you personally. Humor me."

Vin frowned. She remained near the back of the room, standing near the door, still half convinced she should run.

"Well?" Arriev asked.

"We need this contract, Your Grace," Camon said. "Without it we won't be able to continue our canal shipping operations. Your contract would give us a much needed period of stability—a chance to maintain our caravan boats for a time while we search for other contracts."

Arriev studied Camon for a moment. "Surely you can do better than that, Lord Jedue. Laird said that you were very persuasive—let me hear you *prove* that you deserve our patronage."

Vin prepared her Luck. She could make Arriev more in-

clined to believe . . . but something restrained her. The situation felt wrong.

"We are your best choice, Your Grace," Camon said. "You fear that my house will suffer economic failure? Well, if it does, what have you lost? At worst, my narrowboats would stop running, and you would have to find other merchants to deal with. Yet, if your patronage is enough to maintain my house, then you have found yourself an enviable long-term contract."

"I see," Arriev said lightly. "And why the Ministry? Why not make your deal with someone else? Surely there are other options for your boats—other groups who would jump at such rates."

Camon frowned. "This isn't about money, Your Grace, it is about the victory—the showing of confidence—that we would gain by having a Ministry contract. If you trust us, others will too. I *need* your support." Camon was sweating now. He was probably beginning to regret this gamble. Had he been betrayed? Was Theron behind the odd meeting?

The obligator waited quietly. He could destroy them, Vin knew. If he even suspected that they were scamming him, he could give them over to the Canton of Inquisition. More than one nobleman had entered a Canton building and never returned.

Gritting her teeth, Vin reached out and used her Luck on the obligator, making him less suspicious.

Arriev smiled. "Well, you have convinced me," he suddenly declared.

Camon sighed in relief.

Arriev continued, "Your most recent letter suggested that you need three thousand boxings as an advance to refurbish your equipment and resume shipping operations. See the scribe in the main hallway to finish the paperwork so that you may requisition the necessary funds."

The obligator pulled a sheet of thick bureaucratic paper from a stack, then stamped a seal at the bottom. He proffered it to Camon. "Your contract."

Camon smiled deeply. "I knew coming to the Ministry was the wise choice," he said, accepting the contract. He stood,

nodding respectfully to the obligator, then motioned for Vin to open the door for him.

She did so. *Something is wrong. Something is* very *wrong.* She paused as Camon left, looking back at the obligator. He was still smiling.

A happy obligator was always a bad sign.

Yet, no one stopped them as they passed through the waiting room with its noble occupants. Camon sealed and delivered the contract to the appropriate scribe, and no soldiers appeared to arrest them. The scribe pulled out a small chest filled with coins, and then handed it to Camon with an indifferent hand.

Then, they simply left the Canton building, Camon gathering his other attendants with obvious relief. No cries of alarm. No tromping of soldiers. They were free. Camon had successfully scammed both the Ministry and another crewleader.

Apparently.

Kelsier stuffed another one of the little red-frosted cakes into his mouth, chewing with satisfaction. The fat thief and his scrawny attendant passed through the waiting room, entering the entryway beyond. The obligator who had interviewed the two thieves remained in his office, apparently awaiting his next appointment

"Well?" Dockson asked. "What do you think?"

Kelsier glanced at the cakes. "They're quite good," he said, taking another one. "The Ministry has always had excellent taste—it makes sense that they would provide superior snacks."

Dockson rolled his eyes. "About the girl, Kell."

Kelsier smiled as he piled four of the cakes in his hand, then nodded toward the doorway. The Canton waiting room was growing too busy for the discussion of delicate matters. On the way out, he paused and told the obligator secretary in the corner that they needed to reschedule.

Then the two crossed through the entry chamber—passing the overweight crewleader, who stood speaking with a scribe.

Kelsier stepped out onto the street, pulled his hood up against the still falling ash, then led the way across the street. He paused beside an alleyway, standing where he and Dockson could watch the Canton building's doors.

Kelsier munched contentedly on his cakes. "How'd you find out about her?" he asked between bites.

"Your brother," Dockson replied. "Camon tried to swindle Marsh a few months ago, and he brought the girl with him then, too. Actually, Camon's little good-luck charm is becoming moderately famous in the right circles. I'm still not sure if he knows what she is or not. You know how superstitious thieves can get."

Kelsier nodded, dusting off his hands. "How'd you know she'd be here today?"

Dockson shrugged. "A few bribes in the right place. I've been keeping an eye on the girl ever since Marsh pointed her out to me. I wanted to give you an opportunity to see her work for yourself."

Across the street, the Canton building's door finally opened, and Camon made his way down the steps surrounded by a group of "servants." The small, short-haired girl was with him. The sight of her made Kelsier frown. She had a nervous anxiety to her step, and she jumped slightly whenever someone made a quick move. The right side of her face was still slightly discolored from a partially healed bruise.

Kelsier eyed the self-important Camon. *I'll have to come up with something particularly suitable to do to that man.*

"Poor thing," Dockson muttered.

Kelsier nodded. "She'll be free of him soon enough. It's a wonder no one discovered her before this."

"Your brother was right then?"

Kelsier nodded. "She's at least a Misting, and if Marsh says she's more, I'm inclined to believe him. I'm a bit surprised to see her using Allomancy on a member of the Ministry, especially inside a Canton building. I'd guess that she doesn't know that she's even using her abilities."

"Is that possible?" Dockson asked.

Kelsier nodded. "Trace minerals in the water can be burned, if just for a tiny bit of power. That's one of the rea-

sons the Lord Ruler built his city here—lots of metals in the ground. I'd say that . . ."

Kelsier trailed off, frowning slightly. Something was wrong. He glanced toward Camon and his crew. They were still visible in the near distance, crossing the street and heading south.

A figure appeared in the Canton building's doorway. Lean with a confident air, he bore the tattoos of a high prelan of the Canton of Finance around his eyes. Probably the very man Camon had met with shortly before. The obligator stepped out of the building, and a second man exited behind him.

Beside Kelsier, Dockson suddenly grew stiff.

The second man was tall with a strong build. As he turned, Kelsier was able to see that a thick metal spike had been pounded tip-first through each of the man's eyes. With shafts as wide as an eye socket, the nail-like spikes were long enough that their sharp points jutted out about an inch from the back of the man's clean-shaven skull. The flat spike ends shone like two silvery disks, sticking out of the sockets in the front, where the eyes should have been.

A Steel Inquisitor.

"What's *that* doing here?" Dockson asked.

"Stay calm," Kelsier said, trying to force himself to do the same. The Inquisitor looked toward them, spiked eyes regarding Kelsier, before turning in the direction that Camon and the girl had gone. Like all Inquisitors, he wore intricate eye tattoos—mostly black, with one stark red line—that marked him as a high-ranking member of the Canton of Inquisition.

"He's not here for us," Kelsier said. "I'm not burning anything—he'll think that we're just ordinary noblemen."

"The girl," Dockson said.

Kelsier nodded. "You say Camon's been running this scam on the Ministry for a while. Well, the girl must have been detected by one of the obligators. They're trained to recognize when an Allomancer tampers with their emotions."

Dockson frowned thoughtfully. Across the street, the Inquisitor conferred with the other obligator, then the two of them turned to walk in the direction that Camon had gone. There was no urgency to their pace.

"They must have sent a tail to follow them," Dockson said.

"This is the Ministry," Kelsier said. "There'll be two tails, at least."

Dockson nodded. "Camon will lead them directly back to his safe house. Dozens of men will die. They're not all the most admirable people, but . . ."

"They fight the Final Empire, in their own way," Kelsier said. "Besides, I'm not about to let a possible Mistborn slip away from us—I want to talk to that girl. Can you deal with those tails?"

"I said I'd become boring, Kell," Dockson said. "Not sloppy. I can handle a couple of Ministry flunkies."

"Good," Kelsier said, reaching into his cloak pocket and pulling out a small vial. A collection of metal flakes floated in an alcohol solution within. Iron, steel, tin, pewter, copper, bronze, zinc, and brass—the eight basic Allomantic metals. Kelsier pulled off the stopper and downed the contents in a single swift gulp.

He pocketed the now empty vial, wiping his mouth. "I'll handle that Inquisitor."

Dockson looked apprehensive. "You're going to try and take him?"

Kelsier shook his head. "Too dangerous. I'll just divert him. Now, get going—we don't want those tails finding the safe house."

Dockson nodded. "Meet back at the fifteenth crossroad," he said before taking off down the alley and disappearing around a corner.

Kelsier gave his friend a count of ten before reaching within himself and burning his metals. His body came awash with strength, clarity, and power.

Kelsier smiled; then—burning zinc—he reached out and yanked firmly on the Inquisitor's emotions. The creature froze in place, then spun, looking back toward the Canton building.

Let's have a chase now, you and I, Kelsier thought.

We arrived in Terris earlier this week, and, I have to say, I find the countryside beautiful. The great mountains to the north—with their bald snowcaps and forested mantles—stand like watchful gods over this land of green fertility. My own lands to the south are mostly flat; I think that they might look less dreary if there were a few mountains to vary the terrain.

The people here are mostly herdsmen—though timber harvesters and farmers are not uncommon. It is a pastoral land, certainly. It seems odd that a place so remarkably agrarian could have produced the prophecies and theologies upon which the entire world now relies.

3

CAMON COUNTED HIS COINS, DROPPING the golden boxings one by one into the small chest on his table. He still looked a bit stunned, as well he should have. Three thousand boxings was a fabulous amount of money—far more than Camon would earn in even a very good year. His closest cronies sat at the table with him, ale—and laughter—flowing freely.

Vin sat in her corner, trying to understand her feelings of dread. Three thousand boxings. The Ministry should never have let such a sum go so quickly. Prelan Arriev had seemed too cunning to be fooled with ease.

Camon dropped another coin into the chest. Vin couldn't decide if he was being foolish or clever by making such a display of wealth. Underworld crews worked under a strict agreement: Everyone received a cut of earnings in proportion to their status in the group. While it was sometimes tempting to kill the crewleader and take his money for yourself, a successful leader created more wealth for everyone. Kill him

prematurely, and you would cut off future earnings—not to mention earn the wrath of the other crewmembers.

Still, three thousand boxings . . . that would be enough to tempt even the most logical thief. It was all wrong.

I have to get out of here, Vin decided. *Get away from Camon, and the lair, in case something happens.*

And yet . . . leave? By herself? She'd never been alone before; she'd always had Reen. He'd been the one to lead her from city to city, joining different thieving crews. She loved solitude. But the thought of being by herself, out in the city, horrified her. That was why she'd never run away from Reen; that was why she'd stayed with Camon.

She couldn't go. But she had to. She looked up from her corner, scanning the room. There weren't many people in the crew for whom she felt any sort of attachment. Yet, there were a couple that she would be sorry to see hurt, should the obligators actually move against the crew. A few men who hadn't tried to abuse her, or—in very rare cases—who had actually shown her some measure of kindness.

Ulef was at the top of that list. He wasn't a friend, but he was the closest thing she had now that Reen was gone. If he would go with her, then at least she wouldn't be alone. Cautiously, Vin stood and moved along the side of the room to where Ulef sat drinking with some of the other younger crewmembers.

She tugged on Ulef's sleeve. He turned toward her, only slightly drunk. "Vin?"

"Ulef," she whispered. "We need to go."

He frowned. "Go? Go where?"

"Away," Vin whispered. "Out of here."

"Now?"

Vin nodded urgently.

Ulef glanced back at his friends, who were chuckling among themselves, shooting suggestive looks at Vin and Ulef.

Ulef flushed. "You want to go somewhere, just you and I?"

"Not like that," Vin said. "Just . . . I need to leave the lair. And I don't want to be alone."

Ulef frowned. He leaned closer, a slight stink of ale on his breath. "What is this about, Vin?" he asked quietly.

Vin paused. "I . . . think something might happen, Ulef," she whispered. "Something with the obligators. I just don't want to be in the lair right now."

Ulef sat quietly for a moment. "All right," he finally said. "How long will this take?"

"I don't know," Vin said. "Until evening, at least. But we have to go. *Now.*"

He nodded slowly.

"Wait here for a moment," Vin whispered, turning. She shot a glance at Camon, who was laughing at one of his own jokes. Then she quietly moved through the ash-stained, smoky chamber into the lair's back room.

The crew's general sleeping quarters consisted of a simple, elongated corridor lined with bedrolls. It was crowded and uncomfortable, but it was far better than the cold alleyways she'd slept in during her years traveling with Reen.

Alleyways that I might have to get used to again, she thought. She had survived them before. She could do so again.

She moved to her pallet, the muffled sounds of men laughing and drinking sounding from the other room. Vin knelt down, regarding her few possessions. If something did happen to the crew, she wouldn't be able to come back to the lair. Ever. But, she couldn't take the bedroll with her now—it was far too obvious. That left only the small box that contained her personal effects: a pebble from each city she'd visited, the earring Reen said Vin's mother had given her, and a bit of obsidian the size of a large coin. It was chipped into an irregular pattern—Reen had carried it as some kind of good luck charm. It was the only thing he'd left behind when he'd snuck away from the crew half a year before. Abandoning her.

Just like he always said he would, Vin told herself sternly. *I never thought he'd actually go—and that's exactly why he had to leave.*

She gripped the bit of obsidian in her hand and pocketed the pebbles. The earring she put in her ear—it was a very simple thing. Little more than a stud, not even worth stealing, which was why she didn't fear leaving it in the back room. Still, Vin had rarely worn it, for fear that the ornamentation would make her look more feminine.

She had no money, but Reen had taught her how to scavenge and beg. Both were difficult in the Final Empire, especially in Luthadel, but she would find a way, if she had to.

Vin left her box and bedroll, slipping back out into the common room. Maybe she was overreacting; perhaps nothing would happen to the crew. But, if it did . . . well, if there was one thing Reen had taught her, it was how to protect her neck. Bringing Ulef was a good idea. He had contacts in Luthadel. If something happened to Camon's crew, Ulef could probably get her and him jobs on—

Vin froze just inside the main room. Ulef wasn't at the table where she had left him. Instead, he stood furtively near the front of the room. Near the bar. Near . . . Camon.

"What is this!" Camon stood, his face red as sunlight. He pushed his stool out of the way, then lurched toward her, half drunk. "Running away? Off to betray me to the Ministry, are you!"

Vin dashed toward the stairwell door, desperately scrambling around tables and past crewmembers.

Camon's hurled wooden stool hit her square in the back, throwing her to the ground. Pain flared between her shoulders; several crewmembers cried out as the stool bounced off of her and thumped against the floorboards nearby.

Vin lay in a daze. Then . . . something within her— something she knew of but didn't understand—gave her strength. Her head stopped swimming, her pain becoming a focus. She climbed awkwardly to her feet.

Camon was there. He backhanded her even as she stood. Her head snapped to the side from the blow, twisting her neck so painfully that she barely felt herself hit the floor again.

Camon bent over, grabbing her by the front of her shirt and pulling her up, raising his fist. Vin didn't pause to think or to speak; there was only one thing to do. She used up all of her Luck in a single furious effort, pushing against Camon, calming his fury.

Camon teetered. For a moment, his eyes softened. He lowered her slightly.

Then the anger returned to his eyes. Hard. Terrifying.

"Damn wench," Camon muttered, grabbing her by the

shoulders and shaking her. "That backstabbing brother of yours never respected me, and you're the same. I was too easy on you both. Should have . . ."

Vin tried to twist free, but Camon's grip was firm. She searched desperately for aid from the other crewmembers—however, she knew what she would find. Indifference. They turned away, their faces embarrassed but not concerned. Ulef still stood near Camon's table, looking down guiltily.

In her mind, she thought she heard a voice whispering to her. Reen's voice. *Fool! Ruthlessness—it's the most logical of emotions. You don't have any friends in the underworld. You'll never have any friends in the underworld!*

She renewed her struggles, but Camon hit her again, knocking her to the ground. The blow stunned her, and she gasped, breath knocked from her lungs.

Just endure, she thought, mind muddled. *He won't kill me. He needs me.*

Yet, as she turned weakly, she saw Camon looming above her in the caliginous room, drunken fury showing in his face. She knew this time would be different; it would be no simple beating. He thought that she intended to betray him to the Ministry. He wasn't in control.

There was murder in his eyes.

Please! Vin thought with desperation, reaching for her Luck, trying to make it work. There was no response. Luck, such as it was, had failed her.

Camon bent down, muttering to himself as he grabbed her by the shoulder. He raised an arm—his meaty hand forming another fist, his muscles tensing, an angry bead of sweat slipping off his chin and hitting her on the cheek.

A few feet away, the stairwell door shook, then burst open. Camon paused, arm upraised as he glared toward the door and whatever unfortunate crewmember had chosen such an inopportune moment to return to the lair.

Vin seized the distraction. Ignoring the newcomer, she tried to shake herself free from Camon's grip, but she was too weak. Her face blazed from where he'd hit her, and she tasted blood on her lip. Her shoulder had been twisted awkwardly, and her side ached from where she'd fallen. She clawed at

Camon's hand, but she suddenly felt weak, her inner strength failing her just as her Luck had. Her pains suddenly seemed greater, more daunting, more . . . demanding.

She turned toward the door desperately. She was close—painfully close. She had nearly escaped. Just a little farther . . .

Then she saw the man standing quietly in the stairwell doorway. He was unfamiliar to her. Tall and hawk-faced, he had light blond hair and wore a relaxed nobleman's suit, his cloak hanging free. He was, perhaps, in his mid-thirties. He wore no hat, nor did he carry a dueling cane.

And he looked very, very angry.

"What is this?" Camon demanded. "Who are you?"

How did he get by the scouts . . . ? Vin thought, struggling to get her wits back. Pain. She could deal with pain. *The obligators . . . did they send him?*

The newcomer looked down at Vin, and his expression softened slightly. Then he looked up at Camon and his eyes grew dark.

Camon's angry demands were cut off as he was thrown backward as if had been punched by a powerful force. His arm was ripped free from Vin's shoulder, and he toppled to the ground, causing the floorboards to shake.

The room fell quiet.

Have to get away, Vin thought, forcing herself up to her knees. Camon groaned in pain from a few feet away, and Vin crawled away from him, slipping beneath an unoccupied table. The lair had a hidden exit, a trapdoor beside the far back wall. If she could crawl to it—

Suddenly, Vin felt an overwhelming peace. The emotion slammed into her like a sudden weight, her emotions squished silent, as if crushed by a forceful hand. Her fear puffed out like an extinguished candle, and even her pain seemed unimportant.

She slowed, wondering why she had been so worried. She stood up, pausing as she faced the trapdoor. She breathed heavily, still a little dazed.

Camon just tried to kill me! the logical part of her mind warned. *And someone else is attacking the lair. I have to get away!* However, her emotions didn't match the logic. She felt . . . serene. Unworried. And more than a little bit curious.

Someone had just used Luck on her.

She recognized it somehow, even though she'd never felt it upon her before. She paused beside the table, one hand on the wood, then slowly turned around. The newcomer still stood in the stairwell doorway. He studied her with a critical eye, then smiled in a disarming sort of way.

What is going on?

The newcomer finally stepped into the room. The rest of Camon's crew remained sitting at their tables. They looked surprised, but oddly unworried.

He's using Luck on them all. But . . . how can he do it to so many at once? Vin had never been able to store up enough Luck to do more than give the occasional, brief push.

As the newcomer entered the room, Vin could finally see that a second person stood in the stairwell behind him. This second man was less imposing. He was shorter, with a dark half beard and close-cropped straight hair. He also wore a nobleman's suit, though his was less sharply tailored.

On the other side of the room, Camon groaned and sat up, holding his head. He glanced at the newcomers. "Master Dockson! Why, uh, well, this is a surprise!"

"Indeed," said the shorter man—Dockson. Vin frowned, realizing she sensed a slight familiarity to these men. She recognized them from somewhere.

The Canton of Finance. They were sitting in the waiting room when Camon and I left.

Camon climbed to his feet, studying the blond newcomer. Camon looked down at the man's hands, both of which were lined with strange, overlapping scars. "By the Lord Ruler . . ." Camon whispered. "The Survivor of Hathsin!"

Vin frowned. The title was unfamiliar to her. Should she know this man? Her wounds still throbbed despite the peace she felt, and her head was dizzy. She leaned on the table for support, but did not sit.

Whoever this newcomer was, Camon obviously thought him important. "Why, Master Kelsier!" Camon sputtered. "This is a rare honor!"

The newcomer—Kelsier—shook his head. "You know, I'm not really interested in listening to you."

Camon let out an "urk" of pain as he was thrown backward again. Kelsier made no obvious gesture to perform the feat. Yet, Camon collapsed to the ground, as if shoved by some unseen force.

Camon fell quiet, and Kelsier scanned the room. "The rest of you know who I am?"

Many of the crewmembers nodded.

"Good. I've come to your lair because you, my friends, owe me a great debt."

The room was silent save for Camon's groans. Finally, one of the crewmen spoke. "We . . . do, Master Kelsier?"

"Indeed you do. You see, Master Dockson and I just saved your lives. Your rather incompetent crewleader left the Ministry's Canton of Finance about an hour ago, returning directly to this safe house. He was followed by two Ministry scouts, one high-ranking prelan . . . and a single Steel Inquisitor."

No one spoke.

Oh, Lord . . . Vin thought. She'd been right—she just hadn't been fast enough. If there was an Inquisitor—

"I dealt with the Inquisitor," Kelsier said. He paused, letting the implication hang in the air. What kind of person could so lightly claim to have "dealt" with an Inquisitor? Rumors said the creatures were immortal, that they could see a man's soul, and that they were unmatched warriors.

"I require payment for services rendered," Kelsier said.

Camon didn't get up this time; he had fallen hard, and he was obviously disoriented. The room remained still. Finally, Milev—the dark-skinned man who was Camon's second—scooped up the coffer of Ministry boxings and dashed forward with it. He proffered it to Kelsier.

"The money Camon got from the Ministry," Milev explained. "Three thousand boxings."

Milev is so eager to please him, Vin thought. *This is more than just Luck—either that, or it's some sort of Luck I've never been able to use.*

Kelsier paused, then accepted the coin chest. "And you are?"

"Milev, Master Kelsier."

"Well, Crewleader Milev, I will consider this payment satisfactory—assuming you do one other thing for me."

Milev paused. "What would that be?"

Kelsier nodded toward the near-unconscious Camon. "Deal with him."

"Of course," Milev said.

"I want him to live, Milev," Kelsier said, holding up a finger. "But I don't want him to enjoy it."

Milev nodded. "We'll make him a beggar. The Lord Ruler disapproves of the profession—Camon won't have an easy time of it here in Luthadel."

And Milev will dispose of him anyway as soon as he thinks this Kelsier isn't paying attention.

"Good," Kelsier said. Then he opened the coin chest and began counting out some golden boxings. "You're a resourceful man, Milev. Quick on your feet, and not as easily intimidated as the others."

"I've had dealings with Mistings before, Master Kelsier," Milev said.

Kelsier nodded. "Dox," he said, addressing his companion, "where were we going to have our meeting tonight?"

"I was thinking that we should use Clubs's shop," said the second man.

"Hardly a neutral location," Kelsier said. "Especially if he decides not to join us."

"True."

Kelsier looked to Milev. "I'm planning a job in this area. It would be useful to have the support of some locals." He held out a pile of what looked like a hundred boxings. "We'll require use of your safe house for the evening. This can be arranged?"

"Of course," Milev said, taking the coins eagerly.

"Good," Kelsier said. "Now, get out."

"Out?" Milev asked hesitantly.

"Yes," Kelsier said. "Take your men—including your former leader—and leave. I want to have a private conversation with Mistress Vin."

The room grew silent again, and Vin knew she wasn't the only one wondering how Kelsier knew her name.

"Well, you heard him!" Milev snapped. He waved for a group of thugs to go grab Camon, then he shooed the rest of

the crewmembers up the stairs. Vin watched them go, growing apprehensive. This Kelsier was a powerful man, and instinct told her that powerful men were dangerous. Did he know of her Luck? Obviously; what other reason would he have for singling her out?

How is this Kelsier going to try and use me? she thought, rubbing her arm where she'd hit the floor.

"By the way, Milev," Kelsier said idly. "When I say 'private,' I mean that I don't want to be spied on by the four men watching us through peek-holes behind the far wall. Kindly take them up into the alley with you."

Milev paled. "Of course, Master Kelsier."

"Good. And, in the alleyway you'll find the two dead Ministry spies. Kindly dispose of the corpses for us."

Milev nodded, turning.

"And Milev," Kelsier added.

Milev turned back again.

"See that none of your men betray us," Kelsier said quietly. And Vin felt it again—a renewed pressure on her emotions. "This crew already has the eye of the Steel Ministry—do not make an enemy of me as well."

Milev nodded sharply, then disappeared into the stairwell, pulling the door closed behind him. A few moments later, Vin heard footsteps from the peek room; then all was still. She was alone with a man who was—for some reason—so singularly impressive that he could intimidate an entire room full of cutthroats and thieves.

She eyed the bolt door. Kelsier was watching her. What would he do if she ran?

He claims to have killed an Inquisitor, Vin thought. *And . . . he used Luck. I have to stay, if just long enough to find out what he knows.*

Kelsier's smile deepened, then finally he laughed. "That was *far* too much fun, Dox."

The other man, the one Camon had called Dockson, snorted and walked toward the front of the room. Vin tensed, but he didn't move toward her, instead strolled to the bar.

"You were insufferable enough before, Kell," Dockson said. "I don't know how I'm going to handle this new reputa-

tion of yours. At least, I'm not sure how I'm going to handle it and maintain a straight face."

"You're jealous."

"Yes, that's it," Dockson said. "I'm terribly jealous of your ability to intimidate petty criminals. If it's of any note to you, I think you were too harsh on Camon."

Kelsier walked over and took a seat at one of the room's tables. His mirth darkened slightly as he spoke. "You saw what he was doing to the girl."

"Actually, I didn't," Dockson said dryly, rummaging through the bar's stores. "Someone was blocking the doorway."

Kelsier shrugged. "Look at her, Dox. The poor thing's been beaten nearly senseless. I don't feel any sympathy for the man."

Vin remained where she was, keeping watch on both men. As the tension of the moment grew weaker, her wounds began to throb again. The blow between her shoulder blades— that would be a large bruise—and the slap to her face burned as well. She was still a little dizzy.

Kelsier was watching her. Vin clinched her teeth. Pain. She could deal with pain.

"You need anything, child?" Dockson asked. "A wet handkerchief for that face, perhaps?"

She didn't respond, instead remaining focused on Kelsier. *Come on. Tell me what you want with me. Make your play.*

Dockson finally shrugged, then ducked beneath the bar for a moment. He eventually came up with a couple of bottles.

"Anything good?" Kelsier asked, turning.

"What do you think?" Dockson asked. "Even among thieves, Camon isn't exactly known for his refinement. I have socks worth more than this wine."

Kelsier sighed. "Give me a cup anyway." Then he glanced back at Vin. "You want anything?"

Vin didn't respond.

Kelsier smiled. "Don't worry—we're far less frightening than your friends think."

"I don't think they were her friends, Kell," Dockson said from behind the bar.

"Good point," Kelsier said. "Regardless, child, you don't have anything to fear from us. Other than Dox's breath."

Dockson rolled his eyes. "Or Kell's jokes."

Vin stood quietly. She could act weak, the way she had with Camon, but instincts told her that these men wouldn't respond well to that tactic. So, she remained where she was, assessing the situation.

The calmness fell upon her again. It encouraged her to be at ease, to be trusting, to simply do as the men were suggesting. . . .

No! She stayed where she was.

Kelsier raised an eyebrow. "That's unexpected."

"What?" Dockson asked as he poured a cup of wine.

"Nothing," Kelsier said, studying Vin.

"You want a drink or not, lass?" Dockson asked.

Vin said nothing. All her life, as long as she could remember, she'd had her Luck. It made her strong, and it gave her an edge over other thieves. It was probably why she was still alive. Yet, all that time, she'd never really known what it was or why she could use it. Logic and instinct now told her the same thing—that she needed to find out what this man knew.

However he intended to use her, whatever his plans were, she needed to endure them. She had to find out how he'd grown so powerful.

"Ale," she finally said.

"Ale?" Kelsier asked. "That's it?"

Vin nodded, watching him carefully. "I like it."

Kelsier rubbed his chin. "We'll have to work on that," he said. "Anyway, have a seat."

Hesitant, Vin walked over and sat down opposite Kelsier at the small table. Her wounds throbbed, but she couldn't afford to show weakness. Weakness killed. She had to pretend to ignore the pain. At least, sitting as she was, her head cleared.

Dockson joined them a moment later, giving Kelsier a glass of wine and Vin her mug of ale. She didn't take a drink.

"Who are you?" she asked in a quiet voice.

Kelsier raised an eyebrow. "You're a blunt one, eh?"

Vin didn't reply.

Kelsier sighed. "So much for my intriguing air of mystery."

Dockson snorted quietly.

Kelsier smiled. "My name is Kelsier. I'm what you might

call a crewleader—but I run a crew that isn't like any you've probably known. Men like Camon, along with his crew, like to think of themselves as predators, feeding off of the nobility and the various organizations of the Ministry."

Vin shook her head. "Not predators. Scavengers." One would have thought, perhaps, that so close to the Lord Ruler, such things as thieving crews would not be able to exist. Yet, Reen had shown her that the opposite was true: Powerful, rich nobility congregated around the Lord Ruler. And, where power and riches existed, so did corruption—especially since the Lord Ruler tended to police his nobility far less than he did the skaa. It had to do, apparently, with his fondness for their ancestors.

Either way, thieving crews like Camon's were the rats who fed on the city's corruption. And, like rats, they were impossible to entirely exterminate—especially in a city with the population of Luthadel.

"Scavengers," Kelsier said, smiling; apparently he did that a lot. "That's an appropriate description, Vin. Well, Dox and I, we're scavengers too . . . we're just a higher quality of scavenger. We're more well-bred, you might say—or perhaps just more ambitious."

She frowned. "You're noblemen?"

"Lord, no," Dockson said.

"Or, at least," Kelsier said, "not full-blooded ones."

"Half-breeds aren't supposed to exist," Vin said carefully. "The Ministry hunts them."

Kelsier raised an eyebrow. "Half-breeds like you?"

Vin felt a shock. *How . . . ?*

"Even the Steel Ministry isn't infallible, Vin," Kelsier said. "If they can miss you, then they can miss others."

Vin paused thoughtfully. "Milev. He called you Mistings. Those are some kind of Allomancer, right?"

Dockson glanced at Kelsier. "She's observant," the shorter man said with an appreciative nod.

"Indeed," Kelsier agreed. "The man did call us Mistings, Vin—though the appellation was a bit hasty, since neither Dox nor I are technically Mistings. We do, however, associate with them quite a bit."

Vin sat quietly for a moment, sitting beneath the scrutiny

of the two men. Allomancy. The mystical power held by the nobility, granted to them by the Lord Ruler some thousand years before as a reward for their loyalty. It was basic Ministry doctrine; even a skaa like Vin knew that much. The nobility had Allomancy and privilege because of their ancestors; the skaa were punished for the same reason.

The truth was, however, that she didn't really know what Allomancy was. It had something to do with fighting, she'd always assumed. One "Misting," as they were called, was said to be dangerous enough to kill an entire thieving team. Yet, the skaa she knew spoke of the power in whispered, uncertain tones. Before this moment, she'd never even paused to consider the possibility that it might simply be the same thing as her Luck.

"Tell me, Vin," Kelsier said, leaning forward with interest. "Do you realize what you did to that obligator in the Canton of Finance?"

"I used my Luck," Vin said quietly. "I use it to make people less angry."

"Or less suspicious," Kelsier said. "Easier to scam."

Vin nodded.

Kelsier held up a finger. "There are a lot of things you're going to have to learn. Techniques, rules, and exercises. One lesson, however, cannot wait. *Never* use emotional Allomancy on an obligator. They're all trained to recognize when their passions are being manipulated. Even the high nobility are forbidden from Pulling or Pushing the emotions of an obligator. You are what caused that obligator to send for an Inquisitor."

"Pray the creature never catches your trail again, lass," Dockson said quietly, sipping his wine.

Vin paled. "You didn't kill the Inquisitor?"

Kelsier shook his head. "I just distracted him for a bit— which was quite dangerous enough, I might add. Don't worry, many of the rumors about them aren't true. Now that he's lost your trail, he won't be able to find you again."

"Most likely," Dockson said.

Vin glanced at the shorter man apprehensively.

"Most likely," Kelsier agreed. "There are a lot of things we

don't know about the Inquisitors—they don't seem to follow the normal rules. Those spikes through their eyes, for instance, should kill them. Nothing I've learned about Allomancy has ever provided an explanation for how those creatures keep living. If it were only a regular Misting Seeker on your trail, we wouldn't need to worry. An Inquisitor . . . well, you'll want to keep your eyes open. Of course, you already seem pretty good at that."

Vin sat uncomfortably for a moment. Eventually, Kelsier nodded to her mug of ale. "You aren't drinking."

"You might have slipped something in it," Vin said.

"Oh, there was no need for me to sneak something into your drink," Kelsier said with a smile, pulling an object out of his suit coat pocket. "After all, you're going to drink this vial of mysterious liquid quite willingly."

He set a small glass vial on the tabletop. Vin frowned, regarding the liquid within. There was a dark residue at its bottom. "What is it?" she asked.

"If I told you, it wouldn't be mysterious," Kelsier said with a smile.

Dockson rolled his eyes. "The vial is filled with an alcohol solution and some flakes of metal, Vin."

"Metal?" she asked with a frown.

"Two of the eight basic Allomantic metals," Kelsier said. "We need to do some tests."

Vin eyed the vial.

Kelsier shrugged. "You'll have to drink it if you want to know any more about this Luck of yours."

"You drink half first," Vin said.

Kelsier raised an eyebrow. "A bit on the paranoid side, I see."

Vin didn't respond.

Finally, he sighed, picking up the vial and pulling off the plug.

"Shake it up first," Vin said. "So you get some of the sediment."

Kelsier rolled his eyes, but did as requested, shaking the vial, then downing half of its contents. He set it back on the table with a click.

Vin frowned. Then she eyed Kelsier, who smiled. He knew

that he had her. He had shown off his power, had tempted her with it. *The only reason to be subservient to those with power is so that you can learn to someday take what they have.* Reen's words.

Vin reached out and took the vial, then she downed its contents. She sat, waiting for some magical transformation or surge of power—or even signs of poison. She felt nothing.

How . . . anticlimactic. She frowned, leaning back in her chair. Out of curiosity, she felt at her Luck.

And felt her eyes widen in shock.

It was there, like a massive golden hoard. A storage of power so incredible that it stretched her understanding. Always before, she had needed to be a scrimp with her Luck, holding it in reserve, using up morsels sparingly. Now she felt like a starving woman invited to a high nobleman's feast. She sat, stunned, regarding the enormous wealth within her.

"So," Kelsier said with a prodding voice. "Try it. Soothe me."

Vin reached out, tentatively touching her newfound mass of Luck. She took a bit, and directed it at Kelsier.

"Good." Kelsier leaned forward eagerly. "But we already knew you could do that. Now the real test, Vin. Can you go the other way? You can dampen my emotions, but can you enflame them too?"

Vin frowned. She'd never used her Luck in such a way; she hadn't even realized that she could. Why was he so eager?

Suspicious, Vin reached for her source of Luck. As she did so, she noticed something interesting. What she had first interpreted as one massive source of power was actually two different sources of power. There were different types of Luck.

Eight. He'd said there were eight of them. But . . . what do the others do?

Kelsier was still waiting. Vin reached to the second, unfamiliar source of Luck, doing as she'd done before and directing it at him.

Kelsier's smile deepened, and he sat back, glancing at Dockson. "That's it then. She did it."

Dockson shook his head. "To be honest, Kell, I'm not sure what to think. Having one of you around was unsettling enough. Two, though . . ."

Vin regarded them with narrowed, dubious eyes. "Two what?"

"Even among the nobility, Vin, Allomancy is modestly rare," Kelsier said. "True, it's a hereditary skill, with most of its powerful lines among the high nobility. However, breeding alone doesn't guarantee Allomantic strength.

"Many high noblemen only have access to a single Allomantic skill. People like that—those who can only perform Allomancy in one of its eight basic aspects—are called Mistings. Sometimes these abilities appear in skaa—but only if that skaa has noble blood in his or her near ancestry. You can usually find one Misting in . . . oh, about ten thousand mixed-breed skaa. The better, and closer, the noble ancestry, the more likely the skaa is to be a Misting."

"Who were your parents, Vin?" Dockson asked. "Do you remember them?"

"I was raised by my half brother, Reen," Vin said quietly, uncomfortable. These were not things she discussed with others.

"Did he speak of your mother and father?" Dockson asked.

"Occasionally," she admitted. "Reen said that our mother was a whore. Not out of choice, but the underworld . . ." She trailed off. Her mother had tried to kill her, once, when she was very young. She vaguely remembered the event. Reen had saved her.

"What about your father, Vin?" Dockson asked.

Vin looked up. "He is a high prelan in the Steel Ministry."

Kelsier whistled softly. "Now, *that's* a slightly ironic breach of duty."

Vin looked down at the table. Finally, she reached over and took a healthy pull on her mug of ale.

Kelsier smiled. "Most ranking obligators in the Ministry are high noblemen. Your father gave you a rare gift in that blood of yours."

"So . . . I'm one of these Mistings you mentioned?"

Kelsier shook his head. "Actually, no. You see, this is what made you so interesting to us, Vin. Mistings only have access to one Allomantic skill. You just proved you have two. And, if you have access to at least two of the eight, then you have access to the rest as well. That's the way it works—if you're an

Allomancer, you either get one skill or you get them all."

Kelsier leaned forward. "You, Vin, are what is generally called a Mistborn. Even amongst the nobility, they're incredibly rare. Amongst skaa . . . well, let's just say I've only met one other skaa Mistborn in my entire life."

Somehow, the room seemed to grow more quiet. More still. Vin stared at her mug with distracted, uncomfortable eyes. *Mistborn.* She'd heard the stories, of course. The legends.

Kelsier and Dockson sat quietly, letting her think. Eventually, she spoke. "So . . . what does this all mean?"

Kelsier smiled. "It means that you, Vin, are a very special person. You have a power that most high noblemen envy. It is a power that, had you been born an aristocrat, would have made you one of the most deadly and influential people in all of the Final Empire."

Kelsier leaned forward again. "But, you weren't born an aristocrat. You're not noble, Vin. You don't have to play by their rules—and that makes you even *more* powerful."

Apparently, the next stage of my quest will take us up into the highlands of Terris. This is said to be a cold, unforgiving place—a land where the mountains themselves are made of ice.

Our normal attendants will not do for such a trip. We should probably hire some Terris packmen to carry our gear.

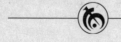

4

"YOU HEARD WHAT HE SAID! He's planning a job." Ulef's eyes shone with excitement. "I wonder which of the Great Houses he's going to strike."

"It'll be one of the most powerful ones," said Disten, one

of Camon's head pointmen. He was missing a hand, but his eyes and ears were among the keenest in the crew. "Kelsier never bothers himself with small-time jobs."

Vin sat quietly, her mug of ale—the same one Kelsier had given her—still sitting mostly full on the tabletop. Her table was crowded with people; Kelsier had let the thieves return to their home for a bit before his meeting began. Vin, however, would have preferred to remain by herself. Life with Reen had accustomed her to loneliness—if you let someone get too close, it would just give them better opportunities to betray you.

Even after Reen's disappearance, Vin had kept to herself. She hadn't been willing to leave; however, she also hadn't felt the need to become familiar with the other crewmembers. They had, in turn, been perfectly willing to let her alone. Vin's position had been precarious, and associating with her could have tainted them by association. Only Ulef had made any moves to befriend her.

If you let someone get close to you, it will only hurt more when they betray you, Reen seemed to whisper in her mind.

Had Ulef even really been her friend? He'd certainly sold her out quickly enough. In addition, the crewmembers had taken Vin's beating and sudden rescue in stride, never mentioning their betrayal or refusal to help her. They'd only done what was expected.

"The Survivor hasn't bothered himself with *any* jobs lately," said Harmon, an older, scraggly-bearded burglar. "He's barely been seen in Luthadel a handful of times during the last few years. In fact, he hasn't pulled any jobs since . . ."

"This is the first one?" Ulef asked eagerly. "The first since he escaped the Pits? Then it's bound to be something spectacular!"

"Did he say anything about it, Vin?" Disten asked. "Vin?" He waved a stumpy arm in her direction, catching her attention.

"What?" she asked, looking up. She had cleaned herself slightly since her beating at Camon's hand, finally accepting a handkerchief from Dockson to wipe the blood from her face. There was little she could do about the bruises, however. Those still throbbed. Hopefully, nothing was broken.

"Kelsier," Disten repeated. "Did he say anything about the job he's planning?"

Vin shook her head. She glanced down at the bloodied handkerchief. Kelsier and Dockson had left a short time ago, promising to return after she'd had some time to think about the things they had told her. There was an implication in their words, however—an offer. Whatever job they were planning, she was invited to participate.

"Why'd he pick you to be his twixt, anyway, Vin?" Ulef asked. "Did he say anything about that?"

That's what the crew assumed—that Kelsier had chosen her to be his contact with Camon's . . . Milev's . . . crew.

There were two sides to the Luthadel underground. There were the regular crews, like Camon's. Then there were . . . the *special* ones. Groups composed of the extremely skillful, the extremely foolhardy, or the extremely talented. Allomancers.

The two sides of the underworld didn't mix; regular thieves left their betters alone. However, occasionally one of these Misting crews hired a regular team to do some of its more mundane work, and they would choose a twixt—a go-between—to work with both crews. Hence Ulef's assumption about Vin.

Milev's crewmembers noticed her unresponsiveness, and turned to another topic: Mistings. They spoke of Allomancy with uncertain, whispered tones, and she listened, uncomfortable. How could she be associated with something they held in such awe? Her Luck . . . her Allomancy . . . was something small, something she used to survive, but something really quite unimportant.

But, such power . . . she thought, looking in at her Luck reserve.

"What's Kelsier been doing these last few years, I wonder?" Ulef asked. He had seemed a bit uncomfortable around her at the beginning of the conversation, but that had passed quickly. He'd betrayed her, but this was the underworld. No friends.

It didn't seem that way between Kelsier and Dockson. They appeared to trust each other. A front? Or were they simply one of those rare teams that actually didn't worry about each other's betrayal?

The most unsettling thing about Kelsier and Dockson had

been their openness with her. They seemed willing to trust, even accept, Vin after a relatively short time. It couldn't be genuine—no one could survive in the underworld following such tactics. Still, their friendliness was disconcerting.

"Two years . . ." said Hrud, a flat-faced, quiet thug. "He must have spent the entire time planning for this job."

"It must be some job indeed. . . ." Ulef said.

"Tell me about him," Vin said quietly.

"Kelsier?" Disten asked.

Vin nodded.

"They didn't talk about Kelsier down south?"

Vin shook her head.

"He was the best crewleader in Luthadel," Ulef explained. "A legend, even among the Mistings. He robbed some of the wealthiest Great Houses in the city."

"And?" Vin asked.

"Someone betrayed him," Harmon said in a quiet voice.

Of course, Vin thought.

"The Lord Ruler himself caught Kelsier," Ulef said. "Sent Kelsier and his wife to the Pits of Hathsin. But *he escaped.* He escaped from the Pits, Vin! He's the only one who ever has."

"And the wife?" Vin asked.

Ulef glanced at Harmon, who shook his head. "She didn't make it."

So, he's lost someone too. How can he laugh so much? So honestly?

"That's where he got those scars, you know," Disten said. "The ones on his arms. He got them at the Pits, from the rocks on a sheer wall he had to climb to escape."

Harmon snorted. "That's not how he got them. He killed an Inquisitor while escaping—that's where he got the scars."

"I heard he got them fighting one of the monsters that guard the Pits," Ulef said. "He reached into its mouth and strangled it *from the inside.* The teeth scraped his arms."

Disten frowned. "How do you strangle someone from the inside?"

Ulef shrugged. "That's just what I heard."

"The man isn't natural," Hrud muttered. "Something hap-

pened to him in the Pits, something bad. He wasn't an Allomancer before then, you know. He entered the Pits a regular skaa, and now . . . Well, he's a Misting for sure—if he's even human anymore. Been out in the mists a lot, that one has. Some say that the real Kelsier is dead, that the thing wearing his face is . . . something else."

Harmon shook his head. "Now, that's just plantation-skaa foolishness. We've all gone out in the mists."

"Not in the mists outside the city," Hrud insisted. "The mistwraiths are out there. They'll grab a man and take his face, sure as the Lord Ruler."

Harmon rolled his eyes.

"Hrud's right about one thing," Disten said. "That man isn't human. He might not be a mistwraith, but he's not skaa either. I've heard of him doing things, things like only *they* can do. The ones that come out at night. You saw what he did to Camon."

"Mistborn," Harmon muttered.

Mistborn. Vin had heard the term before Kelsier had mentioned it to her, of course. Who hadn't? Yet, the rumors about Mistborn made stories of Inquisitors and Mistings seem rational. It was said that Mistborn were heralds of the mists themselves, endowed with great powers by the Lord Ruler. Only high noblemen could be Mistborn; they were said to be a secret sect of assassins who served him, only going out at night. Reen had always taught her that they were a myth, and Vin had assumed he was right.

And Kelsier says I—like he himself—am one of them. How could she be what he said? Child of a prostitute, she was nobody. She was nothing.

Never trust a man who tells you good news, Reen had always said. *It's the oldest, but easiest, way to con someone.*

Yet, she did have her Luck. Her Allomancy. She could still sense the reserves Kelsier's vial had given her, and had tested her powers on the crewmembers. No longer limited to just a bit of Luck a day, she found she could produce far more striking effects.

Vin was coming to realize that her old goal in life—simply

staying alive—was uninspired. There was so much more she could be doing. She had been a slave to Reen; she had been a slave to Camon. She would be a slave to this Kelsier too, if it would lead her to eventual freedom.

At his table, Milev looked at his pocket watch, then stood. "All right, everyone out."

The room began to clear in preparation for Kelsier's meeting. Vin remained where she was; Kelsier had made it quite clear to the others that she was invited. She sat quietly for a bit, the room feeling far more comfortable to her now that it was empty. Kelsier's friends began to arrive a short time later.

The first man down the steps had the build of a soldier. He wore a loose, sleeveless shirt that exposed a pair of well-sculpted arms. He was impressively muscular, but not massive, and had close-cropped hair that stuck up slightly on his head.

The soldier's companion was a sharply dressed man in a nobleman's suit—plum vest, gold buttons, black overcoat—complete with short-brimmed hat and dueling cane. He was older than the soldier, and was a bit portly. He removed his hat upon entering the room, revealing a head of well-styled black hair. The two men were chatting amiably as they walked, but they paused when they saw the empty room.

"Ah, this must be our twixt," said the man in the suit. "Has Kelsier arrived yet, my dear?" He spoke with a simple familiarity, as if they were longtime friends. Suddenly, despite herself, Vin found herself liking this well-dressed, articulate man.

"No," she said quietly. Though overalls and a work shirt had always suited her, she suddenly wished that she owned something nicer. This man's very bearing seemed to demand a more formal atmosphere.

"Should have known that Kell would be late to his own meeting," the soldier said, sitting down at one of the tables near the center of the room.

"Indeed," said the suited man. "I suppose his tardiness leaves us with a chance for some refreshment. I could so use something to drink. . . ."

"Let me get you something," Vin said quickly, jumping to her feet.

"How gracious of you," the suited man said, choosing a

chair next to the soldier. He sat with one leg crossed over the other, his dueling cane held to the side, tip against the floor, one hand resting on the top.

Vin walked to the bar and began rummaging for drinks.

"Breeze . . ." the soldier said with a warning tone as Vin selected a bottle of Camon's most expensive wine and began pouring a cup.

"Hum . . . ?" the suited man said, raising an eyebrow.

The soldier nodded toward Vin.

"Oh, very well," the suited man said with a sigh.

Vin paused, wine half poured, and frowned slightly. *What am I doing?*

"I swear, Ham," the suited man said, "you are dreadfully stiff sometimes."

"Just because you can Push someone around doesn't mean you should, Breeze."

Vin stood, dumbfounded. *He . . . used Luck on me.* When Kelsier had tried to manipulate her, she'd felt his touch and had been able to resist. This time, however, she hadn't even realized what she was doing.

She looked up at the man, thinning her eyes. "Mistborn."

The suited man, Breeze, chuckled. "Hardly. Kelsier's the only skaa Mistborn you're likely to ever meet, my dear—and pray you never are in a situation where you meet a noble one. No, I am just an ordinary, humble Misting."

"Humble?" Ham asked.

Breeze shrugged.

Vin looked down at the half-full cup of wine. "You Pulled on my emotions. With . . . Allomancy, I mean."

"I Pushed on them, actually," Breeze said. "Pulling makes a person less trusting and more determined. Pushing on emotions—Soothing them—makes a person more trusting."

"Regardless, you controlled me," Vin said. "You made me fetch you a drink."

"Oh, I wouldn't say that I *made* you do it," Breeze said. "I just altered your emotions slightly, putting you in a frame of mind where you'd be more likely to do as I wished."

Ham rubbed his chin. "I don't know, Breeze. It's an interesting question. By influencing her emotions, did you take

away her ability to choose? If, for instance, she were to kill or steal while under your control, would the crime be hers or yours?"

Breeze rolled his eyes. "There's really no question to it at all. You shouldn't think about such things, Hammond—you'll hurt your brain. I offered her encouragement, I simply did it through an irregular means."

"But—"

"I'm not going to argue it with you, Ham."

The beefy man sighed, looking a little bit forlorn.

"Are you going to bring me the drink . . . ?" Breeze asked hopefully, looking at Vin. "I mean, you're already up, and you're going to have to come back this direction to reach your seat anyway. . . ."

Vin examined her emotions. Did she feel irregularly drawn to do as the man asked? Was he manipulating her again? Finally, she simply walked away from the bar, leaving the drink where it was.

Breeze sighed. He didn't stand to go get the drink himself, however.

Vin walked tentatively toward the two men's table. She was accustomed to shadows and corners—close enough to eavesdrop, but far enough away to escape. Yet, she couldn't hide from these men—not while the room was so empty. So, she chose a chair at the table beside the one that the two men were using, then sat cautiously. She needed information—as long as she was ignorant, she was going to be at a severe disadvantage in this new world of Misting crews.

Breeze chuckled. "Nervous little thing, aren't you?"

Vin ignored the comment. "You," Vin said, nodding to Ham. "You're a . . . a Misting too?"

Ham nodded. "I'm a Thug."

Vin frowned in confusion.

"I burn pewter," Ham said.

Again, Vin looked at him questioningly.

"He can make himself stronger, my dear," Breeze said. "He hits things—particularly other people—who try to interfere with what the rest of us are doing."

"There's much more to it than that," Ham said. "I run general security for jobs, providing my crewleader with manpower and warriors, assuming such are necessary."

"And he'll try and bore you with random philosophy when it isn't," Breeze added.

Ham sighed. "Breeze, honestly, sometimes I don't know why I . . ." Ham trailed off as the door opened again, admitting another man.

The newcomer wore a dull tan overcoat, a pair of brown trousers, and a simple white shirt. However, his face was far more distinctive than his clothing. It was knotted and gnarled, like a twisted piece of wood, and his eyes shone with the level of disapproving dissatisfaction only the elderly can display. Vin couldn't quite place his age—he was young enough that he wasn't stooped over, yet he was old enough that he made even the middle-aged Breeze look youthful.

The newcomer looked over Vin and the others, huffed disdainfully, then walked to a table on the other side of the room and sat down. His steps were marked by a distinct limp.

Breeze sighed. "I'm going to miss Trap."

"We all will," Ham said quietly. "Clubs is very good, though. I've worked with him before."

Breeze studied the newcomer. "I wonder if I could get *him* to bring my drink over. . . ."

Ham chuckled. "I'd pay money to see you try it."

"I'm sure you would," Breeze said.

Vin eyed the newcomer, who seemed perfectly content to ignore her and the other two men. "What's he?"

"Clubs?" Breeze asked. "He, my dear, is a Smoker. He is what will keep the rest of us from being discovered by an Inquisitor."

Vin chewed on her lip, digesting the new information as she studied Clubs. The man shot her a glare, and she looked away. As she turned, she noticed that Ham was looking at her.

"I like you, kid," he said. "The other twixts I've worked with have either been too intimidated to talk to us, or they've been jealous of us for moving into their territory."

"Indeed," Breeze said. "You're not like most crumbs. Of

course, I'd like you a great deal more if you'd go fetch me
that glass of wine. . . ."

Vin ignored him, glancing at Ham. "Crumb?"

"That's what some of the more self-important members of
our society call lesser thieves," Ham said. "They call you
crumbs, since you tend to be involved with . . . less inspired
projects."

"No offense intended, of course," Breeze said.

"Oh, I wouldn't ever take offense at—" Vin paused, feeling
an irregular desire to please the well-dressed man. She glared
at Breeze. "Stop that!"

"See, there," Breeze said, glancing at Ham. "She still re-
tains her ability to choose."

"You're hopeless."

They assume I'm a twixt, Vin thought. *So Kelsier hasn't
told them what I am. Why?* Time constraints? Or, was the secret too valuable to share? How trustworthy were these men?
And, if they thought her a simple "crumb," why were they being so nice to her?

"Who else are we waiting upon?" Breeze asked, glancing
at the doorway. "Besides Kell and Dox, I mean."

"Yeden," Ham said.

Breeze frowned with a sour expression. "Ah, yes."

"I agree," Ham said. "But, I'd be willing to bet that he feels
the same way about us."

"I don't even see why he was invited," Breeze said.

Ham shrugged. "Something to do with Kell's plan, obviously."

"Ah, the infamous 'plan,' " Breeze said musingly. "What
job could it be, what indeed . . . ?"

Ham shook his head. "Kell and his cursed sense of drama."

"Indeed."

The door opened a few moments later, and the one they
had spoken of, Yeden, entered. He turned out to be an unas-
suming man, and Vin had trouble understanding why the
other two were so displeased about his attendance. Short with
curly brown hair, Yeden was dressed in simple gray skaa
clothing and a patched, soot-stained brown worker's coat. He
regarded the surroundings with a look of disapproval, but he

was nowhere near as openly hostile as Clubs, who still sat on the other side of the room scowling at anyone who looked in his direction.

Not a very big crew, Vin thought. *With Kelsier and Dockson, that makes six of them.* Of course, Ham had said that he led a group of "Thugs." Were the men at this meeting simply representatives? The leaders of smaller, more specialized groups? Some crews worked that way.

Breeze checked his pocket watch three more times before Kelsier finally arrived. The Mistborn crewleader burst through the door with his cheery enthusiasm, Dockson sauntering along behind. Ham stood immediately, smiling broadly and clasping hands with Kelsier. Breeze stood as well, and while his greeting was a bit more reserved, Vin had to admit that she had never seen any crewleader welcomed so happily by his men.

"Ah," Kelsier said, looking toward the other side of the room. "Clubs and Yeden too. So, everyone's here. Good—I absolutely loathe being made to wait."

Breeze raised an eyebrow as he and Ham settled back into their chairs, Dockson taking a seat at the same table. "Are we to receive any explanation for your tardiness?"

"Dockson and I were visiting my brother," Kelsier explained, walking toward the front of the lair. He turned and leaned back against the bar, scanning the room. When Kelsier's eyes fell on Vin, he winked.

"Your brother?" Ham said. "Is Marsh coming to the meeting?"

Kelsier and Dockson shared a look. "Not tonight," Kelsier said. "But he'll join the crew eventually."

Vin studied the others. They were skeptical. *Tension between Kelsier and his brother, perhaps?*

Breeze raised his dueling cane, pointing the tip at Kelsier. "All right, Kelsier, you've kept this 'job' secret from us for eight months now. We know it's big, we know you're excited, and we're all properly annoyed at you for being so secretive. So, why don't you just go ahead and tell us what it is?"

Kelsier smiled. Then he stood up straight, waving a hand toward the dirty, plain-looking Yeden. "Gentlemen, meet your new employer."

This was, apparently, quite a shocking statement.

"*Him?*" Ham asked.

"Him," Kelsier said with a nod.

"What?" Yeden asked, speaking for the first time. "You have trouble working with someone who actually has morals?"

"It's not that, my dear man," Breeze said, setting his dueling cane across his lap. "It's just that, well, I was under the strange impression that you didn't *like* our types very much."

"I don't," Yeden said flatly. "You're selfish, undisciplined, and you've turned your backs on the rest of the skaa. You dress nicely, but on the inside you're dirty as ash."

Ham snorted. "I can already see that this job is going to be *great* for crew morale."

Vin watched quietly, chewing on her lip. Yeden was obviously a skaa worker, probably a member of a forge or textile mill. What connection did he have with the underground? And . . . how would he be able to afford the services of a thieving crew, especially one as apparently specialized as Kelsier's team?

Perhaps Kelsier noticed her confusion, for she found him looking at her as the others continued to speak.

"I'm still a little confused," Ham said. "Yeden, we're all aware of how you regard thieves. So . . . why hire us?"

Yeden squirmed a bit. "Because," he finally said, "everyone knows how effective you are."

Breeze chuckled. "Disapproving of our morals doesn't make you unwilling to make use of our skills, I see. So, what is the job, then? What does the skaa rebellion wish of us?"

Skaa rebellion? Vin thought, a piece of the conversation falling into place. There were two sides to the underworld. The far larger portion was made up of the thieves, crews, whores, and beggars who tried to survive outside of mainstream skaa culture.

And then there were the rebels. The people who worked against the Final Empire. Reen had always called them fools—a sentiment shared by most of the people, both underworlders and regular skaa, that Vin had met.

All eyes slowly turned to Kelsier, who leaned back against the bar again. "The skaa rebellion, courtesy of its leader, Yeden, has hired us for something very specific."

"What?" Ham asked. "Robbery? Assassination?"

"A little of both," Kelsier said, "and, at the same time, neither one. Gentlemen, this isn't going to be a regular job. It's going to be different from anything any crew has ever tried to pull. We're going to help Yeden overthrow the Final Empire."

Silence.

"Excuse me?" Ham asked.

"You heard me right, Ham," Kelsier said. "That's the job I've been planning—the destruction of the Final Empire. Or, at least, its center of government. Yeden has hired us to supply him with an army, then provide him with a favorable opportunity to seize control of this city."

Ham sat back, then shared a glance with Breeze. Both men turned toward Dockson, who nodded solemnly. The room remained quiet for a moment longer; then the silence was broken as Yeden began to laugh ruefully to himself.

"I should never have agreed to this," Yeden said, shaking his head. "Now that you say it, I realize how ridiculous it all sounds."

"Trust me, Yeden," Kelsier said. "These men have made a habit of pulling off plans that seem ridiculous at first glance."

"That may be true, Kell," Breeze said. "But, in this case, I find myself agreeing with our disapproving friend. Overthrow the Final Empire . . . that is something that skaa rebels have been working toward for a thousand years! What makes you think that we can achieve anything where those men have failed?"

Kelsier smiled. "We'll succeed because we have vision, Breeze. That's something the rebellion has always lacked."

"Excuse me?" Yeden said indignantly.

"It's true, unfortunately," Kelsier said. "The rebellion condemns people like us because of our greed, but for all their high morals—which, by the way, I respect—they never get anything done. Yeden, your men hide in woods and in hills,

plotting how they'll someday rise up and lead a glorious war against the Final Empire. But your kind has no idea how to develop and execute a proper plan."

Yeden's expression grew dark. "And *you* have no idea what you are talking about."

"Oh?" Kelsier said lightly. "Tell me, what has your rebellion accomplished during its thousand-year struggle? Where are your successes and your victories? The Massacre of Tougier three centuries ago, where seven thousand skaa rebels were slaughtered? The occasional raid of a traveling canal boat or the kidnapping of a minor noble official?"

Yeden flushed. "That's the best we can manage with the people we have! Don't blame my men for their failures—blame the rest of the skaa. We can't ever get them to help. They've been beaten down for a millennium; they haven't got any spirit left. It's difficult enough to get one in a thousand to listen to us, let alone rebel!"

"Peace, Yeden," Kelsier said, holding up a hand. "I'm not trying to insult your courage. We're on the same side, remember? You came to me specifically because you were having trouble recruiting people for your army."

"I'm regretting that decision more and more, thief," Yeden said.

"Well, you've already paid us," Kelsier said. "So it's a little late to back out now. But, we'll get you that army, Yeden. The men in this room are the most capable, most clever, and most skilled Allomancers in the city. You'll see."

The room grew quiet again. Vin sat at her table, watching the interaction with a frown. *What is your game, Kelsier?* His words about overthrowing the Final Empire were obviously a front. It seemed most likely to her that he intended to scam the skaa rebellion. But . . . if he'd already been paid, then why continue the charade?

Kelsier turned from Yeden to Breeze and Ham. "All right, gentlemen. What do you think?"

The two men shared a look. Finally Breeze spoke. "Lord Ruler knows, I've never been one to turn down a challenge. But, Kell, I do question your reasoning. Are you sure we can do this?"

"I'm positive," Kelsier said. "Previous attempts to overthrow the Lord Ruler have failed because they lacked proper organization and planning. We're thieves, gentlemen—and we're extraordinarily good ones. We can rob the unrobbable and fool the unfoolable. We know how to take an incredibly large task and break it down to manageable pieces, then deal with each of those pieces. We know how to get what we want. These things make us perfect for this particular task."

Breeze frowned. "And . . . how much are we getting paid for achieving the impossible?"

"Thirty thousand boxings," Yeden said. "Half now, half when you deliver the army."

"Thirty thousand?" Ham said. "For an operation this big? That will barely cover expenses. We'll need a spy among the nobility to watch for rumors, we'll need a couple of safe houses, not to mention someplace big enough to hide and train an entire army. . . ."

"No use haggling now, thief," Yeden snapped. "Thirty thousand may not sound like much to *your* type, but it's the result of decades of saving on our part. We can't pay you more because we don't have anything more."

"It's good work, gentlemen," Dockson noted, joining the conversation for the first time.

"Yes, well, that's all great," Breeze said. "I consider myself a nice enough fellow. But . . . this just seems a bit too altruistic. Not to mention stupid."

"Well . . ." Kelsier said, "there might be a little bit more in it for us. . . ."

Vin perked up, and Breeze smiled.

"The Lord Ruler's treasury," Kelsier said. "The plan, as it stands now, is to provide Yeden with an army and an opportunity to seize the city. Once he takes the palace, he'll capture the treasury and use its funds to secure power. And, central to that treasury . . ."

"Is the Lord Ruler's atium," Breeze said.

Kelsier nodded. "Our agreement with Yeden promises us half of the atium reserves we find in the palace, no matter how vast they may be."

Atium. Vin had heard of the metal, but she had never actu-

ally seen any. It was incredibly rare, supposedly used only by noblemen.

Ham was smiling. "Well, now," he said slowly, "that's almost a big enough prize to be tempting."

"That atium stockpile is supposed to be enormous," Kelsier said. "The Lord Ruler sells the metal only in small bits, charging outrageous sums to the nobility. He *has* to keep a huge reserve of it to make certain he controls the market, and to make certain he has enough wealth for emergencies."

"True . . ." Breeze said. "But, are you sure you want to try something like this so soon after . . . what happened the last time we tried getting into the palace?"

"We're going to do things differently this time," Kelsier said. "Gentlemen, I'll be frank with you. This isn't going to be an easy job, but it *can* work. The plan is simple. We're going to find a way to neutralize the Luthadel Garrison—leaving the area without a policing force. Then, we're going to throw the city into chaos."

"We've got a couple of options on how to do that," Dockson said. "But we can talk about that later."

Kelsier nodded. "Then, in that chaos, Yeden will march his army into Luthadel and seize the palace, taking the Lord Ruler prisoner. While Yeden secures the city, we'll pilfer the atium. We'll give half to him, then disappear with the other half. After that, it's his job to hang on to what he's grabbed."

"Sounds a little dangerous for you, Yeden," Ham noted, glancing at the rebel leader.

He shrugged. "Perhaps. But, if we do, by some miracle, end up in control of the palace, then we'll have at least done something no skaa rebellion has ever achieved before. For my men, this isn't just about riches—it isn't even about surviving. It's about doing something grand, something wonderful, to give the skaa hope. But, I don't expect you people to understand things like that."

Kelsier shot a quieting glance at Yeden, and the man sniffed and sat back. *Did he use Allomancy?* Vin wondered. She'd seen employer-crew relationships before, and it seemed that Yeden was much more in Kelsier's pocket than the other way around.

Kelsier turned back to Ham and Breeze. "There's more to all this than simply a show of daring. If we do manage to steal that atium, it will be a sound blow to the Lord Ruler's financial foundation. He depends on the money that atium provides—without it, he could very well be left without the means to pay his armies.

"Even if he escapes our trap—or, if we decide to take the city when he's gone to minimize having to deal with him—he'll be financially ruined. He won't be able to march soldiers in to take the city away from Yeden. If this works right, we'll have the city in chaos anyway, and the nobility will be too weak to react against the rebel forces. The Lord Ruler will be left confused, and unable to mount a sizable army."

"And the koloss?" Ham asked quietly.

Kelsier paused. "If he marches those creatures on his own capital city, the destruction it would cause could be even more dangerous than financial instability. In the chaos, the provincial noblemen will rebel and set themselves up as kings, and the Lord Ruler won't have the troops to bring them into line. Yeden's rebels will be able to hold Luthadel, and we, my friends, will be very, very rich. Everyone gets what they want."

"You're forgetting the Steel Ministry," Clubs snapped, sitting almost forgotten at the side of the room. "Those Inquisitors won't just let us throw their pretty theocracy into chaos."

Kelsier paused, turning toward the gnarled man. "We will have to find a way to deal with the Ministry—I've got a few plans for that. Either way, problems like that are the things that we—as a crew—will have to work out. We have to get rid of the Luthadel Garrison—there's no way we'll be able to get anything done with them policing the streets. We'll have to come up with an appropriate way to throw the city into chaos, and we'll have to find a way to keep the obligators off our trail.

"But, if we play this right, we might be able to force the Lord Ruler to send the palace guard—maybe even the Inquisitors—into the city to restore order. That will leave the palace itself exposed, giving Yeden a perfect opportunity to strike. After that, it won't matter what happens with the

Ministry or the Garrison—the Lord Ruler won't have the money to maintain control of his empire."

"I don't know, Kell," Breeze said, shaking his head. His flippancy was subdued; he seemed to be honestly considering the plan. "The Lord Ruler got that atium somewhere. What if he just goes and mines some more?"

Ham nodded. "No one even knows where the atium mine is."

"I wouldn't say *no one*," Kelsier said with a smile.

Breeze and Ham shared a look.

"You know?" Ham asked.

"Of course," Kelsier said. "I spent a year of my life working there."

"The Pits?" Ham asked with surprise.

Kelsier nodded. "That's why the Lord Ruler makes certain nobody survives working there—he can't afford to let his secret out. It's not just a penal colony, not just a hellhole where skaa are sent to die. It's a mine."

"Of course . . ." Breeze said.

Kelsier stood up straight, stepping away from the bar and walking toward Ham and Breeze's table. "We have a chance here, gentlemen. A chance to do something great— something no other thieving crew has ever done. We'll rob from the Lord Ruler himself!

"But, there's more. The Pits nearly killed me, and I've seen things . . . differently since I escaped. I see the skaa, working without hope. I see the thieving crews, trying to survive on aristocratic leavings, often getting themselves—and other skaa—killed in the process. I see the skaa rebellion trying so hard to resist the Lord Ruler, and never making any progress.

"The rebellion fails because it's too unwieldy and spread out. Anytime one of its many pieces gains momentum, the Steel Ministry crushes it. That's not the way to defeat the Final Empire, gentlemen. But, a small team—specialized and highly skilled—has a hope. We can work without great risk of exposure. We know how to avoid the Steel Ministry's tendrils. We understand how the high nobility thinks, and how to exploit its members. We can do this!"

He paused beside Breeze and Ham's table.

"I don't know, Kell," Ham said. "It's not that I'm disagreeing with your motives. It's just that . . . well, this seems a bit foolhardy."

Kelsier smiled. "I know it does. But you're going to go along with it anyway, aren't you?"

Ham paused, then nodded. "You know I'll join your crew no matter what the job. This sounds crazy, but so do most of your plans. Just . . . just tell me. Are you serious about overthrowing the Lord Ruler?"

Kelsier nodded. For some reason, Vin was almost tempted to believe him.

Ham nodded firmly. "All right, then. I'm in."

"Breeze?" Kelsier asked.

The well-dressed man shook his head. "I'm not sure, Kell. This is a bit extreme, even for you."

"We need you, Breeze," Kell said. "No one can Soothe a crowd like you can. If we're going to raise an army, we'll need your Allomancers—and your powers."

"Well, that much is true," Breeze said. "But, even still . . ."

Kelsier smiled, then he set something on the table—the cup of wine Vin had poured for Breeze. She hadn't even noticed that Kelsier had grabbed it off of the bar.

"Think of the challenge, Breeze," Kelsier said.

Breeze glanced at the cup, then looked up at Kelsier. Finally, he laughed, reaching for the wine. "Fine. I'm in."

"It's impossible," a gruff voice said from the back of the room. Clubs sat with folded arms, regarding Kelsier with a scowl. "What are you really planning, Kelsier?"

"I'm being honest," Kelsier replied. "I plan to take the Lord Ruler's atium and overthrow his empire."

"You can't," the man said. "It's idiocy. The Inquisitors will hang us all by hooks through our throats."

"Perhaps," Kelsier said. "But think of the reward if we succeed. Wealth, power, and a land where the skaa can live like men, rather than slaves."

Clubs snorted loudly. Then he stood, his chair toppling backward onto the floor behind him. "No reward would be enough. The Lord Ruler tried to have you killed once—I see that you won't be satisfied until he gets it right." With that, the

older man turned and stalked in a limping gait from the room, slamming the door behind him.

The lair grew quiet.

"Well, guess we'll need a different Smoker," Dockson said.

"You're just going to let him go?" Yeden demanded. "He knows everything!"

Breeze chuckled. "Aren't you supposed to be the moral one in this little group?"

"Morals doesn't have anything to do with it," Yeden said. "Letting someone go like that is foolish! He could bring the obligators down on us in minutes."

Vin nodded in agreement, but Kelsier just shook his head. "I don't work that way, Yeden. I invited Clubs to a meeting where I outlined a dangerous plan—one some people might even call stupid. I'm not going to have him assassinated because he decided it was too dangerous. If you do things like that, pretty soon nobody will come listen to your plans in the first place."

"Besides," Dockson said. "We wouldn't invite someone to one of these meetings unless we trusted him not to betray us."

Impossible, Vin thought, frowning. He had to be bluffing to keep up crew morale; nobody was that trusting. After all, hadn't the others said that Kelsier's failure a few years before—the event that had sent him to the Pits of Hathsin—had come because of a betrayal? He probably had assassins following Clubs at that very moment, watching to make certain he didn't go to the authorities.

"All right, Yeden," Kelsier said, getting back to business. "They accepted. The plan is on. Are you still in?"

"Will you give the rebellion's money back if I say no?" Yeden asked.

The only response to that was a quiet chuckle from Ham. Yeden's expression darkened, but he just shook his head. "If I had any other option . . ."

"Oh, stop complaining," Kelsier said. "You're officially part of a thieving crew now, so you might as well come over here and sit with us."

Yeden paused for a moment, then sighed and walked over to sit at Breeze, Ham, and Dockson's table, beside which Kelsier was still standing. Vin still sat at the next table over.

Kelsier turned, looking over toward Vin. "What about you, Vin?"

She paused. *Why is he asking me? He already knows he has a hold over me. The job doesn't matter, as long as I learn what he knows.*

Kelsier waited expectantly.

"I'm in," Vin said, assuming that was what he wanted to hear.

She must have guessed correctly, for Kelsier smiled, then nodded to the last chair at the table.

Vin sighed, but did as he indicated, standing and walking over to take the last seat.

"Who is the child?" Yeden asked.

"Twixt," Breeze said.

Kelsier cocked an eyebrow. "Actually, Vin is something of a new recruit. My brother caught her Soothing his emotions a few months back."

"Soother, eh?" Ham asked. "Guess we can always use another of those."

"Actually," Kelsier noted, "it seems she can Riot people's emotions as well."

Breeze started.

"Really?" Ham asked.

Kelsier nodded. "Dox and I tested her just a few hours ago."

Breeze chuckled. "And here I was telling her that she'd probably never meet another Mistborn besides yourself."

"A second Mistborn on the team . . ." Ham said appreciatively. "Well, that increases our chances somewhat."

"What are you saying?" Yeden sputtered. "Skaa can't be Mistborn. I'm not even sure if Mistborn exist! *I've* certainly never met one."

Breeze raised an eyebrow, then laid a hand on Yeden's shoulder. "You should try not to talk so much, friend," he suggested. "You'll sound far less stupid that way."

Yeden shook off Breeze's hand, and Ham laughed. Vin, however, sat quietly, considering the implications of what Kelsier had said. The part about stealing the atium reserves was tempting, but seizing the city to do it? Were these men really that reckless?

Kelsier pulled a chair over to the table for himself and sat

down on it the wrong way, resting his arms on the seatback. "All right," he said. "We have a crew. We'll plan specifics at the next meeting, but I want you all to be thinking about the job. I have some plans, but I want fresh minds to consider our task. We'll need to discuss ways to get the Luthadel Garrison out of the city, and ways that we can throw this place into so much chaos that the Great Houses can't mobilize their forces to stop Yeden's army when it attacks."

The members of the group, save Yeden, nodded.

"Before we end for the evening, however," Kelsier continued, "there is one more part of the plan I want to warn you about."

"More?" Breeze asked with a chuckle. "Stealing the Lord Ruler's fortune and overthrowing his empire aren't enough?"

"No," Kelsier said. "If I can, I'm going to kill him too."

Silence.

"Kelsier," Ham said slowly. "The Lord Ruler is the Sliver of Infinity. He's a piece of God Himself. You can't kill him. Even *capturing* him will probably prove impossible."

Kelsier didn't reply. His eyes, however, were determined.

That's it, Vin thought. *He has to be insane.*

"The Lord Ruler and I," Kelsier said quietly, "we have an unsettled debt. He took Mare from me, and he nearly took my own sanity as well. I'll admit to you all that part of my reason for this plan is to get revenge on him. We're going to take his government, his home, and his fortune from him.

"However, for that to work, we'll have to get rid of him. Perhaps imprison him in his own dungeons—at the very least, we'll have to get him out of the city. However, I can think of something far better than either option. Down those pits where he sent me, I Snapped and came to an awakening of my Allomantic powers. Now I intend to use them to kill him."

Kelsier reached into his suit pocket and pulled something out. He set it on the table.

"In the north, they have a legend," Kelsier said. "It teaches that the Lord Ruler isn't immortal—not completely. They say he can be killed with the right metal. The Eleventh Metal. That metal."

Eyes turned toward the object on the table. It was a thin bar

of metal, perhaps as long and wide as Vin's small finger, with straight sides. It was silvery white in color.

"The Eleventh Metal?" Breeze asked uncertainly. "I've heard of no such legend."

"The Lord Ruler has suppressed it," Kelsier said. "But it can still be found, if you know where to look. Allomantic theory teaches of ten metals: the eight basic metals, and the two high metals. There is another one, however, unknown to most. One far more powerful, even, than the other ten."

Breeze frowned skeptically.

Yeden, however, appeared intrigued. "And, this metal can somehow kill the Lord Ruler?"

Kelsier nodded. "It's his weakness. The Steel Ministry wants you to believe that he's immortal, but even he can be killed—by an Allomancer burning this."

Ham reached out, picking up the thin bar of metal. "Where did you get it?"

"In the north," Kelsier said. "In a land near the Far Peninsula, a land where people still remember what their old kingdom was called in the days before the Ascension."

"How does it work?" Breeze asked.

"I'm not sure," Kelsier said frankly. "But I intend to find out."

Ham regarded the porcelain-colored metal, turning it over his fingers.

Kill the Lord Ruler? Vin thought. The Lord Ruler was a force, like the winds or the mists. One did not kill such things. They didn't live, really. They simply *were*.

"Regardless," Kelsier said, accepting the metal back from Ham, "you don't need to worry about this. Killing the Lord Ruler is my task. If it proves impossible, we'll settle for tricking him outside of the city, then robbing him silly. I just thought that you should know what I'm planning."

I've bound myself to a madman, Vin thought with resignation. But that didn't really matter—not as long as he taught her Allomancy.

I don't even understand what I'm supposed to do. The Terris philosophers claim that I'll know my duty when the time comes, but that's a small comfort.

The Deepness must be destroyed, and apparently I'm the only one who can do so. It ravages the world even now. If I don't stop it soon, there will be nothing left of this land but bones and dust.

5

"AHA!" KELSIER'S TRIUMPHANT FIGURE POPPED up from behind Camon's bar, a look of satisfaction on his face. He brought his arm up and thunked a dusty wine bottle down on the countertop.

Dockson looked over with amusement. "Where'd you find it?"

"One of the secret drawers," Kelsier said, dusting off the bottle.

"I thought I'd found all of those," Dockson said.

"You did. One of them had a false back."

Dockson chuckled. "Clever."

Kelsier nodded, unstoppering the bottle and pouring out three cups. "The trick is to never stop looking. There's *always* another secret." He gathered up the three cups and walked over to join Vin and Dockson at the table.

Vin accepted her cup with a tentative hand. The meeting had ended a short time earlier, Breeze, Ham, and Yeden leaving to ponder the things Kelsier had told them. Vin felt that she should have left as well, but she had nowhere to go. Dockson and Kelsier seemed to take it for granted that she would remain with them.

Kelsier took a long sip of the rubicund wine, then smiled. "Ah, that's *much* better."

Dockson nodded in agreement, but Vin didn't taste her own drink.

"We're going to need another Smoker," Dockson noted.

Kelsier nodded. "The others seemed to take it well, though."

"Breeze is still uncertain," Dockson said.

"He won't back out. Breeze likes a challenge, and he'll never find a challenge greater than this one." Kelsier smiled. "Besides, it'd drive him insane to know that we were pulling a job that he wasn't in on."

"Still, he's right to be apprehensive," Dockson said. "I'm a little worried myself."

Kelsier nodded his agreement, and Vin frowned. *So, are they serious about the plan? Or is this still a show for my sake?* The two men seemed so competent. Yet, overthrowing the Final Empire? They'd sooner stop the mists from flowing or the sun from rising.

"When do your other friends get here?" Dockson asked.

"A couple days," Kelsier said. "We'll need to have another Smoker by then. I'm also going to need some more atium."

Dockson frowned. "Already?"

Kelsier nodded. "I spent most of it buying OreSeur's Contract, then used my last bit at Tresting's plantation."

Tresting. The nobleman who had been killed in his manor the week before. *How was Kelsier involved? And, what was it Kelsier said before about atium?* He'd claimed that the Lord Ruler kept control of the high nobility by maintaining a monopoly on the metal.

Dockson rubbed his bearded chin. "Atium's not easy to come by, Kell. It took nearly eight months of planning to steal you that last bit."

"That's because you had to be delicate," Kelsier said with a devious smile.

Dockson eyed Kelsier with a look of slight apprehension. Kelsier just smiled more broadly, and finally Dockson rolled his eyes, sighing. Then he glanced at Vin. "You haven't touched your drink."

Vin shook her head.

Dockson waited for an explanation, and eventually Vin was

forced to respond. "I don't like to drink anything I didn't prepare myself."

Kelsier chuckled. "She reminds me of Vent."

"Vent?" Dockson said with a snort. "The lass is a bit paranoid, but she's not *that* bad. I swear, that man was so jumpy that his own heartbeat could startle him."

The two men shared a laugh. Vin, however, was only made more uncomfortable by the friendly air. *What do they expect from me? Am I to be an apprentice of some sort?*

"Well, then," Dockson said, "are you going to tell me how you plan on getting yourself some atium?"

Kelsier opened his mouth to respond, but the stairs clattered with the sound of someone coming down. Kelsier and Dockson turned; Vin, of course, had seated herself so she could see both entrances to the room without having to move.

Vin expected the newcomer to be one of Camon's crewmembers, sent to see if Kelsier was done with the lair yet. Therefore, she was completely surprised when the door swung open to reveal the surly, gnarled face of the man called Clubs.

Kelsier smiled, eyes twinkling.

He's not surprised. Pleased, perhaps, but not surprised.

"Clubs," Kelsier said.

Clubs stood in the doorway, giving the three of them an impressively disapproving stare. Finally, he hobbled into the room. A thin, awkward-looking teenage boy followed him.

The boy fetched Clubs a chair and put it by Kelsier's table. Clubs settled down, grumbling slightly to himself. Finally, he eyed Kelsier with a squinting, wrinkle-nosed expression. "The Soother is gone?"

"Breeze?" Kelsier asked. "Yes, he left."

Clubs grunted. Then he eyed the bottle of wine.

"Help yourself," Kelsier said.

Clubs waved for the boy to go fetch him a cup from the bar, then turned back to Kelsier. "I had to be sure," he said. "Never can trust yourself when a Soother is around— especially one like him."

"You're a Smoker, Clubs," Kelsier said. "He couldn't do much to you, not if you didn't want him to."

Clubs shrugged. "I don't like Soothers. It's not just Allomancy—men like that . . . well, you can't trust that you aren't being manipulated when they are around. Copper or no copper."

"I wouldn't rely on something like that to get your loyalty," Kelsier said.

"So I've heard," Clubs said as the boy poured him a cup of wine. "Had to be sure, though. Had to think about things without that Breeze around." He scowled, though Vin had trouble determining why, then took the cup and downed half of it in one gulp.

"Good wine," he said with a grunt. Then he looked over at Kelsier. "So, the Pits really did drive you insane, eh?"

"Completely," Kelsier said with a straight face.

Clubs smiled, though on his face the expression had a decidedly twisted look. "You mean to go through with this, then? This so-called job of yours?"

Kelsier nodded solemnly.

Clubs downed the rest of his wine. "You've got yourself a Smoker then. Not for the money, though. If you're really serious about toppling this government, then I'm in."

Kelsier smiled.

"And don't smile at me," Clubs snapped. "I hate that."

"I wouldn't dare."

"Well," Dockson said, pouring himself another drink, "that solves the Smoker problem."

"Won't matter much," Clubs said. "You're going to fail. I've spent my life trying to hide Mistings from the Lord Ruler and his obligators. He gets them all eventually anyway."

"Why bother helping us, then?" Dockson asked.

"Because," Clubs said, standing. "The Lord's going to get me sooner or later. At least this way, I'll be able to spit in his face as I go. Overthrowing the Final Empire . . ." He smiled. "It's got style. Let's go, kid. We've got to get the shop ready for visitors."

Vin watched them go, Clubs limping out the door, the boy pulling it closed behind them. Then she glanced at Kelsier. "You knew he'd come back."

He shrugged, standing and stretching. "I hoped. People are

attracted to vision. The job I'm proposing . . . well, it just isn't the sort of thing you walk away from—at least, not if you're a bored old man who's generally annoyed at life. Now, Vin, I assume that your crew owns this entire building?"

Vin nodded. "The shop upstairs is a front."

"Good," Kelsier said, checking his pocket watch, then handing it to Dockson. "Tell your friends that they can have their lair back—the mists are probably already coming out."

"And us?" Dockson asked.

Kelsier smiled. "We're going to the roof. Like I told you, I have to fetch some atium."

By day, Luthadel was a blackened city, scorched by soot and red sunlight. It was hard, distinct, and oppressive.

At night, however, the mists came to blur and obscure. High noble keeps became ghostly, looming silhouettes. Streets seemed to grow more narrow in the fog, every thoroughfare becoming a lonely, dangerous alleyway. Even noblemen and thieves were apprehensive about going out at night—it took a strong heart to brave the foreboding, misty silence. The dark city at night was a place for the desperate and the foolhardy; it was a land of swirling mystery and strange creatures.

Strange creatures like me, Kelsier thought. He stood upon the ledge that ran around the lip of the flat-roofed lair. Shadowed buildings loomed in the night around him, and the mists made everything seem to shift and move in the darkness. Weak lights peeked from the occasional window, but the tiny beads of illumination were huddled, frightened things.

A cool breeze slipped across the rooftop, shifting the haze, brushing against Kelsier's mist-wetted cheek like an exhaled breath. In days past—back before everything had gone wrong—he had always sought out a rooftop on the evening before a job, wishing to overlook the city. He didn't realize he was observing his old custom this night until he glanced to the side, expecting Mare to be there next to him, as she always had been.

Instead, he found only the empty air. Lonely. Silent. The mists had replaced her. Poorly.

He sighed and turned. Vin and Dockson stood behind him on the rooftop. Both looked apprehensive to be out in the mists, but they dealt with their fear. One did not get far in the underworld without learning to stomach the mists.

Kelsier had learned to do far more than "stomach" them. He had gone among them so often during the last few years that he was beginning to feel more comfortable at night, within the mists' obscuring embrace, than he did at day.

"Kell," Dockson said, "do you *have* to stand on the ledge like that? Our plans may be a bit crazy, but I'd rather not have them end with you splattered across the cobblestones down there."

Kelsier smiled. *He still doesn't think of me as a Mistborn,* he thought. *It will take some getting used to for all of them.*

Years before, he had become the most infamous crewleader in Luthadel, and he had done it without even being an Allomancer. Mare had been a Tineye, but he and Dockson . . . they had just been regular men. One a half-breed with no powers, the other a runaway plantation skaa. Together, they had brought Great Houses to their knees, stealing brashly from the most powerful men in the Final Empire.

Now Kelsier was more, so much more. Once he had dreamed of Allomancy, wishing for a power like Mare's. She had been dead before he'd Snapped, coming to his powers. She would never see what he would do with them.

Before, the high nobility had feared him. It had taken a trap set by the Lord Ruler himself to capture Kelsier. Now . . . the Final Empire itself would shake before he was finished with it.

He scanned the city once more, breathing in the mists, then hopped down off the ledge and strolled over to join Dockson and Vin. They carried no lights; ambient starlight diffused by the mists was enough to see by in most cases.

Kelsier took off his jacket and vest, handing them to Dockson, then he untucked his shirt, letting the long garment hang loose. The fabric was dark enough that it wouldn't give him away in the night.

"All right," Kelsier said. "Who should I try?"

Dockson frowned. "You're sure you want to do this?"

Kelsier smiled.

Dockson sighed. "Houses Urbain and Teniert have been hit recently, though not for their atium."

"Which house is the strongest right now?" Kelsier asked, squatting down and undoing the ties on his pack, which rested by Dockson's feet. "Who would no one consider hitting?"

Dockson paused. "Venture," he finally said. "They've been on top for the last few years. They keep a standing force of several hundred men, and the local house nobility includes a good two dozen Mistings."

Kelsier nodded. "Well, that's where I'll go, then. They're certain to have some atium." He pulled open the pack, then whipped out a dark gray cloak. Large and enveloping, the cloak wasn't constructed from a single piece of cloth—rather, it was made up of hundreds of long, ribbonlike strips. They were sewn together at the shoulders and across the chest, but mostly they hung separate from one another, like overlapping streamers.

Kelsier threw on the garment, its strips of cloth twisting and curling, almost like the mists themselves.

Dockson exhaled softly. "I've never been so close to someone wearing one of those."

"What is it?" Vin asked, her quiet voice almost haunting in the night mists.

"A Mistborn cloak," Dockson said. "They all wear the things—it's kind of like a . . . sign of membership in their club."

"It's colored and constructed to hide you in the mist," Kelsier said. "And it warns city guards and other Mistborn not to bother you." He spun, letting the cloak flare dramatically. "I think it suits me."

Dockson rolled his eyes.

"All right," Kelsier said, bending down and pulling a cloth belt from his pack. "House Venture. Is there anything I need to know?"

"Lord Venture supposedly has a safe in his study," Dockson said. "That's where he'd probably keep his atium stash. You'll find the study on the third floor, three rooms in from the upper southern balcony. Be careful, House Venture keeps

about a dozen hazekillers in addition to its regular troops and Mistings."

Kelsier nodded, tying on the belt—it had no buckle, but it did contain two small sheaths. He pulled a pair of glass daggers from the bag, checked them for nicks, and slid them into the sheaths. He kicked off his shoes and stripped off his stockings, leaving himself barefoot on the chill stones. With the shoes also went the last bit of metal on his person save for his coin pouch and the three vials of metals in his belt. He selected the largest one, downed its contents, then handed the empty vial to Dockson.

"That it?" Kelsier asked.

Dockson nodded. "Good luck."

Beside him, the girl Vin was watching Kelsier's preparations with intense curiosity. She was a quiet, small thing, but she hid an intensity that he found impressive. She was paranoid, true, but not timid.

You'll get your chance, kid, he thought. *Just not tonight.*

"Well," he said, pulling a coin from his pouch and tossing it off the side of the building. "Guess I'll be going. I'll meet you back at Clubs's shop in a bit."

Dockson nodded.

Kelsier turned and walked back up onto the roof's ledge. Then he jumped off the building.

Mist curled in the air around him. He burned steel, second of the basic Allomantic metals. Translucent blue lines sprang into existence around him, visible only to his eyes. Each one led from the center of his chest out to a nearby source of metal. The lines were all relatively faint—a sign that they pointed to metal sources that were small: door hinges, nails, and other bits. The type of source metal didn't matter. Burning iron or steel would point blue lines at all kinds of metal, assuming they were close enough and large enough to be noticeable.

Kelsier chose the line that pointed directly beneath him, toward his coin. Burning steel, he Pushed against the coin.

His descent immediately stopped, and he was thrown back up into the air in the opposite direction along the blue line. He reached out to the side, selected a passing window clasp, and Pushed against it, angling himself to the side. The careful

nudge sent him up and over the lip of the building directly across the street from Vin's lair.

Kelsier landed with a lithe step, falling into a crouch and running across the building's peaked roof. He paused in the darkness at the other side, peering through the swirling air. He burned tin, and felt it flare to life in his chest, enhancing his senses. Suddenly the mists seemed less deep. It wasn't that the night around him grew any lighter; his ability to perceive simply increased. In the distance to the north, he could just barely make out a large structure. Keep Venture.

Kelsier left his tin on—it burned slowly, and he probably didn't need to worry about running out. As he stood, the mists curled slightly around his body. They twisted and spun, running in a slight, barely noticeable current beside him. The mists knew him; they claimed him. They could sense Allomancy.

He jumped, Pushing against a metal chimney behind him, sending himself in a wide horizontal leap. He tossed a coin even as he jumped, the tiny bit of metal flickering through the darkness and fog. He Pushed against the coin before it hit the ground, the force of his weight driving it downward in a sharp motion. As soon as it hit the cobblestones, Kelsier's Pushing forced him upward, turning the second half of his leap into a graceful arc.

Kelsier landed on another peaked wooden rooftop. Steelpushing and Ironpulling were the first things that Gemmel had taught him. *When you Push on something, it's like you're throwing your weight against it,* the old lunatic had said. *And you can't change how much you weigh—you're an Allomancer, not some northern mystic. Don't Pull on something that weighs less than you unless you want it to come flying at you, and don't Push on something heavier than you unless you want to get tossed in the other direction.*

Kelsier scratched his scars, then pulled his mistcloak tight as he crouched on the roof, the wooden grain biting his unshod toes. He often wished that burning tin didn't enhance all of the senses—or, at least, not all of them at once. He needed the improved eyesight to see in the darkness, and he made good use of the improved hearing as well. However, burning

tin made the night seem even more chilly to his overly sensitive skin, and his feet registered every pebble and wooden ripple they touched.

Keep Venture rose before him. Compared with the murky city, the keep seemed to blaze with light. High nobles kept different schedules from regular people; the ability to afford, even squander, lamp oil and candles meant that the wealthy didn't have to bow before the whims of season or sun.

The keep was majestic—that much was visible simply from the architecture. While it maintained a defensive wall around the grounds, the keep itself was more an artistic construction than a fortification. Sturdy buttressings arched out from the sides, allowing for intricate windows and delicate spires. Brilliant stained-glass windows stretched high along the sides of the rectangular building, and they shone with light from within, giving the surrounding mists a variegated glow.

Kelsier burned iron, flaring it strong and searching the night for large sources of metal. He was too far away from the keep to use small items like coins or hinges. He'd need a larger anchor to cover this distance.

Most of the blue lines were faint. Kelsier marked a couple of them moving in a slow pattern up ahead—probably a pair of guards standing on the rooftop. Kelsier would be sensing their breastplates and weapons. Despite Allomantic considerations, most noblemen still armed their soldiers with metal. Mistings who could Push or Pull metals were uncommon, and full Mistborn were even more so. Many lords thought it impractical to leave one's soldiers and guards relatively defenseless in order to counter such a small segment of the population.

No, most high noblemen relied on other means to deal with Allomancers. Kelsier smiled. Dockson had said that Lord Venture kept a squad of hazekillers; if that was true, Kelsier would probably meet them before the night was through. He ignored the soldiers for the moment, instead focusing on a solid line of blue pointing toward the keep's lofty top. It likely had bronze or copper sheeting on the roof. Kelsier flared his iron, took a deep breath, and Pulled on the line.

With a sudden jerk, he was yanked into the air.

Kelsier continued to burn iron, pulling himself toward the keep at a tremendous speed. Some rumors claimed that Mistborn could fly, but that was a wistful exaggeration. Pulling and Pushing against metals usually felt less like flying than it did like falling—only in the wrong direction. An Allomancer had to Pull hard in order to get the proper momentum, and this sent him hurtling toward his anchor at daunting speeds.

Kelsier shot toward the keep, mists curling around him. He easily cleared the protective wall surrounding the keep's grounds, but his body dropped slightly toward the ground as he moved. It was his pesky weight again; it tugged him down. Even the swiftest of arrows angled slightly toward the ground as it flew.

The drag of his weight meant that instead of shooting right up to the roof, he swung in an arc. He approached the keep wall several dozen feet below the rooftop, still traveling at a terrible speed.

Taking a deep breath, Kelsier burned pewter, using it to enhance his physical strength much in the same way that tin enhanced his senses. He turned himself in the air, hitting the stone wall feet-first. Even his strengthened muscles protested at the treatment, but he stopped without breaking any bones. He immediately released his hold on the roof, dropping a coin and Pushing against it even as he began to fall. He reached out, selecting a source of metal above him—one of the wire housings of a stained-glass window—and Pulled on it.

The coin hit the ground below and was suddenly able to support his weight. Kelsier launched himself upward, Pushing on the coin and Pulling on the window at the same time. Then, extinguishing both metals, he let momentum carry him the last few feet up through the dark mists. Cloak flapping quietly, he crested the lip of the keep's upper service walkway, flipped himself up over the stone railing, and landed quietly on the ledge.

A startled guard stood not three paces away. Kelsier was upon the man in a second, jumping into the air, Pulling slightly on the guard's steel breastplate and throwing the man off balance. Kelsier whipped out one of his glass daggers, allowing the strength of his Ironpull to bring him toward the

guard. He landed with both feet against the man's chest, then crouched and sliced with a pewter-enhanced swing.

The guard collapsed with a slit throat. Kelsier landed lithely beside him, ears straining in the night, listening for sounds of alarm. There were none.

Kelsier left the guard to his gurgling demise. The man was likely a lesser nobleman. The enemy. If he were, instead, a skaa soldier—enticed into betraying his people in exchange for a few coins . . . Well, then, Kelsier was even happier to send such men into their eternity.

He Pushed off the dying man's breastplate, hopping up off the stone service walkway and onto the rooftop itself. The bronze roof was chill and slick beneath his feet. He scurried along it, heading toward the southern side of the building, looking for the balcony Dockson had mentioned. He wasn't too worried about being spotted; one purpose of this evening was to steal some atium, the tenth and most powerful of the generally known Allomantic metals. His other purpose, however, was to cause a commotion.

He found the balcony with ease. Wide and broad, it was probably a sitting balcony, used to entertain small groups. It was quiet at the moment, however—empty save for two guards. Kelsier crouched silently in the night mists above the balcony, furled gray cloak obscuring him, toes curling out over the side of the roof's metallic lip. The two guards chatted unwittingly below.

Time to make a bit of noise.

Kelsier dropped to the ledge directly between the guards. Burning pewter to strengthen his body, he reached out and fiercely Steelpushed against both men at the same time. Braced as he was at the center, his Push threw the guards away in opposite directions. The men cried out in surprise as the sudden force threw them backward, hurling them over the balcony railing into the darkness beyond.

The guards screamed as they fell. Kelsier threw open the balcony doors, letting a wall of mist fall inward around him, its tendrils creeping forward to claim the darkened room beyond.

Third room in, Kelsier thought, moving forward in a crouching run. The second room was a quiet, greenhouse-like

conservatory. Low beds containing cultivated bushes and small trees ran through the room, and one wall was made up of enormous floor-to-ceiling windows to provide sunlight for the plants. Though it was dark, Kelsier knew that the plants would all be of slightly different colors than the typical brown—some would be white, others ruddy, and perhaps even a few light yellow. Plants that weren't brown were a rarity cultivated and kept by the nobility.

Kelsier moved quickly through the conservatory. He paused at the next doorway, noting its lighted outline. He extinguished his tin lest his enhanced eyes be blinded when he entered the lit room, and threw open the door.

He ducked inside, blinking against the light, a glass dagger in each hand. The room, however, was empty. It was obviously a study; a lantern burned on each wall beside bookcases, and it had a desk in the corner.

Kelsier replaced his knives, burning steel and searching for sources of metal. There was a large safe in the corner of the room, but it was too obvious. Sure enough, another strong source of metal shone from inside the eastern wall. Kelsier approached, running his fingers along the plaster. Like many walls in noble keeps, this one was painted with a soft mural. Foreign creatures lounged beneath a red sun. The false section of wall was under two feet square, and it had been placed so that its cracks were obscured by the mural.

There's always another secret, Kelsier thought. He didn't bother trying to figure out how to open the contraption. He simply burned steel, reaching in and tugging against the weak source of metal that he assumed was the trapdoor's locking mechanism. It resisted at first, pulling him against the wall, but he burned pewter and yanked harder. The lock snapped, and the panel swung open, revealing a small safe embedded in the wall.

Kelsier smiled. It looked small enough for a pewter-enhanced man to carry, assuming he could get it out of the wall.

He jumped up, Ironpulling against the safe, and landed with his feet against the wall, one foot on either side of the open panel. He continued to Pull, holding himself in place, and flared his pewter. Strength flooded his legs, and he flared his steel as well, Pulling against the safe.

He strained, grunting slightly at the exertion. It was a test to see which would give out first—the safe, or his legs.

The safe shifted in its mountings. Kelsier Pulled harder, muscles protesting. For an extended moment, nothing happened. Then the safe shook and ripped free of the wall. Kelsier fell backward, burning steel and Pushing against the safe to get out of the way. He landed maladroitly, sweat dripping from his brow as the safe crashed to the wooden floor, throwing up splinters.

A pair of startled guards burst into the room.

"About time," Kelsier noted, raising a hand and Pulling on one of the soldier's swords. It whipped out of the sheath, spinning in the air and streaking toward Kelsier point-first. He extinguished his iron, stepping to the side and catching the sword by its hilt as momentum carried it past.

"Mistborn!" the guard screamed.

Kelsier smiled and jumped forward.

The guard pulled out a dagger. Kelsier Pushed it, tearing the weapon out of the man's hand, then swung, shearing the guard's head from his body. The second guard cursed, tugging free the release tie on his breastplate.

Kelsier Pushed on his own sword even as he completed his swing. The sword ripped from his fingers and hissed directly toward the second guard. The man's armor dropped free—preventing Kelsier from Pushing against it—just as the first guard's corpse fell to the ground. A moment later, Kelsier's sword planted itself in the second guard's now unarmored chest. The man stumbled quietly, then collapsed.

Kelsier turned from the bodies, cloak rustling. His anger was quiet, not as fierce as it had been the night he'd killed Lord Tresting. But he felt it still, felt it in the itching of his scars and in the remembered screams of the woman he loved. As far as Kelsier was concerned, any man who upheld the Final Empire also forfeited his right to live.

He flared his pewter, strengthening his body, then squatted down and lifted the safe. He teetered for a second beneath its weight, then got his balance and began to shuffle back toward the balcony. Perhaps the safe held atium; perhaps it didn't. However, he didn't have time to search out other options.

He was halfway through the conservatory when he heard footsteps from behind. He turned to see the study flooding with figures. There were eight of them, each one wearing a loose gray robe and carrying a dueling cane and a shield instead of a sword. Hazekillers.

Kelsier let the safe drop to the ground. Hazekillers weren't Allomancers, but they were trained to fight Mistings and Mistborn. There wouldn't be a single bit of metal on their bodies, and they would be ready for his tricks.

Kelsier stepped back, stretching and smiling. The eight men fanned into the study, moving with quiet precision.

This should be interesting.

The hazekillers attacked, dashing by twos into the conservatory. Kelsier pulled out his daggers, ducking beneath the first attack and slicing at a man's chest. The hazekiller jumped back, however, and forced Kelsier away with a swing of his cane.

Kelsier flared his pewter, letting strengthened legs carry him back in a powerful jump. With one hand, he whipped out a handful of coins and Pushed them against his opponents. The metal disks shot forward, zipping through the air, but his enemies were ready for this: They raised their shields, and the coins bounced off the wood, throwing up splinters but leaving the men unharmed.

Kelsier eyed the other hazekillers as they filled the room, advancing on him. They couldn't hope to fight him in an extended battle—their tactic would be to rush him at once, hoping for a quick end to the fight, or to at least stall him until Allomancers could be awakened and brought to fight. He glanced at the safe as he landed.

He couldn't leave without it. He needed to end the fight quickly as well. Flaring pewter, he jumped forward, trying an experimental dagger swipe, but he couldn't get inside his opponent's defenses. Kelsier barely ducked away in time to avoid getting cracked on the head by the end of a cane.

Three of the hazekillers dashed behind him, cutting off his retreat into the balcony room. *Great*, Kelsier thought, trying to keep an eye on all eight men at once. They advanced on him with careful precision, working as a team.

Gritting his teeth, Kelsier flared his pewter again; it was running low, he noticed. Pewter was the fastest-burning of the basic eight metals.

No time to worry about that now. The men behind him attacked, and Kelsier jumped out of the way—Pulling on the safe to tug himself toward the center of the room. He Pushed as soon as he hit the ground near the safe, launching himself into the air at an angle. He tucked, flipping over the heads of two attackers, and landed on the ground beside a well-cultivated tree bed. He spun, flaring his pewter and raising his arm in defense against the swing he knew would come.

The dueling cane connected with his arm. A burst of pain ran down his forearm, but his pewter-enhanced bone held. Kelsier kept moving, driving his other hand forward and slamming a dagger into his opponent's chest.

The man stumbled back in surprise, the motion ripping away Kelsier's dagger. A second hazekiller attacked, but Kelsier ducked, then reached down with his free hand, ripping his coin pouch off of his belt. The hazekiller prepared to block Kelsier's remaining dagger, but Kelsier raised his other hand instead, slamming the coin pouch into the man's shield.

Then he Pushed on the coins inside.

The hazekiller cried out, the force of the intense Steelpush throwing him backward. Kelsier flared his steel, Pushing so hard that he tossed himself backward as well—away from the pair of men who tried to attack him. Kelsier and his enemy flew away from each other, hurled in opposite directions. Kelsier collided with the far wall, but kept Pushing, smashing his opponent—pouch, shield, and all—against one of the massive conservatory windows.

Glass shattered, sparkles of lanternlight from the study playing across its shards. The hazekiller's desperate face disappeared into the darkness beyond, and mist—quiet, yet ominous—began to creep in through the shattered window.

The other six men advanced relentlessly, and Kelsier was forced to ignore the pain in his arm as he ducked two swings. He spun out of the way, brushing past a small tree, but a third hazekiller attacked, smashing his cane into Kelsier's side.

The attack threw Kelsier into the tree bed. He tripped, then

collapsed near the entrance to the lit study, dropping his dagger. He gasped in pain, rolling to his knees and holding his side. The blow would have broken another man's ribs. Even Kelsier would have a massive bruise.

The six men moved forward, spreading to surround him again. Kelsier stumbled to his feet, vision growing dizzy from pain and exertion. He gritted his teeth, reaching down and pulling out one of his remaining vials of metal. He downed its contents in a single gulp, replenishing his pewter, then burned tin. The light nearly blinded him, and the pain in his arm and side suddenly seemed more acute, but the burst of enhanced senses cleared his head.

The six hazekillers advanced in a sudden, coordinated attack.

Kelsier whipped his hand to the side, burning iron and searching for metal. The closest source was a thick silvery paperweight on a desk just inside the study. Kelsier flipped it into his hand, then turned, arm held toward the advancing men, falling into an offensive stance.

"All right," he growled.

Kelsier burned steel with a flash of strength. The rectangular ingot ripped from his hand, streaking through the air. The foremost hazekiller raised his shield, but he moved too slowly. The ingot hit the man's shoulder with a crunch, and he dropped, crying out.

Kelsier spun to the side, ducking a staff swing and putting a hazekiller between himself and the fallen man. He burned iron, Pulling the ingot back toward him. It whipped through the air, cracking the second hazekiller in the side of the head. The man collapsed as the ingot flipped into the air.

One of the remaining men cursed, rushing forward to attack. Kelsier Pushed the still airborne ingot, flipping it away from him—and away from the attacking hazekiller, who had his shield raised. Kelsier heard the ingot hit the ground behind him, and he reached up—burning pewter—and caught the hazekiller's cane mid-swing.

The hazekiller grunted, struggling against Kelsier's enhanced strength. Kelsier didn't bother trying to pull the weapon free; instead he Pulled sharply on the ingot behind him, bringing it toward his own back at a deadly speed. He

twisted at the last moment, using his momentum to spin the hazekiller around—right into the ingot's path.

The man dropped.

Kelsier flared pewter, steadying himself against attacks. Sure enough, a cane smashed against his shoulders. He stumbled to his knees as the wood cracked, but flared tin kept him conscious. Pain and lucidity flashed through his mind. He Pulled on the ingot—ripping it out of the dying man's back—and stepped to the side, letting the impromptu weapon shoot past him.

The two hazekillers nearest him crouched warily. The ingot snapped into one of the men's shields, but Kelsier didn't continue Pushing, lest he throw himself off balance. Instead, he burned iron, wrenching the ingot back toward himself. He ducked, extinguishing iron and feeling the ingot whoosh through the air above him. There was a crack as it collided with the man who had been sneaking up on him.

Kelsier spun, burning iron then steel to send the ingot soaring toward the final two men. They stepped out of the way, but Kelsier tugged on the ingot, dropping it to the ground directly in front of them. The men regarded it warily, distracted as Kelsier ran and jumped, Steelpushing himself against the ingot and flipping over the men's heads. The hazekillers cursed, spinning. As Kelsier landed, he Pulled the ingot again, bringing it up to smash into a man's skull from behind.

The hazekiller fell silently. The ingot flipped a few times in the darkness, and Kelsier snatched it from the air, its cool surface slick with blood. Mist from the shattered window flowed by his feet, curling up around his legs. He brought his hand down, pointing it directly at the last remaining hazekiller.

Somewhere in the room, a fallen man groaned.

The remaining hazekiller stepped back, then dropped his weapon and dashed away. Kelsier smiled, lowering his hand.

Suddenly, the ingot was Pushed from his fingers. It shot across the room, smashing through another window. Kelsier cursed, spinning to see another, larger group of men pouring into the study. They wore the clothing of noblemen. Allomancers.

Several of them raised hands, and a flurry of coins shot toward Kelsier. He flared steel, Pushing the coins out of the way. Windows shattered and wood splintered as the room was sprayed with coins. Kelsier felt a tug on his belt as his final vial of metal was ripped away, Pulled toward the other room. Several burly men ran forward in a crouch, staying beneath the shooting coins. Thugs—Mistings who, like Ham, could burn pewter.

Time to go, Kelsier thought, deflecting another wave of coins, gritting his teeth against the pain in his side and arm. He glanced behind him; he had a few moments, but he was never going to make it back to the balcony. As more Mistings advanced, Kelsier took a deep breath and dashed toward one of the broken, floor-to-ceiling windows. He leapt out into the mists, turning in the air as he fell, and reached out to Pull firmly on the fallen safe.

He jerked in midair, swinging down toward the side of the building as if tied to the safe by a tether. He felt the safe slide forward, grinding against the floor of the conservatory as Kelsier's weight pulled against it. He slammed against the side of the building, but continued to Pull, catching himself on the upper side of a windowsill. He strained, standing upside down in the window well, Pulling on the safe.

The safe appeared over the lip of the floor above. It teetered, then fell out the window and began to plummet directly toward Kelsier. He smiled, extinguishing his iron and pushing away from the building with his legs, throwing himself out into the mists like some insane diver. He fell backward through the darkness, barely catching sight of an angry face poking out of the broken window above.

Kelsier Pulled carefully against the safe, moving himself in the air. Mists curled around him, obscuring his vision, making him feel as if he weren't falling at all—but hanging in the middle of nothingness.

He reached the safe, then twisted in the air and Pushed against it, throwing himself upward.

The safe crashed into the cobblestones just below. Kelsier Pushed against the safe slightly, slowing himself until he eventually jerked to a halt in the air just a few feet above the

ground. He hung in the mists for a moment, ribbons from his cloak curling and flapping in the wind, then let himself drop to the ground beside the safe.

The strongbox had been shattered by the fall. Kelsier pried open its mangled front, tin-enhanced ears listening to calls of alarm from the building above. Inside the safe, he found a small pouch of gemstones and a couple of ten-thousand boxing letters of credit, all of which he pocketed. He felt around inside, suddenly worried that the night's work had been for naught. Then his fingers found it—a small pouch at the very back.

He pulled it open, revealing a grouping of dark, beadlike bits of metal. Atium. His scars flared, memories of his time in the Pits returning to him.

He pulled the pouch tight and stood. With amusement, he noticed a twisted form lying on the cobblestones a short distance away—the mangled remains of the hazekiller he'd thrown out the window. Kelsier walked over, and retrieved his coin pouch with a tug of Ironpulling.

No, this night was not a waste. Even if he hadn't found the atium, any night that ended with a group of dead noblemen was a successful one, in Kelsier's opinion.

He gripped his pouch in one hand and the bag of atium in the other. He kept his pewter burning—without the strength it lent his body, he'd probably collapse from the pain of his wounds—and dashed off into the night, heading toward Clubs's shop.

TOR BOOKS *by*

THE STORMLIGHT ARCHIVE

The Way of Kings
Words of Radiance

With more than ten years spent in research, world-building, and writing, The Stormlight Archive is a true epic in the making, a multi-volume masterpiece in the grand tradition of The Wheel of Time®.

THE MISTBORN SERIES

Mistborn
The Well of Ascension
The Hero of Ages

This modern fantasy classic dares to ask a simple question: What if the hero of prophecy fails, and the Dark Lord takes over? What follows is a story full of surprises and political intrigue, driven by a memorable heist crew.

The Alloy of Law

Three hundred years after the events of the Mistborn trilogy, the world is on the verge of modernity, but one scion returning from the Roughs discovers that the civilized world isn't as civilized as he'd thought.